THE MIND WHISPERER

By

R. B. Hill

Copyright © 2025 R. B. HILL

ISBN:

Dedication

This book is dedicated to all the people who have stood by me through thick and thin, through the ups and downs, through the good times and the bad. Whether you have been a friend, a mentor, a family member, or even a stranger, your unwavering support has meant the world to me.

To my readers who have taken the time to pick up this book and delve into its pages, I am eternally grateful for your support and for giving my words a chance to be heard.

If you are reading this, then you are a part of this dedication. Thank you for being a part of my life and for helping me to make this dream a reality.

Acknowledgment

Reflecting on the journey that brought 'Mind Whisperer' to life fills me with gratitude for the countless individuals who supported me along the way. Writing this book has truly been a labour of love, and I couldn't have accomplished it without the encouragement and inspiration of so many amazing people.

First and foremost, I want to express my deepest thanks to my family for always believing in me.

I also want to show my appreciation for those who supported my first book, 'Notice Me.' Sharing my personal memoir was profound, and the encouragement I received from readers made that journey incredibly special. As I move into fiction with 'Mind Whisperer,' I am thrilled to unveil a new side of my writing. I must also express deep gratitude to my editor and publisher for their expertise and guidance. Your professionalism and vision were crucial in bringing this project to life.

To all who have read, reviewed, or simply cheered me on, thank you for believing in the message of 'Mind Whisperer.' I hope this book strikes a chord with you and sparks a deeper appreciation for the incredible potential of the mind.

And lastly, to all readers who pick up this book, thank you for allowing me to share my thoughts with you. Your journey is just as significant as the words within these pages, and I hope you discover wisdom and comfort within them.

With heartfelt appreciation,

R. B. Hill.

R. B. Hill

Table of Contents

Chapter 1
The Silent Observer

Mark Jennings stepped off the bus, his footsteps in perfect time with the rhythm of suburban life that pulsed around him. The mid-morning sun bathed Maple Street in a warm glow, highlighting the neat hedges and flower-filled porches of the homes he passed. As Mark made his way home, his average build and short brown hair made him blend effortlessly into his surroundings; even his stride seemed calibrated to avoid attracting attention.

"Another day," he muttered to himself, a faint smile tugging at his lips. He savoured the comforting predictability of his routine. His hands slipped into the pockets of his unremarkable slacks. Mark's presence was like a familiar song, gently playing in the background of the neighbourhood's daily bustle.

A block away, Sarah stood by the coffee shop window, her fingers drumming an absent beat on the paper cup. Her eyes, weighed down by sleepless nights, flickered over the blurred figures in the spreadsheet before her.

"Stuck in this job... going nowhere... I can't do this anymore," she whispered, her words barely rising above the hum of the espresso machine.

"Come on, Sarah," she urged herself, her voice barely a breath. "Think of the rent, the bills... but what about happiness?" She tugged at her collar, the fabric suddenly feeling tight, as if it were woven from the very threads of her mounting stress.

Passers-by swept around her, lost in their own worlds, but she felt rooted to the spot, weighed down by indecision. Her heart raced at the thought of marching into her boss's office to quit, but the uncertainty of the future held her back.

"Is financial security worth drowning in spreadsheets every day?" she muttered to the empty chair across from her, wondering if there was more to life than this. The thought of breaking free was exhilarating, like the first breath after a deep dive into water, terrifying and thrilling in equal measure.

Her phone buzzed with an email notification, another reminder of the relentless pace of corporate life. Sarah's hand hovered over the device, her mind caught in a tug-of-war between the yearning for freedom and the need for stability.

"Maybe just one more day," she reasoned, though her voice lacked conviction. "But is that what I said yesterday?" The internal debate raged on, leaving her trapped in a loop of hesitation and self-doubt.

"Or maybe," she continued, the words emerging with newfound clarity, "it's time to choose myself." The possibility hung in the air, a fragile hope stirring amidst the chaos of her thoughts.

Mark Jennings observed the world around him, tuning into its subtle cues, a furrowed brow, a quickened step, a shallow breath. As he walked the familiar streets of his neighbourhood, his gaze landed on Sarah. Her distress was as obvious to him as words on a page.

"Excuse me," Mark said softly, stepping closer and offering a warm, reassuring presence like a blanket on a cold day. "It seems like you could use someone to talk to."

Startled, Sarah looked up. Her eyes reflected a storm of emotions. "I'm fine," she stammered, but the tremor in her voice betrayed her.

"Sometimes 'fine' is just another word for 'I'm standing at a crossroads,' isn't it?" Mark said, his tone gentle, inviting her to trust without pressuring her.

She hesitated for a moment, then exhaled, a sound heavy with the weight of her unspoken thoughts. "It's my job," she confessed. "I feel like I'm suffocating there. Every spreadsheet feels like it's draining the life out of me."

"Ah," Mark said softly, understanding colouring his voice. "The quiet struggle between passion and practicality. You're wondering if the safety net is worth sacrificing your spirit."

Sarah's eyes widened. "Yes! Exactly that. How did you...?" She trailed off, searching his face for an explanation.

"Let's just say I've had a lot of time to observe the world," Mark said with a small smile. "I've learned to listen, not just to what people say, but to what they don't say."

"Nobody's ever...," Sarah paused, finding comfort in his calm demeanour. "Nobody's ever put it like that before. But even if I leave, then what? Where does that leave me?"

"Uncertainty is often the canvas for new beginnings," he replied. "Maybe it's not about where it leaves you, but about where you choose to go from there."

"Choose to go..." Sarah repeated, her voice a blend of hope and hesitation, echoing the depth of her internal conflict.

"Exactly," Mark said, his tone encouraging. "Your choices define your journey, not your fears."

"Thank you," Sarah murmured, her shoulders relaxing ever so slightly. "I didn't expect to find clarity sitting on a park bench today."

"Sometimes, the universe has a funny way of sending us what we need," Mark said with a knowing nod. "Even if it's through a stranger with an ear for listening."

"Listening must be your superpower," Sarah chuckled, her smile genuine for the first time.

"Perhaps," Mark agreed, his smile widening. "And maybe your superpower is waiting to be discovered."

Mark tilted his head, his gaze piercing beneath the surface of Sarah's composed exterior. She nervously fidgeted with the hem of her blouse, a small habit she thought no one noticed.

"Sarah," he began softly, "I sense there's more troubling you than just the decision to stay or leave."

Startled, she looked up, shocked by the accuracy of his statement. How could this stranger see through her so clearly?

"Your mind is like a storm," he continued, "but in that storm, I see a glimmer of opportunity. A promotion's on the horizon. If you can hold on a little longer, it will come."

Sarah blinked, taken aback. Her lips parted in disbelief. "A promotion?" she repeated, incredulous. "How could you know about that? I haven't told anyone, not even my closest friends. It's just a faint hope, a whisper in my own mind."

"Sometimes, whispers travel on the wind," Mark said, his eyes twinkling with a mixture of wisdom and mischief. "And sometimes, people just need someone to remind them that their hopes are heard."

"Are you some kind of mind reader?" she asked, half joking but with a hint of seriousness. The idea was absurd, yet here he was, pulling her deepest fears and desires into the open as if they were written in the air.

"Let's just say I'm observant," Mark replied, a playful grin on his face. "But really, Sarah, consider what your heart is telling you. Is it fear that holds you back, or the courage to face what lies ahead?"

His words struck a chord deep inside her, resonating with a truth she had been reluctant to face. The possibility of a promotion had been the only thread keeping her tied to a job that drained her. But here, Mark was, affirming that her silent wish might just come true.

"Courage," she whispered, the word unfamiliar yet oddly empowering. "Maybe... maybe I do have some left after all."

"Everyone has a well of courage," Mark assured her, his voice steady and confident. "Sometimes, it just takes someone to help us find it."

Sarah mulled over his words, the seed of hope taking root in her mind. Though it seemed far-fetched, his conviction sparked something inside her, a flicker of excitement at what might lie ahead if she could just hold on.

Her fingers interlaced, tension knotting her shoulders. "How do you do that? Do you know things about me? It's... not normal."

Mark's gaze met hers with calm assurance. "I have a unique ability," he began, choosing his words carefully. "It's like tuning into a frequency that others can't hear. Your thoughts and feelings are broadcast loud and clear to me."

"Are you serious?" Sarah asked, her voice wobbling with a mix of scepticism and curiosity.

"Very much so," Mark said, his brown eyes sincere. "I've never wanted to scare anyone with it; I only ever want to help."

"Help," Sarah repeated, a hesitant smile tugging at her lips. "Well, you've certainly got my attention."

"Sometimes we all need a little reassurance," Mark said gently. "A reminder that we're not as lost as we think."

Sarah took a deep breath, filling her lungs with air that felt like the first honest breath she'd taken in months. "It's just... this job. It's grinding me down. The politics, the long hours, it feels like I'm losing pieces of myself every day I stay."

"Feeling trapped does that to people," Mark said with a knowing nod. "But remember, you're more than your job, Sarah. You're strong, capable. It sounds to me like you're on the verge of a breakthrough."

"Maybe," Sarah murmured, her voice small but slowly gaining strength. "But how do you deal with the fear? The uncertainty?"

"By trusting yourself," Mark replied. "And knowing that sometimes, the universe nudges us exactly where we need to be."

"Trust," Sarah mused, turning the word over in her mind, trying to fit it into place. "That's a tall order."

"Maybe," Mark agreed. "But not impossible."

"Nothing's impossible, huh?" Sarah said with a dry laugh, her voice light but not bitter. A flicker of excitement danced in her eyes, a spark of hope amidst the uncertainty.

"Exactly," Mark said, his voice soft yet encouraging. "Just think about it, Sarah. What's the harm in holding on just a little longer?"

"Thoughts are what got me into this mess," she said with a wry smile, though her tone had softened. "Okay, Mark the Mind-Reader, I'll think it over."

"Good," Mark replied, his smile infectious. "Remember, whatever you decide, it's your choice. I believe you'll make the right one."

As Mark leaned back on the park bench, his gaze never left Sarah's thoughtful face. The autumn leaves rustled softly in the breeze, and for a moment, time seemed to pause, waiting for her to digest the possibility of hope.

"Listen," Mark began, breaking the silence gently, like a soft wave lapping against the shore. "I've seen this before. There was this guy, Tom, who felt just like you, trapped in a job that was draining him, ready to throw in the towel." He watched Sarah's eyes, noticing the flicker of curiosity that sparked within them.

"Tom?" she echoed, intrigued.

"Yeah," Mark continued, "he was on the verge of quitting. But he didn't. Three months later, he got the promotion he'd been aiming for. Not only that, he ended up leading a project that completely changed things for him. It gave him a real sense of purpose, you know?"

Sarah's eyes widened slightly, her mind visibly working through what he'd said. "So, what happened? Did he stay with the company?"

"Better," Mark smiled, the warmth in his expression matching the tone of his story. "He started his own firm eventually. It was a risk, sure, but it paid off. He found happiness." His voice held a melodic reassurance, each word carrying the promise of new possibilities.

"Really?" A small, disbelieving chuckle escaped Sarah's lips, mingling with the intrigue she felt. "And you predicted all of that?"

"Not exactly," Mark clarified, his eyes twinkling with sincerity. "I helped him see the possibilities. Just like I'm trying to do for you."

Sarah shifted in her seat, her posture uncurling from its previously defensive position. "It's hard to imagine something like that happening to me," she admitted, her voice shaking slightly with a mixture of doubt and wonder.

"Sometimes," Mark said, leaning in a little closer, "the hardest part isn't the struggle itself. It's allowing ourselves to believe we're worthy of the good things that can come after."

She considered his words, letting them wash over her like a soothing balm. "That sounds... nice," Sarah conceded, the corners of her mouth lifting ever so slightly.

"Nice can be real," Mark reassured her. "Change is scary, but it also brings new beginnings. You're standing at a crossroads, Sarah. And sometimes, the best path isn't the easiest one."

"New beginnings, huh?" She repeated the phrase, her scepticism beginning to soften as the idea took root.

"Exactly," Mark said, reaching out to gently tap the watch on her wrist, an unspoken reminder of time and its relentless forward march. "Every second is a fresh opportunity to steer your life in the direction you want it to go."

A brief silence passed between them, the hum of the park's chatter filling the spaces in their conversation. Sarah inhaled deeply, her chest rising and falling with a new rhythm. When she spoke again, her voice was steadier, now carrying a cautious optimism.

"Okay, Mark. Maybe there's something to this after all. Maybe holding on... isn't such a bad idea."

"Maybe it's the beginning of something wonderful," he replied, encouraging her to embrace the uncertainty with courage.

"Maybe," she echoed, the word now laced with a spark of hope, just waiting to grow with the right nurturing.

"Take your time," Mark suggested, his voice as gentle as the breeze rustling through the leaves above them. "No rush to decide. Mull it over. Do what feels right for you, Sarah."

She looked at him, her eyes reflecting the maelstrom of thoughts behind them. "But how can I be sure? I've been so... uncertain lately."

"Certainty is a luxury, often just out of reach," Mark acknowledged, his head tilting slightly. "But trust yourself. You know more than you think."

"Trust me..." she repeated, rolling the words around in her mind like unfamiliar flavours on her tongue.

"Exactly." He nodded, his eyes steady. "And whatever you decide, just remember I'm here. If you ever need to talk, or if you just want someone to listen, I'll be around."

"Thank you, Mark," Sarah said, the weight in her chest feeling a little lighter at his words. "I... I can't believe you just came up to me out of nowhere. Why?"

"Sometimes," Mark said with a small, knowing smile, "the universe nudges us to where we're needed most. Today, it nudged me here. To you."

A genuine smile tugged at Sarah's lips, the first one in what felt like ages. "Well, I'm grateful for that nudge. And for you. You have this... incredible gift."

Mark's face softened. "We all have gifts, Sarah. Some are just easier to see. Yours might be waiting just past this rough patch."

"Maybe it is," she conceded, feeling her heart quicken at the thought.

"Maybe," he echoed, standing up from the bench and offering her his hand. She took it, feeling the strength and warmth in his grip.

"Promise me one thing?" Mark asked as she stood to join him.

"Sure, what's that?"

"Think about it. Really think about it. When you're ready, choose the path that will make you happy, not just the one that seems safe."

"Okay, I promise," she said, her voice stronger now. The park around them seemed brighter somehow; the colours more vivid.

"Good." Mark released her hand, but his reassuring presence lingered in the air. "Take care, Sarah."

"Mark?" She called out as he began to walk away.

He turned back, an inquisitive arch to his brow.

"Thank you. I mean it. For everything today," Sarah said, clasping her hands together as a symbol of her sincerity.

"Anytime, Sarah," he replied with a nod. With a slight wave, he blended back into the suburban scenery, leaving her alone with her thoughts and the seed of hope now planted in her heart.

As Sarah watched him disappear into the crowd, she realised that while the future was shrouded in uncertainty, it was also filled with people like Mark, unexpected guardians whose paths crossed hers just when she needed it most.

With a deep breath, she whispered a vow to the wind, "I'll think it through. And I'll find my way."

Chapter 2
Fractured Shadows

Mark Jennings stepped onto the dew-speckled lawn, the soft glow of the morning sun casting a warm light over the modest suburban homes that lined Elmwood Street. His hands, ever in search of something to fix or fiddle with, found solace in the familiar texture of the newspaper as he picked it up from the driveway. He offered a nod and a half-smile to Mrs. Peterson, who was struggling with her overeager poodle across the street. The neighbourhood hummed with its usual rhythm, a comforting symphony of sprinklers and distant lawnmowers.

"Morning, Mark!" Mr. Howard bellowed from next door, his voice booming over the hedge.

"Good morning, Mr. Howard," Mark replied, his tone neutral, betraying neither irritation nor enthusiasm. The exchange, like clockwork, was part of the unspoken social contract of suburbia.

As Mark folded the paper under his arm, his gaze inadvertently fell on a figure ambling down the sidewalk opposite his house, an odd contrast to the meticulously kept hedges and pristine walkways. Nathan Walker's silhouette stood out against the neat tableau of the neighbourhood. His dark, untamed hair flopped over his forehead, a rebellious defiance to the tidy uniformity around him. A worn leather jacket hung off his lean frame, the elbows frayed, speaking of many days and nights spent in corners far less sheltered than these.

"Another one lost in the storm," Mark muttered to himself, recognising the signs of a soul adrift.

Nathan's face, when he finally lifted it from the contemplation of his scuffed boots, was a canvas of brooding thoughts. His dark eyes flickered with an intensity that felt almost out of place in the pastel serenity of the suburban morning. Eyes that had seen more than their fair share of shadows, reflecting a mind weighed down by troubles extending well beyond the white picket fences.

"Life's got you by the collar, eh?" Mark said softly, though Nathan was far enough away not to hear him. It was a statement laced with empathy, not judgment; Mark knew all too well the weight that invisible burdens could place on a person's shoulders.

"Seems like he could use a friend," Mark thought, quietly storing away the observation like a bookmark in the story of his day, ready to revisit when the time was right. There was a quiet determination in his stance, a resolve that came not from a desire to meddle, but from the understanding that sometimes, the smallest gesture could turn the page on someone's darkest chapter.

"Hey, is that...?" Mr. Howard's voice trailed off as he followed Mark's gaze.

"Someone new," Mark replied simply, "or perhaps just someone who's been here all along, waiting to be noticed."

"Looks like trouble, if you ask me," Mr. Howard scoffed, shaking his head as he retreated into the sanctuary of his manicured garden.

"Or maybe trouble's been following him," Mark whispered to no one in particular, his words as much an observation as a reminder of his own purpose. It was easy to mistake a storm cloud for the storm itself. But Mark, with his unique way of seeing the world, recognised Nathan's distress as a cry for help, muffled by pride and circumstance, not as an omen of chaos.

In the stillness of the morning, Mark's daily routine unfolded with seamless predictability. Yet within the mundane was the seed of an extraordinary encounter, one that promised to breach the walls of two very different worlds.

Mark strolled along the winding path that cut through the suburban park, his hands casually tucked into his jacket pockets. With each step, he absorbed the details around him: the dew-speckled grass glistening in the morning sun, the soft hum of a distant lawn mower, and the laughter of children playing by the pond. It was as though the world moved to a gentle, predictable rhythm, a cadence Mark found both comforting and grounding.

As he rounded a bend, his eyes landed on a solitary figure sitting on a bench ahead. Nathan's silhouette was unmistakable against the backdrop of vibrant greenery, a stark contrast to the lively atmosphere of the park. His posture was slumped, his head bowed as if carrying an invisible weight. Even from this distance, Mark noted the faraway look in Nathan's eyes, hollowed with a sadness that silently resonated across the space between them.

"Hey there," Mark called out as he approached, his voice carrying a warmth that seemed to brush away the chill in the air. Nathan's head snapped up, a flash of surprise crossing his features before they quickly settled into guarded lines.

"Sorry, didn't mean to startle you," Mark continued, offering a tentative smile. He stopped a few paces away, careful not to intrude on the solitude Nathan had wrapped himself in.

"Did you want something?" Nathan's voice was wary, a hint of defensiveness woven through his words.

"Just saw you sitting here, thought you might like some company," Mark replied, studying Nathan's face for any sign of welcome or rejection. "It's a nice day to be outside, isn't it?"

Nathan hesitated, his gaze flickering over Mark's unassuming appearance. "I guess," he finally conceded, the sharpness in his tone softening ever so slightly. "You always talk to strangers in the park?"

"Only when my gut tells me they might need a friend," Mark replied lightly, though there was a sincerity in his words that was unmistakable. He took a small step forward, closing the gap just enough to offer his presence without intruding.

"Your gut, huh?" Nathan scoffed, but a hint of a genuine smile tugged at the corner of his mouth. "What makes you think I need a friend?"

"Sometimes, people wear their hearts not on their sleeves, but in their eyes," Mark said quietly, his voice carrying a wisdom that seemed to stretch beyond his years. "And right now, yours are telling me you've got a lot on your mind."

Nathan glanced away, the fleeting amusement vanishing as quickly as it had appeared. His fingers curled around the bench, knuckles whitening with the force of his grip. "Maybe I do," he murmured, almost to himself.

"Mind if I sit?" Mark gestured to the empty space beside Nathan, his movements deliberate and unhurried.

"Suit yourself," Nathan replied, his tone indifferent but lacking any real resistance.

Taking the invitation for what it was, Mark sat down on the bench, allowing the shared silence of the morning to envelop them. They sat together, two strangers brought together by chance, or perhaps by something more. Nathan's initial wariness hadn't entirely dissipated, but in the quiet space between them, it seemed to ease, bit by bit, like mist giving way to sunlight.

"Mark," he offered after a moment, extending his hand in introduction.

"Nathan," came the reply, accompanied by a tentative handshake that spoke volumes of the fragile beginnings of trust.

And there, amidst the ordinariness of suburbia, an extraordinary connection began to take root, one that promised to grow into something neither of them could have predicted.

Nathan's fingers drummed an erratic beat on the weathered wood of the bench, a staccato rhythm echoing the turmoil within him. His head hung low, a lock of dark hair falling over his furrowed brow as he muttered, "Can't keep going like this... nowhere to turn."

Mark, seated beside him, observed with quiet intensity. The subtle vibrations of Nathan's distress seemed to permeate the air, stirring

Mark's innate empathy. He leaned in slightly, his presence a silent offer of solidarity.

"Feels like you're stuck in a maze with no way out, doesn't it?" Mark's voice was soft but carried an undercurrent of reassurance.

Nathan's drumming stopped, and he cast a sidelong glance at Mark, surprise flickering in his eyes.

"Yeah, exactly," he exhaled, the words slipping out almost like a confession.

"Been there myself," Mark said, shifting his body towards Nathan, closing the gap between them with the warmth of understanding. "Sometimes, all it takes is someone who can listen. Someone who gets it."

Nathan's shoulders, once hunched in defence, dropped ever so slightly. It was as if the simple recognition of his struggle had lightened the weight he carried. He exhaled deeply, a sound that seemed to carry the burden of his woes. "I don't even know where to begin..."

"Start by just being," Mark suggested, an encouraging smile tugging at the corners of his mouth. "The rest will follow when you're ready."

"Being what?" Nathan asked, his tone a mixture of scepticism and curiosity.

"Being here, now, with whatever you've got." Mark's hand reached out, gently resting on Nathan's arm, a touch meant to ground him and remind him of the moment they shared. "And knowing that's enough for a start."

For a moment, Nathan remained still under Mark's touch, then nodded almost imperceptibly, as though conceding to the truth in Mark's words. The beginnings of trust, fragile as morning dew, shimmered between them.

Mark studied Nathan for a moment, the young man's eyes tracing the patterns of autumn leaves skittering across the path. He took a small step forward, his presence unobtrusive yet undeniably empathetic.

"Hey," he said softly, his voice threaded with concern. "Are you okay?"

Nathan's gaze snapped up, irritation flashing across his features as if the question were an intrusion he wasn't prepared for. "I'm fine," he muttered, the words sharp and hollow. His hands clenched into fists on his thighs, knuckles whitening with the force.

"Doesn't look like 'fine' to me," Mark pressed gently, unfazed by the brusqueness. "You look like someone carrying the weight of the world on their shoulders."

"Look, I don't need it," Nathan cut himself off, jaw working as though chewing over his next words. "Thanks, but you should mind your own business."

"Sometimes," Mark continued, undeterred by the rebuff, "our own business is helping others. It's hard to watch someone in pain and do nothing."

"Who says I'm in pain?" Nathan's voice rose slightly, defensive. He looked away, his body language shouting for solitude.

"Your eyes," Mark replied simply, his tone steady and sure. "They tell a story you might not be ready to voice. And that's okay. But if you ever do want to share it, I'm here to listen."

"Great, a mind reader," Nathan scoffed, though the sarcasm barely masked the flicker of interest that betrayed his indifferent exterior. "What else do my eyes say?"

"They say you're tired," Mark said, stepping closer, respecting the distance but offering solace. "Tired of fighting whatever battle you're facing alone."

"Maybe I am," Nathan admitted reluctantly, his shoulders sagging as though the admission had drained some tension from him. "But why would you care? You don't even know me."

"Because everyone deserves someone who cares," Mark replied, his smile gentle and reassuring. "No strings attached."

The Mind Whisperer

Nathan studied Mark's face, scepticism battling with the raw glimmer of hope daring to surface. "You're serious, aren't you?"

"Deadly." Mark's eyes twinkled with sincerity. "So, what do you say? Want to talk about what's weighing you down?"

Mark leaned back on the bench, the wood creaking beneath him. He looked at Nathan, who sat rigid as though bracing against an invisible storm. The air between them was thick with unspoken words.

"Once," Mark began, breaking the silence like a pebble skimming across a still pond, "I found myself in a place not too different from where you might be now."

Nathan's eyes flickered to Mark, a silent invitation to continue despite his earlier resistance.

"Surrounded by people, yet utterly alone. It felt like I was looking at life through a window, never able to step inside." Mark's voice was even, though it carried an undercurrent of raw honesty.

"Is that supposed to make me feel better?" Nathan asked, sarcasm laced with curiosity.

"It's not about feeling better," Mark countered softly. "It's about knowing someone else has navigated through the fog. Sometimes, just knowing that is enough to take the next breath."

"Next breath," Nathan muttered, his gaze dropping to his fidgeting hands. "Feels like I'm suffocating, you know?"

"Because it's like the world expects you to be a certain way, to follow a script you never agreed to?" Mark offered, watching Nathan's reactions closely.

"Exactly!" Nathan exclaimed, surprised. His eyes met Mark's, and for a moment, there was a spark of recognition , the feeling of being understood.

"Your thoughts," Mark continued, tapping his temple gently, "they can be loud, drowning everything else out. It's hard to tell which are yours and which have been… implanted by loss or fear."

"Implanted..." Nathan echoed softly. "How do you know this?"

"Because I've listened to many thoughts, seen patterns." Mark's admission hung between them, neither boast nor confession. "And because sometimes, it takes one to know one."

"Know one what?" Nathan furrowed his brow, his interest piqued further.

"Someone who fights battles no one else can see," Mark clarified, leaning slightly forward, bridging the gap with empathy.

"Like a mind reader?" Nathan asked, half-joking, half-hoping.

"More like a heart listener," Mark corrected with a small smile. "I don't read minds. But I do pay attention. And right now, all I'm doing is listening to you."

"Listening," Nathan repeated, the word strange yet comforting. "No one does that anymore."

"I do," Mark asserted. "And I'll keep doing it for as long as you need."

"Nobody's ever said anything like that to me before," Nathan admitted, the walls around him beginning to crumble as he considered the possibility of a genuine connection.

"Then let me be the first," Mark said warmly. "Let's start a new pattern, one where you talk, and I listen. No judgments. Just two people sharing the same space, understanding a bit of each other's worlds."

For the first time since they met, Nathan's mouth twitched into the beginnings of a reluctant smile. The idea of being heard, truly heard, seemed to ignite a faint fire in his eyes. A glimmer of hope, perhaps, in a reality that had been too dark for far too long.

Mark reached over, his hand hovering before gently settling on Nathan's hunched shoulder. "I believe people are essentially good," he began, his voice soft and melodic, weaving through the crisp park air. "It's the world around us that can cast long shadows over our hearts."

The Mind Whisperer

Nathan's shoulder tensed under Mark's touch, but he didn't pull away. Instead, he tilted his head slightly, a mixture of scepticism and curiosity flickering across his features.

"Sounds like a fairy tale," Nathan scoffed, though his voice lacked conviction. "People aren't good. Not in my experience."

"Maybe," Mark conceded, his thumb tracing small, reassuring circles on Nathan's shoulder. "But sometimes, our experiences are too narrow, too... focused on the pain we've endured. It blinds us to everything else, the possibility of kindness without ulterior motives."

"Kindness..." Nathan mumbled, the word brittle, like dried leaves scattered beneath autumn trees.

"Exactly," Mark affirmed, nodding. "And I want to offer you that, no strings attached. I'm here, Nathan, ready to listen. Ready to help." His brown eyes, earnest and unwavering, met Nathan's guarded gaze.

"Help me with what?" Nathan challenged, though his voice wavered like a leaf caught in a light breeze, betraying his longing for the very thing he questioned.

"Whatever battles you're fighting inside," Mark said, his tone brimming with compassion. "The ones that keep you up at night, that paint your days grey. You don't have to face them alone."

A silence stretched between them, filled only by the distant laughter of children and the rustling whispers of wind through the trees. Nathan's eyes flickered, his hard exterior beginning to crack as he considered the sincerity radiating from Mark.

"Have you ever felt like the world was just... too much?" Nathan asked, the words escaping him like prisoners breaking free after a long confinement.

"Many times," Mark replied without hesitation. "I know what it's like to feel overwhelmed, to feel like you're drowning in a sea of noise and chaos." He paused, letting the truth of his words sink in. "You see, my mind... it operates differently. I feel other people's emotions and pain deeply. It can be a lot to bear."

Nathan's eyes locked onto Mark's with a newfound intensity. "You get it," he whispered, almost to himself. A shiver ran through him, not from the cool air, but from the recognition of a kindred spirit.

"I do," Mark confirmed, the bond between them now palpable, a bridge built on mutual understanding. "And I'm not going anywhere, Nathan. We can share the load, make it a little lighter for both of us."

"Share the load..." Nathan echoed, the idea foreign yet oddly comforting. For a fleeting moment, his slumped posture straightened as if the weight he carried had become just a bit more bearable.

"Let's walk this path together," Mark offered, extending a hand toward Nathan, an invitation to stand side by side. "One step at a time. Who knows? Maybe we'll find that the world has hidden pockets of light we've been missing all along."

With a hesitant nod, Nathan reached out, taking Mark's hand in his own, a tangible sign of trust. The connection was made, two souls recognising the echo of their own despair in each other, finding comfort in the shared silence that followed.

Nathan's grip on Mark's hand was a lifeline, grounding him in the present. They stood for a moment, not speaking, as the park around them hummed with the quiet life of dusk, children laughing in the distance, the rustle of leaves in a gentle breeze. Then, in unison, they began to walk, their steps slow and measured.

"Never thought I'd... you know, talk about this stuff," Nathan murmured, his voice rough like gravel but tinged with wonder. "Especially not with a stranger."

"Sometimes strangers see us more clearly than we see ourselves," Mark replied, his words soft but sure. He felt Nathan's pulse through the clasp of their hands, a nervous rhythm seeking calm.

"Is it always like this for you?" Nathan asked, stealing a glance at Mark. "Feeling everything from everyone?"

"Mostly," Mark admitted, a wry smile tugging at his lips. "But sometimes, I find someone who needs to be heard more than others. Like you."

A laugh, brittle but genuine, escaped Nathan. "Lucky me."

"Maybe lucky us," Mark suggested. "You needed to talk, and I needed to listen. Seems like the universe aligns once in a while."

"Aligns, huh?" There was scepticism in Nathan's voice, but it was lighter now, edged with curiosity rather than dismissal.

"Sure," Mark encouraged. "The stars, fate, cosmic coincidence, whatever you want to call it."

"Never put much stock in fate." Nathan's stride grew more confident, his voice steadier. "But I can't deny... there's something weirdly right about this. About you."

"Nothing weird about it," Mark assured him. "Just two people finding each other at the right time."

"Guess so." Nathan's eyes were searching as he looked at Mark. "You really think people are good? Deep down?"

"I do," Mark said without hesitation, his conviction clear. "Even when they're lost or hurting, there's goodness in them. Sometimes, it just takes a little digging to find it."

"Digging..." Nathan echoed, contemplative. "I've done a lot of that. Mostly unearthing crap."

"Maybe you've been using the wrong tools," Mark offered with a gentle chuckle. "Let me help. Together, we might unearth something better."

"Like what?" The question was a challenge, but also an invitation.

"Hope, for starters," Mark said, squeezing Nathan's hand in reassurance. "Understanding. A future that doesn't look so bleak."

"Hope," Nathan tested the word, rolling it around like something unfamiliar but not unpleasant. "Been a long time since I felt that."

"Then let's rediscover it together," Mark said, his tone imbued with excitement. "It's a journey, Nathan. And every journey begins with a single step."

"Step by step, huh?" Nathan's lips twitched into the ghost of a smile, the first genuine one Mark had seen.

"Exactly," Mark confirmed, his heart swelling with the knowledge that he had reached Nathan, even if it was just the outer edges of his fortified walls.

They walked on, the silence between them no longer heavy with unsaid words but filled with possibility. As the sun dipped below the horizon, painting the sky in shades of pink and orange, Nathan seemed to stand a little taller, the shadows of his turmoil softening in the fading light.

"Okay, Mark," Nathan finally said, his voice barely above a whisper but resolute. "Let's see where this path leads."

And with that simple acquiescence, the fragile bud of their newfound companionship began to open, promising the warmth of kinship and the potential to blossom into something neither of them had expected, a friendship forged in understanding and shaded with hope.

Chapter 3
The Reluctant Guide

Mark paced the living room, his mind churning with thoughts of Nathan. Every furrow in the young man's brow, every downturned corner of his mouth, was etched into Mark's memory. They spoke of a silent despair that clung to him, relentless and heavy.

The air hung thick with the scent of fresh coffee, a small, mundane comfort that did little to cut through Mark's growing concern.

"I can't just let it lie," he murmured to himself, feeling Nathan's pain as though it were his own. The empathy that so often weighed on him now served as his driving force. Watching from the sidelines wasn't enough. He had to dive into the heart of Nathan's suffering and uncover whatever was holding him captive.

He reached for his phone, its cool surface grounding him for a moment. With practiced ease, he dialled Susan's number, each ring drawing him closer to the truth he hoped to find.

"Hey, Susan," he said as soon as she answered, his voice steady but tinged with urgency. "I need your help with something important."

"Mark?" Her voice was warm but edged with concern. "What's happened?"

"It's Nathan. There's more to his story than we know. I can feel it," he said, words spilling out faster now. "I think we need to start digging a bit deeper."

A pause followed. Mark could almost hear her thinking, could almost see the way she'd be nodding slowly.

"You mean looking into his past?" she asked, her intuition as sharp as ever.

"Exactly." He leaned against the back of the sofa, gripping the phone tighter. "I believe there's something hidden there, something that's holding him back. And I can't just watch him keep struggling."

Susan's sigh crackled through the line, filled with understanding. "Alright, Mark. You know I'm with you. What do you need?"

"Your insight. Your support. Maybe even a bit of that stubborn streak of yours," he said, allowing himself a small smile. The thought of her standing beside him, even at a distance, brought a flicker of hope.

"Then I'm in. We'll tackle this together. Do you have any idea where to begin?"

Her voice now carried the spark of shared purpose, the kind that always lit the way when they teamed up.

"Nothing solid just yet. But I was thinking…"

"Of reaching out to people who knew him before? Friends, family, anyone who might fill in the gaps?" she offered.

"Exactly," Mark replied, the weight on his chest easing just a little. It meant everything to know he wasn't doing this alone.

"Leave it to me, big brother. I'll compile a list and make some calls. We'll get to the bottom of this," Susan declared, her protective instincts evident in the firm set of her jaw.

"Thanks, Sue," Mark exhaled, his voice heavy with gratitude. "This means the world."

"Anything for you, Mark. And anything to help Nathan," she affirmed, the unspoken promise between them as solid as a vow.

With their plan taking shape and Susan by his side, Mark ended the call, a new sense of hope stirring within him. Together, they would uncover the layers of Nathan's life, searching for the truth buried beneath. It was a daunting path ahead, but for Nathan's sake, they would face it with unwavering determination.

The Mind Whisperer

Mark's fingers flew over the keyboard, the rhythmic tap-tap of the keys a comforting sound in the quiet of his home office. With every stroke, he started to sketch out the framework for their investigation on the screen before him. The cursor blinked back at him as he paused to think through their next step.

"First things first," he began, the soft glow of his webcam casting a warm light on his face. "We need to understand Nathan's history: his family, childhood experiences, friendships."

"Right," Susan nodded earnestly on the other end, her face framed by the familiar backdrop of her book-lined study. "Every person's life is a story, and every story has its pivotal chapters. We find those, and we unlock the keys to Nathan's present."

"Keys..." Mark repeated, the word resonating with him. He opened a new document, quickly typing out headings: Family, Friends, Education, Employment. Beneath each, he left space for bullet points, ready to fill them in later.

"School records might be a good starting point," Susan suggested, her eyes lighting up with the thrill of the investigation. "Teachers are the quiet observers. They can see the hurts we don't."

"Brilliant," Mark agreed, admiration evident in his voice. "They'll know sides of Nathan that even we haven't seen. I'll add that to our list."

"And then there's employment," Susan continued. "Colleagues, bosses people who might have noticed changes in behaviour we can't. It's all part of the puzzle."

"Patterns," Mark said thoughtfully, typing faster now. "Patterns tell the story. And patterns in behaviour often hold the answers."

"Exactly!" Susan leaned closer to the camera, her enthusiasm practically vibrating through the screen. "We're looking for pieces, Mark. Fragments of Nathan's life. It's like... like putting together a jigsaw puzzle without the picture on the box."

"Which means we're assembling the picture one piece at a time." Mark stopped typing and met her gaze through the camera, his expression steady. "But we've got to be careful, Sue. Not everyone will want to talk. People have their reasons for keeping things quiet."

"True," she agreed, a small frown crossing her face, "but we know how to handle that, don't we? Besides," her smile returned, fierce and confident, "we're doing this for Nathan. To help him heal. No door left unknocked; no stone left unturned."

"Agreed. Empathy is our guide," Mark said, his resolve hardening. "Let's start with Nathan's friends those who've drifted away might be more willing to speak now."

"Friends, it is." Susan grabbed a notepad from her desk, pen at the ready. "I'll take the lead with the initial contact. You're better at reading between the lines during interviews."

"Deal," Mark nodded gently. "Your people skills, my... instinct. We make a good team."

"Always have, always will," Susan replied, her voice rich with pride and affection.

"Okay, let's recap." Mark leaned back in his chair, his eyes scanning the notes on his screen. "We'll reach out to Nathan's old friends discreetly, gather what we can from public records, schools, workplaces. We'll stay sensitive, stay sharp."

"Sharp as tacks," Susan grinned. "Watch out, world, the Jennings siblings are on the case!"

"Indeed," Mark chuckled, a weight lifting from his chest. "For Nathan, we'll get to the bottom of this. And maybe, just maybe, we'll find a way forward for him."

"Let's do it," Susan declared, her determination matching his own.

"Let's." Mark reached out and ended the call, the sound of the click marking the beginning of their heartfelt journey into the unknown corners of Nathan's life.

Susan flipped open her laptop, the soft light from the screen illuminating her focused expression. "I've got a list of Nathan's friends from his social media before he went off the radar," she said, her fingers tapping quickly over the keyboard.

"Perfect." Mark leaned in, his mind already sorting through possibilities, each lead a potential breakthrough. "Start with those who interacted with him most. They'll have the clearest memories."

"Got it." Susan dialled the first number with practised ease, holding the phone between her shoulder and ear. She shot Mark a quick, reassuring smile as the first call connected. "Hi, is this Jamie? ... Yes, my brother and I are trying to understand a situation involving Nathan Walker. We were hoping you could spare a few moments for a chat."

Mark watched her, tuning into the subtle shifts in her voice, the way her eyebrows furrowed or relaxed. He caught the rhythm of her words, the pauses that spoke volumes, and the laughter genuine or strained that revealed more than words alone.

"Can you tell us about any significant changes you noticed in Nathan over the past year?" Susan continued, her warmth coaxing openness like sunlight on a blooming flower.

Mark's instincts kicked in, quietly predicting the flow of the conversation, sensing where hesitations might lie or where a breakthrough could occur. His anticipation grew with every nod Susan gave, each one a silent signal that they were uncovering something meaningful.

"Thank you so much, Jamie. Your perspective means a lot to us," Susan said as she ended the call, her face a mix of excitement and contemplation as she turned to Mark. "He mentioned a falling out with someone close to Nathan, but he didn't know the specifics."

"Let's keep digging," Mark suggested, his voice calm but filled with anticipation. His heart raced at the thought of the next lead. "Who's next?"

"Emma she was close to him in college." Susan dialled once more, her tone shifting to match the gravity of the upcoming conversation. "Hello, Emma? My name's Susan Jennings. I'm looking into some things concerning Nathan Walker…"

Mark listened closely, aware that silence could sometimes reveal just as much as words. When Susan hit a wall, unable to extract more than vague, noncommittal responses, she glanced at Mark, a silent question in her eyes.

"Ask her about Nathan's hobbies and passions," Mark suggested quietly. "Sometimes joy speaks louder than pain."

"Emma," Susan's voice softened, "can you share anything about what Nathan loved doing? Any particular interests or activities?" Her tone was gentle, inviting openness.

The shift in approach worked. Emma's guarded tone began to melt as she reminisced about Nathan's passion for astronomy, the late-night stargazing sessions that seemed like distant memories now.

"Thank you, Emma. That's really helpful," Susan said, her voice thoughtful as she ended the call. "Stargazing… maybe there's something in that, Mark."

"It could be a metaphorical compass," Mark mused, a flicker of hope igniting in his chest. "Maybe we'll find what he's been searching for among the stars."

"Or maybe we'll find who he's been missing," Susan added, her intuition in perfect sync with his. They exchanged a look, their resolve deepening as they connected yet another dot.

"Next?" Mark asked, eager to continue their search.

"His former colleague, Ben," Susan replied, dialling once more. As the phone rang, Mark closed his eyes, bracing himself to navigate yet another conversation with his unique sense of intuition.

"Ben, hi, this is Susan Jennings. We're piecing together some information about Nathan Walker. Could we ask you a few questions?"

As Susan engaged with Ben, Mark felt the weight of their mission pressing upon him. But there was also a thrill, an undercurrent of exhilaration, as every word brought them closer to understanding Nathan's world one piece at a time.

"I understand your hesitation, Ben," Susan's voice was steady and calm, "but any insight you have could be the key to helping Nathan find his way back."

Mark scribbled frantically in his notebook, his fingers almost dancing across the page. He had always been meticulous about details each note was a breadcrumb, leading them closer to a breakthrough.

"Look, Susan," came Ben's gruff voice over the speakerphone, tinged with reluctance, "I ain't seen the guy in months. We didn't exactly part on speaking terms."

"Could you tell us what happened?" Susan asked gently, her patience unwavering as she carefully probed.

"Work stuff, y'know? Disagreements. Ego clashes." There was a pause, then a heavy sigh. "Nathan took things... hard."

"Disagreements about what, Ben?" Mark interjected, sensing there was more to the story.

"Projects, deadlines," Ben muttered, then added, as though the words were being pulled from him, "And there was this one night something about the stars..."

"Go on," Susan encouraged softly.

"Damn astronomy project we were bidding on. Nathan wanted it bad and said it meant everything to him. When we lost it to Anderson Corp, he just... broke."

"Thank you, Ben," Susan said, her voice warm with a quiet triumph. Mark felt it too another piece of the puzzle had slid into place.

"Anything else you remember could help," Mark pressed, not willing to let the conversation slip away just yet.

"Sorry, that's all I've got. And frankly, I'd like to stay out of it now," Ben's voice grew distant, signalling the end of his willingness to cooperate.

"Understood. Thank you for your time," Susan concluded, ending the call. They sat in silence for a moment, the weight of Ben's words lingering in the air.

"Stars again," Mark noted, tapping his pen against his notebook. His mind raced, seeing patterns where others saw only confusion.

"Seems they're more than just a hobby," Susan mused, leaning back in her chair as she glanced at the remaining names on the list. "Next?"

"Let's try his aunt, Marianne. Maybe she can shed some light on this stargazing angle," Mark suggested, his eyes fixed on the phone, ready to dive into the next conversation.

"Hello, Marianne? This is Susan Jennings..." Her voice flowed into another familiar rhythm, a comfort to Mark as he settled into the moment.

But as the conversation unfolded, Marianne's resistance was clear, even to Mark's finely tuned senses. She skirted around direct answers, her tone laced with an undercurrent of weariness.

"Please, Marianne," Susan's plea was gentle but insistent, "this isn't about dredging up the past it's about helping Nathan now."

"Child, I've put those days behind me," Marianne's voice wavered, a hint of old pain leaking through. "Nathan was always a dreamer, chasing after comets and constellations. But dreams can turn to nightmares, and some things are best left alone."

"Even a nightmare can hold the key to waking up," Mark said quietly, his voice a calm anchor amidst the storm of their search. The depth of his words surprised even him, but he spoke from the heart.

There was a long pause on the other end of the line. Then, finally, Marianne spoke again, her voice slow and deliberate. "You remind me of him, you know. That same fire. All right, I'll tell you what I can."

As Susan continued the conversation, Mark's pen flew across the paper, capturing every word with precision. They were drawing closer to the heart of Nathan's mystery, piece by piece, like stitching together a vast, fragmented tapestry of secrets waiting to be uncovered.

Mark shuffled through the notes, his fingers tracing the lines of text as though they might reveal something beyond the ink. Susan, perched on the edge of the sofa, was surrounded by a clutter of documents, her laptop aglow in the dim light.

"Listen to this," Mark said, tapping a note with emphasis. "Nathan had a job at a local garage during high school. That's where he got into cars something about them calmed him."

"Calmed him, or gave him an escape?" Susan pondered aloud, her gaze flitting from the screen to her brother. "Maybe both." She clicked through several tabs, her search history a breadcrumb trail in their pursuit. "Okay, here's something. He won a regional science fair there's a small article in the town's digital archives. It mentions his fascination with astronomy."

"Passion can be a double-edged sword," Mark murmured, recalling Nathan's tortured expression when they first met. "It either lifts you up or cuts deep when it's lost."

Susan nodded, her eyes reflecting the glow of the screen. "Losing a dream, or not being able to follow it... that could be a piece of his despair."

"Right," Mark agreed, feeling the excitement building between them. The puzzle was intricate, but every piece mattered. "There must be records, something from the school or the contest that might give us more insight."

"Let's see what we can find," Susan proposed, her fingers dancing over the keys with practised ease.

Moments later, she exhaled sharply. "Got it! His high school grades and attendance records. But there are gaps semesters with missing data."

"Patterns," Mark said, leaning in to examine the anomalies. "Sometimes it's not what's there, but what's missing that tells the story."

"Exactly," Susan responded, her voice tinged with determination. "We need to understand those gaps. I'll request his employment history next."

"Good, good," Mark nodded, his mind already racing ahead. "And I'll look for any legal records maybe parking tickets, event permits for the science fair, anything that could have his name on it."

"Or court documents," Susan added, her voice laced with concern. "If there were any family issues custody battles, restraining orders... those could have left scars."

"Scars that we can heal," Mark affirmed, his empathy bolstering his resolve.

"Or at least understand," Susan corrected gently, always the realist to his idealist.

Their shared endeavour was more than just an investigation; it was a lifeline they hoped to extend to Nathan. Mark could feel the weight of each discovery, the tremor of potential breakthroughs mingling with the frustration of elusive truths.

"Here goes nothing," Susan said, submitting a query for the legal records. They both held their breath, waiting for the electronic world to yield its secrets.

"Something's coming up," Mark whispered, almost afraid to break the spell.

"Then let's dive in," Susan declared, her smile fierce and fearless. Together, they plunged back into the depths of Nathan's past, determined to surface with the understanding he so desperately needed.

Mark tapped his finger against the stack of printouts, each one a dead end. "Nothing here but false starts," he muttered, rifling through the pages.

Susan leaned back, her own pile of documents scattered around her. She exhaled sharply, a lock of blonde hair falling over her eyes. "It's like looking for a needle in a haystack made entirely of needles, all irrelevant."

"Except," Mark said, his voice steady despite the setbacks, "haystacks don't have patterns. This does." His finger paused on a school record, tapping thoughtfully.

"Patterns?" Susan tilted her head, curiosity piqued.

"Look at the dates," he urged, drawing her attention to the timeline they had created. "Every winter, Nathan's performance drops. Every spring, it rises again."

"Seasonal affective disorder?" she suggested, a spark of excitement in her tone.

"Or something happening in those months," Mark countered, his eyes narrowing as he connected the dots. "Something cyclical."

"Let's call Mrs. Henderson again," Susan proposed, reaching for the phone. "She might not have thought it was important, but she did mention Nathan always seemed different after the holidays."

"Exactly," Mark nodded, watching as Susan dialled the number. The pulse of hope was palpable between them.

"Mrs. Henderson? Hi, it's Susan Jennings again. Yes, about Nathan Walker. May we ask you some more questions?"

As Susan spoke, Mark reviewed the notes they'd taken from their first call with Mrs. Henderson. His mind was a whirlwind, thoughts and theories colliding and reforming with every new piece of information.

"Thank you so much," Susan said warmly into the phone. "That detail about his father moving out every January could be significant."

"Father moved out every January?" Mark repeated, his voice rising with the realisation. "Moved out or... kicked out?"

"Would you say there was tension in the household during these times, Mrs. Henderson? I see," Susan scribbled more notes, her brow furrowing.

"Ask her about the science fair," Mark interjected suddenly, remembering the event permit he'd seen Nathan's name on.

"Mrs. Henderson, do you remember anything about Nathan participating in a science fair during his senior year?"

"An accident?" Susan's voice dropped to a whisper, and she glanced up at Mark, alarm in her eyes. "He never mentioned an accident."

"Thank you, Mrs. Henderson. This has been very helpful," Susan said, wrapping up the call. She put the phone down, her hands trembling slightly.

"An accident at the science fair," Mark mused, connecting another dot. "And every January, his father leaves."

"Trauma layered upon trauma," Susan murmured, her protective instincts flaring. "We're starting to understand why Nathan built such high walls."

"Understanding is the first step to helping him heal," Mark replied, his determination unwavering. "These are not just coincidences. They're chapters of his life story, and we're going to read every page."

"Let's keep going," Susan said, her blue eyes shining with resolve. "We've got more calls to make, more records to find. We're getting closer, Mark. I can feel it."

"Me too," Mark agreed, his heart heavy yet hopeful. "For Nathan, we'll turn over every stone."

Together, they dove back into the fray, their synergy a beacon in the murky waters of Nathan's past.

Mark leaned over the cluttered kitchen table, his finger tracing a line through the sea of scribbled notes that covered it. "Mrs. Henderson mentioned Dr. Elbridge, Nathan's high school science teacher. He might have more insights about the accident," he said, his voice steady with focus.

"Right," Susan nodded, her blonde hair falling over her shoulder as she jotted down the name in her notebook. "He's retired now, but I bet the school district can give us his contact info."

"Then there's the janitor, Mr. Kline," Mark added, recalling a detail from one of the interviews. "He was close to Nathan and might know more personal stuff."

"Exactly! And what about Lily? She was listed as his emergency contact at one of his old jobs," Susan suggested, enthusiasm lighting up her face.

"Good memory." Mark gave an approving nod, his excitement mirroring hers.

"Let's divvy up," Susan proposed, standing and stretching her petite frame. "I'll take Dr. Elbridge and Mr. Kline. You try to get a hold of Lily."

"Deal," Mark agreed, already reaching for his phone. His hands, usually calm and controlled, betrayed a slight tremor a physical manifestation of the emotional investment he'd made in this case.

"Remember, empathy is your superpower, Mark," Susan reminded him gently, placing a comforting hand on his arm. "Use it to connect with them."

He smiled, a warmth spreading through him at her words. "I've got this, Susan."

"Hey," she caught his eye, "we're doing good here. We're really onto something."

He knew she was right; they were a formidable team. Her belief in him was unwavering, and it bolstered his resolve. "For Nathan," he affirmed, feeling the weight of responsibility settle firmly on his shoulders.

"Okay, let's do this," Susan declared, picking up her phone as well.

The siblings worked in tandem, their calls punctuating the quiet room with a rhythm of hope. With each conversation, they wove a more comprehensive tapestry of Nathan's life, each thread a possible key to unlocking the mystery of his despair.

Hours passed, and as the sun began to set, painting the room in hues of orange and gold, Mark and Susan reconvened. They shared their findings, each piece of the puzzle eliciting nods of understanding and determined looks.

"Dr. Elbridge remembers Nathan well. He said the accident shook the whole school, especially Nathan," Susan reported, her voice tinged with sorrow.

"Meanwhile, Lily… she hinted at something, something big that happened right after graduation. But she clammed up wouldn't go into details over the phone," Mark disclosed, frustration creeping into his tone.

"Sounds like we need to meet with her in person," Susan assessed, her mind already strategising their next move.

"Agreed," Mark said, tapping his finger on the table, the gears in his mind turning. "We'll approach gently; let her see we only want to help Nathan."

"Tomorrow, first thing," Susan decided, closing her notebook with a snap. "No time to waste."

"Every moment counts," Mark echoed, standing up and stretching his back, feeling the strain of the long hours. Yet, fatigue did not touch the sense of purpose that coursed through him.

"Mark," Susan said softly, reaching out to squeeze his hand. "You're amazing, you know that? Nathan's lucky to have you in his corner."

"Couldn't do it without you, Sue," he replied, giving her hand a grateful squeeze.

Together, they stood in the quiet aftermath of their productive day, the bonds of sibling love and shared mission stronger than ever. They were ready to tackle whatever came next, driven by the knowledge that their actions had the power to alter the course of Nathan's troubled life.

"Let's find the truth," Mark stated resolutely, the last rays of sunlight casting a halo around him.

"Let's bring Nathan home," Susan added, equally resolved.

And with that, the Jennings siblings prepared for the morrow, united in their determination to unearth the secrets buried deep within Nathan's past.

Chapter 4
Healing Hands

Mark Jennings stepped into the bustling main corridor of the hospital, the sharp scent of antiseptic blending with the quiet urgency that lingered in the air, heavy like a thick fog. The linoleum floors became a racetrack for figures in scrubs, darting from room to room, their faces drawn with the day's triumphs and burdens. He moved with quiet confidence, his medium build weaving through the human torrent, dodging gurneys and sidestepping anxious family members in a practiced dance.

"Watch it!" a doctor barked, brushing past Mark, a clipboard gripped tightly like a lifeline.

"Sorry," Mark mumbled, his focus undisturbed. His short brown hair barely ruffled in the flurry of activity around him, his calm presence standing in stark contrast to the chaos of the emergency department.

A sudden commotion broke out near the nurses' station, and Mark's sharp eyes immediately caught sight of her the woman whose reputation for boundless compassion preceded her, even amid this whirlwind of need.

Clara Reynolds was at the centre of it, her wavy brown hair cascading over her shoulders, her eyes wide with concern as she knelt beside a patient who had collapsed onto the tiled floor.

"Can someone grab me the crash cart?" Clara called, her voice cutting through the noise like a clear bell.

"Right away, Nurse Reynolds!" A nearby attendant scrambled to comply.

"Stay with me," Clara whispered to the patient, her hand steady on their wrist, checking their pulse. She glanced up, her gaze a silent command, directing the chaos around her with nothing more than a look her authority gentle but unmistakable.

"Give them some air, please," she instructed the bystanders, carving a small bubble of space in the crowded corridor.

Mark paused, instinctively drawn to the scene. His eyes absorbed every detail: the patient's ashen complexion, the sweat beading on their brow, and the determination in Clara's posture as she worked tirelessly to stabilise the patient. Her focus was unwavering, every movement imbued with purpose, but also with a quiet hope.

"Anything I can do to help?" a passing technician asked, ready to lend a hand.

"Keep the crowd back and check their oxygen stats," Clara replied without missing a beat, her attention never leaving her patient.

The patient gasped a good sign. Clara offered a brief smile, the first flicker of reassurance. "That's it, just keep breathing," she murmured, her tone soft but firm, laced with warmth that seemed to radiate beyond the sterile walls of the emergency room.

Mark stood at a respectful distance, unnoticed in the frenzy, but acutely aware of the unfolding drama. His heart went out to the patient on the floor and to Clara, whose every action radiated a quiet, steadfast dedication to both healing and comforting. Amid the hospital's orchestrated pandemonium, Clara Reynolds was a beacon of hope a steady anchor in a storm of uncertainty.

"Clara, do you need"

"I've got it covered, thanks," she answered a passing offer, never breaking her focus from the task at hand.

The emergency began to subside as quickly as it had flared up. The patient's colour improved, their breathing grew steadier, and Clara rose to her feet, her composure as intact as if she'd simply been taking a routine blood pressure reading. She patted the patient's hand gently before making a note on their chart, her efficiency a testament to years of experience.

"Good job, everyone," she said with a grateful smile, surveying the team that had gathered.

As the tension eased, Mark moved closer. It was time to introduce himself and offer his own brand of help, however unique it might be. Clara might not realise it yet, but their paths were about to intersect in ways neither of them could foresee, drawn together by a shared mission to bring light to the darkest corners.

Mark watched as Clara moved through the aftermath of the crisis, expertly rearranging supplies on the crash cart with the precision that only comes from years spent in emergencies. To an outsider, she appeared the picture of composure, but Mark's perceptiveness cut through the surface. He noticed the tremor in her fingers, the slight tightness around her eyes a silent testament to the emotional storm she'd weathered.

"Excuse me," Mark said quietly, stepping into her peripheral vision. His approach was measured, non-threatening designed not to startle or add to the day's stress. "Clara?"

She turned, her kind eyes briefly flashing with surprise before settling into the warmth that had become second nature to her. "Yes? Can I help you?" Her voice held the faintest quiver, subtle but discernible to someone who listened as intently as Mark did.

"I hope so," he replied softly, his tone gentle. "I couldn't help but notice how well you handled everything just now. It's... it's quite remarkable." Tentatively, he reached out, his fingers brushing lightly against her arm a soft, reassuring touch, meant to bridge the gap between them.

"Thank you," she said, offering him a weary smile. She paused, momentarily setting aside the task at hand. "But it's really just part of the job."

"Maybe so, but not everyone carries it with your grace," Mark said, his gaze steady and unwavering. "I'm actually here to see Nathan

Walker. I believe I can assist him. And perhaps, if you're willing, you might be able to help me too."

"Assist you?" Clara repeated, her brow furrowing slightly. Her initial scepticism was tempered by genuine curiosity, and despite her exhaustion, there was an undeniable spark of interest in her eyes.

"Yes," Mark said, his voice earnest and sincere. "I have a… let's call it a unique perspective. And I think it could be beneficial for Nathan. For all of us."

"Unique perspective?" Clara tilted her head, considering him. "Well, that does sound intriguing. Tell me more."

"Alright, Clara," Mark began, his arms folded as he leaned slightly forward, "I have this ability... to understand people. To sense their emotions, really. It's not something I can explain easily, but I can tune into their feelings almost before they even realise them themselves."

"Like some kind of mind reader?" Clara asked, her scepticism lacing her words even as her curiosity grew.

"More like an empath," Mark corrected gently. "It's not about reading minds. It's a deep connection to someone's emotional state."

Clara's posture softened, and the professional distance between them seemed to lessen, replaced by genuine intrigue. "And you believe this can help Nathan?"

"I do," Mark said, his voice steady. "I believe that everyone has their own rhythm an emotional frequency. If I can tune into his, maybe I can reach him, help him find his way through whatever's tormenting him."

"Torment…" Clara echoed, her voice trailing off as she stared down the corridor, lost in thought. She sighed deeply before looking back at Mark. "You know, every day I see so much pain, so much suffering. It feels like a weight that never lifts." Her gaze met his again, vulnerable but fierce. "I became a nurse because I wanted to make a difference.

But sometimes it feels like I'm just putting band-aids on gaping wounds."

"Clara," Mark said softly, taking a step closer, his voice gentle but unwavering. "What you do... it matters. You give people hope. That's not a band-aid; that's healing."

"Maybe," she conceded, a fragile smile flickering at the corners of her lips. "But hope's a tricky thing. It slips through my fingers some days. It's fleeting."

"Understandable," Mark nodded. "But that's why we're having this conversation. To hold onto that hope together. To not let it slip away."

"Is that what you do?" Clara asked, her gaze searching his face. "Hold onto hope for others?"

"In a way," he replied. "I try to amplify it, to reinforce it. Because sometimes, all it takes is one person believing in someone to turn things around."

"Sounds exhausting," Clara said, her tone softer now, less guarded.

"It can be," Mark said with a small, wry smile. "But it's worth it. Every single time."

"Then maybe," Clara said, a spark of determination rekindling within her, "just maybe, you could use a partner in this mission of yours."

"Nothing would please me more," Mark said, his relief evident in his smile.

"Alright," Clara breathed out, nodding decisively. "Let's do this. Let's give hope a fighting chance."

"Clara," Mark began, his gaze steady on her, "I've been trying to understand Nathan's situation better. There's a lot about his past that seems to be haunting him."

She hesitated for a moment, then sighed, pulling a strand of wavy brown hair behind her ear. "Nathan... he lost his sister in a car accident about two years ago. She was just a teenager, full of life. They were close inseparable, really. After she passed, a part of him just… shut down." Her voice dropped to a whisper, heavy with shared grief.

"Did he ever talk about it?" Mark asked, his voice barely above a whisper, as if the question itself carried weight too heavy to bear.

"Only once," Clara replied, her voice steady but tinged with sorrow. "And even then, it was like he hit a wall. He said her name Lily and then went silent. You could see the pain in his eyes, the guilt. He believes he should have been able to protect her."

Mark nodded slowly, taking in the tragic revelation. "Survivor's guilt can be crippling. It's like living in a shadow that you can't escape."

"Exactly," Clara agreed, her kind eyes reflecting the understanding that only someone who had witnessed such suffering could possess. "That shadow has been following Nathan around, consuming everything in its path. He needs more than traditional therapy. He needs someone who can reach into that darkness and pull him out."

"How would you describe his mental state?" Mark pressed, wanting to grasp the full extent of Nathan's pain.

"Volatile at times, but mostly..." Clara hesitated, searching for the right words. "Mostly just hollow. Like he's here but not really present. Going through the motions without actually feeling anything." Her hands moved as she spoke, emphasising the emptiness she saw in Nathan, as if she could physically grasp the essence of his suffering.

"Then we need to find a way to bring him back. To give him something to hold on to," Mark said, his voice filled with determination.

"Hope," Clara uttered firmly. "We need to rekindle hope in him, Mark. Without that, there's no moving forward."

"Hope can be powerful," Mark acknowledged, his mind spinning with ideas.

"More than you know," Clara responded, her conviction unwavering. "If we can bring even a sliver of hope back into Nathan's life, maybe we can start to heal those wounds that have been left open for far too long."

"Then let's do that together," Mark said, reaching out to her, the beginning of an unspoken partnership forming between them.

"Agreed," Clara nodded, her posture one of unyielding resolve. "We'll do whatever it takes to help Nathan find his way out of the dark. We owe him that much."

"Thank you, Clara," Mark said, his gratitude clear in his voice. "With your insight and compassion, I truly believe we can make a difference."

"Let's hope so," she replied, her eyes now alight with a fierce determination. "For Nathan's sake."

Mark's gaze lingered on Clara, noting the gentle lines etched into her face the marks of years of selfless care. The hospital's harsh fluorescent lights bathed them both in a clinical glow, but there was a warmth in the bond that was forming between them.

"Clara," Mark asked, his voice quieter now, almost reflective, "have you ever felt like you were meant to cross paths with someone?"

"Often," she replied, her tone carrying the weight of years spent in service. "It's as if there are invisible threads connecting us to the people who need us most."

"Exactly," he said, a faint smile tugging at the corner of his lips. "Like us, here, now. I believe we're meant to help Nathan together."

"Mark, I..." Clara hesitated, searching his face as if she could read something deeper in his expression. "I see something in you. A genuine desire to heal, not just the mind, but the soul."

"That's all I've ever wanted," he said softly, his sincerity clear. "To use this... ability of mine to do something good."

The Mind Whisperer

Their conversation flowed effortlessly between them, a dance of words and shared understanding. Clara spoke of her late-night worries for patients, her mind racing long after her shift had ended, while Mark revealed his fears of misinterpreting situations due to his unusual ability to sense people's emotions.

"Sometimes, I think I'm too close to their pain," Clara confessed, her voice barely audible amidst the hospital's chaos.

"Maybe that's your gift," Mark suggested gently. "You feel with them, Clara. That's rare and beautiful."

She looked away for a moment, as if considering his words, before returning her gaze to him with a quiet, resolute expression. "Mark, I want to help you with Nathan," she said. "Tell me what you need from me."

"Your understanding of him, from a medical perspective, is crucial," Mark said, his hands moving animatedly, reflecting his thoughts. "We can tackle this together your insight, and my... whatever it is I do," he chuckled softly, a slight self-deprecation in his tone.

"Empathy," she offered, her smile softening the tension in the air. "And an extraordinary ability to connect."

A patient's call briefly interrupted their conversation, but Clara was quick to refocus on Mark, her attention unwavering.

"Let's dive into the heart of his despair," she said, her voice resolute. "Together, we'll peel back the layers of his grief and find a way to let light back into his life."

"Clara, that means the world to me," Mark replied, excitement evident in his eyes. "With your compassion and my... empathy, we could really make a difference."

"Then it's settled." Clara extended her hand, not just in agreement, but as a symbol of their newly forged alliance.

As they shook hands, Mark felt the weight of possibility of hope and healing. For Nathan, for themselves, and for the very essence of what it meant to truly care.

"Thank you, Clara," Mark said, his voice full of gratitude. A smile tugged at his lips, easing the worry that had clung to him since arriving. "I've been trying to reach him, to understand what he's going through, but it feels like navigating a labyrinth in the dark."

"None of us can do it alone," Clara replied, her tone full of hope. "Sometimes, all we need is someone to share the load, to shine a light when the path gets murky."

Mark nodded, feeling the weight on his shoulders lighten, if only a little, with her words. "Exactly. And your light... it could be what guides Nathan out of his darkness."

"Then let's not waste any more time," she said, her voice filled with resolve. The determination in her eyes matched the certainty in his heart.

"Agreed. I'll gather everything I've learned about him so far. Maybe together, we can identify the patterns, the triggers anything that might help."

"Let's meet after my shift ends tomorrow," Clara suggested. "We'll lay everything out and start connecting the dots."

"Tomorrow," Mark echoed, already formulating plans in his mind, his thoughts racing with potential strategies.

"Remember, though," Clara added, her hand resting briefly on his arm, as though to ground him, "we're dealing with a person, not just a puzzle to be solved. Patience and care are key."

"Of course," Mark assured her, his gaze steady. "Patience and care."

As they began to part ways, Mark turned back. "Clara?"

"Yes?"

The Mind Whisperer

"Thank you. Truly."

She smiled warmly, the connection between them still palpable despite the distance beginning to grow. "We're in this together, Mark. Remember that."

With a final nod, Mark watched her disappear around the corner before heading towards the exit. His pace was now driven by purpose, his steps lighter, energised by the partnership they had just formed. The hospital's incessant hum seemed to fade into the background, overshadowed by a singular focus: saving Nathan Walker.

As the automatic doors slid open to the cool night air, Mark paused for a moment, breathing in deeply. The first stars of evening twinkled above him, as if offering a silent promise reminding him that even in the vastness of the universe, two people with a common purpose could indeed make a world of difference.

For a fleeting moment, he allowed himself to feel the warmth of hope that filled him. Then, with renewed determination, he set off into the night, ready to face the challenges ahead.

Chapter 5
Strength In Numbers

The sun had barely risen when Susan Jennings slipped into the kitchen, the soft morning light casting a warm glow on her shoulder-length blonde hair. The scent of freshly brewed coffee filled the air, mingling with the quiet resolve she felt as she leaned against the counter, her thoughts focused on the task ahead. As a fiercely protective sister, her loyalty to Mark was matched only by her concern for Nathan's well-being. She understood her brother's gift better than anyone else, but the weight of Nathan's struggles made her question how much they could truly help him.

"Can we really make a difference?" she murmured softly to herself, her warm smile laced with worry.

Down the hall, in the guest room, Clara Reynolds was folding the corner of a clean sheet with meticulous care. As a nurse, her hands were skilled in offering comfort and healing, yet as she smoothed out the wrinkles, a hint of scepticism clouded her kind eyes. She believed in Mark's unique abilities, certainly, but helping Nathan seemed like a challenge beyond anyone's reach.

"Is it enough to just be there for him?" Clara wondered, tucking the last corner into place.

At the community centre, Angela Pierce surveyed the empty space that would soon be filled with the hustle and bustle of daily activities. Her freckles stood out boldly in the harsh fluorescent light, a stark contrast to the shadow of doubt that crossed her face. She ran the place like a well-oiled machine, but the thought of guiding someone as troubled as Nathan back to calmer waters left her uneasy.

"Can we reach him before he drifts too far away?" Angela asked herself, her hands clasping and unclasping in anticipation.

The Mind Whisperer

Marie Thompson sat at the edge of her bed, her curly black hair framing her face as she held a small, framed photograph of her family. Her soft-spoken voice often masked the turmoil within, and now, postpartum depression cast a long shadow over her confidence. She sought Mark's guidance just as much as Nathan did, and the idea of being someone else's anchor seemed daunting.

"Am I strong enough to help when I'm still seeking help myself?" Marie whispered to the stillness of her room.

As the clock struck ten, Mark Jennings stood at the head of his dining room table, which was cleared of everything except a notepad and several pens. His medium build and short brown hair gave no indication of the storm of thoughts he navigated daily with his unique gift. He looked around at the faces of his gathered allies, each of them carrying their own blend of hope and hesitation.

"Thank you all for being here," Mark began, his voice steady but laced with excitement. "I know we're stepping into unknown territory with Nathan. Yes, it's going to be tough, but I've seen what we're capable of when we work together."

Susan nodded, her initial doubts gradually fading under the influence of her brother's optimism.

"Each of us brings something special to the table," Mark continued, locking eyes with each person in turn. "Clara, your compassion as a nurse is unmatched. Angela, you have a rare gift for making people feel at home. Marie, your journey through darkness gives you insights that others might lack. And Susan, your understanding of my gift makes you an irreplaceable part of this team."

Their eyes met his, and a silent understanding passed between them as his words began to take root.

"Individually, we can do good, but together, we can change Nathan's world," Mark said, his belief ringing clear. "We have a chance to show him that he's not alone, that we're here for him, and that we'll stand with him every step of the way."

A collective breath seemed to lift the room, and the air hummed with renewed purpose. They were more than individuals with doubts; together, they were a beacon of possibility.

"Let's do this for Nathan," Mark declared, and the room erupted in a chorus of agreement, their scepticism slowly giving way to a shared sense of mission.

Mark's living room, once a place of quiet contemplation, had transformed into a buzzing hub of ideas and discussion. The soft glow of the table lamp cast a comforting aura as the team huddled around, papers scattered across the surface like leaves in an autumn breeze. Despite the warmth of the room, an undercurrent of tension still hummed beneath their words.

"Okay," Mark said, his voice steady and inviting, "let's hear what's on everyone's mind. We can't move forward until we address our concerns."

Susan bit her lip, folding her arms across her chest. "I believe in what we're doing, I do, but I'm just not sure how Nathan will react. He's... well, he's a tough nut to crack." Her forehead creased with worry, revealing the weight of her uncertainty.

Clara nodded, her eyes filled with empathy. "And how do we even begin? My nursing skills are one thing, but this? It's so personal, so complex. Are we truly prepared for the emotional toll this might take?"

Angela Pierce leaned forward, her hands clasped tightly together. "There's also the question of privacy. We want to help Nathan, but we must respect his boundaries. It's a delicate balance, and I fear we might overstep without meaning to."

Marie Thompson's gaze drifted to the window, where the night sky promised secrets of its own. "I've been where Nathan is in that darkness. Sometimes, the last thing you want is someone trying to pull you out of it before you're ready. We need to be mindful of that."

Mark listened attentively to each concern, nodding thoughtfully. "These are all valid points," he acknowledged. "But remember, we're not here to force change on Nathan. We're here to offer support, to be his allies on whatever path he chooses. Now, let's focus on how we can do that effectively."

They gathered closer, the brainstorming session unfolding like a map of uncharted territory. Ideas bounced back and forth, the energy in the room growing with each new suggestion.

"What if we start by just being present?" Susan suggested. "Simple things, like meeting for coffee or taking a walk in the park. Casual, no pressure."

"Exactly!" Clara exclaimed, her enthusiasm sparking. "We could each take turns, ensuring he has a support system without overwhelming him."

"And perhaps we can get involved in some community activities," Angela offered. "Nothing too invasive, just opportunities for Nathan to feel connected, to remind him that there's a world outside his struggles."

"Support groups," Marie chimed in, her voice quieter but no less determined. "Not pushing him to join, but making the information available. Letting him know he has options."

"Great ideas, everyone," Mark encouraged, his eyes alight with pride and hope. "It's not about grand gestures; it's about showing Nathan the simple, consistent acts of kindness. We'll build trust through patience and understanding."

The excitement in the room was palpable, each member eager to contribute to Nathan's recovery. They were different people, united by a common cause, and in that unity, they found strength.

"Alright," Mark concluded, his smile infectious. "Let's put these plans into action. For Nathan."

A chorus of assent filled the room, each voice reinforced by the others. Together, they stood on the brink of something powerful, ready to transform their collective care into real support for someone who needed it most.

Mark tapped a pen against the notepad, excitement buzzing in the air like electricity. The circle of allies around him was a patchwork of motivation and skill. "We've got a wealth of knowledge here," he said, meeting each pair of eyes in turn. "Let's focus on how we can leverage that for Nathan."

Clara leaned forward, her brown hair tumbling over her shoulders as she clasped her hands together. "I'll take the lead on health checks. With my medical background, I can help monitor his physical well-being. Casual 'accidental' run-ins at the grocery store or coffee shop, just to check in, and to see if there are any signs of neglect."

"Perfect, Clara. That's exactly the kind of subtle support we need." Mark scribbled notes, Clara nodding in satisfaction.

Angela, with her deep ties to the community, spoke next. "I'm your link to local resources. I can discreetly make sure he receives information about job opportunities, counselling services, and even community events that might catch his interest."

"Angela, that's invaluable," Mark said, clearly impressed by her network. "You'll be our anchor in the community."

Marie interjected softly, but with fervour behind her words. "I understand the shadows Nathan's walking through. I... I've been there, in a way." Her gaze was steady, and her vulnerability tangible. "Let me be the one to reach out to support groups. No pressure, but if he needs them, he'll know where to find them."

"Thank you, Marie. Your empathy will be a light in the dark for Nathan." Mark made another note, feeling the pieces coming together.

"Then it's settled," Mark declared, his voice rising with determination. "Clara, you're on health checks. Angela, you'll weave the community fabric. And Marie, you're the beacon for emotional support."

Their nods were synchronised, a small orchestra of agreement. Each person had a role to play in the symphony of Nathan's recovery.

"Let's reconvene next week, same time," Mark said, his tone brimming with anticipation. "Keep your eyes open and your hearts ready. We're doing something special here."

The room echoed with a resounding "Yes!" As they dispersed, the energy didn't dissipate; it followed them out the door, a promise of hope and a plan of action that would change Nathan's world, one subtle, caring step at a time.

Mark watched as the team settled into a semi-circle of couches and armchairs, the soft lighting of his living room casting a cocoon around them. Susan fiddled with her pen, a sign of nerves that betrayed her usual confidence as a retired police officer. Clara held her steaming mug close, the aroma of chamomile tea mingling with the tension in the air. Angela leaned back, her eyes reflecting the weight of community expectations, while Marie's hands rested on her lap, her fingers tracing patterns over the fabric of her skirt.

"Thank you all for being here," Mark began, his voice steady and reassuring. "I know we have different strengths, but it's our shared commitment to Nathan that unites us."

"I must admit," Susan said, breaking the silence that followed Mark's words, "this isn't like any case I've worked on before. Usually, there are clear leads and evidence... but this, helping Nathan, it feels like we're grasping at smoke."

"Smoke can be corralled, directed," Clara replied, her medical background giving her a calm, analytical edge. "If we understand the winds, the environment, we can predict its path. Nathan's health, both mental and physical, is a puzzle, but not an unsolvable one."

Angela nodded, her earlier reserve melting away. "Community is like that too. It seems nebulous, but there's a rhythm, a pattern to how people connect. I can tap into that and find the support Nathan doesn't even know he needs."

"Patterns, yes," Marie whispered, more to herself than to the others. "The patterns of the mind when cloaked in darkness they're familiar to me. If we can illuminate just one thread for Nathan, it might lead him out of the labyrinth."

Mark smiled, his heart warming at the sight of their earnest faces. "That's exactly the kind of hope and insight that will make the difference."

"But what if he rejects our help?" Susan's question hung heavy in the air. "What if he decides we're meddling and pushes us away?"

"Then we respect his boundaries," Mark answered, mindful of the delicate nature of their endeavour. "We offer support without insistence. Our presence alone can be a beacon."

"Boundaries," Clara repeated, nodding slowly. "I'm used to pushing for answers, for healing. This requires... a softer touch."

"Soft but persistent," Angela added, her voice firm. "We stay present, visible in his life. We ensure he knows we're here when he's ready, without overwhelming him."

"Exactly," Marie affirmed, sitting up a little straighter. "We become his safety net woven tightly enough to catch him, but with enough give so he doesn't feel trapped."

"Does everyone feel comfortable with this approach?" Mark asked, scanning their faces for any signs of hesitance.

"Comfortable? Maybe not entirely," Susan admitted with a short laugh. "But committed? Absolutely."

Clara raised her mug in a silent salute, her agreement clear in her steady gaze.

"Committed," echoed Angela, the corners of her mouth lifting in a determined smile.

"Committed," Marie confirmed, her voice stronger now, carrying the weight of her resolve.

"Then let's move forward together," Mark said, feeling the energy in the room shift from uncertainty to resolute purpose. "For Nathan."

"For Nathan," they echoed, a chorus of solidarity that filled the space with promise and the strength of their newfound camaraderie.

Mark unrolled a large calendar across the mahogany dining table, its blank squares staring up at them like a challenge. "We need to map out our milestones," he said, tapping a pen against today's date.

"First things first, we establish contact within the week," Susan suggested, leaning forward. Her analytical mind was already sorting the timeline into neat, achievable segments.

"Agreed," Mark said, circling the date seven days from now. "But let's set up a system of check-ins every three days. Progress reports, concerns, any changes in Nathan's demeanour."

"Every three days sounds reasonable," Clara chimed in, her fingers drumming on the smooth wood. "It gives us time to observe and react without being overbearing."

"By the end of the month," Angela interjected, pointing to a date with determination etched on her face, "we should have a solid understanding of his routines, his haunts, and who he trusts."

"Which leads us to strategy," Mark transitioned, feeling the energy build as they dove headfirst into planning. "Ideas?"

"Community outreach," Angela started confidently. "I've got ties with local groups that can help us create a network of support around him."

"Good, good!" Mark scribbled notes beside the timeline. "Susan?"

"Data is our friend," she replied, her eyes alight with fervour. "Let's compile what we know about Nathan patterns, history, and potential triggers and cross-reference it with psychological studies. Knowledge is power."

"Excellent." Mark nodded, impressed by her thoroughness.

"Clara, you're on medical watch," he continued. "Keep an eye out for signs of decline or improvement. Anything physical that might clue us into his state of mind."

"Of course," Clara agreed solemnly, the gravity of her responsibility clear.

"And Marie," Mark turned to her with an encouraging smile, "you've been where he is. Your insight could be the key to reaching him."

Marie nodded, her own struggles fuelling her empathy. "I'll draft up some talking points things that would've made me feel heard and not judged."

"Let's also set up a shared document," Susan added, as practical as ever. "Real-time updates, so we're all in the loop. No overlaps or gaps in our approach."

"Brilliant," Mark commended, his admiration for their synergy growing.

"Then it's settled," Angela stated, her voice carrying a note of triumph. "We've got our timeline, our roles, and the beginnings of a solid plan."

"Remember, we're doing this for Nathan. But also," Mark paused, letting his gaze settle on each of them, "for anyone out there who's felt as lost as he does now."

Their nods were synchronised, a silent pact forming around the table. They had their mission, and they had their resolve. Now, it was time to put their strategy into action.

The Mind Whisperer

Mark rose to his feet, the uncertainty of earlier now a distant memory, as he addressed his newly assembled team. "I know we've all taken different paths to get here," he said, the evening light casting long shadows across the living room walls. "But our journeys have converged for a reason to help someone who's stumbling in the dark."

"More than just help, Mark," Angela chimed in, her eyes alight with a fervour that seemed to pierce through her usually composed exterior. "We're going to be Nathan's beacon until he finds his own way again."

"Exactly," Susan added, her voice steady and resolute. "Our collective strength will guide him. We won't let him slip through the cracks not on our watch."

A chorus of agreement filled the room, each voice echoing the same sentiment. Clara's hands were folded neatly in her lap, but her posture radiated readiness. Marie clasped her hands tightly, as though holding onto the hope they were all nurturing.

"None of us can do this alone," Marie said softly, her gaze unwavering. "But together? We're unstoppable."

"Unstoppable," Clara echoed, her voice imbued with the weight of their collective resolve.

"Then let's make a promise, right here and now," Mark urged, extending his hand towards the centre of the group. "That we'll see this through for Nathan, and for everyone else who needs someone to fight for them when they've lost the strength."

One by one, hands joined atop his Angela's, Susan's, Clara's, then Marie's each one firm and unwavering. The pact was silent, but stronger than any vow spoken aloud.

"Let's show the world what a little kindness and teamwork can do," Angela said, a smile tugging at the corners of her mouth.

"Tomorrow, we start fresh," Mark concluded, his words settling over them like a blanket of assurance. "Tonight, we rest knowing we are united in purpose."

As they withdrew their hands, the room hummed with an electric sense of anticipation. They had laid the groundwork, formed their bonds, and sparked a plan that had the potential to change everything.

"Remember, though," Susan cautioned as they began to gather their notes and belongings. "It won't be easy. We'll likely face hurdles we can't foresee, moments that will test our resolve."

"True," Mark agreed, acknowledging the road ahead with a nod. "Nathan's struggle is complex, and there are no quick fixes. But we're prepared for the long haul, aren't we?"

"Absolutely," Clara confirmed, her voice resolute.

"Whatever it takes," Marie added, determination etched into her features.

"Then let's call it a night," Mark suggested. "We have our strategy, and tomorrow, we begin implementing it. Step by step, we'll find a way to bring Nathan back from the brink."

As the team filed out, the room seemed to hum with the residue of their commitment. Their alliance was more than just an agreement it was a lifeline, woven for Nathan, strand by resilient strand.

Outside, the sky had deepened to a rich indigo, stars emerging like distant promises. The chapter closed with the team dispersing into the night, the stillness punctuated only by their departing footsteps and whispered vows carried on the wind. Ahead lay a thicket of challenges and unknowns, but they moved forward with courage and conviction, bound by unity.

It was this bond, forged in the heart of a cosy living room, that would carry them into tomorrow and beyond, as they embarked on their extraordinary mission to save a soul adrift.

Chapter 6
Seeking Truths

The office was a sanctuary of calm, the soft blue and green hues on the walls creating a serene atmosphere. Clara's desk, typically a landscape of organised chaos, had been cleared to make space for her team. She sat at the head, her wavy brown hair framing her face, exuding an air of quiet authority.

"Right, everyone, let's get started," Clara said, her voice calm yet firm, filling the small room with an unspoken command. The chairs around her creaked as the team settled in, notebooks opened, pens poised, and eyes focused.

Mark Jennings took a deep breath, centring himself amidst the expectant gazes. His short brown hair seemed even more untamed than usual, a sign of the long hours he'd spent reflecting on Nathan Walker an enigma wrapped in a puzzle.

"Thanks, Clara," Mark began, leaning forward, his hands clasped together on the table. "I've been trying to connect with Nathan, really tune into what's going on beneath the surface. It's like… he's broadcasting on a frequency that's difficult to pin down."

Clara nodded, encouraging him to continue.

"His emotions are a tangled web," Mark said, his brow furrowing in concentration. "There's a lot of pain, a sense of loss so profound it's almost tangible. But there's something else, too: barriers he's built for protection. They're formidable."

"How do you suggest we navigate those barriers?" Clara asked gently, her kind eyes reflecting the concern they all shared for the young man whose presence often seemed dark and brooding.

"Carefully," Mark replied, locking eyes with each person in the room. "We can't rush this. Nathan's trust is a rare commodity, and once it's lost, I doubt we'll ever regain it."

"Can you sense anything specific?" Clara pressed, her voice soft yet insistent. "Any particular event or memory that might help us understand him better?"

Mark closed his eyes for a moment, letting the silence stretch as he searched his mind for the elusive threads of Nathan's inner turmoil. When he spoke again, his voice carried a sombre weight.

"His childhood... there's a shadow there. A deep sadness that clings to him, but it's obscured almost like he's buried it himself. We need to help him unearth it, but it has to be on his terms."

"Then that's what we'll do," Clara declared, her voice firm with resolve. "We'll give Nathan the time and space he needs. Our support will be unwavering, and when he's ready, we'll be here to help him face whatever comes."

A fresh energy filled the room, a synergy of purpose binding them together. They were more than just a team; they were guardians of a fragile trust, committed to guiding Nathan through the labyrinth of his past with patience and compassion. And with Mark's unique insight leading the way, they were one step closer to shedding light on the shadows that haunted Nathan Walker.

As Mark's words settled in the air, Susan reached into her satchel, her movement almost reverent. She pulled out a stack of worn photographs and laid them gently on Clara's desk, which had now become their makeshift headquarters. The team leaned in, their faces a mosaic of concentration and concern, as they studied the images hoping they might unlock the secrets of Nathan's guarded heart.

"Found these tucked away in a box at the back of his closet," Susan explained, her voice soft but tinged with excitement. "Nathan, with some other kids looks like from when he was about ten."

The team gathered around, drawn together like moths to a flame. There was Nathan, much younger but unmistakably him, with the same unruly dark hair, standing on the edge of a group of children at a birthday party. Balloons and streamers painted the background in festive colours, but Nathan's stance set him apart, like a shadow on the edges of the celebration.

"Look at his eyes," Angela murmured, pointing to a photo where a young Nathan stared into the camera, his expression unreadable. "Even surrounded by friends, there's a... a loneliness there."

"Exactly," Susan said, picking up on Angela's observation. "And this one," she continued, flipping to another picture where Nathan stood on the outskirts of a soccer game. "He's there, but not really part of it, you know?"

The photos passed from hand to hand, each team member studying Nathan's youthful face for clues anything that might help them understand the web of shadows that seemed to enshroud his present.

"Speaking of not really being part of things," Angela began, breaking the spell cast by the photographs. She took a deep breath, her freckles standing out against her fair skin in the warm light of the desk lamp. "I've been talking to some people who lived near Nathan when he was growing up. They remember him as the kid who always kept to himself."

"Did they say why?" Clara asked, her brows knitting together in concern.

"Bits and pieces. One neighbour mentioned hearing shouting from his house late at night. Another recalled a time when Nathan showed up at school with a bruise on his cheek, but he brushed it off as a fall." Angela paused, the weight of her words hanging heavy in the air. "No one pried back then, but it's clear there were issues at home."

Susan's hands clenched tightly around the photographs, a protective instinct flaring within her as she thought of her own brother and the struggles he'd faced. "We have to be careful how we handle this," she said, her tone firm. "Nathan's built walls for a reason."

"Agreed," Clara nodded, her resolve mirroring Susan's. "But these photos, your conversations, Angela these are pieces of a puzzle we're starting to piece together."

"Let's keep going," Mark added, his voice steady despite the emotional undercurrents. "For Nathan. We'll do this with empathy, respect... and hope."

The team exchanged determined glances, their shared purpose uniting them. They were more than just investigators; they were keepers of a fragile trust, standing at the threshold of a past that needed to be brought to light with the utmost care. With photographs spread before them and whispered stories lingering in their minds, they pressed on determined to help Nathan find the peace he so clearly deserved.

Clara leaned forward in her chair, the dim light of the desk lamp casting a warm glow around the room. Her eyes, always full of compassion, scanned the faces of her companions before she spoke. "We can't ignore the academic and social aspects of Nathan's life," she said, tapping a pen against the edge of her notepad. "Perhaps reaching out to his former teachers or schoolmates could give us more context. They might remember details that have been overlooked."

"Good point," Susan chimed in, tucking a loose strand of hair behind her ear as she considered the suggestion. "School can be such a formative place. Both good and bad memories are made there."

Mark nodded thoughtfully, his gaze drifting from the now silent photographs to the eager faces of his friends. "The echoes of those years often linger longer than we realise," he murmured softly.

"Exactly," Clara agreed, her voice carrying a note of determination. "If we can trace back through those years, perhaps we'll gain a better understanding of the struggles Nathan has faced."

Angela leaned back in her chair, crossing her arms but nodding in agreement. "It's worth a try. Those connections could open doors we didn't even know were there."

The Mind Whisperer

The room was charged with a collective sense of resolve when Mark gently cleared his throat, drawing their attention. His brow furrowed slightly, a sign of the gears turning in his mind. "I've been thinking," he began, carefully selecting his words. "If I try to connect with Nathan's emotions, really get to the heart of them, we might uncover memories or traumas he's buried deep within."

"Are you sure about that?" Angela asked, her tone laced with concern. "That sounds intense, even for you, Mark."

"It is intense," Mark acknowledged, his fingers tracing the grain of the wooden table. "But I feel it's necessary. There are shadows in Nathan's past that need to be brought to light, and I believe I can help unearth them."

"Can you handle that, though? Delving into someone else's pain?" Susan asked, her protective nature surfacing.

"His pain is already here," Mark replied, tapping his temple and then his chest. "I sense it every time I'm near him. It's just a matter of reaching out and touching it."

"Then we trust you to take that step," Clara said with quiet confidence. "If anyone can do this with the sensitivity it requires, it's you, Mark."

"Thank you," Mark murmured, visibly buoyed by their support. "I won't push too hard. We're walking a delicate line, and I don't want to break the thread of trust Nathan has extended."

"Let's plan carefully, then," Clara suggested. "We'll make sure Nathan feels comfortable and knows he's not alone in this."

"Agreed," Susan said firmly. "We're doing this together, as a team."

The word "team" seemed to carry more weight in that moment, a collective force that bound them together. As they nodded in agreement, the gravity of their mission settled upon them, not as a burden, but as a shared commitment to guide Nathan toward healing.

A renewed energy filled the room one of hope, understanding, and the unwavering human connection that united them all.

Susan leaned forward, her blonde hair catching the soft glow of the office light as she tapped her pen against her notepad. "I think I should start compiling a list of teachers, classmates, neighbours... anyone who might've known Nathan well," she said, her voice carrying the same determined tone that often marked her protective stance toward her brother.

"Are you sure we can get them to talk?" Clara asked, her fingers idly twirling a lock of her wavy brown hair. "People can be tight-lipped about these things."

"Discretion is my middle name," Susan replied with a wink. "I'll approach it as an old friend just walking down memory lane. No one needs to know the real reason behind my curiosity."

"Good idea," Clara nodded. "Keep it light, and they're more likely to open up."

"Exactly." Susan scribbled a note, her warm smile betraying none of the anxiety she felt. "I'll make some calls and send out a few feelers. See what comes back."

"Meanwhile," Clara began, her gaze intense with purpose, "I have access to some hospital records that are kept confidential. There might be something there about Nathan's past medical history, psychological evaluations, anything that could fill in the gaps for us."

"Isn't that a breach of privacy?" Susan asked, her voice steady but cautious.

"Normally, yes," Clara conceded, meeting Susan's eyes with a seriousness that mirrored the gravity of their task. "But I have a feeling Nathan's been through the system more than once, and if there's a pattern or something we've missed, it's worth looking into."

The Mind Whisperer

"Clara, are you sure you want to take that risk?" Mark interjected, his brow furrowed with concern.

"Absolutely," Clara said firmly. "If we're going to help Nathan, we need the whole picture. And I'm willing to go the extra mile to get it."

"Alright, then," Susan chimed in, her determination matching Clara's resolve. "We cover all bases. Leave no stone unturned."

"Exactly," Clara echoed. "We have to tread carefully, but the truth is what will free him from whatever shadows he's hiding in."

"Then let's get to work," Mark said, standing up and stretching his arms above his head. "Time is of the essence, and Nathan doesn't even know how much he needs us right now."

"Let's hope our little investigation sheds some much-needed light on his past," Susan added, already flipping through her contacts on her phone.

"Every piece of the puzzle helps," Clara agreed, her kind eyes reflecting a steely resolve. "No matter how small."

With the plan in place, the energy in the room was palpable. Each team member was fuelled by the urgency of their mission. They were a mosaic of strengths united by a common goal: to bring clarity to Nathan's murky past and, hopefully, peace to his troubled present.

The room hummed with a low-level tension, a collective breath held as they circled back to the core of their mission: Nathan. Mark leaned against Clara's desk, his gaze fixed on the worn carpet as he organised his thoughts.

"Guys," he began, lifting his eyes to meet his companions, "we can't just bombard Nathan with all this. It's... it's gotta be delicate."

Susan paused, her finger hovering over her phone screen. "He's like a stray cat. Skittish. If we come at him too fast, he'll bolt. We've got to earn his trust first."

64

"Exactly," Angela agreed, nodding vigorously. She tucked a loose strand of auburn hair behind her ear and leaned forward in her chair, elbows on her knees. "We need to create a space where he feels safe, not cornered." Her voice was soft but insistent, carrying the weight of her experience from her days of counselling at the community centre.

"Safe space..." Clara mused, tapping her pen against her lips. "That could mean different things. But for Nathan, I think it means familiarity perhaps a bit of nostalgia."

"Something low-key," Mark suggested, his hands gesturing as if to shape the idea physically. "Where he doesn't feel like there's any pressure on him."

"Like what?" Susan asked, curiosity sparking in her expression.

Angela's face lit up with inspiration. "What about a small get-together? Nothing fancy, just a casual event." She spread her hands, as though unveiling her vision. "We invite a few people from his past just the ones he had good relationships with. Keep it light, reminiscing about the good old days."

"Sort of a mini reunion?" Clara chimed in, her excitement growing. "I love that! It's genius, Angela. It's neutral ground, and it won't feel like an intervention."

"Plus," Mark added, a rare smile breaking through his usual solemn demeanour, "it might jog some buried memories and give us more pieces to the puzzle without him feeling like he's under a microscope."

"Right, and I'll make sure it's somewhere he feels comfortable," Angela continued, already picturing how she would arrange the event. "Somewhere familiar maybe even the community centre. He's been there before with me; it's a start."

"Exactly!" Susan exclaimed, finally putting down her phone and clasping her hands together in determination. "And we'll be there to support him, no matter what surfaces. It's perfect."

"Then it's settled," Clara said, standing up as if to cement the decision. "Angela, you organise the gathering. Susan, keep working on your list, but focus on the positives from his past. And I'll handle the records search."

"Operation 'Nostalgia' is underway," Mark declared, a glimmer of hope in his eyes. "Let's help Nathan find his way back to himself."

They each felt the weight of responsibility, the importance of their task, but also the thrill of possibility. They were united, a team ready to guide Nathan through the shadows of his past toward the light of truth and healing. With careful steps and compassionate hearts, they embarked on their quest to unlock the mystery of Nathan Walker.

Mark leaned forward, resting his elbows on the scratched surface of Clara's desk, his gaze meeting each pair of eyes in turn. "We need a strategy," he said with quiet conviction, his voice steady despite the flutter of anticipation in his chest. "A plan that plays to our strengths."

"Divide and conquer?" Susan suggested, a spark of eagerness lighting up her expressive face.

"Exactly," Mark nodded, glancing at his sister with pride. "Susan, you have a knack for finding people. You could reach out to those from Nathan's past, gently probe for insights without stirring up too much dust."

"Consider it done," she replied, pulling out a small notebook and pen, ready to jot down names and strategies.

Clara, whose nurturing instincts had always been her compass, spoke next. "And I'll take on the hospital records. If there's anything there to find about Nathan's past, I'll find it."

"Thank you, Clara." Mark smiled with gratitude. His attention shifted to Angela, who was already mentally organising the gathering. "Angela, you're the heart of this community. Can you handle the event?"

"Of course," Angela responded confidently, her mind racing through potential themes and decorations that would create a warm backdrop for remembrance. "I'll make sure it's an event that feels like homecoming, not an interrogation."

"Brilliant," Mark affirmed, leaning back in his chair. The dynamic between them crackled with shared purpose. They weren't just a team they were a constellation of care, drawn together by a common need to heal and help.

"Okay, team," Susan chimed in, her voice vibrant with excitement, "Operation 'Nostalgia' is officially in motion!"

They stood up, the scrape of their chairs against the floor a chorus of readiness. Each of them wore an expression of determination, tempered by a clear understanding of the delicate task ahead. They exchanged nods the silent language of comrades embarking on a crucial mission.

"Remember, we're doing this for Nathan," Mark reminded them, his voice carrying the empathy that guided his every action. "Let's bring him some peace."

"Absolutely," Clara agreed, her kind eyes reflecting a fierce resolve.

"Every piece of the puzzle helps," Angela added, her freckles seeming to dance with her determination.

"Alright, let's get to work," Susan declared, her blonde hair swishing as she turned toward the door, phone already in hand.

One by one, they left Clara's office, each step echoing their commitment to the cause. As the door closed behind them, the room seemed to hold the weight of their collective hope: to light the dark corners of Nathan's memory, revealing the truths hidden within.

Mark lingered for a moment, taking a deep breath as he absorbed the gravity of their endeavour. He felt the familiar thrum of intuition the same feeling that had always guided him toward those in need of his gift. With a final glance at the empty chairs, he stepped out into the hallway, his stride purposeful.

Chapter 7
Labyrinth Of Secrets

"Okay, so we've hit a wall, but that doesn't mean we're out of options," said Mark, his voice carrying the same steady resolve it had when they'd first begun. For hours, they had combed through every fragment of Nathan's life, determined to unpick the shadowy threads of his past threads that clung to him like cobwebs. Each revelation, each secret unearthed, had drawn them closer to the core of Nathan's struggle. Now, under the dim glow of Susan's desk lamp, they felt the weight of everything they'd uncovered.

"Every piece matters, no matter how small," Susan agreed, her fingers lightly brushing the collection of photographs and notes they'd amassed. Her eyes, sharp and observant, missed nothing lit with the fierce protectiveness she held for those she cared about. She turned back to Nathan's box of belongings, her hands moving with gentle care, as though the memories inside might stir at her touch.

"Whoa what's this?" Her voice cut through the silence as her fingers found the edge of something hidden beneath a loose floorboard in the old chest. She pulled free a weathered diary, its leather cover cracked, the pages yellowed with age. The air around them stilled, heavy with anticipation.

"Found something?" Nathan asked, leaning in, his dark fringe falling into his eyes as he examined the object in her hands.

"Looks like a diary. Is it yours?" she asked, tilting her head to catch his reaction. His expression remained blank, unreadable yet a flicker passed through his eyes. Recognition? Or fear?

"Never seen it before," he said far too quickly. Susan knew a lie when she heard one. She opened the book to reveal scrawled handwriting cryptic entries that hinted at buried pain and sketches that seemed to leap from the paper, raw and unsettling.

"Look at this," she murmured, her voice tinged with concern as she pointed to a drawing of a house, twisted and distorted by shadows. It seemed to writhe on the page.

"This is intense. Nathan, do you recognise this?"

Nathan swallowed hard, his throat dry, as if the image summoned ghosts he'd tried to forget. "It's... complicated."

"Complicated how?" Mark leaned in, his curiosity sharpening.

"It doesn't matter. It's old news," Nathan muttered. But his voice faltered betraying the storm the diary had awakened.

"Old news that feels very much alive," Susan replied softly. "Nathan, whatever it is we're here. We'll face it together."

"Let's keep going," Mark said, his tone gentle but firm. He knew how tightly Nathan's memories were wound unravelling them was the first step towards healing.

The group gathered close, heads nearly touching as they pored over the diary. Page by page, they began to decode the entries each one a breadcrumb leading further into the labyrinth of Nathan's past, a past riddled with pain and secrets long buried.

"Look at these dates," Susan pointed, her finger tracing a line of faded ink. "They're all around the same time of year. And these sketches they repeat."

"Whatever happened, it left a deep scar," Mark murmured, his voice laced with empathy.

"We'll figure this out, Nathan. You're not alone anymore."

Nathan looked up. In the faces around him, he saw something unexpected: hope. A hope he'd thought long extinguished.

Later, in Mark's living room, the fading daylight spilled across the coffee table, illuminating the diary's pages. They were a patchwork of disturbing illustrations and cryptic ramblings pages that pulsed with unspoken truths.

"Right," Mark said, flipping through the book. "Nathan, do any of these sketches look familiar?"

Nathan peered down, brow furrowed. "It's like trying to remember a dream blurry, but... familiar."

Susan slid a page closer. "These symbols repeat. And the handwriting changes it becomes more erratic here."

"Stress indicators," Clara added, her years of nursing giving her insight. "He was clearly under immense pressure when he wrote these."

"Or scared witless," Angela muttered, eyes narrowed. She tapped a sketch of a house. "This shows up again and again. It must mean something."

"Wait" Clara sat upright, eyes alight. "That house I've heard of it. There's a place on the edge of town. People say it's haunted."

"Haunted?" Marie raised an eyebrow, sceptical but intrigued. "Don't tell me we're adding ghosts into this."

"Legends start somewhere," Clara said firmly. "The place has been abandoned for decades. Locals say it's cursed people go there and... they change."

Susan looked between Clara and the diary. "Could this place be part of Nathan's past?"

"Everything's connected," Mark said quietly, his knack for seeing patterns kicking in. "We just have to follow the threads."

"Then we're going," Nathan said, surprising even himself. "If there are answers there, I want them."

"Are you sure?" Mark asked. "We don't know what we're walking into."

Nathan offered a crooked smile. "My whole life's a mystery. What's one more puzzle to solve?"

The room vibrated with resolve. They might be stepping into darkness, but they were no longer doing it alone. The haunted house called to them and with it, the promise of answers.

Mark broke the silence. "Alright, then." He rummaged through a drawer and pulled out several heavy-duty torches. "We'll need light." The soft clicks of switches echoed as he tested each one.

"Got my camera," Susan added, patting the strap slung across her shoulder. She unzipped her kit bag to reveal a DSLR camera and a range of lenses. "For documentation or anything that's... not quite normal."

"Here take these." Angela handed out batteries like sweets. Her kitchen had become a makeshift supply station, stacked with snacks and bottled water.

"You think of everything," Marie said, slotting a battery into her torch.

Angela shrugged. "Old Girl Guide habits."

Clara held up a digital recorder. "If there are whispers I want to catch them." Her hands were steady, but her eyes shone with anticipation.

"Looks like we're ready. Stick close," Mark said, casting a glance at Nathan, who nodded silently, burdened by the weight of what lay ahead.

The drive was quiet, tension hanging thick in the air. A murmur of directions here, a shared granola bar there until the house loomed into view. Its silhouette against the dusk sky was jagged and ominous.

"Here we are," Nathan murmured as the car engine fell silent. The chill in the air was sharp, tinged with damp and decay. The house towered above them its windows like dead eyes, its porch sagging under the strain of memory.

"Look at this place..." Susan breathed, snapping photos of ivy that clawed at the crumbling brick like desperate fingers.

"It's watching us," Angela muttered, tightening her rucksack straps.

"Or waiting," Marie added, a shiver running down her spine.

"Shall we?" Mark gestured to the entrance, torch beam cutting into the gloom. He stepped forward. The porch creaked beneath his weight, a groan of protest.

"Careful," Clara warned, voice hushed as they followed.

"Stay together," Mark said, pushing open the heavy front door. It groaned open with an agonised squeal that echoed through the house.

"Into the belly of the beast," Nathan said, a smirk disguising the tightness in his chest.

"Let's find those answers," Susan replied, gripping her camera tighter. The air inside was stale, musty. The door slammed shut behind them with a final thud.

"Alright, team," Mark said, his voice calm despite the weight of silence. "We'll cover more ground if we split up. Nathan and I will take the basement. The rest of you upstairs."

"Be careful," Susan replied, her worry more than just for physical dangers.

"Always," Mark said with a smile that didn't quite reach his eyes.

As the group split, Nathan's tension was palpable. The basement steps creaked underfoot, the air colder, heavier with each descent.

"This place gives me the creeps," Nathan muttered, torchlight flickering.

"Focus. Look for anything out of place," Mark said, though he knew the real threat was already within Nathan memories clawing to be remembered.

The Mind Whisperer

Upstairs, Susan led the way. Clara, Angela, and Marie followed closely. The floorboards moaned under their weight.

"Look at this," Clara whispered, pointing to strange carvings on the bannister. "These symbols they're intentional."

"Some kind of code?" Angela suggested, scanning for patterns.

"Or a cry for help," Marie murmured, clutching her own fear like a shield.

"Photograph everything," Susan instructed, her camera clicking. Maybc, just maybe, the lens would catch more than what the eye could see.

Back in the basement, Mark and Nathan came across an old chest its wood warped by time, but the carvings on its lid were clear and precise.

"A family crest?" Mark asked, running his fingers across the emblem. "Feels significant."

"Feels like something straight out of a horror film," Nathan replied but the joke was hollow. The past was catching up with him.

Suddenly, a light flickered above them, casting erratic shadows against the stone walls. A guttural whisper seemed to emanate from nowhere and everywhere at once, causing both men to freeze.

"Did you hear that?" Nathan asked, every muscle taut.

"Hard not to," Mark replied, his uncanny senses peeling back the layers of sound, searching for its source.

Meanwhile, upstairs, the women felt the house stir around them. A picture frame tilted on the wall without being touched, its once-clear faces now blurred by the passage of time.

"Is it just me, or did that move?" Marie whispered, her anxiety spiking.

"Definitely not just you," Angela confirmed, her practical nature warring with the unexplainable.

"Something doesn't want us here," Clara observed, the nurse in her recognising the signs of fear.

"Or something does," Susan countered, her protective instincts flaring. "Maybe it's trying to communicate."

"Let's keep going," Clara said, steadying her breath. "For Nathan."

As they pressed on, every creak and groan of the house tightened the knot of suspense in their chests. The atmosphere thickened with dread, the line between natural and supernatural blurring with each step.

"Are we really doing this?" Marie murmured, half to herself, half to the unseen presences she felt crowding around them.

"We have to," Susan said firmly, her resolve strengthening the group. "For Nathan."

"Right," Angela echoed, squaring her shoulders. "For Nathan."

The energy in the house seemed to shift in response, the air crackling as though the mystery they sought was alive, pulsing through the walls, guiding them deeper into the labyrinth of Nathan's haunted past.

In the dusky basement, Mark ran his hands along the cold stone wall, his fingertips sensitive to the smallest anomaly.

"Here," he murmured, pressing gently against a faint outline. A low click echoed through the damp air as a section of the wall creaked open, revealing a hidden room steeped in the musty scent of long-buried secrets.

"Good Lord," Nathan breathed, his torch beam flickering across an array of items frozen in time. Dust particles danced like tiny spirits in the light.

"Let's see what we've got," Mark said, his voice steady, though Nathan could sense his excitement as they stepped inside.

<h1 align="center">The Mind Whisperer</h1>

The room was a museum of memories, each artefact a fragment of someone's life. Nathan hesitated at the threshold, the weight of history pressing heavily on him. He watched as Mark picked up a faded photograph of a smiling woman who bore an uncanny resemblance to him.

"Is this...?" Nathan began, his voice catching.

"Looks like she could be family," Mark replied gently, empathy shining in his eyes.

"Mum," Nathan whispered, the word escaping from a place deep inside him. The air seemed to hum, as if the shadows whispered her name.

"Look at this," Mark said, holding out a delicate silver locket. It swung like a pendulum from his fingers, its secrets waiting to be revealed.

"Open it," Nathan urged, stepping closer.

With reverence, Mark unlatched the locket to reveal two tiny photographs one of a man Nathan didn't recognise, and the other of a younger Nathan himself. His breath caught in his chest.

"I don't remember this..."

"Let's keep looking," Mark said softly, placing the locket in Nathan's palm. "There might be more clues."

Meanwhile, upstairs, the thud of a heavy book falling to the floor drew the women's attention to a towering bookcase.

"Did you see that?" Clara's voice trembled as she pointed to the book that seemed to have leapt of its own accord.

"Something's behind there," Susan said, her detective instincts sparking to life. She gripped the shelf and pulled. With a grinding noise, it shifted, revealing a narrow passage cloaked in darkness.

"Angela, the camera!" Marie called, clutching her torch like a lifeline.

"Got it," Angela replied, heart pounding as she began to film their descent into the unknown.

"Be careful," Clara warned, her nurse's training reminding her of every possible hazard.

"Always am," Susan quipped with a wink, emboldened by the thrill of the chase.

The secret chamber at the end of the passage was sparse save for a single journal resting on a stone pedestal. Its leather cover was cracked, the pages brittle and yellowed.

"This is it," Susan announced, flipping through the aged pages. "It's about the fire the one that changed everything for Nathan."

"Read it aloud," Marie urged, curiosity overcoming fear.

Susan began, her voice growing stronger as she read: "14th June. The night of flames... the night I lost everything dear to me..."

As the sorrowful story unfolded, the women exchanged glances. Understanding settled over them like dust. This was the key the event that had shaped Nathan's entire life.

"Mark needs to see this," Angela said firmly, snapping the camera shut. Their resolve solidified, shielding them against the chill that whispered from the very walls.

"Let's go," Clara agreed, her professional calm belying her racing heart. "For Nathan."

Together, they retraced their steps, the journal clutched tightly in Susan's hands a fragile beacon of hope in the deepening gloom.

"Did you hear that?" Angela whispered, halting mid-step, her eyes wide.

Susan raised a finger to her lips and nodded. The air thickened with unease as the creak of a floorboard overhead echoed like a warning shot.

"Someone's here," Clara murmured, scanning the shadows with clinical precision.

"Quick behind here," Marie hissed, ushering them into a shadowed alcove.

They huddled together, breaths shallow, hearts racing. Susan's pulse thundered in her ears. Mark's abilities often gave them the upper hand but without him, they felt utterly exposed.

Downstairs, in the hidden room, Mark's head snapped up. His eyes met Nathan's.

"We're not alone," he said quietly. Despite the adrenaline flooding his system, his voice was calm. His autism heightened his senses in moments like this, honing his awareness of the intruders above.

"Hide," Nathan whispered, shoving Mark gently towards an old armoire. They slipped inside just as footsteps began descending the basement stairs.

"Who would come here?" Nathan breathed, struggling to contain his fear.

"Shh," Mark replied, focusing on the vibrations in the floor.

Upstairs, the women strained to hear. A soft tread moved from room to room, deliberate and slow. Dust motes shimmered in the fractured light streaming through boarded windows, lending the scene an eerie, dreamlike quality.

"Could it be the police?" Marie whispered.

"Or Lucas Morgan," Angela suggested, recalling the journalist's relentless pursuit of a story.

"Either way, we can't be caught," Susan said firmly, clutching the journal. "This changes everything for Nathan."

"Look!" Clara nudged her, pointing towards the doorway. A tall, imposing shadow flitted past.

"Who is that?" Marie mouthed, her eyes wide.

"Wait do you see that?" Angela squinted, her hand gripping Susan's arm.

"Is that...?" Susan began, her words fading as the shadow paused seeming to turn directly towards their hiding place.

"Stay still," Angela breathed, her community centre experience kicking in, guiding her calm in the face of fear.

"Always am," Susan replied with a wink, emboldened by the thrill of discovery.

As the tragic tale unfolded, the women exchanged glances, a dawning understanding reflected in their eyes. This was the key to Nathan's tormented soul the event that had cast a long shadow over his entire life.

"Mark needs to see this," Angela said firmly, snapping the camera shut. Their shared resolve steeled them against the eerie chill that seemed to seep from the very walls, whispering of the sorrow that had once consumed the house.

"Let's go," Clara agreed, her professional composure concealing the thunder of her heartbeat. "For Nathan."

Together, they retraced their steps, the journal clutched tightly in Susan's hands a fragile beacon of hope in the surrounding gloom.

Chapter 8
Wolves At The Door

Mark Jennings stood on the makeshift stage, calm amidst a sea of anxious murmurs and uneasy whispers. The crowd at the annual Mind and Mysteries Conference had gathered around him, eyes wide with anticipation, waiting for the promised demonstration of his extraordinary abilities. But Lucas Morgan had his own agenda.

"Tell us, Mr. Jennings," Lucas's voice sliced through the chatter, its sharpness cutting into the thick tension of the room. His greying hair barely registered under the harsh, unforgiving lights of the auditorium. "How exactly do you explain these so-called predictions of yours? Are they not simply the product of manipulation and cold reading?"

The question hung in the air, sharp and accusing. The audience shifted uncomfortably, their interest quickly soured by the scepticism in Lucas's tone. The murmurs grew louder, tinged with doubt.

"Lucas, my abilities are not up for debate here," Mark responded, his voice steady, controlled unfazed by the rising tide of hostility. The adrenaline coursing through his veins didn't show. "I've helped countless people with my insights. Take Mrs. Henley, for example, who avoided a disastrous business decision because of my prediction."

A few heads nodded in recognition of the well-known case, where Mark's foresight had saved a local bakery from investing in a fraudulent venture. But Lucas wasn't done.

"Convenient anecdotes, Mr. Jennings," Lucas pressed, his voice dripping with condescension. "But where is the science? Where is the evidence?"

"Science hasn't yet understood the full extent of the human mind, Lucas," Mark countered, meeting Lucas's gaze with unwavering confidence, his voice like steel. "Just because something can't be explained doesn't mean it isn't real."

"Or maybe," Lucas snapped back, "it just means you're an incredibly skilled con artist."

A ripple of gasps ran through the crowd as the room's atmosphere grew colder, each word sinking like a stone in Mark's chest.

"Consider Jenny Carter," Mark said, his voice cutting through the tension. "She was on the verge of leaving her husband. I sensed the deep-rooted issues in their relationship, and now they're attending counselling, working through their problems together."

"Isolated cases don't prove legitimacy!" Lucas shot back, his scepticism mounting like a palpable force. The room seemed to tighten around them.

"Nor do they prove deceit, Lucas," Mark said, calm as ever. His tone was firm, devoid of doubt. "I've dedicated my life to helping people. My aim is never to exploit, but to aid those who need it."

"Your 'gift' or whatever you want to call it " Lucas gestured broadly to the audience, as if dismissing the whole concept, "will be exposed for the sham it truly is."

"Then let the truth speak for itself," Mark replied, his confidence undiminished. "The lives I've touched, the people who've benefited from my help that is the real evidence."

The crowd watched, mesmerised by the exchange. In the battle of words, Mark was the eye of the storm calm, focused, and resolute in his conviction, unwavering even in the face of relentless attack.

Lucas Morgan sat across from Marianne Wilkes in a small, dimly lit coffee shop. His pen tapped rhythmically against the notepad, his eyes never leaving her. Marianne, clearly uncomfortable, twisted a lock of her hair nervously, unable to meet his gaze.

"Mrs. Wilkes," Lucas began, his voice smooth, yet laced with an undercurrent of authority, "you sought Mark Jennings' guidance last year, didn't you?"

"Yes," she whispered, her voice shaky. "My son was missing. The police had no leads. I didn't know where else to turn."

"And Mr. Jennings," Lucas pressed, his voice softening just enough to feign empathy, "he gave you a location?"

"More like... a feeling," Marianne's voice trembled as she recalled the events. "He held my hand and said he sensed water, a park, laughter... It led us to the lakeside amusement park. That's where we found Robbie, playing by the docks."

Lucas leaned in, his eyes narrowing. "Did you ever consider it might have been a lucky guess?"

Tears welled in Marianne's eyes, threatening to spill over. "It doesn't matter," she whispered, her voice thick with emotion. "My boy came home because of him."

"Thank you for your time, Mrs. Wilkes." Lucas scribbled a note quickly, then stood to leave, leaving behind a stunned Marianne, her emotions raw and her eyes brimming with gratitude.

Scene after scene played out in much the same way. Lucas interviewed former clients of Mark Jennings, determined to uncover something anything that would discredit him. But with each interview, the journalist's frustration deepened. None of his subjects could provide the solid proof he needed to substantiate his claims.

Eventually, Lucas stood outside the modest façade of Mark's home, the weight of his task pressing heavily on his shoulders. The frustration of his fruitless search was now palpable.

"Come in, Lucas," Mark greeted, stepping aside to allow the journalist entry. His home was humble, with none of the ostentation one might expect from someone who claimed to possess supernatural gifts. It was simple, unassuming a reflection of the man himself.

"Mind if I look around?" Lucas asked, though his tone implied it wasn't really a question.

"Be my guest," Mark replied, gesturing toward the rooms with an open-handed invitation. Mark folded his arms, watching closely as Lucas rummaged through drawers, inspected bookshelves crowded with philosophy and psychology texts, and rifled through personal papers.

"Looking for something in particular?" Mark asked, his voice amused, though his eyes betrayed a glimmer of weariness.

"Anything that shows how you do it," Lucas muttered, flipping through a notebook filled with doodles and random thoughts, looking for any clue to disprove Mark's abilities.

"Find what you're seeking?"

"Nothing yet," Lucas grumbled, clearly frustrated. He slammed the notebook down on the counter and turned on Mark, eyes fierce. "If you've got nothing to hide, prove it. Let me test you."

Mark didn't flinch. His expression remained serene. "Alright," he said, sitting down at the kitchen table. "What's the test?"

"Think of a number between one and a hundred," Lucas instructed, pulling out a small recorder. "Don't tell me. Just concentrate on it."

Mark locked eyes with him. "Done."

"Is it... seventeen?"

Mark smiled slightly. "No."

"Damn it," Lucas muttered under his breath, frustration simmering just beneath the surface.

"Lucas," Mark said softly, "I can't read minds, nor can I predict random numbers. My gift isn't about that. It's about connection. It's about feeling people's needs, their emotions, their intentions."

"Convenient excuse," Lucas sneered, his voice thick with contempt.

"Believe what you want," Mark replied, rising from the table. "But I'll continue helping those who come to me. Whether you call me a fraud or not doesn't change the lives I've touched."

Lucas switched off his recorder, the weight of his failure heavy in his pocket. The confrontation had ended, but the quest for truth his truth was far from over.

As Mark watched Lucas leave, his hands clenched at his sides. The frustration that had been bubbling under the surface for so long finally began to crest. Lucas had left, but the sting of his scepticism remained, lingering like a shadow in Mark's otherwise peaceful home.

"Can you believe it, Susan?" Mark's voice echoed through the living room, his usual composure crumbling under the weight of the accusation. "After everything I've done, the lives I've touched... he still sees me as nothing more than a charlatan!"

Susan looked up from her cup of tea, her eyes mirroring the storm raging in her brother's heart. "It's not about you, Mark," she said softly, her hand reaching out to steady his trembling ones. "Lucas's quest for truth blinds him. He can't see the forest for the trees."

"But how can he ignore the good?" Mark's voice cracked, his gaze falling to the floor as he turned away. He appeared dejected, framed by the room where so many had found solace. "I've seen it in their eyes, Susan the relief, the hope... How can he deny that?"

"Because sometimes," Susan replied, her words heavy with unwavering belief in her brother, "people are afraid of what they don't understand. Fear dictates their actions, not compassion."

Mark sank onto the couch, his head in his hands. "What if he's right? What if I'm just fooling myself?"

"Mark," Susan moved beside him, her presence comforting and familiar. "Look at me." When he did, in her eyes he found all he needed to remember. "You have a gift, Mark. A rare and beautiful gift. You've used it to help countless people through their darkest moments. Don't let one man's doubt undo all of that."

He drew in a long, steadying breath, the air filling his lungs like balm to his frayed spirit. "But how do I continue, Sue? How do I keep going when every step forward is met with suspicion?"

"By remembering why you started," she said firmly. "Think back to the first person you helped, without even realising what you were doing. Remember the look on their face when they realised they weren't alone. That's your compass, Mark. Let it guide you, not the fear or doubt of others."

Mark nodded slowly, the knot in his chest beginning to loosen. "I just wish he could see..."

"Maybe one day he will," Susan said, standing and offering him her hand. "But until then, you have work to do. People to help. Don't give up on them because of him."

"Thank you, Susan," Mark murmured, accepting her hand and allowing her unshakable faith to seep into his veins. She was right. This wasn't the end of his journey, merely a detour. With each step forward, he would carry with him the certainty of her belief, and the knowledge that his gift was meant for far more than the approval of sceptics.

"Let's show Lucas Morgan what you're made of," Susan declared, a fire igniting in her eyes that matched the renewed determination in Mark's heart. Together, they would stand tall against the tide of doubt, their bond unbreakable, their mission clear.

Lucas Morgan sat beneath the sterile white glow of a coffee shop's fluorescent lights, the hum of the refrigeration unit blending with the soft jazz trickling through the speakers above. Across from him, a woman in her mid-fifties fidgeted, her fingers tracing the rim of her untouched latte.

"Mr. Morgan, I just don't see how this helps," she began, her voice tinged with discomfort. "Mark, he was so sure... so convincing."

"Ms. Hammond," Lucas said, leaning forward, his recorder placed carefully between them. "I understand this is difficult, but it's crucial to establish the full truth about Mr. Jennings' predictions."

She sighed, a sound filled with weary disappointment. "He told me my husband would overcome his illness, that we'd have years ahead of us." Her eyes darted away, finding solace in the swirling patterns of her untouched drink. "Three weeks later, my world fell apart. The cancer... it spread too fast."

"Did you confront Mark about this?" Lucas asked, his pen poised above his notepad, ready to capture her words.

"Once. He said that sometimes the future changes, that he only sees possibilities. But that doesn't pay for the funeral costs, does it?" Her bitterness was evident, the taste of broken promises lingering in her voice.

"Thank you for sharing your story," Lucas said, his tone professional as the journalist within him filed away her testimony. Another piece of the puzzle had fallen into place, and with it, the cracks in Mark's façade seemed to widen.

Mark Jennings stood outside the glass doors of the *Sentinel-Times*, fists clenched at his sides as he drew a deep breath. Inside, he knew, was the man determined to discredit him at every turn. With Susan's words echoing in his mind, Mark pushed the door open and strode purposefully into the bullpen.

"Mr. Jennings," an intern called out, startled by the urgency in Mark's movements.

"Where's Morgan?" Mark demanded, his voice firm, controlled yet trembling with underlying tension.

"His office, but "

Without waiting for permission, Mark navigated the maze of desks until he reached the door marked "Lucas Morgan." Without knocking, he flung it open, finding Lucas hunched over a mountain of notes and clippings.

"Mark, what are you " Lucas began, surprised by the sudden intrusion.

"Enough, Lucas!" Mark's voice filled the room, commanding attention. "This campaign against me it has to stop."

"Mark, I'm uncovering the truth," Lucas replied, standing up, his defensive tone betraying the uncertainty gnawing at him.

"The truth?" Mark's laugh was hollow, devoid of humour. "You're fixated on the few times I couldn't help, ignoring all the good that's come from my gift."

"Gift? Is that what you call it?" Lucas challenged, his words sharp. "For every success, there's someone like Ms. Hammond."

"Life is complex, Lucas!" Mark shot back, his hands slicing through the air to punctuate his point. "I never claimed perfection. People find hope, guidance, comfort. Isn't that worth something?"

"Hope based on falsehoods is dangerous," Lucas retorted, his scepticism a shield, impenetrable.

"Look deeper!" Mark implored, his voice softening but still laced with intensity. "Lives have changed. Despair has turned to hope. Why can't you focus on the positive impact? On helping those in need?"

"Because I can't ignore the possibility of manipulation," Lucas admitted, his journalistic instinct refusing to yield.

"Then come with me," Mark suggested, his offer hanging between them like a challenge. "See for yourself. Witness the work I do. Maybe then you'll understand."

Lucas stared at Mark, the moment stretching out. Could he step into Mark's world, confront his own scepticism, or would he only solidify his doubts?

"Alright, Mark," Lucas finally said, his voice tinged with cautious curiosity. "I'll take you up on that."

"Good," Mark nodded, an uneasy truce settling between them. "Let's start tomorrow."

As Mark left Lucas's office, a flicker of hope stirred within him. Perhaps this was the chance he needed to prove to both Lucas and himself that he was not a fraud, but simply a man trying to use his unique gift for the greater good.

Lucas Morgan stood in the centre of Mark Jennings's modest living room, a sheaf of papers clenched in his hand like an accusation. The air was thick with tension, the light filtering through the curtains casting long shadows that seemed to heighten the moment's gravity.

"Explain these," Lucas demanded, his voice sharp, as he tossed the documents onto the coffee table. They scattered across the surface testimonies, failed predictions, all stark evidence laid before Mark.

Mark's stomach tightened as he scanned the pages. Here were the silent ghosts of his past, the rare but haunting failures that had slipped through the cracks of his extraordinary ability. He looked up at Lucas, his expression strained.

"Everyone makes mistakes," Mark said, his tone defensive but undercut with uncertainty. "No one is perfect, not even me."

"Is that an admission, then?" Lucas leaned forward, his eyes narrowing as grey strands of hair caught the light. "An admission that this 'gift' of yours is nothing more than a well-orchestrated ruse?"

Mark's hands trembled slightly as he picked up one of the papers, a report of a prediction gone awry that had led to heartbreak instead of healing. He remembered the weight of their expectations, the hope in their eyes when they came to him, and the crushing burden when he couldn't deliver.

"Look," Mark insisted, his voice shaking but determined, "I've helped countless people. These... these are just outliers."

"Outliers?" Lucas repeated, his voice a bitter sneer. "Or perhaps they're evidence of the truth? You can't hide behind your successes forever."

Mark's composure cracked, and the calm façade began to splinter. Raw, palpable fear took its place. He thought of all the good he'd done, of the lives touched by his gift, but the seeds of doubt planted by Lucas's relentless investigation were starting to sprout, twisting his thoughts.

"Am I a fraud?" The question slipped from Mark's lips before he could stop it, a vulnerable whisper that filled the room with its echo. His eyes searched Lucas's face for a glimmer of compassion, but found only the cold pursuit of justice.

"Only you can answer that, Mark," Lucas replied, his voice softer now, but still unwavering. "But if you're deceiving these people, knowingly or not, it's my job to bring that to light."

The confrontation reached its peak, a crescendo in a symphony that had been building ever since Lucas set his sights on exposing Mark's secrets. The journalist's determination was unyielding, and the potential destruction of Mark's reputation was mere collateral damage in his pursuit of truth.

"Maybe I am fooling myself," Mark confessed, his shoulders slumping as he sank into the couch, his gaze falling to the floor. In his heart, he knew the good he'd achieved, but Lucas's words gnawed at his confidence. Could his life's work truly be tainted by doubt?

"Then stop," Lucas urged, standing tall over him, his silhouette casting a long shadow. "Stop before more people get hurt."

"Even if I wanted to," Mark whispered, his voice breaking, "I don't know if I can." His hands gripped together, seeking comfort in the familiar sensation of his skin   the only certainty he had left.

"Then we have more to discuss," Lucas said, his tone final, as though this battle were far from over.

As Lucas turned to leave, Mark watched him go, the setting sun casting long, creeping shadows across the room   a mirror to the darkening of his soul. Was he truly out of touch with reality, or was it Lucas who couldn't see the light of truth? Only time would tell, but for now, the seeds of self-doubt had taken root and were beginning to grow.

The murmur of the gathered crowd filled the air, a palpable tension threading through the auditorium as Mark and Lucas took their positions on stage. The harsh lights above cast stark shadows, their faces frozen masks of determination and uncertainty.

"Good evening, everyone," the moderator's voice rang out, tight with anticipation. "Tonight, we witness a pivotal moment as two men lay their convictions bare for all to see."

Mark adjusted his microphone, fingers brushing the cool metal, steadying his breath. Across from him, Lucas remained a statue, his eyes sharp, calculating, and cold.

"Mr. Jennings," the moderator began, turning first to Mark. "You claim to have helped countless individuals with your abilities. Can you explain how you do it?"

Mark leaned forward, his hands clasped in front of him. "It's not something I do," he began, his voice steady despite the rapid drumming of his heart. "It's something I feel. A connection to others that guides me, helps them find clarity."

"And yet, Mr. Morgan has raised concerns about the validity of your predictions," the moderator pressed, casting a glance at Lucas, who nodded curtly.

Lucas interjected before Mark could speak. "Predictions that have sometimes proven false, leading to consequences for those involved. Isn't that right, Mr. Jennings?"

Mark met Lucas's gaze, his eyes betraying the inner turmoil he'd been battling. "I've never claimed to be infallible," he admitted, his voice softening. "My efforts are always in the spirit of guidance, not certainty."

"Guidance that can mislead, perhaps?" Lucas challenged, his voice rising with intensity.

"Enough!" Mark's outburst cut through the tension, his fists clenched as he fought to regain his composure. "I've seen the good that's come from my gift. People reunited, lives changed for the better. That's what drives me."

A hushed whisper rippled through the crowd, their eyes flicking back and forth between the two men, like spectators at a tennis match.

"Mr. Morgan, your response?" the moderator asked, inviting Lucas to speak, though it was clear Lucas had been prepared to continue without prompting.

"Drive should not excuse recklessness," Lucas retorted firmly. "And hope should not be built on shaky foundations. My investigation has uncovered "

"Allegations," Mark interjected, desperation creeping into his voice. "Not proof. My work is not a science; it's a form of compassion."

"Or manipulation," Lucas shot back, his words hanging in the air, causing a stir among the audience.

"Let's allow the audience to ask some questions, shall we?" the moderator interjected, sensing the growing tension.

One by one, questions from the crowd filtered through some sceptical, others supportive. Mark answered each with sincerity, while Lucas countered with pointed scepticism.

The Mind Whisperer

As the debate drew to a close, the moderator summarised the exchange. "It seems we've reached an impasse. Mr. Jennings stands by his abilities, while Mr. Morgan remains unconvinced of their legitimacy."

Mark's gaze swept over the crowd, searching for an ally in the sea of faces. His breath caught when he noticed a figure standing at the back of the room, a shadow hidden in uncertainty.

"Before we conclude," the moderator announced, "each man will have a final opportunity to address the audience."

Mark rose, his legs unsteady, but his resolve unwavering. "I stand before you, not as a miracle worker, but as a man striving to make a difference. Whether or not you believe in my abilities, know this my intention has always been to serve for the greater good."

Lucas stood next, his posture rigid with conviction. "Intentions may be noble, but deception intentional or not can shatter lives. We must demand proof, not just promises."

The moderator nodded solemnly. "Thank you both. It is now up to you, the public, to decide. Good night."

The applause came, but Mark barely heard it. His eyes were fixed on the mysterious figure, whose presence seemed to hold the key to the ordeal that had enveloped him.

"Is he a fraud or a saviour?" a voice murmured nearby, summing up the question that lingered in the minds of everyone in the room.

As the curtain fell, obscuring Mark and Lucas from view, the chapter closed, leaving the audience hanging on the edge of uncertainty desperate to uncover the truth hidden within the enigma that was Mark Jennings.

Chapter 9
Masks Unveiled

Mark Jennings adjusted his tie with meticulous care, a slight tremor of anticipation coursing through his fingers. The polished brass handle of the restaurant's front door felt cool and substantial beneath his palm as he pushed it open. He stepped into the opulent embrace of "Le Ciel Étoilé," a name that promised celestial dining experiences. Tonight, he was to meet Victoria Green, a rendezvous that stirred both excitement and unease in his heart.

The maître d' greeted him with a practised smile, but Mark hardly noticed. His senses were already reaching out for Victoria's familiar presence amid the soft clinking of fine china and the low murmur of conversation. With each step he took on the plush carpet, the weight of expectation grew heavier upon his shoulders.

"Good evening, sir," said a waiter, brushing past with a tray of sparkling champagne flutes.

"Evening," Mark replied absently, his gaze sweeping across the room's elegant décor. Crystal chandeliers cast a warm glow over mahogany panelling and tables draped in white linen, each a flawless island of conviviality in a vast sea of wealth and privilege.

As he moved forward, he scanned the faces and postures around him, tuning into the muted hum of thoughts that provided a constant backdrop to his life. Couples leaned towards one another in intimate conversation, business associates laughed over shared jokes, and somewhere within this tapestry of human interaction, Victoria awaited him.

"Is Madame already here?" he asked softly, almost to himself, as if the answer might be revealed in the intricate swirls of the parquet floor.

A well-dressed patron raised a glass in cheer to a companion, while a woman's silvery laughter floated above the gentle cadence of piano music. Mark's finely honed instincts his uncanny ability to interpret the nuances of social interplay guided his attention to a secluded table in the far corner of the restaurant, offering privacy and discretion.

"Ah, there she is," he murmured, his eyes locking onto the poised figure of Victoria Green. Her flowing blonde hair cascaded down her back in waves of careful perfection, the dim light catching the glint of her diamond earrings. She sat alone, a queen in her meticulously crafted domain, awaiting her guest.

"Excuse me," Mark said politely, sidestepping a passing server as he navigated the maze of tables. Each step brought him closer to the woman whose intentions remained obscured, a puzzle his mind was eager yet hesitant to solve. He felt the vibrations of energy in the room, the ebb and flow of unspoken narratives dancing just out of reach of ordinary perception.

"Victoria Green," he thought, a mix of respect and wariness coursing through him. "What secrets lie behind those sapphire eyes?"

As he approached her table, the rest of the world faded away, the ambient noise diminishing to a whisper. Mark's journey through the restaurant had been a subtle dance, but now, standing at the precipice of discovery, he braced himself for whatever the night had in store.

A soft smile a rare curling of his lips that seldom graced his public persona touched his features as he neared the secluded table where Victoria sat. Warmth glimmered in his eyes, reflecting the pleasure he gained from aiding those who sought his insight. He extended his hand towards her, the motion fluid and confident.

"Victoria," he greeted, his voice carrying an undercurrent of excitement. "It's good to see you again."

"Mark!" Victoria responded, her brightness somewhat diminished, failing to reach her eyes. She stood, taking his hand in both of hers. Her grip was firm, yet carried a coolness that belied the warmth of her words. "I've been looking forward to this meeting with such anticipation."

"Have you?" Mark chuckled lightly, releasing her hands as they settled into their chairs. His senses, ever attuned to the subtlest nuances, picked up on an underlying tension beneath her polished veneer, though he couldn't quite place it.

"Absolutely," Victoria continued, tilting her head slightly as she regarded him with what seemed to be admiration. "The way you helped me last time was… remarkable. I've told all my friends about your incredible abilities."

"Helping is what I do," Mark replied, the corners of his mouth twitching upward with modesty. "I'm just glad to be of service."

"Your humility is one of your many endearing qualities," Victoria praised, her voice imbued with an enthusiasm that felt almost excessive. She leaned forward, her sapphire gaze locked onto his. "Really, Mark, I can't thank you enough for guiding me through that rough patch. You have a gift."

"Thank you, Victoria," he replied, brow furrowing slightly as he sensed the undercurrents of her praise. He felt the familiar tug of empathy urging him to reach out, yet an inner voice warned him to tread carefully.

"Shall we order?" Victoria suggested, gesturing gracefully towards the menu with her perfectly manicured hand, her practiced smile in place. "I believe tonight's special is truly out of this world."

"Sounds perfect," Mark agreed, his mind subtly probing the edges of Victoria's enthusiasm, searching for the sincerity he hoped would be evident.

"Have you tried the truffled lobster here?" Victoria asked, her eyes sparkling with a hint of something Mark found difficult to decipher.

The Mind Whisperer

"No, I can't say I have," Mark replied, unfolding his napkin onto his lap. The soft clink of cutlery and the murmur of conversations created an intimate cocoon at their secluded table.

"Mark, you really must. It's divine," she enthused, the word rolling off her tongue like a promise of untold delights. "Speaking of divine, I've been reflecting a lot on your talents. You know, how incredibly unique they are."

Mark nodded, taking a sip of water. "Well, each person bears their own strengths, I suppose."

"Indeed, but not everyone can do what you do." Victoria's gaze was intent, increasingly calculating. "Imagine the possibilities if your gift could be shared on a larger scale."

"Shared?" Mark echoed, sensing the conversation shift imperceptibly.

"Absolutely," Victoria purred. "Think about it. You could influence so many more lives, help countless people with your… insight."

"Helping people is one thing," Mark said slowly, uneasy as he sensed the tendrils of her ambition weaving through her words. "But it's quite another to use it for."

"For the greater good?" Victoria finished for him, her lips curving into a smile that didn't quite reach her eyes. "Of course; I mean for the greater good. What else could I be alluding to?"

"Right," Mark murmured, though a sliver of doubt crept into his thoughts.

"Besides," Victoria continued, leaning in closer as if to share a secret, "think of the recognition you'd receive. You could be celebrated, revered even."

"Recognition isn't important to me," he responded, his voice firm yet polite. "I just want to do what's right."

"Of course, of course," she quickly backtracked, waving a dismissive hand. "But surely, you understand the potential to shape the world?"

"Shape the world?" Mark repeated, the phrase echoing uncomfortably within him. Fleeting images of gentle guidance twisting into manipulation flickered in his mind, prompting him to push the unsettling thought aside.

"Perhaps," Victoria pressed, her tone insistent. "You haven't considered all the ways your abilities could benefit others or even yourself."

"I believe I have a clear understanding," Mark replied, meeting her gaze steadily. A new sharpness had entered her features, a glint of something unspoken lurking in the depths of her sapphire eyes.

"Mark, don't you see? You could be..." Victoria trailed off, fingers drumming lightly against the white tablecloth.

"Could be what?" he prompted, heart racing as he began to sense the magnitude of her hidden agenda.

"Powerful," she whispered, the word hanging between them like a veiled threat.

"Power," Mark repeated softly, a frown creasing his forehead. Power had never been his goal; the very notion felt at odds with the essence of who he was. He felt the steady rhythm of his empathy disrupted by a growing dissonance with each probing question from Victoria.

"Exactly," Victoria said, leaning back in her chair, satisfied with the seed she believed she had planted. "Think about it, Mark. Really consider the power at your fingertips."

Mark's spoon clattered against his saucer, the sound sharper than intended. He realised with a sudden wave of trepidation that the anticipation and excitement he had felt upon arrival had been overshadowed by an uneasy apprehension. Victoria's ambitions were becoming clearer, and for the first time, he wondered whether his gift his blessing could also become his greatest challenge.

The fine china rattled as Victoria leaned forward, her voice dropping to a conspiratorial whisper. "Mark, I've been using the insights you provided," she said, her eyes gleaming with a fervour bordering on mania.

Mark's brow furrowed, his spoon poised mid-air. "Using them? How?" The restaurant around them faded into a blur, the clang of glasses and muted conversations falling away as he focused on her admission.

"Your predictions, your uncanny ability to know what people are going to do it's been… invaluable." She spread her hands wide, as if to showcase the breadth of her scheme. "I've made decisions, investments, and moves in my social circles based entirely on what you told me."

A coldness settled into Mark's stomach, a sharp breath freezing in his lungs. "But those sessions were meant to help you understand yourself better, not..." He trailed off, unable to articulate the depth of her betrayal.

"Oh, sweet, naive Mark," Victoria purred. "Did you genuinely think I'd let such a gift go unexploited? You're a gold mine, and I've been reaping the benefits."

Disappointment crashed over him like a wave. He had trusted her, believed in her desire for growth and improvement. He stared at her, struggling to reconcile the woman he thought he knew with the one who sat before him, draped in deceit as one might wear an expensive shawl.

"Victoria, I can't believe you'd do this," he managed to voice, strained with the effort to remain calm. The gentle touch he was known for had hardened into a clenched fist upon the tablecloth.

"Believe it, darling," she said, a flash of triumph dancing across her features. "And there's so much more."

Mark shook his head slowly, peering into her eyes cold stars against a velvet night and found no remorse there. It dawned on him how little he truly understood about the shadows lurking in someone like Victoria Green. It was a darkness that his own light could not penetrate.

"Is there anything real about you?" he asked, each word carrying the immense weight of shattered trust. "Or is everything just a game?"

"Real? Of course it's real," she snapped back. "It's as real as the power you wield without even realising its potential."

His heart raced, not with the thrill of discovery but with the sharp sting of betrayal. "This isn't what my abilities are for," he said, realisation settling heavily upon him: his mission to help others had been compromised. "I wanted to make a difference, not be part of... whatever this is."

"Too late for second thoughts," Victoria replied coolly. "You're in this whether you like it or not."

Mark recognised then that the path ahead would be fraught with danger. As he gazed across the table at Victoria, her face glowing with the thrill of control, he understood the true cost of his gift. In that moment, he made a silent vow: he would not allow his abilities to be tainted by greed and ambition not by anyone, not even Victoria Green.

"Consider it a compliment," Victoria purred, swirling her wine with an air of nonchalance that belied the seriousness of her confession. "You've been quite the asset, Mark far more valuable than you can imagine."

"An asset?" Mark's voice blended disbelief with hurt. "Is that all I am to you?"

"Please." She waved a dismissive hand. "Don't be so melodramatic. It's unbecoming. You should feel flattered that someone of my standing finds such… innovative uses for your little parlour trick."

"Helping people isn't a 'parlour trick,'" he countered, hands clenched beneath the table. The elegant atmosphere of the restaurant seemed to close in around them, the walls echoing the tightening grip of Victoria's ambitions.

"Helping people is a noble cause," she conceded with a hollow smile. "But let's not pretend you weren't benefitting from our little arrangement. You've sampled more of this world's luxuries since meeting me than ever before."

Mark wrestled with the complexity of his emotions. His heart ached with betrayal while concern for those he aimed to help surged within him. "I never wanted this," he said quietly. "My only wish was to make a positive impact, not to be part of someone's scheme."

"Darling, everyone plays a part in someone else's scheme," Victoria replied, her tone dripping with condescension. "The sooner you realise that, the better off you'll be."

"Perhaps," Mark murmured, although his thoughts vehemently disagreed with her perspective. He searched for any sign of the friend he thought he knew in Victoria's eyes, only to find the cold glint of ambition.

"Look at it this way," she continued, leaning forward. "You're a player on a grand stage now. Isn't that exciting?"

"Exciting isn't the word I'd use," he retorted, his sense of purpose warring against the shock of deceit. "What you view as a game, I see as people's lives lives I'm meant to protect, not exploit."

"Protect, exploit it's all semantics, really." Victoria shrugged, sipping her wine as if discussing nothing more significant than the weather. "What matters is how you wield the power you possess. And, dear Mark, you have far more power than you realise."

His resolve flickered like a candle in the wind, threatened by the storm of doubts swirling within him and Victoria's relentless persuasion. Yet, somewhere deep within, a spark of defiance remained a determination to stay true to the core of who he was, regardless of the storm raging around him.

Mark's chair scraped against the polished floor, a grating sound mirroring the turmoil within. He stood abruptly, his posture rigid with tension, met by Victoria's arched eyebrow, her façade of concern as fragile as the porcelain before them.

"Victoria," he began, voice steady despite the inner maelstrom. "I need to understand why. Why would you twist something meant for good into a personal agenda?"

She set down her wine glass with a soft clink, studying him with a clinical curiosity that sent shivers down his spine. "Because, Mark, opportunity knocks but once. You have this… gift," she said, her fingers dancing in the air as if to pluck the word from some invisible source. "Yet you've been playing in the minor leagues. I'm offering you a chance in the big leagues."

Mark shook his head, his brown hair barely stirring with the motion. "At what cost?" he pressed, voice rising in pitch. "What about those I was supposed to help? What becomes of our integrity?"

"Integrity won't put you on the map, darling," Victoria countered smoothly. Her smile had a razor's edge, slicing through the fabric of their relationship with every dismissive flick of her wrist. "This world devours the weak, the altruistic. You're neither not if you seize the opportunity."

He paced before her table, each step punctuating his internal debate. His gift his curse had always been about connection, about alleviating the hidden pains and silent screams of those around him. Now, here stood Victoria, draped in elegance and deceit, offering him a devil's bargain.

"Enough." The word was a thunderclap, sudden and jarring in the hushed ambience of the restaurant. Patrons turned, eyes widening as forks hovered mid-air.

"Enough," he repeated, softer yet resolute. "I won't let you or anyone else corrupt my ability. It's not a tool for manipulation it's a responsibility."

"Is it, Mark?" Victoria's tone was patronising, her gaze penetrating. "Or is it simply about control? Who wields the power and sets the rules?"

"Perhaps it is about control," he admitted, meeting her gaze unwaveringly. "But not in the way you think. I control how I use my abilities and with whom I share them. And right now, Victoria, it's evident that person isn't you."

"What will you do then, Mark?" she challenged, leaning back in her chair, a picture of nonchalance. "Will you walk away? Hide from the world and its shadows?"

"No." His response was resolute a lifeline cast into the sea of doubt. "I'll continue my mission, but with eyes wide open. You've unveiled the darker side of human nature, Victoria. Yet I won't allow it to deter me. I refuse to let it define who I am."

"Brave words," she conceded, tilting her head. "Let's hope they're not just words, for your sake."

Mark didn't flinch at the veiled threat. Instead, he squared his shoulders, his decision crystallising into an unwavering core. "They're not. This is where I stand firm. I'll safeguard the gift I've been given, Victoria, and I'll use it to help, not harm."

"Very well," she said, a fleeting trace of respect flickering in her eyes before being extinguished by her relentless ambition. "We'll see how long your resolve lasts, Mark Jennings."

With that, he turned and strode away, leaving behind the opulent trappings of the restaurant, the echo of Victoria's laughter, and any lingering doubts about his path forward.

Mark's footsteps echoed against the marble floor as he walked away from Victoria, each step a declaration of his newfound resolve. He hadn't gone far before her voice, smooth as silk yet cold as ice, stopped him in his tracks.

"Mark," she called out, her tone sharp with a warning that could shatter the thick tension in the air. He paused but did not turn to face her. "You do realise what you're up against, don't you?"

He sensed her rise from her chair, her presence looming like a storm cloud on the horizon. "People like me don't take kindly to threats," she continued. "And make no mistake, darling, your little declaration was a threat."

Mark turned slowly, confronting her directly. Her smirk was a slash against her impeccably made-up features, eyes glinting with the confidence of someone who has always wielded power. "So, this is it then? Intimidation?" he asked, his voice steady despite the adrenaline coursing through his veins.

"Consider it friendly advice." Victoria stepped closer, perfume wafting over him, an attempt to ensnare him in her fragrant trap. "If you expose me or interfere with my plans, it won't just be your reputation on the line. I have resources and connections… You can't even imagine the doors I can close for you."

"Or the ones I can open," Mark countered, feeling the weight of his abilities more acutely than ever. His gift wasn't merely a tool; it was a profound responsibility one he could not afford to yield to someone so reckless with the lives of others.

Victoria laughed, a cold, mirthless sound that chipped away at the restaurant's cosy ambience. "Open them if you can," she challenged. "But remember, for every move you make, I'll be two steps ahead. This isn't a game, sweetheart. It's chess, and I've been playing it far longer than you."

Her words hung in the air, a gauntlet thrown before him. Mark felt the sting of betrayal not just from Victoria's deception, but from the painful realisation that his own naivety had allowed this to unfold. How many others would see his gift merely as a means to their end?

"Are you done?" he asked, his heart pounding fiercely in his chest.

"For now." She scrutinised him with a final, piercing gaze. "Just remember, Mark sometimes, the king is the most vulnerable piece on the board."

With that, she turned on her heel, leaving Mark alone amid the chatter of unsuspecting diners. The clinking of glasses and clattering of cutlery formed a dissonant backdrop to the turmoil brewing within him.

As he stood there, the ghost of her smirk lingering in the air, doubt crept into the corners of his determination. Could he truly navigate this treacherous terrain where every friend might be a foe, every truth could mask a lie?

The question haunted him as he exited the restaurant. The door closed behind him with a soft thud that echoed ominously, reminiscent of a countdown an inevitable confrontation lingering just beyond the horizon. The cool night air brushed against his skin, whispering secrets and warnings. As one chapter closed, readers would be left gripping the edges of their seats, eagerly wondering what move Mark Jennings would take next.

Chapter 10
Hidden Conspiracies

The fading daylight cast a warm, golden hue through the sheer curtains of Susan's living room, where a solemn circle of friends had gathered. The scent of freshly brewed coffee mingled with a tense expectancy, clinging to the air like static. Mark stood at the centre of the room, brow furrowed in concentration, every pair of eyes fixed on him.

"Thanks for coming on such short notice," he began, his voice laced with a tremor of nerves. He wasn't speaking merely as a brother or friend he was their anchor in the deepening unknown.

Angela leaned forward on the edge of the couch, her hands wrapped tightly around a steaming mug. "We're all here for Nathan," she said. Her gaze flicked briefly to the young man in question, who sat partially cloaked in shadow the very image of anxious anticipation.

"Right," Mark said, nodding his thanks to her before turning to the rest of the group. He slid his hands into the pockets of his jeans, searching for steadiness in the familiar fabric as he marshalled his thoughts. "What I've uncovered about Nathan's past it's not just a string of bad luck. It's deliberate. Calculated."

Susan instinctively moved closer to her brother, her presence steadying. "What do you mean, Mark?" she asked quietly, though the steel in her gaze betrayed a fierce resolve.

"Everything that's happened to Nathan," Mark said, lifting his head to meet their eyes in turn, "the losses, the estrangement from his family, the trouble with the law... None of it was coincidental."

A collective gasp rippled through the room. Mark felt the swell of confusion and concern pressing in like a tide. Reaching out with his mind, he brushed gently against their thoughts, offering reassurance without words. His condition had always granted him an almost preternatural connection an unspoken empathy.

"Someone's been orchestrating it all," he continued, his voice growing firmer. "Someone with the power and reach to manipulate events from behind the scenes. Nathan has been targeted. And they're not finished."

"Targeted?" Marie's voice quivered, her face pale. "But why? Why him?"

"That's what we need to uncover," Mark replied, his resolve hardening. "This goes deeper than we imagined. It's dangerous."

"Then it's a good thing we're not just any group of friends," Angela said, her voice edged with steel. "We're a team. And we'll get to the bottom of this for Nathan."

Mark met Nathan's gaze, offering a silent vow. Whatever lay ahead, they would face it together. In unity, they would find their strength bound by loyalty, driven by the pursuit of justice. Nathan sat motionless, the room's shadows seeming to close in around him as Mark's words hung thick and oppressive in the air. His chest rose and fell in rapid, shallow breaths; his hands trembled, betraying the storm within. His eyes once guarded by scepticism blinked furiously, his expression a portrait of disbelief.

He looked up at Mark, searching for a lifeline.

"Mark," he said, his voice cracked and hushed, "how can this... how can it be true?"

Mark stepped forward, deliberate and composed, radiating a calmness that felt almost tangible. He placed a firm hand on Nathan's shoulder a grounding, steadying gesture.

"I know it's hard to accept," he said gently. "But I'm here. We all are. You're not facing this alone."

Nathan nodded, the weight of those words anchoring him as warmth from Mark's touch seemed to seep through his very skin, tethering him to the present.

From her seat, Clara leaned forward, her gaze sharp and unwavering. "We need to act," she declared, slicing through the haze of shock that lingered. "Whatever's behind this won't wait for us to catch our breath."

"Dig deeper?" Susan echoed, glancing between Clara and Nathan.

"Exactly," Clara affirmed. "The truth is buried beneath layers of lies. We owe it to Nathan to strip it all away, to shine a light so blinding that whoever's been pulling the strings can't hide anymore."

"Peel back the shadows," Marie murmured, her voice quiet but resolute.

"Shadows, lies none of it matters," Clara pressed on, unflinching. "We'll confront every secret. Together."

Nathan, buoyed by the fire in Clara's voice, straightened his spine. The disbelief clouding his features began to lift, replaced by the first glimmers of resolve. The truth was a labyrinth, and they stood at its entrance. But with Mark's guidance and Clara's conviction, perhaps they truly had a chance.

Angela shifted, the creak of the leather couch breaking the silence. Concern coloured her features, each freckle seeming to stand out in the soft lamplight. She turned to Nathan, meeting his eyes.

"Look, we can't go into this blind," she said, running a hand through her auburn hair. "I've got contacts in law enforcement good people who owe me favours. They might help us understand what we're up against and keep us one step ahead."

Mark nodded, a calm intensity in his eyes. He read people instinctively, and now his gift lent gravity to Angela's words.

"She's right," he said, his voice both firm and reassuring. "We need every piece of intel we can get. Friends in the right places might give us the edge we need. This isn't just about uncovering the truth anymore it's about protecting ourselves from whatever's stalking Nathan's past."

Nathan's shoulders loosened fractionally. The prospect of official backup gave him something to cling to an anchor in the chaos.

"Then it's settled," Angela said, her freckles glowing with renewed purpose. "I'll make the calls first thing tomorrow. We'll get the support we need."

With the decision made, a fresh current of energy surged through the room. They all knew the path ahead would be fraught with danger, but their alliance sealed here tonight was rooted in trust and a shared determination to unearth the truth. With Angela's resourcefulness and Mark's insight, they were carving a way through the darkness.

Susan leaned forward from her perch on the arm of the overstuffed sofa, the lamplight catching in her blonde hair like a halo. She looked around at each of them, every face drawn with worry, united in purpose.

"Listen," she said, her voice calm and clear amid the storm of thoughts, "we have to stay vigilant. Every shadow, every unfamiliar face there's a chance we're being watched." Her eyes settled on Nathan, softening. "Especially you. The past has a way of creeping back when you least expect it."

Nathan nodded, his dark eyes swimming with unspoken fears. He ran a hand through his unruly hair, the gesture betraying his inner conflict.

"Surveillance..." Marie said softly, her voice trembling yet steady. She sat upright, gripping a cushion as though to anchor herself against rising fear. "I never imagined... But I'm with you. All of you. Every step of the way."

The weight of her words settled heavily over the room. Despite her quiet voice and recent struggles with postpartum depression, Marie's resolve shone through. She would not falter.

"Whatever it takes," she added, her black curls framing a face now carved with determination. "We'll help Nathan. We'll drag the truth into the light, no matter how deep the shadows go."

A collective breath hung suspended in the room, charged with conviction. They were more than a group of friends now. They were a family united by purpose, bound by loyalty and they would stop at nothing to protect one of their own and expose the darkness that threatened to consume them.

Mark stood up abruptly, the movement drawing the attention of everyone in Susan's cosy living room. His gaze swept over his companions, intense and purposeful, as each face reflected concern and quiet resolve. He cleared his throat, the gesture underscoring the weight of what he was about to say.

"Listen," Mark began, his voice steady with the calm of someone who had seen into others' minds. "We need to be strategic about this. The conspiracy we're dealing with… it's like a hydra. Cut off one head, and two more grow back."

He paced in a small circle before turning to face them again, the evening sun catching the strands of his short brown hair through the window.

"Clara, Angela you both have the connections and skills we need. I think you should focus on gathering more evidence. We need to understand exactly what we're facing."

Clara nodded, her nurse's instincts kicking in, ready to triage the situation. "You can count on us, Mark. We'll leave no stone unturned."

Angela's freckled face was firm with determination. "We've got this," she said, her fists clenching slightly, as though ready to take on the darkness herself.

"Susan, Marie," Mark continued, his tone softening, "Nathan will need you more than ever. Emotional support, reassurance it's crucial. You both know how heavy the truth can be."

Susan reached out and took Nathan's hand, her blonde hair haloed by the dimming light. "Always," she whispered, her protective nature a palpable force in the room.

Marie drew a steadying breath, pushing back her anxiety. "I may be scared, but I won't let that stop me from helping." Her dark eyes met Nathan's, filled with quiet strength and empathy.

Finally, Mark turned inward, acknowledging his own role. "As for me," he said, tapping his temple lightly, "I'll keep using my gift. Whatever secrets are hiding in plain sight I'll find them."

The group exchanged looks, their individual fears merging into a collective resolve. They understood the stakes, the risk, and the necessity of what they were about to do. A nod here, a glance there each gesture sealed their commitment.

"Then it's settled," Clara said, her voice unwavering. "We have our mission."

"Let's get to work," Angela added, standing with an energy that seemed to charge the air.

As they rose, a newfound determination shone in their eyes. The moment had crystallised their purpose they were united not just by the mystery entwining their lives, but by their desire to protect Nathan from the threat hanging over him.

"Thank you," Nathan murmured, finding his voice amidst the storm. "For believing in me… for fighting for me."

"We're in this together," Mark assured him, resting a reassuring hand on his shoulder. "We're stronger as one."

With a final exchange of smiles and firm nods, each person mentally prepared for the task ahead. The room buzzed with anticipation and the silent promise of action.

They were ready.

"Alright, team," Mark said, his voice cutting through the haze of uncertainty. "The road ahead is full of challenges we can't yet see. But we must stay focused." He looked at each of them. "Trust each other. Lean on each other. Our unity is our strength and our shield."

Nathan's hands had stopped trembling, stilled by the weight of Mark's words. "I never realised how much I needed this… this family," he admitted, voice low with emotion.

"Family sticks together," Susan replied, her eyes soft on him. "And watches each other's backs."

"Exactly," Clara added, already collecting her notepad and pen. "We'll find every last scrap of evidence. They won't know what hit them."

Angela nodded, reaching into her bag for her phone. "I've got a few calls to make. My contacts might help illuminate what we've missed." Her brow was furrowed, but her eyes gleamed with determination.

"Let's be careful," Mark warned, scanning each face. "They've managed to stay hidden this long. They're clever. We have to be smarter."

"Subtlety is my middle name," Marie quipped, though her serious expression didn't quite match her tone. "I'll support Nathan and keep everyone grounded. That, I can do."

"Thank you," Nathan said, his voice quiet but sincere. "All of you."

"Time to get moving," Mark said, picking up the thread that bound them together. "We each have our role. Let's begin."

One by one, the group stood, their movements measured, every step filled with purpose. As they dispersed, they shared silent nods and glances gestures charged with understanding and quiet courage.

"Stay safe," Susan called after them, her voice laced with worry.

"Always," came the reply.

The Mind Whisperer

With Mark's steady leadership guiding them, they stepped into the unknown, prepared to unravel the lies and confront the danger head-on. Nathan watched them go, their retreating forms lit with the fragile promise of hope.

Mark lingered by the window, watching until the last car disappeared. The room felt vast now, hollow in their absence. He placed a hand on the cool glass, the chill seeping into his skin, and let himself feel the weight of it all.

"Okay, Mark," he murmured to his reflection, a pale outline against the night outside. "You can do this." His voice echoed faintly in the stillness, a quiet mantra.

His mind flickered through fragments Clara's resolve, Angela's drive, Susan's calm, Marie's steady heart, Nathan's vulnerability. Each image a piece of the larger puzzle. But at its centre lurked a shadow the force behind it all.

Turning away from the window, Mark began to pace, each step a steady rhythm on the carpet. "It's not just about uncovering the truth," he said aloud. "It's about protecting each other from it."

The responsibility was enormous, the conspiracy complex and dangerous. But Mark drew strength from his gift his ability to see through the masks people wore, to untangle thoughts and intentions. It had once been a burden. Now, it was their greatest advantage.

"Whoever you are, whatever you've done," he said to the darkness he could feel rather than see, "I'll find you."

The house was still, save for the soft ticking of the mantel clock, marking time until their next move. Mark listened to the beat of his own heart strong, steady, determined.

Then his phone buzzed. A message from Angela: *Meeting set up with my contact. We're on track.*

Good, Mark replied, thumbs moving quickly. *Keep me posted.*

He slid the phone back into his pocket and looked around Susan's living room no longer a place of comfort, but now their command centre. With a deep breath, he reached for his coat, its familiar weight settling across his shoulders like armour.

"Will we be enough?" he whispered, not as a doubt, but a challenge. The question lingered in the air, heavy with anticipation.

He stepped through the door, locking it behind him. The click of the deadbolt was final a chapter closed.

The road ahead would twist, shadowed by danger. But Mark didn't falter. He walked into the night, his silhouette merging with the darkness. For him and his team, it was no longer a question of *if* they could protect Nathan and reveal the truth.

Only *how*.

And with that, the hunt began.

Chapter 11
Webs Of Deception

Mark's fingers traced the edge of the documents scattered across Clara's mahogany desk, each sheet a breadcrumb leading to Nathan's mysterious disappearance. The late afternoon sun filtered through half-drawn blinds, casting long shadows that seemed to amplify the weight of their task. In the cosy confines of Clara's office, the air was thick with determination.

"Look at this," Clara said, her voice soft but insistent, cutting through the hum of the overhead lights. She held up a sheaf of papers, her wavy brown hair falling over one shoulder as she leaned forward. "I think I've found something."

Mark looked up from the evidence, his sharp gaze catching the subtle shift in Clara's expression, a sign of the concern tightening her kind face. The rest of the team moved closer, their collective breath holding in suspense.

"Hit us with it, Clara," Mark urged, his voice steady yet laced with the excitement he couldn't quite suppress. His empathy resonated with the team's eagerness, in tune with his own pulse.

Clara's finger hovered over a highlighted section on the page. "This corporation," she began, "the one we suspected? I dug into their financials and partnerships." She paused, letting the weight of her discovery settle in the room. "There's a direct link between them and the project Nathan was working on before... before everything fell apart."

A collective gasp rippled through the room. Mark felt the implications of Clara's words settle heavily in his chest, foreboding and ominous.

"Are you saying they're involved in his tragedy?" Mark asked, his voice deceptively calm, masking the torrent of thoughts rushing through his mind.

"More than involved," Clara confirmed, her eyes flashing with fierce intensity. "They funded the very research Nathan claimed was being manipulated. And not just that – there are emails, memos... they were steering the results, demanding specific outcomes, no matter the ethical cost."

"Unbelievable," Mark muttered, though part of him had already begun to piece together the sinister puzzle. He could almost hear the unspoken thoughts of his team, their shock and outrage mirroring his own.

"Can we prove it?" one of the team members asked, a mix of hope and scepticism in their voice.

"Prove it?" Clara echoed, flipping through the evidence with renewed vigour. "With this, we can blow the lid off the entire operation. We just need to tread carefully."

Mark nodded, his analytical mind already mapping their next move. The revelation of the corporation's unethical practices was the linchpin they needed to unravel the mystery of Nathan's tragedy. But with such powerful adversaries, they would have to be strategic.

"Then let's get to work," Mark declared, rallying the team with a conviction that belied the danger ahead. "For Nathan and for every soul caught in their web of deceit. It's time the truth came out."

As the team dove back into the evidence, the room buzzed with the fervour only truth-seekers could understand. United in purpose, emboldened by Clara's discovery, they were ready to face whatever challenges lay ahead. Together, they would expose the conspiracy and restore justice to Nathan's tarnished legacy.

Mark's gaze swept across his team's faces, each etched with determination amidst the clutter of papers and open laptops. His fingers tapped a staccato rhythm on the wooden table, echoing the rapid pace of his thoughts.

"Guys," Mark said suddenly, breaking the silence that had settled over the room like dust on old books. "There's someone out there who knows more. An ex-employee turned whistleblower."

Heads lifted, and the room's energy shifted, palpable with renewed focus.

"Are you sure?" Clara asked, her hand pausing mid-air above a stack of notes.

"I can feel it," Mark replied, leaning in with a tone heavy with conviction. "They're scared, but they want to talk. We just need to reach out the right way, discreetly."

"Getting this person to trust us is key," Susan chimed in from her corner, the blue glow of her laptop illuminating her determined face. "I'll make contact. I've got a secure line we can use."

"Can you guarantee it's untraceable?" one of the team members asked, casting a nervous glance toward the window, as if expecting someone to be watching.

"Absolutely," Susan replied, a hint of pride in her voice. "I've done it before. They won't leave a trace."

"Okay, do it," Mark affirmed, nodding at his sister with a confidence only she could inspire. A mix of excitement and tension filled the room, the gravity of the situation sinking in.

"Let's get to work," Clara said, her gaze fierce. "It's time we shed some light on their darkness."

Susan's fingers flew over the keyboard, each click blending with the room's collective heartbeat. There was no turning back now. With each stroke, they wove their own web a net of truth cast into murky waters, hoping to catch a glimpse of what lurked beneath.

Angela's eyes flicked across the screen, the glow accentuating the determination etched on her freckled face. "Marie, look at this," she said, tapping a line of text in an old news article they'd found buried in an online archive. The article hinted at a pattern of environmental violations by the corporation, all quietly settled out of court.

Marie leaned closer, her curly hair brushing against Angela's arm, her voice tinged with the anxiety that had seemed to cling to her of late. "It's like they've been using their power to sweep everything under the rug."

"Exactly," Angela replied, her tone sharp. "And if we can link this to Nathan's case, we might just have the leverage we need."

"Hey!" Susan called from across the room, her voice slicing through their concentration. "I've got a secure channel open. I'm about to make contact."

"Be careful," Marie murmured, biting her lip as she watched Susan initiate the connection.

"Always am," Susan replied with a grin, though her hands were steady, the seriousness of the moment evident in her every move.

"Hello?" A distorted voice crackled through the speakers, laced with static and caution.

"Hi, you don't know me, but I believe we share a common interest in bringing some truths to light about your former employer," Susan began, her voice measured and calm.

"Who are you? How did you find me?" The wariness in the whistleblower's voice was palpable.

"We're friends of Nathan," Susan explained. "We think you might have information that could help us understand what really happened to him. Can we meet?"

There was a long pause, the tension in the room stretching to breaking point. Then, "Okay. But it has to be somewhere public. Somewhere safe."

"Agreed," Susan said. "How about the old mill on Harper's Lane? It's quiet there this time of year."

"Fine. Tomorrow at noon. And I'll only talk to one of you. No tricks, or I walk."

"No tricks," Susan confirmed. "We want the truth, that's all."

"Until tomorrow, then." The line went dead.

Angela let out a breath she hadn't realised she was holding. "Did that just happen?"

"It did," Susan replied, her blonde hair falling into her eyes as she leaned back in relief. "We've got our meeting."

"Good work, Susan," Marie chimed in, her voice a blend of admiration and fresh anxiety. "But what now? This feels bigger than we thought."

"Now," Angela said, rising to her feet with resolve, "we prepare for what we hope will be the breakthrough we've been waiting for. We're closer to the truth, I can feel it. We're about to blow this whole thing wide open." She turned to Susan, locking eyes with her. "Let's do this for Nathan. For justice."

"Let's do it," Susan echoed, her smile returning, now infused with a renewed sense of purpose.

As the team dispersed to gather more evidence and rest before the pivotal day, the office hummed with quiet anticipation. They were like a constellation of individuals, each shining their light on the shadows that had long veiled Nathan's tragic loss. Together, they felt unstoppable.

The sun hung behind a veil of clouds, casting a muted, mournful light over the abandoned warehouse where Mark, Susan, and Clara waited. The location was remote, a forgotten relic on the outskirts of town, selected for its seclusion.

"Remember, let me do the talking," Susan whispered, her voice barely audible above the rustling of old papers scattered across the floor. She adjusted the cuffs of her jacket a nervous habit she'd developed when preparing for something important.

Mark nodded, his eyes scanning the space with meticulous attention, noting every subtle shift in the air. He could feel the tension, electric and ready to spark. Clara stood beside him, her presence offering him a quiet sense of calm amidst the anxiety that buzzed beneath his skin.

A shadow moved at the far end of the room their signal. A figure stepped into the dim light, their features obscured by a hood.

"Are you the ones?" The voice was distorted, cautious.

"We are," Susan confirmed, stepping forward. "You have information about the corporation?"

The whistleblower's hands trembled as they pulled back their hood, revealing eyes that had witnessed too much. "I worked there for years," they began, their voice thick with the weight of buried memories. "And what I've seen…" They faltered, cracking under the strain of years of silence.

"Tell us," Clara urged gently, her nurturing instinct evident as she sought to soothe the pain woven through the whistleblower's words.

"Projects that should never have seen the light of day," the whistleblower said, their voice low and strained. "Nathan... he stumbled upon one of them. It was an accident, but once he knew, they couldn't let him go public."

"Is that why they…" Mark trailed off, the empathy in his voice cutting straight to the heart of the matter.

"Silenced him? Yes." The word hung in the air like a bullet, punctuating the stillness. "And they won't stop there. Anyone who poses a threat gets the same treatment."

"Can you prove this?" Susan asked, her mind already racing with the possibilities that solid evidence could bring.

"Better than that," the whistleblower replied. They reached into a battered satchel and produced a stack of documents, their edges worn from countless hands. Then, with a precision born of necessity, they extracted a series of recordings digital truths in a world of lies.

"Everything's here. Transactions, internal communications, project files. And these," they tapped the recordings, "are conversations between the higher-ups, discussing Nathan… and others."

Susan accepted the evidence, her fingers brushing against the whistleblower's in a silent gesture of gratitude. She handed the documents to Mark, and in that exchange, a spark of connection passed between them an unspoken promise to bring justice to light.

"Let's get this somewhere safe," Mark said, his voice steady, though a storm of emotions swirled within him. His ability to sense the truth in the whistleblower's words strengthened his resolve.

"Absolutely," Clara agreed, her kind eyes hardening with the resolve of someone who had dedicated her life to healing, now thrust into the heart of a battle for truth.

"Thank you," Susan said to the whistleblower, her voice thick with gratitude and fierce protectiveness. "This… this changes everything."

"Be careful," the whistleblower warned, pulling the hood back over their head. "They're watching. Always watching."

With a final nod, the figure disappeared into the shadows from whence they came. Left in their wake, Mark, Susan, and Clara huddled around the precious evidence, the weight of the conspiracy pressing down on them, even as adrenaline surged through their veins.

"Let's expose them," Susan said, a defiant smile returning to her lips.

"Let's," Mark echoed, his mind already churning with ways to use this new information to protect Nathan and countless others from the insidious corruption that sought to strangle the innocent.

Clara glanced at both siblings, her own determination reflected in their faces. "For Nathan," she whispered.

"For Nathan," they replied in unison, their voices carrying the unwavering hope that had taken root in the gathering darkness.

Mark's phone vibrated against the cold concrete floor of the abandoned warehouse, the sound sharp and jarring in the sudden silence that had descended after their monumental meeting. His hand, steady despite the adrenaline still surging through his veins, reached for it. The screen flickered to life, and the message, displayed in a chillingly anonymous font, sent a shiver down his spine: "They know. You're being watched."

"Clara, Susan," Mark's voice dropped to an urgent whisper, slicing through the thick tension, "we have to go, now!"

Susan's eyes, wide with alarm, met his as she quickly scanned the message on his phone.

Instinctively, her fingers flew over her own device, initiating protocols to wipe any trace of their communication with the whistleblower.

"Who?" Clara asked, her voice steady, though her hands betrayed a slight tremor as she swiftly gathered the documents, packing them into her bag with practiced motions.

"Doesn't matter," Mark replied, his mind racing as he tried to predict their next move. His ability to foresee actions merged with the fear that gnawed at his gut. "We're compromised. That's all we need to know."

"Split up," Susan said decisively, her hacker instincts alert to the danger of digital footprints. "Change everything that can be tracked phones, cards, everything."

"Meet back at," Clara started, but Mark cut her off with a shake of his head.

"No," he interjected, his voice urgent. "Not there. They'll anticipate it. We need somewhere unexpected." His mind swirled, seeking the right location.

"Angela's community centre," Susan suggested, after a brief pause. "It's deserted after hours, and Angela trusts us."

"Good," Clara nodded, stuffing the last of the papers into her bag. "Let's move out."

The trio moved with a swift, coordinated urgency, erasing their presence from the warehouse as best they could. They split outside the rusted metal door, each taking a different direction into the encroaching night.

"Remember, no patterns," Mark reminded them softly, his gaze lingering on Susan for a moment longer. She nodded, her blonde hair catching the scant moonlight, her expression resolute.

"Stay safe," Clara added, her nurturing instincts flaring, even amidst the danger.

"See you soon," Susan replied, then melted into the shadows like a wraith.

Mark took a deep breath and moved swiftly; his footsteps silent on the damp ground. He kept to the darker edges of the streets, every sense heightened, alert to any sound, any sign of pursuit. The knowledge that unseen eyes might be tracking them fuelled his determination, his empathy for Nathan's plight mingling with his own desire for safety.

He could almost feel the watchers, imagined them lurking just out of sight. Yet his mind remained clear, his purpose undiminished. Every step was measured, every turn calculated to throw off any would-be pursuers.

As he navigated the labyrinth of alleys and backstreets, Mark couldn't help but think of Nathan the weight of what rested on their shoulders now. They were his only hope, the last chance for his salvation. They would not let him down. Not when so much was at stake.

"Be smart. Be safe," he muttered to himself, echoing the mantra that had become their creed. And above all, he clung to the belief that, together, they would bring the truth to light.

"Spread everything out. We need to see the big picture," Mark instructed, his voice barely above a whisper as they re-entered Clara's office. The room was small and unassuming, but it had become their command centre in their quest to uncover the layers of Nathan's torment.

Clara laid out the documents with meticulous care on her cluttered desk, her fingers trembling slightly. "Everything the whistleblower gave us is here."

Susan leaned over the papers, her eyes scanning quickly. "These email chains are damning. Look at this one," she exclaimed, pointing to a particular line of text. "It confirms what we suspected about the corporation's involvement."

"Let me see." Mark's hand brushed against Susan's as he took the paper, feeling the urgency building between them. They were close now, so close to the truth it felt tangible like the very air they breathed was thick with revelation.

"God, it's worse than we thought," Clara said, her compassionate heart heavy with worry as she pieced together the timeline of events. Her nursing background had trained her for crisis management, but the scale of this deception overwhelmed even her seasoned nerves.

"Look at this memo." Susan held up another sheet, her hacker's instincts honed in on the hidden patterns within the data. "It mentions a government official high up, very high up."

"Which means this goes beyond corporate greed. This is systemic corruption," Mark concluded, the weight of the conspiracy settling heavily on him. He saw Nathan's haunted expression in his mind's eye, understanding now the depths of the forces that had instilled such fear in the young man's guarded demeanour.

"Can we prove a direct link?" Angela asked, her voice steady, despite the palpable excitement that charged the air around them.

"Right here," Marie chimed in, tapping a section of the document. "This name, this official... they've been safeguarding the corporation's interests for years."

"Unbelievable," Clara muttered, her usually kind eyes darkening with anger. "They've been toying with people's lives as though they're mere chess pieces."

"Exactly," Mark agreed, a resolute spark lighting his gaze. "And Nathan was just a pawn in their game. But not anymore. We're going to expose it all."

"Are we prepared for just how big this could become?" Susan questioned, her stoic face revealing no sign of hesitation.

"We have to be," Mark affirmed, rallying the team with a nod. "For Nathan's sake and for everyone else caught in their web."

"Then let's get to work," Angela said, determination etched into every word. "We'll bring this whole corrupt system crashing down."

The team gathered around the evidence, their collective resolve forming an unbreakable bond. They weren't merely investigators; they were guardians of the truth. And no matter the cost, they would stand united to protect Nathan from any further harm.

Mark paced the length of Clara's office, his hands tightly clasped behind him. The steady hum of the ceiling fan seemed to underscore the gravity of their discussion.

"Alright, we need a plan," he said, coming to a stop and turning to face his companions. "This goes deeper than we imagined, and it's going to take precision to navigate these waters."

Clara leaned forward, elbows resting on the desk, her face a mask of concentration. "We've got one shot at this, Mark. If we slip up..."

"Then we make sure we don't," Mark cut in, his brow furrowed in thought. "They have eyes everywhere, so we'll need allies discreet but powerful."

Susan perked up, her fingers already dancing across her keyboard. "Someone outside their reach, someone with a platform."

"Exactly," Mark agreed, the gears in his mind turning. He paused and then locked eyes with each team member. "There's a journalist, Riley Henderson. They've been sniffing around similar cases for years. If anyone can help us expose this, it's Riley."

"Riley Henderson?" Angela repeated, a spark of recognition lighting her features. "I've read their articles. They're relentless."

"Relentless is exactly what we need," Marie added, nodding. Her fingers tapped a rhythm on the tabletop as she considered the implications.

"Can we trust them?" Clara asked, her voice measured, the question hanging heavily in the air.

Mark's response was immediate, his voice steady. "Riley has integrity. They're in it for the truth, just like us." He glanced around the room, meeting the eyes of each team member. "But we must approach with caution. Nothing too direct. We can't risk leading anyone back here."

"Leave that to me," Susan said confidently, her gaze fixed on her screens. "I'll set up a secure line of communication. No digital footprints."

"Good," Mark nodded in approval. "But be careful. One wrong move and we could spook them, or worse, alert the wrong people."

"Understood," Susan replied, her focus never wavering.

"Angela, Marie, keep digging," Mark instructed. "Every piece of information we uncover is ammunition."

"Got it," they chorused, turning back to the mountain of documents spread across the table.

"Clara," Mark said, turning to her with a reassuring smile. "You keep us grounded. Make sure we don't lose sight of why we're doing this."

"Always," Clara affirmed, her gaze unwavering.

"Alright, team," Mark said, his voice tinged with a mixture of determination and adrenaline. "Let's get to work. We're not just fighting for Nathan now; we're fighting for justice."

The room buzzed with renewed energy. Each member was fuelled by their shared mission. They were a mosaic of skills and resolve, bound together by the common cause of exposing the truth. And with a trusted journalist potentially on their side, their chances had just improved exponentially. The game was on, and they were ready to play.

"Alright, we're set," Susan declared, her fingers flying over the keyboard before she swivelled in her chair to face the rest of the team. "I've arranged a time and place to meet with the journalist."

"Where?" Mark asked, leaning against the edge of Clara's desk, a mixture of anticipation and concern clouding his features.

"An old coffee shop on the outskirts of town. Quiet, unassuming, and more importantly off the corporate radar," Susan replied, a smirk playing on her lips as she relished outsmarting their potential adversaries.

"Good choice," Clara nodded in approval from her seat by the window, sunlight casting a warm glow on her determined features. "It's the perfect spot for a discreet meeting."

"Are we sure they can be trusted?" Angela interjected, her voice tinged with the scepticism that had served her well as an investigator.

"Absolutely," Mark assured her, his eyes flashing with conviction. "This journalist has been a thorn in the side of corrupt power players for years. If anyone wants to see this corporation fall, it's them."

"Plus," Marie added, flipping through her notes, "their articles have enough dirt to bury these people ten times over. They just need the final nail in the coffin, something we can provide."

"Then let's not waste any more time," Mark said, pushing away from the desk and straightening his jacket. The others stood up, suddenly animated by the prospect of action. "We meet with the journalist, lay everything out, and watch the dominoes fall."

"Could this really be it?" Nathan's voice was quiet but underlined with hope, his dark eyes reflecting the gravity of what they were about to do.

"Let's make it happen," Mark said, placing a reassuring hand on Nathan's shoulder. "We'll bring them down and clear your name. You have my word."

"Then let's get moving," Susan urged, her own excitement bubbling to the surface. "The sooner we blow this wide open, the better."

"Agreed," Clara said, standing up and grabbing her coat. "Justice waits for no one."

"Let's do this, for Nathan, for all those who've been silenced, and for the truth," Mark proclaimed, a fierce determination setting his jaw.

With a collective nod, they gathered their things. Their steps synchronised as they headed for the door. The atmosphere was thick with the electricity of impending revelation. Each member of the team was ready to play their part in the intricate dance of deception and exposure.

The Mind Whisperer

"See you on the other side of history," Mark said, offering a wry smile as they stepped into the cool air of the outside world, the weight of destiny pressing down upon them.

Chapter 12
Escape And Pursuit

Mark's breath came in heavy rasps, his chest rising and falling rapidly as he leaned against the cool brick wall. The air was thick with tension, a tangible force that seemed to squeeze the very atmosphere of the dimly lit room where the team had hastily gathered. They were a tableau of resolve, each member sporting bruises and cuts like badges of honour from their skirmish with the shadowy figures threatening the safety of their world.

'Alright, everyone,' Mark said, his voice steady despite the adrenaline that still coursed through his veins. 'We made it out, but we can't let up now. They'll be regrouping and so should we.'

Clara Reynolds, her wavy brown hair cascading over her shoulders, nodded solemnly as she dabbed at a cut on her arm with a piece of sterile gauze. 'Mark's right,' she agreed, her kind eyes scanning the group to ensure everyone was accounted for and relatively unharmed. 'We have an opportunity a lead that could help us take them down for good.'

'Lead?' Nathan queried, arching an eyebrow as he checked his gear, ensuring everything was in place for their next move.

'During our... encounter, I found something,' Clara continued, pulling a crumpled piece of paper from her pocket. The others crowded around as she smoothed it out on a makeshift table, revealing a hastily drawn map. A circle marked a location on the outskirts of town.

'One of them dropped it. I think it's where they're meeting next an abandoned warehouse. Secluded, off the grid. Perfect for whatever they're planning.'

'Then that's where we'll go,' Mark declared, his mind already racing through possible scenarios. He knew the risks but letting the conspirators slip through their fingers was not an option. Not when they were this close.

'Gear up. Ten minutes,' Angela announced, matching Mark's urgency. The team dispersed immediately, each member moving with practised efficiency as they prepared for the battle ahead.

Boots thudded against the concrete floor. Zippers were yanked closed. The clink of metal filled the air as weapons were checked and secured.

'You good?' Susan asked, placing a reassuring hand on Mark's shoulder. Her gaze held concern and a fierce resolve that mirrored his own.

'Never better,' Mark replied, though his pulse thrummed with a heady mix of apprehension and anticipation. They were walking into the unknown but he wasn't alone. He had his team, and together they were unstoppable.

'Let's bring these bastards down,' Marie chimed in, her voice ringing with fierce determination, fortifying their collective resolve.

'Watch each other's backs,' Clara added, standing tall despite the exhaustion clinging to her limbs. She was usually the healer but today, she was as much a warrior as any of them.

'Let's do this,' Mark said, meeting each pair of eyes with a firm nod. As they filed out, the energy between them was electric, a shared current binding them together against whatever dangers lay ahead.

'Remember,' Clara called after them, just before they disappeared into the night, 'we're not just fighting for ourselves. We're fighting for everyone they've hurt and everyone they might hurt.'

With that, they melted into the darkness, a silent promise hanging heavy in the air: they would stop at nothing to unravel the conspiracy looming over their world.

'Mark, stick with me,' Nathan whispered as they moved down a narrow alleyway, swallowed by the shadows. The faint glow of a distant streetlamp carved their silhouettes against the grimy walls.

'Right behind you,' Mark replied, his voice steady despite the adrenaline surging through him. Every sound seemed amplified, every emotion razor-sharp.

Susan's earlier words echoed in his mind   their plan was solid. It had to be. Yet the prickling sensation of uncertainty lingered like a shadow clinging to his back.

'Think we'll make it before them?' Nathan asked, the gravel beneath their feet crunching softly as they moved.

'Hope so,' Mark answered, scanning their surroundings. 'We can't afford any delays.'

'Feels like we're walking straight into a trap, doesn't it?' Nathan muttered, his jaw tight. Trust had never come easy to him   but necessity had forged a bond between them.

'Maybe,' Mark conceded. He didn't believe they'd been misled   his gift, his ability to read the truth behind facades, gave him a sliver of confidence.

'Keep your eyes peeled,' Nathan warned, peering cautiously around a corner. 'I don't fancy getting jumped.'

'Neither do I,' Mark said with a fleeting smile, imagining Susan's fierce scolding if she saw them now.

'Hey, you doing alright?' Nathan checked, his concern genuine. Once unsettled by Mark's gift, now he respected it   and the man who wielded it.

'Focused and ready,' Mark assured him, the weight of responsibility pressing heavy on his shoulders. He was their key to success   their beacon in the dark   a role he bore without hesitation.

'Good,' Nathan said, nodding resolutely. 'Because we've got a job to finish and I'm not letting those bastards win.'

'Agreed,' Mark breathed as the hulking silhouette of the warehouse loomed ahead. It was time to confront the danger head-on, to finish what they had started.

'Let's end this,' Nathan said, determination etched into every line of his face.

'Let's,' Mark echoed, stepping forward into the night.

Mark halted abruptly, his hand shooting out to grip Nathan's arm. 'Stop,' he hissed, his voice low but commanding.

Nathan froze, heart thundering. 'What is it?' he whispered.

'Trap,' Mark said, his gaze sweeping over the seemingly innocuous stretch of alleyway ahead. 'Two more steps and we'd have been caught.'

Under the faint light of a streetlamp, Mark's sharp eyes scanned the shadows.

'Damn. How can you tell?' Nathan asked, straining to see what Mark saw.

'Patterns,' Mark replied, his mind working at lightning speed. 'People always leave patterns. It's a talent noticing what others miss.'

'Right your... gift,' Nathan muttered, still a little uncomfortable with it, though he could hardly deny its effectiveness.

'Follow me,' Mark instructed, steering them down a narrow passageway. The walls closed in, the darkness almost suffocating.

'Where are we going?' Nathan asked, his voice echoing faintly off graffiti-tagged bricks.

'Shortcut. Trust me it's safe.'

'Okay,' Nathan conceded, admiration lacing his tone despite the tension.

They emerged into an open lot strewn with rubbish, the warehouse looming just ahead. Mark paused, surveying the area.

In the distance, the bulky shapes of guards loitered, their stances deceptively casual yet charged with alertness.

'Front door's got a welcoming committee,' Nathan observed dryly.

'Too many eyes,' Mark agreed. 'We need a diversion.'

'Got any ideas that won't get us shot?' Nathan quipped.

'Distraction is key,' Mark murmured, already analysing. 'Something they can't ignore.'

'Like what? A bloody fireworks show?'

'Actually yes. Quieter, though,' Mark said with a ghost of a smile. He picked up a rusted pipe from the ground and, with a practised arm, hurled it across the lot. It collided with a stack of metal drums, sending a clamorous echo ricocheting into the night.

The guards snapped to attention, their lax postures vanishing as they moved towards the noise.

'Now,' Mark hissed, and they sprinted for the entrance.

'Brilliant,' Nathan breathed as they slipped through the doorway, adrenaline surging.

'Quick before they realise it's a ruse,' Mark urged, pulling him along. Inside, darkness smothered them, the air thick with dust and disuse.

'Let's find the others,' Nathan said, his voice tight but steady. 'And finish this.'

'Agreed,' Mark whispered, senses blazing. The truth they sought was within reach he could feel it.

Inside the shadow-draped warehouse, they crouched behind a stack of rotting wooden crates, barely daring to breathe as they surveyed the cavernous space.

'Can you pick up anything from them?' Nathan whispered, nodding towards the guards, still distracted by the diversion.

Mark closed his eyes, reaching out with his mind. It was like dipping fingers into a current of raw thought chaotic, volatile.

He flinched at the contact, the guards' emotions jagged and unfiltered.

'Got something,' Mark murmured. 'One's worrying about his sick daughter. Another's doubting the whole operation. There's fear too fear of being caught.'

'Perfect,' Nathan said grimly, a calculating light in his eyes. 'Fear makes people sloppy.'

'Wait,' Mark warned, lifting a hand. 'There's another. Different. Alert. Suspicious. He won't fall for distractions.'

'Then we improvise,' Nathan said, pulling out a compact, homemade noise maker from his pocket. 'I set this off on the far side should draw Mr Alert away.'

'Good,' Mark said, watching as Nathan crept away, silent as a shadow.

Nathan planted the device among discarded metal scraps, then retreated to Mark's side.

'Three... two... one...' Nathan counted under his breath then activated it remotely.

A series of rapid clicks filled the air, followed by a loud pop and a sizzling crackle.

As anticipated, the guards scattered, their footsteps hammering against the concrete floor as they rushed to investigate the disturbance. Mark watched them go, reading their intentions as they moved, their focus solely on the noise, their guard momentarily down.

"Let's move," Mark said, grasping Nathan's arm. They sprinted across the open ground, their movements swift and silent as shadows in the dim light.

They slipped past the entrance, stepping over a threshold that felt like the border between the known and the unknown. Inside, the air was musty, thick with the scent of oil and rust. Their hearts raced with the exhilaration of trespassing into the very heart of the conspiracy.

"Keep your eyes peeled," Nathan breathed, scanning the gloom. "Any sign of the others?"

"Not yet," Mark replied. His ability wasn't just about reading thoughts; it was about sensing intentions, the vibrations of human presence lingering in the air. Right now, the warehouse felt hollow, but he knew that would not last.

"Stay sharp," Nathan urged, instincts honed from years of navigating perilous situations. "We're not alone in this."

As they delved deeper into the belly of the warehouse, every nerve in their bodies bristled with the electric charge of danger. They were in the lion's den now, and the hunt for truth had never felt more alive.

The warehouse sprawled before them like a slumbering beast, its innards a complex weave of corridors and rooms that seemed to shift and change like a living organism. Mark led the way, his footsteps light against the concrete, as if afraid to wake the giant they had ventured into.

"Left here," he whispered, without needing to see the dead end that awaited them to the right. His mind buzzed with the thoughts that seeped through the walls, guiding him like a compass needle to true north.

"Are you sure?" Nathan asked, his voice low but laced with trust. He followed close behind, senses extended outward, alert for any sign of movement or danger.

"Positive," Mark asserted, eyes scanning the dimly lit pathway. Though the walls were an oppressive grey, he could feel the colourful intentions of those lurking within, painting a mental map only he could read.

"Wait." Mark's hand shot out, halting Nathan just as a faint click echoed through the air. They froze. "Pressure plate," Mark breathed, pointing towards a barely distinguishable seam in the floor.

"Good catch," Nathan said, sidestepping the trap with practised ease.

They continued, a silent dance of avoidance and anticipation. The deeper they went, the more Mark felt the conspiracy's weight pressing down upon them, a tangled web of deceit, each thread vibrating with the pulse of dark intentions.

And then voices.

"Should have been done by now," a rough tone grumbled, filtered through a thin wall that separated them from the speakers.

"Patience," another voice chided, smooth as silk and cold as ice. "The pieces are falling into place."

Mark and Nathan exchanged a glance, the gravity of their discovery sinking in. The conversation beyond the wall offered fragmented insights, but every word confirmed their worst fears. This wasn't mere petty crime; it was something far more sinister.

"Can you make out anything else?" Nathan whispered.

"Plans... shipment... tonight," Mark murmured, piecing together the broken whispers. His heart thudded with a mix of fear and excitement. They stood on the brink of unravelling a plot that could shake the very foundations of their world.

"Tonight," Nathan echoed, his brow furrowed. "We need backup."

"Already on it," Mark affirmed, knowing the rest of their team was converging, drawn together by the gravity of their mission. They were a constellation of determined stars aligning against the darkness.

"Let's find a vantage point," Mark suggested, his voice steady despite the adrenaline coursing through his veins. "We'll know more soon."

With a nod, Nathan followed, both men acutely aware that every step brought them closer to the heart of the conspiracy and to the dangers awaiting them there.

Mark's pulse quickened as they rounded a corner, stepping into an expansive loading bay. The vast space was dimly lit, casting long shadows that merged with the darkness. Ahead, a figure emerged from the gloom, his posture rigid with authority and malice: a conspirator.

"Thought you could sneak around, did ya?" the figure sneered, his eyes narrowing on Mark and Nathan. He was large, broad-shouldered, with a scar tracing down his left cheek a detail Mark's sharp gaze didn't miss.

"Easy," Nathan murmured, tension coiling in his voice like a spring. "We're just looking for some lost property."

Mark's mind raced, reaching out with his gift. Thoughts bombarded him plans, orders, suspicion.

They know too much. The conspirator's hand twitched near his belt, where the outline of a weapon was barely discernible.

"Lost property? Well, isn't that a shame," the man taunted, stepping closer. His thoughts screamed intent; he was moments from action. Mark could almost see the outcome unfold: a struggle, a shout, the echo of a gunshot.

"Behind the crates," Mark said steadily, his words a lifeline to Nathan. They backed away slowly, eyes locked on their adversary.

"Where do you think you're going?" the conspirator barked, following, his hand now openly hovering over his holster.

"Listen," Nathan started, but Mark cut him off with a slight shake of his head. They needed time just a few seconds more.

The tension snapped as the door burst open with a resounding crash. Susan led the way, her determination etched in every feature, followed closely by Angela and Marie, who fanned out with practised ease.

"Drop it!" Susan commanded, her voice slicing through the standoff like a blade.

Angela moved like water, her presence grounding, while Marie's sharp eyes darted around, her maternal instincts fuelling her courage.

The conspirator whirled towards the intrusion, momentarily distracted. It was the opening they needed.

"Go!" Mark shouted, and they lunged forward. Nathan tackled the conspirator from one side while Mark grappled with the arm holding the weapon. Together, they forced his grip open, the gun clattering harmlessly to the floor.

"Marie, secure the gun!" Susan called, while Angela jumped to help restrain the man.

"Got it!" Marie confirmed, snatching the weapon and moving it out of reach.

"Nice timing," Nathan panted, relief threading through his voice as they pinned the conspirator down.

"Always," Susan replied with a tight smile, exchanging a glance with Mark that spoke of years of trust and understanding.

"Are you okay?" Angela asked Mark, concern evident even amidst the adrenaline.

"I am now," he said, returning her gaze with gratitude. They had faced danger, but together, they had turned the tide. The conspirator lay subdued beneath them, his menace diminished by their unity. Their hearts still pounded, but they stood ready for whatever came next a team unbroken.

The clamour of combat echoed through the warehouse as Mark and his companions clashed with the conspirators. Punches were thrown, grapples ensued, every movement a desperate dance of survival.

"Left!" Mark barked, cutting through the din. Nathan ducked instinctively as a crowbar swung where his head had been moments earlier.

"Thanks," he gasped, swinging back with a well-aimed fist that connected with their assailant's midsection.

"Angela, watch your six!" Susan warned, just in time for Angela to pivot and parry a blow aimed at her back.

"Appreciated," she replied, her breath measured even as she countered with a swift kick.

"Keep them off balance!" Marie called, dodging an attack and pushing a stack of crates towards a group of advancing foes.

Mark's mind whirred amidst the chaos, his gift sifting through the mental noise like a beacon. Thoughts, plans, fears all laid bare before him. He closed his eyes for a fraction of a second, focusing on the psychic murmur that revealed more than words ever could.

"Stop!" Mark commanded. The action halted momentarily. "They're afraid of us, of failing. They didn't sign up for this level of resistance."

"Then let's not disappoint them," Susan said, her tone steely as she exchanged blows with a burly opponent.

"Guys, I know why they're here!" Mark interjected, sidestepping an attacker and pushing them into another's path. "It's not just random crime it's about control. Controlling information!"

"Figures," Angela grunted, landing a precise jab. "That's how they've stayed hidden so long."

"More than that," Mark continued, "they're planning a blackout a city-wide blackout to cover their tracks and set their final plan in motion."

"Over my dead body," Nathan declared, grabbing a pipe and using it to fend off two attackers.

"Let's make sure it doesn't come to that," Marie said, her determination unwavering.

"Focus, everyone!" Susan rallied. "Take down this cell and get the word out. We can stop the blackout!"

"Stay sharp!" Mark urged, feeling the pieces fall into place within his mind the strategy, the hierarchy, their desperation.

"Mark, we need you!" Nathan called urgently.

"Coming!" Mark replied, diving back into the fray with renewed vigour, his insights fuelling not just his actions but the entire team's resolve.

"Take this one down and it's a domino effect!" he yelled, sensing their collective energy converging into an unstoppable force.

"Dominoes are falling!" Angela echoed, her voice laced with triumph as another conspirator fell.

"Let's push!" Marie urged, protective instincts morphing into an offensive drive.

"Pushing!" the team responded in unison, conviction growing with each adversary overcome.

"Good work, team!" Susan exclaimed as they gained the upper hand, the tide turning in their favour.

"Let's finish this," Mark said, his thoughts already racing ahead to the next move, the next revelation. Together, they were unstoppable a united front against the shadows.

Mark leaned against the cold metal wall of the warehouse, the din of battle fading to a ringing silence. Sweat and grime streaked his face, but his brown eyes shone with the clarity of victory. He scanned his team, their chests heaving, faces etched with fatigue and triumph.

"Is everyone okay?" Susan asked, her voice steady yet tinged with concern, her gaze lingering a moment longer on Mark.

"Nothing that won't heal," Nathan panted, brushing back his dark hair, earlier scepticism now replaced by solidarity.

"Look at us," Angela said, a broad grin spreading across her freckled face. "We did it. We really did it."

Marie nodded, tucking a strand of curly black hair behind her ear. "But this is just the start. There's more to do, right?"

"Right," Mark agreed, pushing himself off the wall. "The information we've uncovered changes everything. We know who's behind the conspiracy now."

"Who is it?" Susan asked quickly, urgency clear in her tone.

"High-level officials," Mark revealed, "and someone we never expected Victoria Green. She's been playing both sides."

"Victoria? But she came to you for help!" Clara's kind eyes widened with disbelief.

"Part of the act," Mark confirmed grimly. "Her influence runs deep too deep."

"Then we'll go deeper," Nathan said, his brooding demeanour replaced by fiery resolve. "Expose them all."

"Exactly." Mark's gift was already piecing together their next steps. "We need to document everything. Go to the authorities with proof. And Lucas Morgan he'll want a piece of this story."

"Lucas?" Angela tilted her head. "Are you sure we can trust him?"

"He seeks the truth, like we do," Mark said confidently. "And right now, we need someone with his tenacity on our side."

"Then let's not waste time," Marie said, lifting her chin. "Those kids I work with they deserve a future without fear."

"Agreed," Dr Henderson added, clinical detachment now infused with passionate resolve.

"First, we rest. Then we plan," Susan declared, sliding her arm around her brother's shoulders.

"You've led us this far, Mark. Wherever you guide us next we'll follow."

Mark met her gaze, feeling a surge of warmth. His ability wasn't just a tool for navigating peril; it was a beacon for those who believed in the goodness he had always known existed.

"Rest up, team," he instructed, allowing himself a brief respite. "Tomorrow, we bring light to the shadows. Together, we'll rewrite the stars."

A chorus of agreement filled the room. They were more than a team now they were a family, bound by purpose and the courage to stand against the darkness. As they settled in, each found solace in the knowledge that they were no longer fighting alone.

Their mission was only just beginning but their unity made them invincible.

Chapter 13
Darkest Hour

Mark's pulse thundered in his ears, a steady drumbeat synchronised with the urgency propelling him forward. The room ahead was cloaked in shadows, a dim lightbulb flickering hesitantly, casting an eerie glow that seemed to recoil from the corners. He sensed Nathan's presence even before his eyes adjusted to the gloom a dense weight of despair hung thick in the air.

"Hey, Nathan," Mark called softly, his voice a beacon of warmth in the cold expanse.

Nathan was huddled against the far wall, knees drawn to his chest, head buried in his arms. His body was racked with silent tremors, each one a muted echo of the turmoil twisting within his mind.

"Leave me alone," Nathan's muffled voice barely reached him, laced with a pain that tugged at Mark's heart.

Ignoring the plea, Mark crossed the room in steady strides, each step deliberate the way he'd learned to navigate a world that often overwhelmed him. He crouched beside Nathan, the closeness allowing him to feel the other man's anguish as a tangible force.

"Can't do that," Mark said, firm but gentle. "I'm here to help you."

Nathan's hand was clenched into a fist, knuckles white, a physical manifestation of the battle raging within. With deliberate care, Mark extended his own hand, hovering just inches from Nathan's. The air between them crackled with tension, but Mark's resolve remained unshaken.

"Trust me, Nathan." His voice was imbued with empathy, a soothing contrast to the chaos surrounding them. "Let me in."

The Mind Whisperer

For a long moment, Nathan didn't respond. Only their breathing filled the space a shared rhythm in a fractured reality. Then, slowly, Nathan's fingers unfurled, revealing the vulnerability he'd long kept hidden.

Mark gently wrapped his fingers around Nathan's trembling hand skin to skin a connection forged in silence. In that touch, he conveyed a promise: a vow of unwavering support and understanding.

"Feels like you're drowning, doesn't it?" Mark said softly, each word carefully chosen. "But you're not alone. I've got you."

Nathan lifted his head. His dark eyes met Mark's searching, questioning. Fear lingered there, the fear of slipping into darkness, but also a desperate yearning for a lifeline.

"Help me," Nathan whispered, the words escaping the fortress he'd built around himself.

"That's what I'm here for," Mark affirmed, squeezing his hand. The bond between them, though new and fragile, brimmed with potent energy the first flicker of hope against insurmountable odds.

Mark closed his eyes and inhaled deeply, drawing in the musty air of the room. He let their joined hands become a conduit, and as he exhaled, he stepped into the swirling vortex of Nathan's mind. It was like entering a storm each thought a gust of wind, every memory a clap of thunder.

"Can you feel that?" Mark asked, his voice a beacon amid the tempest. "The storm inside you?"

Nathan nodded, his body tense, bracing against the internal gale. "It's… it's tearing me apart."

"Focus on my voice," Mark instructed, even as his own emotions threatened to drag him under. "I'm right here with you."

His mind worked furiously, tracing patterns in the chaos. He pictured himself navigating the labyrinth of Nathan's fears, sidestepping the sharp edges of painful recollections threatening to slice through his resolve.

"Tell me about the darkness," Mark coaxed gently, as though trying to lure a shy creature from hiding. "What does it look like to you?"

"It's… all-consuming," Nathan stammered, his voice steeped in despair. "A black hole that swallows all the light… all the good."

"Then let's find your light," Mark declared, his tone steely with conviction. "There's a spark in there, Nathan. I know it."

As he delved deeper, he encountered walls built by trauma seemingly impenetrable barriers. But Mark's gift was not so easily deterred. He reached out with the tendrils of thought, searching for a crack, a sliver of brightness within the oppressive dark.

"Remember the warmth," Mark urged, painting with his words. "The laughter… those moments when the weight lifted, even if only for a heartbeat."

"It's been cold for so long," Nathan murmured, his voice trembling with effort.

"Then let me be your warmth," Mark said. "Think of me as a safe harbour a respite from the storm."

The encouragement stirred something in Nathan, a flicker in the void. A memory shimmered on the periphery of his mind: a day soaked in sunlight, a smile that didn't quite reach the eyes but was genuine nonetheless.

"There!" Mark exclaimed, seizing the image. "Hold on to that. That's your hope, Nathan. That's your way out."

"Is it enough?" Nathan asked, uncertainty heavy in his voice.

"It's a start," Mark assured him. "Every journey begins with a single step. And I'll walk every inch of it with you."

"Okay," Nathan breathed, a spark of trust blooming in the tightening grip of his hand. "Okay… let's do this."

Together, they clung to the lifeline of that memory. The anguish began to ebb as Mark guided them towards calmer waters towards the promise of dawn after the longest night.

Mark's fingers tightened around Nathan's; a lifeline cast across the chasm threatening to swallow them both. The dim room seemed to press inwards, the shadows pulsing with Nathan's despair. Mark's brow furrowed, his short brown hair damp and sticking to his skin as sweat trickled down his face.

"Concentrate, Nathan," he urged, voice steady despite the chaos. "Focus on my voice."

Nathan's breath came in ragged gasps, his body trembling like a leaf in the wind. Mark could feel the tension in every fibre of him, a testament to the war being waged in his mind.

"Can you hear me, Nathan?" Mark pressed, feeling urgency mount in his chest. His heartbeat pounded in his ears, a relentless rhythm urging him forward.

"Trying," Nathan croaked, barely audible.

"Good. Keep trying," Mark said, drawing upon his deepest reserves of strength.

Then it happened. A spark in the darkness of Nathan's mind. A memory flickered like a candle flame in a draught. Faint, yet to Mark's heightened senses, as clear as a beacon in the night.

"Your sister… her laugh," Mark said, latching onto the image. "Tell me about that day."

Nathan's fear-clouded eyes showed the first glimmer of clarity. "The picnic," he stuttered. "We… we were outside. She laughed when I fell in the creek."

"That's it!" Mark exclaimed, hope rising. "She was there for you, wasn't she? Always your light."

"Yes," Nathan breathed, some peace settling into his expression. "She always made things better."

"Let her laughter guide you now," Mark urged, his own emotions intertwined with Nathan's. "She might not be here, but her love her memory can still be your sanctuary."

"Sanctuary," Nathan echoed, the word like a talisman.

"Exactly," Mark said, sensing the shift. "You're not alone, Nathan. You've never been."

Their focus created an oasis within Nathan's turmoil, the image of his sister's laughter a shield against the darkness. Mark clung to the connection fiercely, willing the shadows to recede.

"Keep this with you," he said, voice resolute. "She's your anchor your proof that there's light beyond the dark."

"Okay," Nathan agreed, stronger now, uplifted by a once-lost joy. "I'll hold on."

The oppressive atmosphere began to ease, relief seeping into the room as they clung to the life raft of memory daring to believe in the promise of salvation.

"Listen to me, Nathan," Mark said, voice thick with emotion. "You're not just a prisoner of your past. You can choose which memories to hold. Your sister wouldn't want you to dwell in this pain."

Nathan's chest heaved with ragged breaths, his fingers twitching in Mark's grasp, mirroring the inner war.

"Her laughter remember the sound? How it could light up a room?" Mark continued, his own heart pounding as he reached out with everything he had.

A flicker crossed Nathan's face. The taut lines of despair loosened slightly as the sound resurfaced bright, bell-like, and full of life.

"Can you hear it, Nathan?" Mark asked, his voice a lifeline.

"Yes," Nathan whispered, barely audible. But there it was light in his eyes, a sign that hope had taken root.

"Good. Hold onto that sound. Let it shield you let it be your armour."

"Armour…" Nathan echoed, locking eyes with Mark a silent plea met with unwavering presence.

"Exactly. Think of her. Of the good times. Let those memories protect you."

Mark watched the change unfold walls crumbling as trust replaced doubt.

"Mark… I " Nathan began, his voice still fragile, but alive with something vital.

"That's it. Keep going. You're doing brilliantly," Mark said, excitement swelling. He was both guide and guardian to a soul clawing back from the edge.

"Thank you," Nathan breathed, the quiet words resonating like a clarion call, sealing the bond between them.

Mark leaned in, never breaking eye contact. He saw the shift in Nathan's gaze barriers giving way to trust.

"Focus on that feeling," he urged. "You're reclaiming your mind, piece by piece."

"Like… like a puzzle?" Nathan asked, the weight of realisation in his whisper.

"Exactly," Mark beamed. "Each memory you choose to embrace is another piece falling into place."

The room pulsed with the energy of healing. Shadows clawed at the edges, faltering under the glow of Nathan's resolve.

"Can you feel it?" Mark asked, nearly chanting. "The light's within your grasp."

Nathan nodded, a faint smile gracing his lips. "It's… warmer. The cold's fading."

Triumph surged through Mark. This was more than progress it was a victory. He felt like a conductor guiding a symphony to crescendo.

"Keep going," he encouraged, squeezing Nathan's hand. "Let the warmth spread. Let it "

A crash shattered the moment. The room recoiled into chaos, serenity ruptured by an unseen force. Both men flinched, wide-eyed.

"What was ?" Nathan began, panic flaring.

"Shh," Mark whispered, heart racing. "Stay with me. Don't let this break your focus."

But even as he said it, Mark knew: the fragile thread binding them was fraying. The shadows, once retreating, were advancing once more hungry to reclaim their hold.

"Mark, I " Fear edged Nathan's words, slicing through the room's tension like a knife.

"Nothing has changed. We're still here, together," Mark said, struggling to maintain the calm authority in his voice. But the noise had been a clear signal: their sanctuary had been breached, and uncertainty now loomed over them a silent spectre, waiting to strike.

Mark's heart pounded a rapid staccato against his ribs, a primal drumbeat in tune with the sudden surge of danger. He tightened his grip on Nathan's hand, as if the physical connection might anchor them both against the encroaching peril.

"Someone's here," Mark whispered, his voice barely more than a breath. His eyes darted around the dimly lit room, searching for shadows within shadows. A floorboard creaked ominously, betraying the presence of their intruder. "They want to use your fear, Nathan. I won't let them."

"Who?" Nathan's voice trembled, the word faltering in a throat constricted by terror.

"Doesn't matter. Trust me." Mark's gaze locked onto Nathan's, willing him to understand. Every synapse in his brain fired with his unique insight into human behaviour now a lifeline. He could almost see the patterns, the potential actions of their unseen adversary playing out before him.

"Window or door?" Mark muttered, his mind racing through scenarios and probabilities. The window was too high, the fall too risky. The door offered a chance but likely lay within the assailant's control.

"Stay behind me," Mark instructed, rising to his feet. His movements were calculated a chess player positioning his pieces with precision. He could predict. He could outthink. This was his realm; his gift made tangible in the tension of the moment.

"Mark, I'm scared," Nathan confessed, his voice choked.

"Feel it. Use it. But don't surrender to it," Mark said, channelling his own fear into razor-sharp focus. "Fear keeps you sharp, but trust keeps you safe. Trust me, Nathan."

He edged towards the door, each step measured and deliberate. The darkness pulsed with anticipation, an invisible force waiting for the slightest misstep. Mark's ears strained for any hint of movement any whisper of intent from the threat that loomed just beyond sight.

A shadow shifted a subtle displacement of darkness that might have gone unnoticed by anyone else. But not by Mark. He caught the faintest glint of light reflecting off something metallic a weapon, perhaps.

"Down!" he hissed, pulling Nathan to the floor just as a dull thud sounded where they had been standing seconds earlier.

"Are we going to make it?" Nathan's words quivered between hope and dread.

"Focus on my voice," Mark commanded, his tone unwavering despite the adrenaline coursing through him. "We're smarter. We're quicker. And we are leaving this place together."

Mark inhaled deeply, centring himself amidst the chaos. It was time to act. With a swift gesture, he signalled for Nathan to crawl towards the door while he readied himself to confront their tormentor head-on. No one would harm Nathan. Not on his watch. The protective fury welling inside him was potent a force as formidable as any physical blow.

"Keep moving," he urged, then sprang forward, every sense honed to perfection by the moment. They were a team: Mark with his gift, Nathan with his newfound courage. Together, they would face the unknown, side by side.

"Stay low," Mark whispered, the muscles in his legs tensed like coiled springs as he eyed the barely discernible figure advancing towards them. "When I say so run for the door."

Nathan's eyes were wide with fear, but he nodded, understanding the gravity of the moment. Mark could feel Nathan's resolve solidifying; it was a silent testament to their growing connection.

"Go!" Mark barked, pushing Nathan toward the exit as he launched himself at the assailant. His body moved on instinct, each motion driven by the need to shield Nathan from harm.

"Who are you?" Mark demanded, even as he dodged a wild swing aimed at his head the assailant's movements full of intent, but lacking precision.

"Doesn't matter!" the attacker grunted, lunging again.

"Wrong answer," Mark countered, leveraging his ability to anticipate the next move. His footwork was nimble, an intricate dance guided by heightened perception. He could almost see the patterns of thought behind each strike, each desperate attempt to overpower him.

"Mark! Look out!" Nathan's shout pierced the scuffle, and Mark dropped to the ground, narrowly avoiding a vicious kick that whistled through the air where his head had just been.

"Thanks!" Mark called back, rolling to regain his footing. The room seemed to shrink, the walls closing in, heavy with the weight of their desperation.

"Stop trying to be a hero," the attacker sneered, though now there was doubt in his voice a crack in the resolve that Mark's intuition seized upon.

"Being a hero is exactly my plan," Mark replied, his words steady despite the pounding in his chest. He feinted left, then struck right, his fist connecting with a satisfying thud against the attacker's ribs.

"Give up yet?" he pressed, taking advantage of the falter in his opponent's stance. But the assailant was stubborn, fuelled by malice, and surged forward with renewed ferocity.

"Never!" came the spit-filled reply, followed by a wild flurry of blows that Mark evaded with a dancer's grace.

"Your mistake," Mark said, ducking under a clumsy punch and stepping in close. With a swift, calculated move, he locked the attacker's arm and twisted sharply. A cry of pain followed, then the clatter of something metallic hitting the floor, and the attacker went limp subdued, for now.

"Come on, we need to get out of here," Mark urged. Nathan, wide-eyed and panting, hovered near the door.

"Is it over?" Nathan's voice trembled with the residue of terror and adrenaline.

"Not yet but the worst has passed," Mark assured him, glancing down at the defeated figure. "We have to keep moving."

"Thank you," Nathan breathed, his gratitude mingling with the lingering fear in his eyes.

"Don't thank me yet. We still have a mystery to solve," Mark said with a grim smile, pulling Nathan up. They stepped over their fallen adversary, determination in their stride.

"Let's find some answers," he added, leading the way into the unknown.

Mark's thoughts honed in, the chaotic noise of the room narrowing to a single, sharp point. The assailant loomed over them, eyes wild with the thrill of the hunt but Mark was undeterred. He could feel Nathan's anxious breaths behind him, a stuttering rhythm that spurred him forward.

"Enough!" Mark bellowed his voice not merely sound, but force, resonating with an authority that surprised even him. Reaching deep within to the core of his being, where his gift pulsed like a living thing he envisioned a wave of energy. With a thrust of will, he released it.

The attacker stumbled back as if struck by an invisible tidal wave, shock registering on their face before they collapsed, overwhelmed by the psychic assault. The metal object, once brandished as a weapon, skittered across the floor now harmless debris.

"Did you just…?" Nathan's voice was a mix of awe and disbelief as he peered down at the defeated foe.

"Sometimes I surprise myself," Mark admitted, chest heaving as he fought to steady his breathing. The surge had drained him, leaving a tremble in his hands he hoped Nathan wouldn't notice.

"Mark, that was… incredible." Nathan's eyes met his no longer guarded, but open, filled with wonder.

"Let's just say it's not something I do every day," Mark replied, offering a weary smile. He extended a hand to help Nathan up. "Come on. We're safe for now."

As they stood side by side, Mark felt the shift between them. The air was charged with a new understanding, an acknowledgement of the ordeal they had endured. Nathan's earlier scepticism had vanished replaced by a fledgling trust that warmed Mark more than he'd expected.

"Thank you," Nathan said again, this time with a strength matching the firm grip he gave Mark's hand. "I don't know how to ever repay you for this."

"Help me solve this mystery, Nathan. That's all the payment I need," Mark replied, matching the pressure of Nathan's grip.

They shared a nod a silent agreement sealed in the aftermath of adrenaline and revelation. Together, they turned towards the door, ready to leave the room that had witnessed the full extent of Mark's gift, and the birth of a partnership forged in danger's crucible.

"Let's go see what other secrets this place is hiding," Mark suggested, a flicker of curiosity lighting his tired eyes.

"Lead the way, mind reader," Nathan said with a chuckle free of mockery, filled only with respect.

And with that, they stepped through the threshold, leaving the shadows behind, moving into the promise of illumination.

Mark leaned heavily against the cool wall, his chest heaving as he fought to normalise his breathing. The room seemed to spin a carousel of shadows and light but he anchored himself in the moment, drawing strength from the solid surface at his back.

"Mark?" Nathan's voice cut through the haze. "You okay?"

"Give me a second," Mark managed, his voice barely above a whisper. He squeezed his eyes shut, trying to push away the vertigo. It wasn't just the physical exertion that had drained him it was the enormity of what had transpired. His mind whirred, piecing together the puzzle of his own abilities.

"Hey take your time." Concern laced Nathan's words, a testament to the shift in their dynamic.

The realisation struck Mark like lightning. His gift this incredible, burdensome ability to delve into the minds of others had saved them… and put them in harm's way. A double-edged sword: one that could protect or provoke, depending on the wielder.

"Mark?" Nathan prompted again, his hand resting gently on Mark's shoulder.

Opening his eyes, Mark met Nathan's gaze. The intensity of his epiphany was reflected there. "I just realised something important, Nathan. My gift… it's not just about saving people."

"What do you mean?" Nathan's brow furrowed, curiosity piqued.

"It's powerful, yes but it's also a beacon. It can draw in forces we may not be ready to face," Mark explained, his voice tinged with awe and apprehension.

"Then we'll be ready. Together," Nathan said firmly, conviction echoing through the confined space.

A smile tugged at the corners of Mark's mouth. "You're right. I can't let fear dictate my actions. This ability… it's a part of me. And I've seen the good it can do."

"Exactly. You've got something special, Mark. Don't forget that," Nathan said, clapping him on the back.

"Special and dangerous," Mark conceded with a nod. "But I won't turn away from those who need help. I'll use this gift to shield others from the darkness no matter what it attracts."

"Then I'm with you every step of the way," Nathan declared, their bond now forged in steel.

"Thank you, Nathan. Your support means more than you know." Mark straightened, rolling his shoulders. The weight of responsibility settled on him but it was a burden he chose to bear.

"All right, partner. Let's get moving. We've got mysteries to solve and lives to save," Nathan said, a spark of excitement lighting his features.

"Lead on," Mark replied, his voice steady and resolute. They were a team now united in purpose, fortified by the trials they had faced.

Together, they would confront whatever lay ahead undaunted by the shadows that sought to ensnare them.

Stepping across the threshold of the room, Mark felt Nathan just behind him. Without looking back, he sensed Nathan pausing casting one final glance at the place that had forged both their fears and their courage. They moved together in silence, the soft shuffle of their feet on worn carpet the only sound in the corridor.

"Mark," Nathan said, his voice tinged with newfound strength, "back there… what you did…"

"Shh," Mark interrupted gently, turning to face him. His eyes locked with Nathan's, conveying an empathy words could scarcely hold. "No need, Nathan. I know."

Nathan nodded, a half-smile twitching at his lips a look that said more than words could.

"Feels like we've crossed some kind of line, doesn't it?" Nathan murmured.

"Crossed and erased it," Mark replied, his voice a low rumble of agreement.

They continued down the hallway. The dim bulbs overhead cast long shadows that danced away from them, as though afraid to touch the bond now binding them. The building's old bones creaked but compared to the danger they had silenced, it sounded like a lullaby.

"Where do we go from here?" Nathan asked.

"Forward," Mark said with a decisive nod. "Always forward." He drew a deep breath, letting it fill his lungs with resolve.

"Into the unknown, then," Nathan said, his voice half-joking but his eyes serious.

"Exactly. But not alone. Together," Mark affirmed, his gaze unwavering.

"United against whatever madness comes next," Nathan added, the gleam of adventure replacing his earlier doubt.

"Whatever it is we face it head-on," Mark said, the promise between them clear.

Chapter 14
Resilience

Mark's hand trembled as he set down the thick envelope their only lead, now reduced to ashes. The smouldering remains filled the air with an acrid scent, making it heavy with defeat. Susan stood frozen beside him, her eyes wide in disbelief, mirroring the stunned expressions etched onto every face in the room.

"Everything… it's all gone." Her voice cracked, barely above a whisper, yet it thundered in the silence of their dimly lit sanctuary.

Angela's hands clenched into fists at her sides. "How could this have happened? Who would do this?"

"Someone who doesn't want us getting any closer," Clara murmured, her kind eyes now shadowed with a steely resolve. She glanced around the group, her gaze lingering on Mark's downcast profile. "We were naïve to think they wouldn't come after us."

Susan reached out and gently touched her brother's arm, pulling his attention from the charred debris. "Mark, we need your insight more than ever. Can you sense anything? Any clue as to who's behind this?"

He lifted his head slowly, brow furrowed as he searched for the elusive whispers of thought that usually danced within reach. But the shock had erected walls in his mind; for once, his gift felt just beyond grasp. "Nothing. It's like they're shrouded in darkness."

Marie wrapped her arms around herself, shadows playing across her worried features. "If they're capable of this, what else are they planning? We have Nathan to think about too."

"Right now, we've got to focus," said Angela, her voice steady despite the flicker of fear in her eyes. "They've set us back, but we can't let them see us crumble. We'll find another way we always do."

"Angela's right," Mark agreed, pushing past the tendrils of self-doubt threatening to overwhelm him. His gift wasn't his only strength; he had his friends, and their shared determination.

"They want to scare us off. But we won't let them. We can't."

"Except now we're back to square one," Susan pointed out, frustration sharp in her tone. "No evidence. No leads."

"Then we'll find new ones." Clara's words cut through the fog of uncertainty. "We need to keep our heads clear and stay focused. We've overcome challenges before."

"Challenges, yes but nothing like this," Marie countered, her voice quivering.

"Which means we'll just have to be smarter. More careful," Mark said, meeting each gaze in turn. "I know it's hard to believe in ourselves when everything feels lost, but I believe in us. In every one of you."

A charged silence settled over the group as each member absorbed Mark's words, drawing strength from the bond between them.

"Okay, then." Susan straightened, a renewed spark in her eyes. "Let's start by figuring out who benefited from destroying our evidence. There must be a trail."

"Agreed," Angela added. "We regroup, reassess, and hit back twice as hard."

"Exactly," Clara nodded. "We've faced darkness before but together, we bring light. Let's get to work."

Their circle tightened, hands reaching out to clasp one another, forging unity amid the chaos. They were a team, bound by purpose and driven by a shared mission. And no setback no matter how devastating could extinguish the fire burning within them.

"Listen," Susan said, her voice steady despite the gravity of the moment. "The ones behind this aren't playing games. They knew exactly what they were targeting."

Mark nodded grimly, pacing the cramped room as the walls seemed to close in. "They're sending a message. This wasn't just about erasing evidence it was intimidation. A warning. They're letting us know they can reach us, hurt us, whenever they choose."

"Which means Nathan's in more danger than ever," Angela concluded, scanning the faces around her, searching for the defiance she knew they all needed now.

"Exactly," Clara agreed. "Let's not kid ourselves we're all targets now. But we can't let fear dictate our next move."

"Then we need a plan. Fast," Marie interjected. She leaned forward, pressing her hands flat against the table that bore the weight of scattered notes and half-empty coffee cups. "We've got to think outside the box come up with something they won't expect."

"Right," Mark said, halting his pacing. "First, we find a new angle on this case something we missed. Anything at all that could lead us back to them."

"Could we go public? Expose them with what we've got?" Susan suggested, but her question was met with headshakes.

"Too risky," Clara countered. "It would make Nathan an even bigger target and all of us too. That's the last thing we need."

"Underground channels, then?" Angela proposed. "We've got contacts who owe us favours. Maybe it's time to call them in."

"Good," Mark said, his mind racing as he assessed their limited options. "Angela, start reaching out quietly. We can't afford any more attention."

"Marie, Susan, I want you two to comb through every scrap of information we've got left. Anything that seems off, even remotely flag it. We'll cross-reference and look for patterns," Clara said, taking the lead on strategy.

"Got it," Marie replied, determination etched into her features.

"Clara and I will work on securing somewhere safe for Nathan to lay low while we sort this out," Mark added. "Off the grid."

"Time's not on our side," Susan reminded them, her gaze fierce. "Every second we waste is another they gain."

"Then let's not waste any more," Clara said, pushing back from the table and standing decisively. "We split up cover more ground. Stay in touch, but be cautious. Use codes if you have to."

"Remember," Mark said, looking each team member in the eye, "we're in this together. No one faces this alone. For Nathan. For all of us."

"Agreed," they echoed in unison, a chorus of resolve amid the threat looming over them.

As they dispersed to their tasks, the air crackled with tense energy. The conspiracy had tried to break them but instead, it had steeled their resolve. They were a unit, each part essential to the whole, and they would not be easily dismantled.

The dim glow of a single bulb cast long shadows across the room, where Mark and his team huddled around the cluttered table. Papers were strewn everywhere each one a potential clue, now seeming more like a taunt in the wake of their setback.

"Are we even sure what we're doing anymore?" Marie's voice trembled, her hands fidgeting with a pen. "It feels like we're just… flailing."

Susan let out a weary sigh. "I thought I knew how to handle situations like this. But every move we make, they're two steps ahead. I don't know if I can keep going."

Clara's eyes, usually sharp with determination, now held a flicker of doubt. "If we can't protect Nathan, what good are we? If we can't outsmart them, what chance does he have?"

Angela shrugged, her confidence shaken. "We've been at this for so long, and it feels like we're no closer to figuring it out. Maybe we're just not cut out for this."

A heavy silence fell, the weight of their shared uncertainty pressing down like a physical force. Mark, with his unique gift, felt it most acutely. He'd always been able to sense the undercurrents the unspoken fears that now screamed in the stillness.

"Guys," Mark began, his voice barely audible, fingers twitching as if to grasp the solution slipping through them. "I can usually see the patterns the paths people take. But this…" He paused, gaze distant as if staring through the walls and into the abyss beyond. "It's like trying to catch smoke with my bare hands."

"Mark, you've got something nobody else has," Susan said softly, placing a steadying hand on his shoulder. "You've guided us this far."

"But what if it's not enough?" His question lingered, heavy with dread the fear of failing Nathan when it mattered most.

"No one expects you to be infallible, Mark," Clara said gently. "We trust your instincts. You've earned that."

"Trust," Mark echoed, rolling the word around his tongue. Trust had never come easily, yet here it was offered freely by those who needed him as much as he needed them.

"Look, we all have our moments," Angela said, a flicker of fire returning to her tone. "But I'll be damned if I let fear decide our fate. We've come too far to back down now."

"Exactly," Marie added, nodding firmly. "Let's focus on what we *can* do. Together."

"Right." Mark's brow smoothed as resolve replaced doubt. "We're not just individuals we're a team. And we're going to use everything we've got to save Nathan."

"Everything we've got," they repeated, the words binding them together once more.

"Let's get back to it then," Mark declared, standing tall despite the weight he bore.

"For Nathan. For the truth."

"For all of us," added Susan, her voice steady and sure.

With that, the shadows in the room seemed to recede slightly, as though pushed back by the collective strength of their renewed commitment. They turned, shoulder to shoulder, to face the conspiracy head-on prepared to unravel its sinister weave, thread by thread.

The room's dim light flickered, mirroring the intensity of the debate that had erupted amongst them. Clara stood, her hands planted firmly on the table, her voice rising above the others.

"We can't just rush in blindly! We need a solid plan something we haven't thought of yet!"

"Time isn't on our side, Clara!" Susan shot back, her eyes flashing with frustration. "Every minute we waste, Nathan's risk grows!"

Mark watched the exchange, tension coiling inside him like a spring. He could almost hear their unspoken thoughts the collision of fear, urgency, and the desperate need to act.

"Enough!" Angela slammed her fist on the table, the sharp crack drawing all eyes to her.

"Arguing is getting us nowhere. We need to be calm and collected."

"Collected?" Marie's voice wavered, her anxiety palpable. "How can we be collected when everything we've tried has brought us here?"

"Because we have to be," Mark interjected, his voice stronger than he felt. "We can't afford to let panic dictate our moves."

The door creaked open.

Edward Collins stepped into the room, his face ghostly pale. All conversation ceased as they turned towards him, sensing the gravity of his presence.

"Edward? What is it? What's happened?" Susan asked, moving towards him with concern etched across her features.

He hesitated, swallowing hard before speaking.

"I've… I've uncovered something. The conspiracy it's not just about silencing dissent or covering up some dirty secret. It's darker. Much darker."

His stern expression faltered for a moment, revealing a glint of genuine fear.

"Go on," Mark urged, the room hanging on Edward's every word.

"They're planning something big. A display of power to make an example of anyone who dares stand against them. I've seen the plans. They involve Nathan."

"An example?" Clara asked, her nurse's instinct to protect life surfacing with an edge of dread.

"Public," Edward choked out the word, as if it were laced with poison. "They want the world to watch as they break him physically and mentally."

A collective gasp filled the room. Suddenly, the air grew thick, heavy with the weight of the revelation.

Mark felt a knot form in his stomach. This wasn't just about saving their friend anymore it was about stopping a public spectacle designed to terrify and suppress countless others.

"Okay," Mark said, drawing strength from the resolve in his companions' faces. "We need to stop this whatever it takes."

"Agreed," Angela replied, her voice calm and controlled. "We can't allow them to use Nathan like this. It's monstrous."

"Then we need to be clever and creative," Susan said, her mind racing. "We can't play by their rules."

"Exactly," Mark nodded. "We'll use my gift, your insights, every resource we have. We'll save Nathan and expose this conspiracy for what it really is."

Their faces, once etched with shock and disbelief, were now hardened with determination. The setback had been devastating, but the new information had become a rallying cry. They would find a way to save Nathan and in doing so, confront the darkness threatening to engulf them all.

Mark paced the dimly lit room, his thoughts a whirlwind of strategies and possibilities. The walls seemed to close in with every revelation, but when he looked at his friends, their eyes met his with a shared, steely resolve. It was time to turn despair into action.

"Alright," Mark began, his voice cutting through the silence like a blade. "We can't let fear dictate our next move. Nathan's counting on us."

"Mark's right," Marie said, her voice still quivering but infused with a newfound strength. "We've come too far to give up now."

"Think, everyone," Susan urged, brow furrowed in concentration. "There has to be something we've overlooked. Some angle we haven't explored."

The group huddled closer, their heads nearly touching as they poured over every scrap of information they'd gathered. Maps, photographs, and scribbled notes covered the table symbols of their tireless effort and determination.

"Wait," Clara said suddenly, her finger tracing a line on one of the maps.

"This route here it bypasses the main security checkpoints. Could it be a way in?"

"Or a way out," Angela added, leaning forward. "If we could get Nathan out that way..."

"Brilliant," Mark exclaimed, eyes lighting up. "It's risky, but it might work. We'll need a distraction something that pulls focus from that area."

"Let's not forget my gift," Mark reminded them, tapping his temple lightly. "If I focus, I can predict their movements, anticipate their actions."

"Exactly!" Susan said, her voice quickening with hope. "And I've been working on hacking into their communication network. If I can break through, we'll know exactly when to move."

"Okay, team," Mark said, planting his hands on the table as he looked at each member of the group.

"We've got a plan taking shape. Let's refine it and iron out the details. We're going to save Nathan and shine a light on this conspiracy once and for all."

As the team buzzed with renewed vigour, working through each element of their plan, a sudden chime from Susan's laptop broke their concentration.

They turned as one, eyes fixed on the flashing screen.

"Guys, you're going to want to see this," Susan said, her voice trembling with a mixture of trepidation and hope. She clicked on the message, and a string of coded text appeared.

"Is that...?" Clara began, her voice trailing off.

"It's a code," Mark confirmed, already reading. "It's from Nathan! He's alive and sending us a message."

"Does it say where he is?" Angela asked, crowding behind Susan to get a better look.

"Not exactly," Susan replied, her fingers flying across the keyboard. "But there's a pattern here a clue to his location. He's smart. He knows we're looking."

"Then what are we waiting for?" Marie said, a spark of hope igniting in her eyes.

"Let's figure out where Nathan is and bring him home."

"Right," Mark agreed, a determined smile forming. "We've got a lead, and we're not going to waste it. Let's get to work."

The room erupted into a flurry of activity. Each person moved with purpose, driven by the glimmer of hope Nathan's message had provided. It was a turning point a sign that the tide might finally be shifting. With their friend's life hanging in the balance, failure was not an option.

Mark's hands trembled slightly as they hovered over the keyboard. Each keystroke felt like a beacon of hope in the dim light. The coded message from Nathan was a lifeline and they were clinging to it with everything they had.

"Easy, Mark," Susan said softly, placing a steadying hand on his shoulder. Their eyes met an unspoken reminder that they were in this together.

"Right. Sorry." He flashed her a grateful smile and returned his focus to the screen. The tension in the room was thick, but beneath it lay a current of unwavering unity.

"Whatever happens, we've got each other's backs," Clara stated, her gaze sweeping the room. It wasn't just a reassurance it was a vow.

"Always," Angela added, her voice strong despite the shadows in her eyes.

Marie nodded, lips pressed into a determined line.

"We're not just a team we're a family. And we don't leave family behind."

Each affirmation bolstered Mark's resolve. These weren't just his friends they were his foundation.

"Okay, I've isolated the repeating patterns," he said, pointing at the screen. "Nathan's trying to tell us something important. We just need to "

A sudden knock at the door cut him off. It was sharp, urgent.

Everyone froze.

No one was supposed to know they were here.

"Who is it?" Susan whispered, her voice barely audible as she reached for the baseball bat they kept by the door.

"Police! Open up!" came the muffled voice on the other side.

Their eyes locked across the room, each reflecting the same question: Friend or foe? With the conspiracy looming large, trust was a risk they could hardly afford.

"Act natural," Mark mouthed, rising to his feet. His heart hammered against his ribs, but his face remained composed. He moved slowly towards the door, every step laden with the weight of the unknown.

The others took up positions out of sight, ready for whatever might come.

Mark reached for the doorknob, he knew the next moments could change everything. Would opening that door lead them closer to saving Nathan or thrust them deeper into peril?

"Here goes nothing," he muttered under his breath and turned it.

The door swung open to reveal...

And there the chapter ended, leaving readers to wonder who stood on the threshold, salvation or destruction, and how the team would face the new challenge that awaited them.

Chapter 15
Inner Demons

Mark Jennings sat alone, the last vestiges of amber sunlight barely penetrating the heavy drapes of his small, yet profoundly sanctuary-like, study. An eclectic expanse of books and papers lay strewn around him, each volume a whispered echo from a different realm of knowledge. The room, a delightful clutter of the esoteric and the everyday, served as a tangible reflection of his mind – a place organised in its apparent disarray, perpetually seeking order amidst the unfathomable. Mark's fingers idly traced the worn spine of a leather-bound book before he paused, his gaze settling on an unseen point as he retreated inward, contemplating the immense scope of his abilities set against the demanding canvas of his conscience.

"Responsibility," he murmured aloud, the word landing with a thud so profound that even the enveloping silence seemed to buckle under its sheer weight. The furrow etched between his brows deepened, sending ripples across the otherwise placid surface of his thoughts as he peered into the vast, sometimes terrifying, depths of his own potential.

His hand instinctively found its way to a well-used journal, the supple leather cover flexing with the familiar ease of a bird's wing poised for flight. Flipping it open, the pages rustled, whispering secrets known only to them. Here lay the intricate map of his extraordinary journey: notes scrawled in moments of urgent insight; sketches etched with painstaking precision, a rich tapestry of interwoven thoughts and deliberate intent.

"Ah, this one," Mark breathed, as if greeting an old and trusted confidante, his finger tracing a diagram with a reverence that was both shaky and deeply felt. A surge of pride swelled within him, a buoyant force amidst the turbulent sea of doubt that perpetually threatened to engulf him. Each page turned was a step back through the corridors of time, a contemplative stroll among memories that were both vividly bright and deeply shadowed.

"Did I do enough?" The question hung suspended in the air, a palpable entity amidst the stillness of the room, desperately seeking an answer that steadfastly refused to materialise. His eyes lingered on a particular sketch, a fleeting moment captured, a potential crisis deftly averted, yet the sense of triumph it depicted felt strangely distant, diluted by the ever-present spectre of uncertainty that shadowed his every action.

"Predictions and actions... merely fragile threads in the complex, unforgiving fabric of consequence," he continued, his voice barely more than a whisper, as if genuinely afraid to disturb the delicate equilibrium of past and future laid bare before him. A soft sigh escaped his lips, a release of pent-up tension that offered no genuine promise of resolution.

"Mark, you've always known the path would be steep," he reassured himself, the comfort of his own words wrapping around him like a familiar, well-loved blanket. Yet, the profound solitude of his study bore silent witness to the inherent isolation of his quest, a solitary figure forever bridging the precarious gap between foresight and fate.

The journal fell open, seemingly of its own accord, to a page Mark wished with every fibre of his being he could simply erase. The edges were noticeably worn, a silent testament to the countless times he had revisited this particular entry. His fingers hovered just above a sketch that conveyed far more than a simple incident; it was a stark, unflinching illustration of his deepest, most enduring regret.

"Elaine," he muttered, and in that single word, the study seemed to physically shrink around him, the walls pressing in with the unbearable weight of that crushing memory. He could see her still, the way she had looked at him with such desperate, heartbreaking hope, her eyes reflecting the earnest promise he had made, a promise he ultimately couldn't possibly keep.

"Please, Mark, tell me it'll be okay," her voice echoed in the chambers of his mind, fractured and distorted by the passage of time, yet still sharp and cutting as shards of glass.

"I... I see a path," he had assured her then, his own voice now sounding painfully naive and ill-equipped to his ears. "Follow my guidance; you'll make it through."

But Elaine didn't make it through. The vision he had so confidently trusted had betrayed him, a rare and devastating misstep in the intricate dance of foresight that he had yet to truly forgive himself for. It was a cruel, constant reminder that even with his extraordinary, almost uncanny abilities, the threads of fate were sometimes hopelessly knotted, frustratingly beyond his reach.

"Dammit!" Mark's clenched fist collided with the surface of the desk, the dull thud a harsh punctuation mark to the raging storm of his inner turmoil. Papers fluttered to the floor like wounded, disoriented birds, their silent descent a poignant testament to his overwhelming frustration.

"Did any of it truly matter?" he demanded of the empty room, desperately seeking an answer from the indifferent shadows that gathered in the corners. "I give them hope, but when that fragile hope crumbles, what then? Comfort? A mere, inadequate bandage on an eternal, festering wound?"

He stood abruptly, beginning to pace the familiar confines of his sanctuary, each measured step a rhythmic beat in the unfolding symphony of his doubts. His mind raced, replaying the countless faces of those he had touched, those he had genuinely helped. But among them, Elaine's face lingered stubbornly, a ghostly, haunting watermark on the canvas of his memories.

"Is this my purpose?" he questioned the deafening silence, his heart heavy with the immense, often unbearable cost of his extraordinary gift. "To merely delay the inevitable?"

Mark's hands sought solace in the worn leather of the chair, gripping it tightly as if it could somehow anchor him amidst the relentless storm of his thoughts. Yet, despite the tempest raging within, a quiet, resolute determination began, tentatively, to take root. He knew with absolute certainty that he couldn't change the past, but the future, however uncertain, was still his to shape, one prediction, one deliberate action at a time. With a deep, steadying breath, he composed himself, ready to face the unfolding pages of his life once more.

Mark's gaze drifted from the scattered papers to a photograph framed in simple, unadorned wood, the glass reflecting back the dim, ambient light of his study. His sister, Susan, captured mid-laugh, her eyes sparkling with genuine mirth and her lips curved in joyous, uninhibited abandon, seemed to radiate warmth and light from within the confines of the frame. He reached out, his fingers gently tracing the edge, feeling a poignant, bittersweet mixture of deep gratitude and lingering guilt.

"Am I asking too much of her?" he whispered to the encompassing stillness, the vivid image of Susan evoking a sudden, overwhelming cascade of complex emotions. "Can she possibly handle the burden of my gift?"

"Mark?" The voice, crisp, clear, and undeniably tender, sliced through his troubled reverie.

He looked up to find Susan standing quietly at the doorway, her head tilted slightly, a clear expression of concern etched upon her features. She stepped closer, her very presence a comforting beacon in the murky, troubled waters of his mind.

"Your face tells a story of a thousand worries," she observed gently, pulling a chair close to his desk and settling in.

Mark sighed, the sheer weight of his thoughts desperately needing an outlet. "Susan, you've always been there for me, unwavering and steadfast, but this path I walk... it's shrouded in shadows, fraught with uncertainty. What if it's simply too much? For both of us?"

"Mark," she replied, her tone firm yet infused with a deep, unwavering gentleness, "you've been given a rare, extraordinary gift. Yes, it undeniably comes with its challenges, its burdens, but think of all those people, the ones whose lives are undeniably better, immeasurably brighter, because you dared to care, because you dared to intervene."

"But the cost," he began, his voice laced with weariness, only to be gently but firmly cut off by her reassuring, knowing smile.

"Look at me, Mark. Really, truly look at me." She took his hands in hers, the simple physical contact grounding him, pulling him back from the precipice of his despair. "Am I not stronger because of you? Haven't we both grown in ways we never, ever thought possible?"

He searched her eyes, seeking the profound truth he so often effortlessly read in the faces of others. And there it was, unwavering, pure, and utterly undeniable.

"You bring hope where there's despair, guidance where there's confusion, a glimmer of light in the deepest darkness. That's not just *something*; that's *everything* to someone who's lost, someone who's utterly adrift," she continued, her conviction burning bright and steady as a flame.

"Hope can be fleeting, Susan. What if,"

"Stop," she implored, squeezing his hands gently but firmly. "You're not a fortune-teller promising fanciful fairy tales and guaranteed happy endings. You offer what no one else on this earth can – a chance. Sometimes, Mark, just sometimes, that's all anyone truly needs."

Mark absorbed her words, letting them slowly seep into the deep, pervasive cracks of his self-doubt. Susan had always been his unwavering anchor, her unshakeable belief in him a constant, comforting presence, even when his own was faltering, threatening to disappear entirely.

"Have faith in yourself, Mark," she urged softly, her voice a soothing balm. "Because I do. Always have, always will."

At that precise moment, her unwavering confidence felt like a lifeline, strong and true, thrown across the vast, terrifying chasm of his deepest fears. His heart swelled with an emotion he couldn't quite articulate, couldn't quite name, but it felt undeniably like the first tentative rays of dawn breaking after a long, arduous night. He nodded, a silent, profound vow passing between them in the quiet stillness of the study.

"Thank you, Susan," he said, a small, genuinely hopeful smile finally tugging at the corners of his lips. "For everything."

"Anytime, big brother," she replied, her own smile a warm, comforting mirror of his. "Now, let's get these papers picked up. Your journey's far from over, Mark, and I'm right here with you, every step of the way."

Together, with a quiet understanding that transcended words, they began the painstaking task of collecting the scattered pages, each one a tangible testament to the past and a silent, hopeful promise for the future.

Mark's steps within the dimly lit study became a rhythmic metronome, the soft, repetitive thud of his soles against the polished hardwood floor an echo of the relentless turmoil churning inside him. He walked the full length of the room, turned sharply on his heel, and walked back again, a caged animal pacing restlessly within the self-imposed confines of its pen.

"Is it really a gift?" he muttered to himself, pausing his restless circuit to run a weary hand through his tousled brown hair. "Or is it just... too much?"

The walls surrounding him were lined with imposing shelves groaning under the weight of countless books, each spine a silent, watchful sentinel to his ceaseless, often fruitless, search for definitive answers. In his mind's eye, however, those very same volumes seemed to murmur insidious questions about the fundamental nature of his extraordinary, sometimes terrifying, ability. Could the profound insights he gleaned so effortlessly from the minds of others be twisted, perhaps even inadvertently, into something dark, something malevolent? It was a question that gnawed relentlessly at him, sharp, insidious teeth of doubt nibbling away at the very core of his resolve.

"Predicting actions, reading thoughts," he articulated aloud, as if the mere act of voicing the words could somehow exorcise the persistent demons that plagued his inner landscape. "It's power, undeniably, but... what if it falls into the wrong hands? What if, God forbid, my hands are the wrong ones?"

He froze abruptly mid-stride, his troubled gaze falling upon the familiar photograph of his sister, Susan. Her image, usually a comforting beacon of unwavering faith, at this precise moment served only to starkly illuminate the vast, terrifying chasm of his profound uncertainty. The sheer weight of potential consequences pressed down upon him, a palpable, suffocating force that threatened to utterly crush his spirit.

"Can I truly bear this?" he whispered, his voice cracking audibly like thin ice giving way underfoot.

Suddenly, and without warning, Mark's legs gave way beneath him, and he crumpled unceremoniously to the floor amidst the chaotic sea of scattered papers, each one a fragile remnant of a life he had touched, a destiny he had influenced. His body shook with silent, convulsive sobs, his shoulders rising and falling in a rhythm entirely disjointed from the steady tempo of his earlier, restless pacing. No sound escaped his lips, but the hot, stinging tears that streaked his cheeks spoke volumes of the deep, unyielding pain he harboured within his soul.

"Is it worth it?" The question was a ragged gasp, a breath expelled from the very depths of his being, raw and desperate. "The good I've done... does it truly outweigh the potential harm I might inadvertently cause?"

There, in the profound quiet of his sanctuary, surrounded by the comforting, if sometimes intimidating, tomes of accumulated knowledge and the scattered remnants of his past, Mark Jennings confronted the sheer enormity of his existence. A man who stood perpetually at the precarious crossroads between two disparate realms – ordinary, everyday life and the extraordinary, often crushing, burden of his unique gift – he grappled fiercely with the very essence of his purpose.

"Help me," he pleaded to the indifferent shadows that gathered in the corners, seeking solace, seeking absolution. "I need to know, with absolute certainty, that I'm doing the right thing."

But the room remained stubbornly silent, offering no tangible response to his anguished, heartfelt cry. It was within this profound, echoing silence that Mark would ultimately have to find his own answer, somewhere between the relentless doubts that plagued him and the unwavering, steadfast support of the sister who believed in him more fiercely than he, in his darkest moments, believed in himself.

Mark dragged a trembling hand across his face, wiping away the last lingering remnants of tears as he forced himself, with a supreme effort, to stand. He desperately needed a lifeline, something solid and reliable to cling to in the turbulent, storm-tossed sea of his own mind. His gaze fell upon a tattered, familiar journal lying open atop the chaotic jumble of papers on his desk. Each page within its worn covers was a powerful testament to the countless lives he'd impacted, a vibrant mosaic of cherished recollections he now instinctively turned to for solace and desperately needed comfort.

"Little Jamie..." he murmured, his voice catching with emotion as he gently caressed the edge of a faded, childlike drawing depicting a young boy with wide, innocent, and profoundly grateful eyes. Mark remembered vividly how his precise prediction had led Jamie's frantic parents directly to the hidden, disused well where the child had been terrifyingly trapped. The overwhelming relief in their voices, the raw, powerful warmth of their subsequent embrace, it all rushed back to him in a sudden, powerful wave, reigniting a fragile spark of hope that had been all but smothered by his persistent, corrosive doubt.

"Mrs. Cartwright," he continued, a faint, wistful smile touching his lips as he recalled the elderly woman's joyous laughter when his timely insights had miraculously reunited her with her long-lost, cherished love. These moments of pure, unadulterated joy and immense relief were not merely fleeting memories; they were powerful beacons, guiding him steadfastly through the oppressive darkness, telling him that maybe, just maybe, he had genuinely made a difference.

With the tender flicker of hope tentatively warming his heart, Mark carefully set the journal aside and stood up, straightening his shoulders. He needed more than just the comforting embrace of his past successes; he needed solidarity, he needed understanding, he needed connection. A place where his gift wasn't perceived as a strange anomaly but a shared, understood experience. Grabbing his coat from the back of the door, he headed out into the crisp, cool evening air, his steps purposeful, towards the community centre that regularly hosted a support group specifically for individuals like him.

"Good evening, Mark," greeted Ms. Simmons, the warm, welcoming facilitator of the group, as he entered the familiar, comforting room. Her genuine smile was a soothing balm to his frayed, raw nerves.

"Evening," Mark replied, offering a small, hesitant wave to the others already gathered in a comforting circle of chairs. There was Tim, whose premonitions came to him in vivid, often unsettling dreams; Lila, who possessed the remarkable ability to feel the emotions of others as if they were undeniably her own; and several more, each with their own unique, often challenging, abilities.

"Rough night?" Tim asked gently, his eyes soft with genuine concern and understanding.

"More like a rough week, to be honest," Mark confessed, taking his usual seat between Lila and a quiet man named Eric, who simply nodded in silent, empathetic understanding.

"Let's start with sharing our triumphs," Ms. Simmons suggested, her voice warm and encouraging. "Sometimes, we get so caught up in our challenges, in the weight of our burdens, that we completely forget the genuine good we've managed to do."

One by one, members of the group began to recount their recent encounters, detailing how they had used their extraordinary gifts to aid those in distress, to offer a helping hand in moments of profound need. As Mark listened, truly listened, he felt the palpable sense of camaraderie in the room envelop him like a warm, comforting embrace. Here, in this shared space, he wasn't alone; here, he was undeniably part of a collective force for good, a shared purpose.

"Your turn, Mark," Lila said gently, her hand finding his in a comforting, understanding gesture.

He took a deep, steadying breath, consciously letting their shared strength flow through him, fortifying his spirit. "I helped find a missing child last month," he began, his voice surprisingly steady, gaining confidence with each word. "And there was an older couple, I predicted a significant health issue before it became dangerously serious. They managed to get the treatment they desperately needed in time."

"See? You're making a genuine, tangible difference," Eric chimed in, his tone earnest and sincere. "We all are, in our own unique ways."

The group nodded in unison, a quiet chorus of heartfelt agreement that visibly buoyed Mark's spirits. This was exactly what he needed: validation, understanding, and acceptance from those who truly understood the immense weight of such gifts and the profound responsibility that inevitably accompanied them. In this safe, shared space, he was powerfully reminded that he wasn't carrying this immense burden alone, that together, they formed a rich, complex tapestry of hope and crucial assistance for those who were utterly lost, utterly in need.

By the end of the meeting, the crushing despair that had plagued Mark earlier had noticeably dissipated, replaced by a newfound, quiet resolve. Yes, the path ahead was undoubtedly fraught with uncertainty, with potential pitfalls, but it was also undeniably lined with extraordinary potential for good. As he bid farewell to the group, stepping back out into the cool, crisp night air, Mark felt the solid ground of purpose firmly beneath his feet once more.

Mark stood utterly motionless before the large study window, his gaze intently following the seemingly aimless path of a lone sparrow as it flitted effortlessly between the skeletal, bare branches of an ancient oak tree. The leaves had long since fallen, gracefully surrendering to the crisp, biting embrace of winter's imminent onset, and in that delicate, intricate dance of bird and bough, Mark found a poignant echo of his own complex existence, perpetually caught between the exhilarating promise of flight and the inevitable, relentless pull of gravity.

"Can I truly change anything?" he whispered to the glass, his warm breath fogging it momentarily. His fingers traced the outline of a solitary droplet as it raced downwards across the pane, merging with others to form tiny, meandering rivulets of uncertainty. "I'm just one person, after all."

The world outside continued its relentless, bustling rhythm of life, people wrapped tightly within the confines of their own narratives, utterly unaware of the man who watched them from his quiet sanctuary with the extraordinary, sometimes burdensome, power to sense their silent struggles, their hidden pains. He pondered, with a complex blend of profound humility and a weary resignation, the vast, intricate web of lives into which he had glimpsed, each fragile thread vibrating with the dizzying potential for either overwhelming joy or crushing despair.

"Even if I can't possibly save everyone," he murmured, his voice barely audible,

"there's meaning in the attempt, isn't there? A profound value in simply trying?"

His question hung suspended in the air, unanswered, yet it was enough, just enough, to still the restless, turbulent tide within him. There were undeniable limits to what he could possibly do, boundaries imposed by the very nature of reality, but those inherent limitations did not, could not, diminish the fundamental value of his efforts, of his unwavering commitment to try.

Each small victory, every precious fragment of averted sorrow, they all mattered, accumulating gradually to form a compelling narrative of hope, a story authored by the unique, extraordinary power of his gift.

The sharp, clear chime of the mail slot suddenly snapped Mark from his deep reverie. He turned abruptly, a flicker of curiosity lifting the corners of his mouth as he approached the front door. There, lying innocuously amidst a scattering of mundane bills and unsolicited advertisements, was an envelope crafted from elegant, cream-coloured paper, its surface adorned with delicate, looping handwriting that was both familiar and intriguing.

"Interesting," he said aloud, a genuine smile tugging at his lips as he immediately recognised the name in the return address.

In the quiet sanctity of his study, Mark carefully slid a finger under the sealed flap and gently unfolded the letter. The words within seemed to leap out at him, vibrant with a palpable sincerity and a heartwarming warmth that immediately resonated with his soul:

"Dear Mark,

I hope this letter finds you well and in good spirits. I've wanted to write to you for some time now, to express my deepest gratitude. Your guidance last year... it truly changed everything for me, in ways I couldn't have possibly imagined. I was utterly lost, adrift in a vast, terrifying sea of confusion and crippling fear, but your prediction, Mark, it was like a powerful lighthouse guiding me safely back to shore, back to solid ground. Because of you, I found the inner strength I desperately needed to face my challenges head-on and, miraculously, to overcome them. My family and I are in a far better place now, happier and healthier than we ever honestly thought possible.

Thank you doesn't seem nearly sufficient, doesn't feel like enough, but from the very bottom of my heart, thank you, Mark. You possess a truly remarkable gift, a power that is both extraordinary and profound, and the kindness, the genuine compassion, with which you wield it is a rare and precious treasure in this often-difficult world.

With deepest and most sincere gratitude,

Eleanor"

As he read Eleanor's heartfelt words, truly absorbed their meaning, Mark's chest swelled with a complex mixture of profound pride and immense, overwhelming relief. Eleanor's words were far more than mere ink on paper; they were tangible, irrefutable proof of the positive, far-reaching ripples he had sent across the intricate fabric of another's life. Her gratitude was a powerful beacon, reigniting the flickering flame of purpose that had threatened to extinguish entirely in his darkest moments of doubt.

"See, Mark? You are genuinely making a difference," he whispered to himself, a newfound vigour, a quiet strength, infusing his voice.

He carefully placed the letter on his desk beside the framed photograph of Susan, allowing its powerful, resonant message to settle deep within his soul, to take root. This was the validation he so desperately needed, the powerful affirmation that his journey, though undeniably fraught with challenges, with moments of profound despair, was one utterly worth continuing.

"Tomorrow is another day," he said, his eyes reflecting the clear, bright spark of renewed determination. "Another chance to change a life, to make a difference."

And with that, he reached out and switched off the lamp, the room gradually descending into a comforting darkness save for the gentle moonlight that spilt through the window, casting a soft, ethereal silver glow over the heartfelt letter that had so powerfully rekindled Mark Jennings' belief in the extraordinary power and profound potential of his out-of-this-world gift.

Mark turned slowly from the letter lying on his desk, the warm echo of Eleanor's heartfelt gratitude still resonating pleasantly in his ears. He was just about to extinguish the last remaining light in his study when a soft, hesitant knock at the door momentarily startled him. He hesitated for a brief moment before opening it to find Nathan standing there, the young man's usual tough, almost impenetrable facade noticeably softened by the raw vulnerability he saw reflected in his eyes.

"Hey, Mark... Can I come in for a second?" Nathan's voice was barely above a whisper, raw and quiet, but it carried the undeniable weight of unspoken troubles, of a heavy burden.

"Of course, Nathan. What's on your mind, mate?" Mark stepped aside immediately, allowing the young man to enter the comforting sanctuary of books, memories, and quiet contemplation.

Nathan shuffled awkwardly into the room, his gaze flickering nervously around the space before eventually landing on a peculiar, eye-catching object atop the bookshelf – a small, intricately carved wooden phoenix. Its delicate wings were outstretched, frozen in a moment of perpetual motion, as if caught mid-rebirth from its own fiery ashes.

"Is that new?" Nathan asked tentatively, pointing towards the symbolic figure.

"Not really," Mark responded, his fingers gently grazing the smooth, cool contours of the wooden phoenix. "It's been with me for quite some time, actually. It's a symbol of resilience, you see. Of rising above despite everything life throws at you."

"Feels like it's mocking me a bit," Nathan chuckled weakly, a humourless sound, but his eyes remained fixed on the symbolic figure with a hint of longing, a touch of wistfulness.

"Mocking? No, Nathan, not at all. It's a powerful reminder that even amidst destruction, amidst the ashes of failure, there's always hope for renewal, for a fresh start. For all of us, without exception." Mark's words seemed to resonate deeply within the quiet room, imbued with the quiet conviction of someone who genuinely believed in second chances, in the possibility of redemption.

Nathan sighed heavily, looking down at his hands, calloused and worn, before meeting Mark's gaze again, a flicker of raw emotion in his eyes. "I don't know if I have that kind of strength left in me, Mark."

"Strength isn't just about standing tall and facing the world alone; it's also about knowing when to ask for help, about being open to the possibility of change, to the need for support," Mark said gently, his voice soft but firm, undeniably reassuring. "You're here, aren't you? You came here tonight. That's a significant start, Nathan."

"Maybe... but what if it's genuinely too late for me, Mark?"

"Look at me, Nathan. Really look at me. It's never, ever too late. Not for anyone." Mark held Nathan's gaze steadily, and for a fleeting moment, he saw it, the faint, almost imperceptible glimmer of hope that had been so frustratingly elusive in the young man's darkened, troubled expression. It was faint, fragile, but it was undeniably there, and it shone with the quiet, persistent possibility of redemption, of a brighter future.

"Thanks, Mark. I, I'll try to remember that, I really will," Nathan murmured, the very beginnings of a small, hesitant smile finally tugging at the corners of his mouth.

"Good man. And remember, Nathan, I'm right here if you ever need to talk, if you ever need someone to listen," Mark offered genuinely, clapping a warm, reassuring hand on Nathan's shoulder.

As Nathan departed, leaving behind him a quiet trail of unspoken gratitude and a palpable sense of relief, Mark turned back to the wooden phoenix, his gaze lingering on its symbolic form. His fingers gently traced the intricately etched feathers, following the delicate curves and flowing lines that spoke of a life continually reborn from adversity, from hardship. With each gentle touch, his own resolve solidified, a silent, powerful promise to himself and to those like Nathan that he would continue to offer guidance, to be a steadfast beacon of hope in their moments of deepest darkness.

"Rise again," Mark whispered to the quiet room, a newfound sense of profound purpose illuminating his face, chasing away the shadows of doubt. His gift wasn't merely a tool for predicting potential outcomes; it was a powerful means to inspire change, to ignite the fragile sparks that could potentially set lives ablaze with renewed purpose, with boundless potential.

And with that, Mark felt genuinely ready to face whatever challenges lay ahead, the small wooden phoenix standing sentinel over a world where mysteries continued to unfold, and destinies awaited those brave enough, those resilient enough, to embrace them fully.

The study was quiet now, a profound stillness settling over the room, the only discernible sound the gentle, rhythmic rustle of paper as Mark carefully turned each worn page of his familiar journal. He paused, reflecting deeply on the extraordinary journey that had brought him to this precise point, the countless faces, the myriad stories, etched indelibly into the fabric of his memory. Every single entry within the journal's pages was a powerful testament to the trials he'd faced, the lessons he'd learned, and the countless lives he'd touched, however briefly.

"Remember Jamie?" Susan's voice broke the comfortable silence, her tone light, almost conversational, but undeniably probing. She leaned casually against the doorframe, watching her brother with an attentive, understanding eye.

Mark looked up, a faint, knowing smile gently tugging at his lips. "Yes, the baker who genuinely thought he'd lost absolutely everything in the fire. But we found the crucial evidence that ultimately saved his business, saved his livelihood."

Susan nodded slowly, stepping fully into the room, her presence immediately comforting and grounding. "You did far more than just that, Mark. You gave him hope, genuine, tangible hope, when he was completely ready to give up, to surrender to despair. That, Mark, was all you, your doing."

"Hope," Mark repeated softly, the word resonating deeply within him like the clear, pure chime of a bell. It had, almost unconsciously, become his mantra, a guiding beacon illuminating his path through the persistent fog of uncertainty that perpetually shrouded each and every case he undertook.

"Every challenge, every setback... they were lessons, weren't they? Crucial learning opportunities," Mark mused aloud, his gaze drifting towards the window where the world outside continued to move at its own relentless, indifferent pace.

"Exactly right, Mark." Susan sat down beside him, her presence a source of quiet strength and unwavering support. "You learned to trust your instincts, to truly listen to that unique, powerful voice inside you, the one only you can hear."

Mark chuckled softly, a genuine, heartfelt sound, shaking his head in disbelieving wonder. "Who would have thought, eh? Me, helping solve mysteries, using my... what did you call it, Sue? My 'superpower'?"

"Because it is, Mark, genuinely, truly is," Susan insisted earnestly, her conviction unwavering. "You see things others simply can't. You feel what they feel, understand what they're going through on a level no one else can."

The memories flooded back, a torrent of emotions and experiences – the unsettling tightness in his chest when danger loomed, the warm, comforting sensation spreading through his veins when joy was just around the corner, a palpable presence. Each emotion a vibrant, distinct colour in the rich, complex tapestry of his mind's eye.

"And you've grown so much, Mark," she continued, a clear note of pride evident in her voice. "Remember how you used to struggle so much with change, with the unexpected? Now you navigate it like a seasoned captain steering confidently through a storm at sea."

"Thanks to you, Sue. Honestly, truly thanks to you." Mark's voice was thick with raw emotion, with profound gratitude. "You always believed in me, always had faith, even when I stumbled, when I fell."

"Because I know you, Mark. The real you, the good man you truly are." She reached out, gently squeezing his hand, a simple gesture that conveyed a world of understanding and affection. "And I'm not the only one, Mark. There are so many out there, more than you realise, who share my unwavering faith in you."

"Sometimes, I still wonder, though..." Mark began, his persistent doubts, like insidious shadows at dusk, slowly creeping back in.

"Then think about Nathan," Susan cut in sharply, her voice firm, almost commanding. "Today, you sparked something in him, Mark. Something real, something hopeful. He left here different than when he came, lighter, more hopeful, more open to the future."

"Perhaps," Mark conceded, allowing himself, just for a precious moment, the luxury of truly believing that he genuinely had made a difference, a real, tangible impact. "It's just hard, isn't it? Hard to see the bigger picture, the wider impact, when you're caught up so completely in the details, in the immediate."

"Then let's focus on the now, Mark," Susan suggested, her eyes gleaming with excitement, with possibility. "You have a gift, Mark. A rare, beautiful, powerful gift. And you use it, selflessly, to bring justice, to uncover truths that are hidden from everyone else, truths that would otherwise remain buried."

"Justice," Mark echoed, rolling the word around in his mind, weighing its significance. It was a heavy responsibility, undeniably, one he had willingly taken up time and time again, despite the personal cost.

"Come on, big brother." Susan stood, pulling him gently to his feet, her energy infectious. "Let's get back to work, eh? There's a whole world out there waiting for your touch, for the magic only you can bring to it."

"Magic," Mark said, the word a quiet whisper of awe, of newfound determination. With a deep, cleansing breath, he stepped forward, ready, truly ready, to face whatever lay ahead, his past victories, his hard-won lessons, now firmly carving the path to new horizons, to new possibilities. His story wasn't finished yet; it was, undeniably, just beginning another compelling chapter.

Chapter 16
Selfless Act

The quaint, almost sacred hush of the library was brutally shattered by a sudden, discordant whisper that pierced through Susan's deep concentration like a shard of glass. Her fingers, which had been delicately tracing the worn spine of an ancient tome on parapsychology, froze mid-motion, suspended in the air. The voice, threaded with a chilling, palpable malice, was unmistakably directed towards her brother, Mark, and their newfound, fragile ally, Nathan.

"Tonight's the night," hissed the unseen speaker, the words dripping with sinister anticipation. "They won't even see it coming, not a chance."

Susan's heart seized violently in her chest, panic flaring instantly like wildfire consuming dry brush as she desperately peered through the dense, confusing labyrinth of towering bookshelves. She caught a fleeting glimpse of a shadowy figure slipping silently between the stacks, just out of reach, just out of sight. Her mind raced furiously, piecing together the chilling fragments of the whispered plot. It didn't take her empathetic brother's extraordinary gift to know, with a sickening certainty, that Mark and Nathan were the intended targets of this unseen threat.

"Mark... Nathan..." she whispered under her breath, a desperate plea, her eyes frantically scanning the room for her brother's familiar, comforting presence and Nathan's typically brooding, distinct silhouette. They were huddled together over a large table in the far corner, seemingly lost in deep conversation, utterly oblivious to the sinister intentions swirling ominously around them, a dark cloud gathering.

"Excuse me," she murmured quickly to the elderly librarian, who looked up with a startled expression, her spectacles perched precariously on her nose. Susan's feet carried her swiftly, almost instinctively, across the checkered floor, her petite frame manoeuvring with an agility born purely of urgent necessity, of raw instinct.

"Mark, Nathan, we need to leave. Now," Susan said, her voice barely above a whisper, a low, urgent tone, but undeniably laced with an uncharacteristic, sharp edge of alarm, of imminent danger.

Mark glanced up immediately, his gentle, perceptive eyes meeting hers. He saw not just fear reflected there, but a fierce, unwavering determination shining back at him, a protective fire. Nathan's dark brows drew together in confusion, a furrow appearing on his brow, but he sensed the undeniable gravity, the sheer urgency, in her tone, in her demeanour.

"What's wrong, Suze?" Mark asked, his voice remarkably calm despite the sudden tension, but undeniably alert, his senses heightened.

"Can't explain right now, Mark, no time," she replied hurriedly, glancing nervously over her shoulder, scanning the room for any sign of pursuit. "We're in danger. We have to get out of here, out of this building, before..."

"Before what, Susan?" Nathan pressed, pushing back abruptly from the table with a harsh scrape of chair legs against the wooden floor, his own unease mounting.

"Someone knows about... your abilities, Mark. And they definitely don't mean well, not at all," she admitted, revealing only as much as was absolutely necessary to spur them into immediate action without causing outright panic, without sending them into a tailspin.

"Understood," Mark responded instantly, standing up with an uncharacteristic swiftness, a sudden, decisive movement that completely belied his usual composed, thoughtful demeanour. His innate ability to read situations, to sense underlying currents, even without actively employing his unique talent, told him, with absolute certainty, that Susan's urgent warning was not, under any circumstances, to be taken lightly.

"Let's go then," Nathan said, his voice surprisingly steady despite the undeniable quickening beat of his heart, the sudden surge of adrenaline. With a mutual, shared nod of understanding, the trio quickly gathered their few belongings, casting wary, nervous glances around the silent, imposing rows of books that suddenly seemed far more ominous than scholarly, far more threatening than comforting.

"Stick close to me, both of you," Susan instructed quietly but firmly, leading the way with a surreptitious glance towards the nearest exit, her escape route. Her mind worked furiously, racing ahead, considering every possible escape route, every potential contingency plan. Her fiercely protective instinct for her brother had kicked into overdrive, a powerful, visceral response, and with Nathan's troubled, complex past, she knew, with a chilling certainty, that they couldn't afford to take any chances whatsoever.

"Everything's going to be okay, I promise," she reassured them, though her own pulse hammered wildly in her ears, a frantic drumbeat against the sudden silence. "Just trust me, okay? Please, just trust me."

"Down this way! Quickly!" Susan hissed, her eyes darting instinctively to the shadowed alcove nestled strategically between towering, laden bookshelves. The library's labyrinthine layout, a confusing maze of accumulated knowledge, now served, ironically, as their unlikely, precarious refuge.

"Wait," Mark cautioned softly, his voice laced with a sudden, instinctive caution, sensing an undercurrent of palpable malice threading through the air, a dark energy. "I feel..."

"Trouble," Susan finished for him, her own heightened senses prickling with a sudden, sharp alarm. At that precise moment, heavy, ominous footsteps echoed loudly, coming from the very direction they had been headed. She peered cautiously around the corner and saw the bulky, imposing silhouette of a man advancing steadily towards them. His movements were purposeful, deliberate, and undeniably predatory.

The Mind Whisperer

In his hand glinted something metallic, something undeniably threatening – a weapon.

"Behind me, now, both of you," she commanded instantly, stepping instinctively in front of her brother and Nathan without a moment's hesitation, without a second thought. Her heart thudded violently against her ribs, a wild, frantic drumbeat in the sudden, tense silence of the library.

"Who is that?" Nathan whispered urgently, trying desperately to peer around Susan's slight, protective frame, straining to see.

"Doesn't matter who he is right now. He's here for us, for one of us, or all of us," Susan said, her voice low, fierce, and resolute. She could feel Mark's raw anxiousness radiating off him in palpable waves, like heat rising from the pavement on a scorching summer day. Nathan's breaths came in short, sharp bursts, betraying his own deep-seated fear despite his typically stoic, controlled facade.

"Stay back!" she warned the approaching figure, standing as tall as her frame would allow despite the undeniable tremor in her legs, the sudden weakness. "We don't want any trouble, mate."

The man chuckled darkly, a chilling sound utterly devoid of any humour, any warmth. "But trouble, my dears, has well and truly found you," he replied, his voice a gravelly, menacing threat that crawled across Susan's skin, sending shivers down her spine.

"Mark, Nathan, whatever happens next, run, just run, at the very first chance you get," Susan instructed urgently, locking eyes with her brother for a fleeting moment to convey a wealth of unspoken urgency, of desperate need. Mark nodded, his thoughts a jumbled, frantic cacophony that only Susan, with her unique connection to him, could possibly interpret – worry for her safety, a readiness to act decisively, an absolute, unwavering trust in her judgement.

"Brave words indeed for such a small, fragile thing," the antagonist sneered, closing the distance between them with a chilling, predatory confidence. Susan could see clearly now the glint was from a knife, a serious blade, the kind with intentions far more sinister, far worse, than merely slicing paper.

"Leave us alone, please, just go," Susan demanded, her voice surprisingly steady, unwavering, even as the cold, sharp edge of fear slid like ice down her spine.

"Can't do that, love," the man replied, and with a swift, sudden motion, he lunged forward, directly at them.

Susan's instincts screamed a primal warning. She reacted instantly, sidestepping with lightning speed, narrowly avoiding the lethal blade that sliced through the air precisely where she had been standing just a heartbeat before. Adrenaline surged violently through her veins, igniting a fierce, fiery courage she hadn't known she possessed. She was undeniably terrified, yes, her heart pounding like a drum, but her fierce, unwavering love for Mark and Nathan was a far stronger force, a powerful motivator, pushing her relentlessly to shield them with every fibre of her being, with every ounce of her strength.

"Run! Now!" she shouted, her voice raw and desperate, hoping against hope that her spontaneous sacrifice would buy them precious, life-saving seconds. The danger was terrifyingly real, immediate, and undeniably present, and Susan Jennings stood resolute, a fragile barrier between it and her family, between the threat and those she loved.

"Think fast!" Susan's voice cracked like a whip as she instinctively hurled her purse, a heavy leather bag, directly at the assailant's face. It was an impromptu, desperate missile, a gamble, but it bought her a crucial heartbeat of time, a moment's reprieve. The man staggered back, cursing loudly and violently as he desperately clawed at the leather bag tangled frustratingly in his hair, momentarily disoriented.

"Get out of here! Both of you! Now!" she screamed to Mark and Nathan, seeing them hesitate, frozen for a terrifying second. For a fleeting moment, her brother's eyes met hers, filled with silent promises of protection, of unwavering support, a telepathic plan unfolding rapidly, instinctively, between them, a connection forged over a lifetime.

The assailant ripped the purse away with a violent jerk, his gaze now fixed solely on Susan with a renewed, terrifying malice, his eyes burning with rage. "Clever girl," he snarled, lunging again, this time more cautiously, more deliberately, having learned from her unexpected move.

Susan's mind raced, working at lightning speed. She frantically scanned her surroundings, the layout of the room, noting the heavy vase on the mantelpiece, the way the late afternoon light from the window cast long, distorted shadows across the wooden floor. Anything, absolutely anything, could potentially become a weapon, a distraction, a chance to survive, a way out.

"Mark! Nathan! Now! Go!" Her voice was a sharp, urgent command that finally spurred them into motion, their footsteps retreating rapidly, echoing slightly, even as Susan braced herself, tightening her muscles, for the attacker's next move, for the inevitable assault.

With a sudden, violent jerk, the man advanced, brandishing the knife with a chilling expertise, clearly accustomed to wielding such a weapon. Susan instinctively ducked swiftly under his outstretched arm, feeling the whoosh of air as the lethal blade missed her by mere inches, a terrifyingly close call. She grabbed the nearest solid object, a thick, heavy book from the low coffee table, and swung it with all her might, all her desperate strength. It connected with a satisfying thud against the attacker's wrist, a bone-jarring impact, sending the knife skittering noisily across the polished wooden floorboards, out of his immediate reach.

"Is that all you got, mate?" she taunted, a feigned bravado masking the raw, debilitating terror that gripped her insides, threatening to overwhelm her.

The attacker hissed in pain and frustration, cradling his injured wrist, his face contorted in anger. His eyes darted instantly towards the fallen knife, then back to Susan, his mind calculating, assessing the situation. But Susan didn't miss a beat, didn't allow him a moment's respite. She kicked the knife further away, a swift, decisive movement, her heart pounding like a frantic drum in her chest, threatening to burst.

"Big mistake, love," he growled, his voice low and dangerous, and with a swift, powerful move, he shoved the heavy coffee table directly towards her. Susan stumbled, her balance faltering precariously as she desperately tried to sidestep the incoming obstacle, the sudden, unexpected assault.

A moment of terrifying suspense hung heavy in the air – would she regain her footing in time, or would she fall prey to the attacker's continued, relentless onslaught?

"Stay back!" Susan warned, finding her ground once more, her stance firming. She eyed the distance between them, between herself and the fallen knife, and between her and her brother and Nathan, now safely, hopefully, behind a locked door, a solid barrier.

"Or what, then? You'll throw another book, will you?" the man sneered, advancing yet again, a cruel smile playing on his lips.

"Whatever it takes, mate. Whatever it takes to protect them," Susan replied, her voice steady, unwavering, her spirit utterly undaunted, unbroken. She knew, with a quiet certainty, that the longer she managed to hold his attention, to occupy him, the further away Mark and Nathan could get, the closer they were to achieving safety, to escaping the immediate danger.

"Very well, then, let's dance, shall we?" he said, a wicked, chilling smile spreading across his face, a mask of pure malice, as he prepared to strike once more, to end this game.

"Mark, Nathan, listen to me, properly!" Susan's voice was firm, urgent, a desperate plea disguised as a command. She kept her gaze locked firmly on the advancing threat, the man moving steadily towards her, while speaking directly to the door behind her, the solid wood feeling cold and reassuring against her back, a tangible, physical barrier between her loved ones and the imminent harm that threatened them. "I need you two to find a way out of there, out of this building, now! Don't wait for me!"

"Are you completely insane, Sue?! We're not leaving you, not a chance!" Nathan's muffled voice came through the thick wood of the door, raw and laden with panic, with fear for her safety.

"Trust me, please, just trust me," she implored, her tone leaving absolutely no room for argument, for doubt, for hesitation. "You know I can handle this, you've seen me. Keep moving, keep quiet, make yourselves scarce, and for heaven's sake, stay together, look out for each other."

She could almost perfectly picture Mark's intent, worried eyes and Nathan's deeply furrowed brow on the other side of that solid door, but there was simply no time for doubts, for second-guessing, for hesitation. They had to believe in her, implicitly, just as she, in this terrifying moment, believed fiercely in herself, in her own ability to survive, to protect them.

"Promise me, Mark! Promise you'll take care of Nathan, that you'll look after him!" She strained desperately to hear his usually soft, gentle voice over the frantic, deafening thudding of her own heart, a wild drumbeat in her ears.

"I promise, Suze," came the faint, muffled reply, wrapped in the warmth of deep, unwavering trust and the unbreakable bond of sibling love.

"Good. Right." Susan bit down hard on her lip, bracing herself physically and mentally for the inevitable confrontation, for the next move. "Now go! Don't look back!"

The silence that followed was an unspoken vow, a sacred pact sealed in the face of imminent danger and profound, unwavering devotion. She knew, with a chilling certainty, that they would follow her command; it was, terrifyingly, the only way to ensure their survival, their escape.

"Endearing, truly," the attacker said mockingly, a cruel smile twisting his features, inching closer with a palpable menace in his every deliberate step. "But it won't save them, not ultimately, and it certainly won't save you, little bird."

"Like hell, it won't," Susan glowered at him, her eyes blazing with fierce defiance, feeling the air around them charge, thicken, with palpable peril. Every second counted now; every breath she drew, every movement she made, was one more for Mark and Nathan, one more chance for them to get away, to reach safety.

"Time's running out, little bird," he taunted, his voice dripping with cruel anticipation, reaching deliberately into his coat, his hand disappearing inside.

Susan's mind raced furiously, a whirlwind of desperate thoughts. The knife was frustratingly out of reach, the room seemingly devoid of any other potential weapons, yet her resolve, her determination, never wavered, never faltered. It was her wits against his brute force, her potential sacrifice against his chilling malice. And she wouldn't yield, not now, not while her brother and Nathan had a fighting chance, a possibility of escaping this nightmare.

"Then we better make this quick," she retorted, her voice surprisingly steady, preparing herself mentally and physically for his next move, for the inevitable attack. The stakes had never been higher, the danger never more immediate, and she was all in, ready to risk absolutely everything for the ones she loved, for the ones who depended on her.

Susan's heart hammered violently in her chest, a rapid, frantic drumbeat echoing the sudden surge of adrenaline that flooded her system, sharpening her senses, preparing her for what was to come.

Her eyes locked onto the advancing figure, the malicious intent in his gaze, in his posture, all too terrifyingly clear.

"Stay back," she warned, her voice surprisingly steady, unwavering, despite the tremor that threatened to betray her inner turmoil, the raw fear that coiled in her gut.

The man sneered, a cruel, humourless twist of his lips, his gaze flickering briefly, dismissively, behind her to where Mark and Nathan had retreated, their hiding place. "You honestly think you can protect them, little girl?" he goaded, his voice dripping with contempt.

"Always," Susan shot back instantly, a fierce, protective determination hardening her features, her resolve absolute. She could clearly see the deep concern etched into Mark's expressive face, the way his lips were pressed into a thin, tight line, his thoughts undoubtedly racing, strategising, worrying. Nathan hovered protectively just behind him, his dark eyes wide with apprehension but filled, undeniably, with a silent vow of unwavering support, of loyalty.

"Very touching, Susan, truly, but ultimately pointless," the man said, closing the remaining distance between them with a chilling, predatory ease, like a hunter cornering his prey.

"Nothing is pointless when it comes to family, mate," she retorted fiercely, her stance resolute, defiant. The words were as much for her own desperate encouragement, a reinforcement of her purpose, as they were a direct challenge to the dangerous man standing before her.

"Mark, Nathan, whatever happens now, whatever you hear, don't come out, not for anything," she called out, her voice strained but clear, not daring to take her eyes off the attacker for even a second.

A soft murmur of protest, a hesitant sound, came from behind her, muffled by the door, but she heard the distinct shuffle of feet obediently moving further away, deeper into their hiding place. A painful lump formed in her throat; her potential sacrifice, her willingness to face this threat alone, was their only viable lifeline, their only chance.

"Look at you, then," the man goaded, circling her slowly, assessing her, like a predator sizing up its quarry. "Ready to play the hero for your brother and his little friend, are we?"

"Someone has to, don't they?" Susan replied sharply, refusing to back down, refusing to show weakness. The air around them crackled with a tangible, electric tension, and for a terrifying moment, everything seemed to hang precariously in the balance, suspended in the tense silence.

"Mark, she's amazing, isn't she? Truly incredible," Nathan's hushed voice barely reached her, a faint sound from behind the door, but the undeniable undercurrent of awe, of profound gratitude, was unmistakable, a balm to her frayed nerves.

"Always has been, Nathan. Always," Mark responded, his thought-laden voice laced with unmistakable pride and something far more profound, something deeper – boundless, unconditional love for his sister.

"Focus on me, mate!" Susan snapped at the attacker, her voice sharp, deliberately diverting his dangerous attention away from the fragile hiding place of her brother and friend.

"You're completely outmatched here, love," he said with a cold, dismissive laugh, but Susan didn't flinch, didn't back down. Her mind worked furiously, racing ahead, plotting her next move, anticipating his, while her body tensed, coiled like a spring, ready to act, ready to defend.

"Maybe," she conceded, a flicker of grim determination in her eyes, "but I'm certainly not outwilled, not by a long shot." With that, she lunged forward suddenly, unexpectedly, catching the man completely off guard, surprising him. It wasn't brute strength she relied on, she had none to spare, but sheer surprise, desperate agility, and the raw, fierce desperation of a sister fighting tooth and nail for her kin, for those she loved.

"Go on, Susan! Get him!" Nathan's voice rang out suddenly, no longer subdued by worry but ignited by the sight of her courage, her defiance.

"Be careful, Suze! Please be careful!" Mark's desperate plea was almost drowned out by the sudden scuffle, the sounds of their struggle, his mental projections flickering rapidly with countless potential scenarios, each one a precarious lifeline she might grasp, a path to safety he desperately hoped she would find.

"Always am, Mark!" she managed to gasp out, her breath coming in ragged bursts, grappling fiercely with the man who was now cursing loudly and violently under his breath, enraged by her unexpected resistance.

"Damn you, woman!" he growled, his voice a low snarl, trying desperately to shake her off, to dislodge her determined grip.

"Better people have tried, mate," she quipped weakly, a flash of her usual humour, even as raw fear gnawed relentlessly at her, a cold, sharp ache in her gut. But beneath the fear, beneath the pain, lay an unbreakable will, a steely, unyielding resolve that she would do absolutely whatever it took, endure whatever she had to, to keep them safe, to ensure their survival.

"Thank you, Susan," Mark's voice, surprisingly clear, broke through the chaos, laced with emotions so strong, so raw, they cut straight to her core, to the heart of her being.

"Thank you... for everything you're doing," echoed Nathan, his voice filled with a profound, heartfelt gratitude, his words reinforcing the sheer magnitude of what she was doing for them, the sacrifice she was making.

"Shut up and stay hidden, both of you!" Susan yelled, feigning exasperation, though her heart swelled with their words, with their belief in her. Their trust, their unwavering belief in her, it fuelled her fight, pushing her beyond limits she never knew she had, giving her strength she didn't think was possible.

The man's grip loosened momentarily, a crucial slip, and she seized the opportunity instantly, throwing her weight against him with all her remaining strength, twisting and turning. As they tumbled together to the ground in a tangled heap, Susan knew, with a grim certainty, that this battle, this terrifying encounter, was far from over, but the bond between them, the strength they drew from their love, from her sacrifice, was something no menace, no threat, could ever truly shatter.

Panting heavily, her lungs burning, Susan lay sprawled awkwardly across the cold, hard floor, her assailant pinned precariously beneath her, his body twisted uncomfortably. The initial, powerful rush of adrenaline was beginning to wear off, leaving behind a sharp, persistent pain in her side, a dull ache spreading. She could hear Mark's urgent, hushed whispers from their hiding place, his voice a complex mix of raw worry and quiet command, a desperate plea.

"Stay down, Susan," he said, his voice barely audible over the sound of her own ragged, desperate breathing, the pounding of her heart.

"Can't... let him... get up," she replied between gasps, each breath a struggle, struggling desperately to maintain her hold on the thrashing, struggling figure below her, trying to keep him immobilised.

"Is he... is he out?" Nathan began, the concern evident even in his unfinished question, in the tremor in his voice.

"Out... for now, I think," Susan grunted, exerting pressure, as she used her legs, her weight, to keep the man pinned, immobilised. Despite the immediate danger, a brief, almost involuntary smile touched her lips at the thought of how they must look to anyone watching, two tangled bodies locked in an awkward, desperate dance of survival.

"Okay, listen carefully, Susan," Mark's voice was more composed now, analytical even in the midst of a crisis, taking control. "You need to move away from him, quickly; we don't know if he's alone, if there are others."

"Right... yes, right." With a significant effort, Susan rolled painfully to the side, away from the unconscious man, her heart pounding against her ribs like a caged bird desperately seeking escape, seeking freedom. The immediate aftermath of her sacrifice, of her desperate act, left them with mere seconds to regroup, to assess the situation, before they would inevitably have to face whatever came next, whatever new threat emerged from the shadows.

Nathan was suddenly, unexpectedly, at her side, kneeling beside her, his hands checking her gently for injuries, his touch surprisingly soft. "You're bleeding, Susan," he noted, his fingers coming away red from where her blouse had been torn, ripped during the struggle.

"Comes with the territory, doesn't it?" Susan quipped weakly, trying to push herself up, to sit upright, despite the pain.

"Easy, Suze," Mark cautioned, appearing beside Nathan to help support her, his hand gentle on her arm. "We need to get out of here, quickly, but we can't rush and make a lot of noise, we'll give ourselves away."

"Helping you is making us sitting ducks, Mark," Nathan murmured with a deep frown, his eyes darting nervously towards the shadowy corners of the room, searching for any signs of additional threats, of unseen dangers.

"Maybe," Susan conceded, wincing visibly as she moved, the pain flaring, "but that's a risk I'm absolutely willing to take, Nathan." A small price, she reasoned silently to herself, a necessary sacrifice, for their safety, for their chance to escape.

"Your loyalty, Susan, it might actually cost us, cost us everything," Nathan said, the sharp edge in his voice betraying his deep-seated fear for her wellbeing, for her life.

"And your healthy scepticism, Nathan, it might just save us in the end," she shot back with a weary, knowing smile, acknowledging his caution. "Let's use that scepticism now, then, to get out of this mess we're in."

"Alright, listen up, we stick to the plan, the one we just made," Mark interjected, taking charge, his voice firm and decisive. "Susan, you'll be in the middle, protected. Nathan, you cover our back, keep an eye out for anything."

They moved as one unit, a makeshift trio bound together by necessity, by shared danger, and by a newfound, fragile kinship forged in crisis. Every step they took was a test of their fortitude, a measure of their resilience, each breath they drew a silent affirmation of their resolve to survive. There was absolutely no room for error, no margin for mistakes, and yet Susan felt strangely calm, an odd, unsettling tranquillity amidst the surrounding chaos, the lingering danger.

"Mark," she whispered, pausing momentarily, turning slightly towards him, "whatever happens now, know that..."

"Save it, Susan," Mark interrupted, his voice firm, cutting her off, his gaze resolute. "We're going to make it through this, all of us. Together."

"Of course we are, Mark," she replied, a quiet certainty in her voice, though her body screamed in protest, every muscle aching, every bruise throbbing. Her actions had consequences, she knew that implicitly. They were now undeniably deeper in the complex web of mystery surrounding Nathan, and there was absolutely no telling what repercussions, what new dangers, awaited them due to her spontaneous, desperate interference.

"Look!" Nathan suddenly hissed, his voice sharp, urgent, pointing towards a sliver of light visible ahead, a beacon in the darkness. "That's our way out! I think it leads outside!"

"Then let's not waste another single second standing here," Susan urged, the pain momentarily forgotten, eclipsed by a sudden surge of desperate hope within her.

"Thank you, Susan," Nathan said quietly, his voice low but sincere, his gratitude cutting through the lingering tension, the fear. "For everything you just did, for saving us."

"Let's save the thanks until we're actually out of here, shall we?" she retorted, managing a weak smile despite the gravity of the situation, despite the danger that still lurked. Together, moving cautiously, silently, they edged towards the light, ready to face the uncertainty, the unknown, that awaited them beyond the shadows, beyond the confines of the library.

The narrow beam of light grew steadily brighter, a powerful, undeniable promise of escape that quickened their steps, spurred them onwards. Susan felt Mark's hand grip hers tightly, a silent vow passing between them, a shared understanding. They were close now, so close; the cool, fresh draft of air that whispered through the opening tasted, undeniably, of freedom, of a chance at survival.

"Almost there," she panted, her voice barely audible over the frantic pounding of her heart, a wild bird trapped in her chest.

"Wait!" Nathan's sharp cry sliced abruptly through the air, halting them instantly in their tracks, freezing them in place.

Susan's head snapped around immediately to see Nathan staring intently at something behind them, back the way they had come; his face was drained of all colour, pale and terrified. A vast, imposing shadow loomed where they had emerged from the library, growing in size and palpable menace with each passing second. The sense of dread was almost overwhelming, a tangible force; it clung to the damp walls of the passage, an unseen spectre of the danger they thought, just moments ago, they had finally left behind.

"Run!" It was all Susan managed to shout before the ground beneath them shuddered violently, a deep, unsettling tremor.

The ancient walls seemed to groan in protest, a sound of immense strain, and a sudden, terrifying cascade of dirt, stone, and debris rained down upon them. Susan shoved Mark instinctively towards the light, her body acting purely on instinct, on a primal need to protect him. "Go, Mark, go, go, go!"

"Come on, Susan! Hurry!" Mark reached desperately for her, his eyes wide with fear, with panic for her safety. But she was already moving, throwing herself forward, propelling herself towards the opening as the passage began to collapse violently behind them, sealing them off from what lay within.

"Mark!" Nathan's voice was lost in the sudden, deafening tumult, a desperate plea muffled, swallowed by the chaos, by the roar of falling rock and earth.

They stumbled unceremoniously into the open air, coughing and gasping desperately for breath, for clean air. Above them, the vast, infinite sky stretched out, a blanket of indifferent stars winking down as if to mock their desperate plight, their narrow escape. They had made it out, they were alive, but the reprieve was terrifyingly short-lived, the relief fleeting.

"Where is he? Nathan?" Susan's voice was hoarse, raw, laced with a sudden, gut-wrenching panic. They scanned the darkness frantically, their hearts sinking with each passing second. Nathan was not with them. He hadn't made it out.

"Back inside," Mark said instantly, anguish and fierce determination warring openly in his tone, in his expression. "We have to go back, we have to..."

"Wait!" Susan held up her hand, silencing him, her ears straining against the sudden, eerie silence that had fallen, listening intently. A faint, rhythmic sound emerged from the pile of rubble, from the collapsed passage – a tapping, rhythmic and strangely insistent.

"Is that...?"

"Code," Mark realised instantly, his face contorting with a mixture of relief and renewed worry as he began to mentally decode the familiar message. "He's alive. Trapped, but he's alive, Suze."

"Help's on the way, Nathan!" Susan shouted back towards the collapsed pile of earth and stone, her voice filled with a forced reassurance, though her eyes betrayed the deep uncertainty, the gnawing fear, that clawed at her, threatening to consume her. How long would it take for help to arrive? Would they reach Nathan in time, before it was too late?

"Stay strong, Nathan!" Mark shouted back towards the silent pile of earth, his voice breaking with emotion, with the strain. "We're not leaving you, mate! We'll get you out!"

"Never," Susan echoed fiercely, her resolve hardening, turning to steel.

But as the first distant sirens wailed, a mournful, approaching sound, drawing closer with every frantic heartbeat, Susan couldn't shake the persistent, gnawing fear that gripped her, a cold, suffocating hand around her heart. Had her sacrifice, her desperate actions, been enough to truly save them all? Or had it merely postponed the inevitable, merely bought them a little time before the true danger caught up with them?

And somewhere in the darkness beyond their sight, hidden threats, unseen enemies, continued to plot, their sinister whispers carried off by the cold night wind, leaving behind a chilling, unsettling promise: this, their ordeal, was far, far from over.

Chapter 17
The Confrontation

Mark Jennings stood utterly alone in the encroaching darkness, the evening mist curling lazily around his feet like spectral, grasping fingers reaching from the gloom that enveloped the surroundings. The decrepit warehouse loomed before him, a silent, imposing monolith holding both the terrifying answers and the inherent dangers of the night that lay ahead. His heart hammered an irregular, frantic beat against his ribs, each powerful thump resonating deeply with the immense weight of what was to come, of the confrontation he knew he had to face. This was it, he realised, the culmination of everything he had worked towards, the final, inevitable confrontation with the elusive mastermind whose insidious conspiracy had woven itself through the very fabric of Mark's life, leaving a trail of destruction in its wake.

He reached out instinctively, pressing a calming hand against the cold, rough brick wall of the warehouse, grounding himself firmly in the present moment, pushing away the swirling uncertainties of the future. His breaths came slow and deliberate now, controlled, the chill, damp air filling his lungs with the sharp, metallic taste of determination, of unwavering resolve. He had always known, deep down, that his unique journey, his extraordinary gift, would inevitably lead him to this precipice of truth and retribution, to this final reckoning. Now, standing on the very brink, his gift hummed beneath his skin, a low, insistent thrumming, a complex symphony of thoughts, emotions, and premonitions that could, he knew, tip the delicate balance between triumph and utter disaster.

"Alright, Mark," he whispered quietly to himself, a silent encouragement, "time to do what you do best. Time to face this head-on."

With measured, cautious steps, Mark approached the hideout's entrance, a rusted, corroded metal door hanging askew on its broken hinges, a silent, foreboding invitation. He pushed it open slowly, the metal groaning loudly in protest, a tortured sound echoing in the stillness, as he slipped inside, swallowed by the darkness. The dimly lit, cavernous room unravelled before him, shadows clinging stubbornly to the corners like dark, malevolent secrets waiting patiently to pounce, to reveal themselves. Mark's senses, already heightened by the surge of adrenaline coursing through his veins, sifted through the oppressive stillness, searching desperately for any hint, any whisper, of imminent danger.

"Any traps laid? Any dirty tricks waiting?" he murmured under his breath, his voice barely audible over the sound of his own careful footsteps echoing slightly in the vast space. It wasn't just his eyes searching the gloom; it was as if his mind extended unseen tendrils into the murky halflight, feeling, sensing, for the lingering impressions, the hidden intentions, left behind by those who had orchestrated this elaborate maze of deception, who had set this trap.

"Come on, Mark. Focus now. You need to focus." He encouraged himself inwardly, knowing full well that his extraordinary, often overwhelming, gift required calm, unwavering concentration to function at its peak, to give him the edge he desperately needed. His eyes swept slowly over the cracked concrete floor, noting the undisturbed dust, a silent betrayer of recent movement, or rather, the lack of it. The rafters high above were shrouded in impenetrable darkness, but Mark sensed no immediate threat lurking there either, no presence waiting to drop down upon him.

"Too quiet, far too quiet," he thought, suppressing the powerful urge to call out, to announce his presence, to break the tension. That, he knew instinctively, would be playing directly into their hands, precisely what they wanted, and he couldn't afford any mistakes, not now, not with Nathan counting on him, waiting for him. Every step he took was measured, calculated, and every breath was controlled, deliberate. He navigated the confusing labyrinth of crates and discarded machinery, old remnants of the building's industrial past, now silent sentinels to his careful, cautious progression deeper into the heart of the warehouse.

"Where are you hiding, then?" he questioned softly, not truly expecting an answer and receiving none, only the echo of his own voice. His mental radar, fine-tuned by years of navigating a world that often overwhelmed his senses with its intensity, detected the faintest, almost imperceptible, shift in the air, a subtle displacement, a lingering energy that spoke volumes to him. Someone had been here very recently, someone was waiting, anticipating his arrival.

"Ready or not," Mark whispered, his resolve hardening like tempered steel, settling firmly within him. "Here I come to find you."

The oppressive stillness shattered suddenly as a figure peeled away from the deep shadows, stepping deliberately into the sparse, weak light that filtered grudgingly through the grimy, broken windows high above. The mastermind's face, etched deeply with lines of arrogance, of cruelty, and chilling malice, twisted into a smirk that didn't quite manage to reach their cold, calculating eyes.

"Mark Jennings," they drawled, their voice dripping with a palpable disdain, with contempt. "You've been quite the persistent thorn in my side, haven't you?"

"Only because you've been planting nothing but toxic weeds," Mark retorted, his voice steady, unwavering, despite the frantic hammering of his heart against his ribs. He focused his intense gaze on the man before him, allowing his keen, empathetic gift to read the micro-expressions that danced fleetingly across the mastermind's features, revealing glimpses of their inner state.

"Oh, come now, Mark," the mastermind said dismissively, circling Mark slowly, deliberately, like a predator sizing up its cornered prey. "We both know perfectly well this is far, far bigger than mere weeds. It's about reshaping the entire garden, fundamentally changing everything."

"By hurting innocent people? By destroying lives?" Mark's brow furrowed deeply, his innate, powerful sense of justice flaring instantly at the thought of the immense harm inflicted by the mastermind's insidious conspiracy, the lives ruined.

"Collateral damage, Mark, is simply inevitable," the mastermind shrugged, the gesture overtly calculated to convey an utter lack of empathy, of indifference. "The greater good, you see, demands sacrifice. Necessary sacrifices."

"Your 'greater good' is nothing but a flimsy facade for your insatiable hunger for power and absolute control," Mark's voice was calm, controlled, but the undeniable undercurrent of cold anger laced his words, giving them weight. "You manipulate and destroy lives, Mark, without a single shred of remorse, without a second thought."

"Such melodrama, Mark, really," the mastermind scoffed dismissively, leaning closer, invading Mark's personal space. "But then, I suppose that's your particular strength, isn't it? Your ability to understand the human condition, to empathise so deeply with the pawns in your little game."

"Understanding people doesn't make them pawns, mate," Mark shot back instantly, his mind racing furiously to keep ahead of the dangerous verbal chess match they were engaged in. "It means recognising their inherent value, their incredible potential to do good in the world, to make a difference."

"Ah, but there, Mark, lies the fundamental difference between you and I," the mastermind replied with a sly, knowing grin, a flicker of amusement in their cold eyes. "I, you see, see their potential to serve *my* ends, to further *my* goals."

"Then you're utterly blind," Mark said, holding the mastermind's gaze steadily, refusing to look away. "Because when people finally realise they're being used, being manipulated, they'll rise up against you. They always do in the end."

"Is that what you honestly think will happen here, Mark? Right now?" The question hung heavy in the air between them, laced with a chilling, venomous mirth, with cruel anticipation.

"I don't just think it, I know it," Mark stated, his confidence surprisingly unshakeable, bolstered by the countless times he had witnessed the sheer resilience, the ultimate triumph, of the human spirit against overwhelming odds. "And I know something else, something crucial. You've profoundly underestimated me, haven't you?"

"Have I now, Mark?" The mastermind's eyebrow arched slowly, deliberately, an implicit challenge woven into the simple, seemingly innocent action.

"Every single step of the way," Mark confirmed, taking a deep, steadying breath, readying himself for whatever physical or psychological assault might come next. "And that, my friend, is ultimately going to be your downfall."

"Your confidence, Mark, is utterly misplaced," the mastermind began, a cold, humourless laugh escaping their lips, echoing slightly in the vast space, as they circled Mark like a hungry shark eyeing its vulnerable prey. "Especially now that I know all about your... special little ability."

Mark's muscles tensed instantly, coiled like a spring, but his expression remained deliberately stoic, unreadable. He had desperately hoped his gift, his unique ability to read emotions, to sense intentions, would remain his secret weapon, his hidden advantage, but now that it was out in the open, exposed, he knew he needed to be even more cautious, even more strategic in his movements.

"Ah, there it is," the mastermind said, a flicker of cruel delight in their eyes as they read Mark's subtle reaction, his internal shift. "The dawning realisation that I've been fully aware of your little secret all along, Mark. Tell me, does it frighten you? Knowing that I might just be utterly immune to your predictive charms, your emotional insights?"

"It doesn't change anything, not really," Mark countered calmly, his mind already working overtime, processing information, mapping out possible outcomes, potential lines of attack and defence, all while keeping up with the verbal jousting. "If anything, it simply confirms what I already suspected. You're afraid, aren't you? Afraid of what I can truly do, of what my gift means."

"Am I?" A wide, unsettling smirk spread slowly across the mastermind's face, a mask of false bravado. "Or am I simply intrigued by the notion of someone like you, with your rather limited gift, believing they can actually stop me? Your gift, Mark, remarkable as it may appear on the surface, has very real, very definite limits. And what exactly happens, Mark, when you push those limits too far? When the strain, the sheer mental burden, becomes simply too much for your fragile mind to bear?"

"Then I guess we'll both find out together, won't we?" Mark said, locking eyes with the mastermind, holding their gaze. Within those cold depths, he saw a fleeting flicker of an intention, a subtle shift in posture, a tightening of muscles that betrayed the next move, the next attack, before it was even made, before it was fully formed.

"Predictable," Mark murmured softly under his breath, a quiet observation, side-stepping smoothly just as the mastermind lunged forward, expecting, clearly, to catch him off guard, to surprise him. Instead, they found only empty air where Mark had stood just moments before, a frustrating void.

"Impossible!" The mastermind stumbled slightly, their carefully constructed composure cracking visibly, a fissure appearing. "How in the name of hell...? You read that from my thoughts? From my mind?"

"Partly," Mark admitted, a flicker of grim satisfaction in his eyes, feeling Nathan's safety, his well-being, anchoring him, grounding him, fuelling his fierce determination to end this, to end the mastermind's reign of terror, once and for all. "But mostly, I read it from your colossal ego, mate. You simply can't resist trying to prove you're smarter, that you're better than everyone else, that you're always one step, one move, ahead. But not this time. This time, you're the one being read."

"Your pathetic parlour tricks won't save you, Mark," the mastermind spat, regaining their balance and their outward composure, their eyes burning with renewed fury. "Nor, I assure you, will they save Nathan."

"Leave him out of this, you hear me?" Mark warned, his voice low, dangerous, and utterly devoid of any humour. Despite the clear, present threat hanging over them both, a powerful surge of protectiveness for Nathan propelled Mark forward, strengthening his resolve. His gift, he realised, wasn't just about seeing possible futures, about predicting outcomes; it was about understanding people on a fundamental level, knowing their next move because he understood their deepest fears, their burning desires, their inherent, often predictable, human nature.

"Very well," the mastermind said, retreating back into the shadows momentarily, a tactical withdrawal, before launching another sharp, verbal jab, a psychological attack. "Let's see precisely how well you fare, Mark, when the stakes are raised considerably, shall we? When the pressure is truly on?"

Mark braced himself, his muscles tensing, ready to use his gift not as a fragile crutch, not as a passive ability, but as an active, guiding force, a sharp weapon. With each calculated word, each deliberate movement from the mastermind, Mark stayed a crucial step ahead, anticipating, dodging, countering, not with brute force, which he lacked, but with the sharpness of his intellect, the speed of his mind, and the unyielding resolve to protect those he cared about, those who depended on him.

The mastermind lunged forward, a sudden, violent blur of motion clearly intended to intimidate, to overwhelm. Mark sidestepped smoothly, narrowly avoiding the brunt of the attack, feeling the rush of air as the blow missed him. The air between them crackled with a palpable tension, each second stretching out, elongated, as if heavily laden with the weight of their dual, conflicting intentions, their desperate struggle.

"Predictable," Mark countered, his voice steady, controlled, despite the surge of adrenaline coursing through him, making his heart pound. "Your anger, your rage, makes you reckless, predictable."

"Shut up!" the mastermind hissed, circling him like a trapped animal, a predator cornered. Their eyes were alight with raw fury, a testament to the sheer chaos swirling violently within them, threatening to break free.

"Anger is a loud emotion, mate," Mark continued calmly, reading the subtle twitch in the mastermind's brow, the tightening of their clenched jaw, seeing the tells. "It screams your moves, your intentions, before you even make them."

"Enough of this utter nonsense!" In a sudden, explosive flash of movement, the mastermind charged again, their fists aimed with lethal precision directly at Mark.

Mark pivoted instantly, the world narrowing to the critical space between actions and reactions, between intention and execution. He caught a wrist, twisting it sharply until he heard a guttural grunt of pain escape his opponent. His opponent recoiled momentarily, but Mark held on tightly, using the momentum of the struggle to land a strategic, painful strike to the ribs.

"Your pride," he breathed, his own movements mirroring the fluid, dangerous dance they had been ensnared in, "it blinds you completely."

"Arrogant fool!" The mastermind recovered quickly, their feet shuffling noisily on the concrete floor, setting the rhythm for another clash, another exchange of blows.

"Isn't that description more fitting for you, perhaps?" Mark parried a sharp jab, feeling the vibrations of the impact travel painfully up his arm. He used the contact, the physical connection, to gauge his adversary's resolve, sensing, feeling, that it wavered just slightly, just enough. "You consistently underestimate those you foolishly consider beneath you, don't you?"

Their exchange became a brutal symphony of grunts, thuds, and sharp intakes of breath, a physical conversation where each blow landed, each movement made, spoke volumes about their intentions, their desperation. Mark absorbed the information, both physical and emotional, his gift allowing him to sense the fissures, the weaknesses, in the mastermind's carefully constructed façade, in their control.

"Stop!" the mastermind gasped, suddenly, desperately.

"Stop what?" Mark ducked smoothly under a wide, wild swing, countering instantly with a swift sweep of the leg that sent the mastermind stumbling awkwardly, off balance. "Or stop proving that you can be read, that you can be predicted, that you can be understood, despite all your efforts?"

They locked arms, a tangled, desperate knot of limbs and wills, each vying fiercely for dominance, for control of the situation. Mark's heart pounded relentlessly in his ears, not from fear, but from the absolute clarity of his purpose, his unwavering determination. He manoeuvred, exploiting a slight overextension on his opponent's part, and twisted sharply, decisively.

"Your ego, Mark, it's your ultimate downfall," Mark said, breathless from the exertion, from the struggle. As they grappled, locked together, the dimly lit room spun crazily around them, every object within it a potential ally or a dangerous enemy. A heavy table was overturned with a crash, papers fluttering like wounded, disoriented birds to the ground.

"Damn you to hell!" the mastermind spat, the veneer of control finally cracking, desperation seeping into their voice, raw and ugly.

"Human nature," Mark replied calmly, pushing forward with a subtle, newfound strength that surprised even himself, a strength drawn not from physical prowess but from deep conviction. "Is my most powerful ally, mate."

Mark and the mastermind paused simultaneously, their breaths coming in heavy, ragged gasps in the charged, electric silence that hung thick in the air between them. Panting, Mark locked eyes with his adversary, searching desperately for even a sliver of humanity within those cold, calculating depths, a hint of the person who had once existed.

"Look at what you've become," Mark implored, his voice steady, unwavering, despite the adrenaline still coursing violently through him, making his hands tremble. "This isn't, doesn't have to be, who you are forever."

A sneer, a mask of contempt, crept onto the mastermind's face, their outward confidence, though now fragile, still stubbornly unshaken. "Spare me your pathetic, sentimental drivel, Mark. It's meaningless here."

"Sentiment, mate, is our strength, not a weakness," Mark countered, wiping a bead of sweat from his brow with a trembling hand. His hands trembled slightly, not from fear, but from the sheer, intense strain of tapping so deeply, so fully, into the furthest reaches of his gift, pushing its limits. "It's what truly connects us, what gives us purpose beyond ourselves, beyond mere survival. You know this, mate, somewhere deep down, somewhere beneath that impenetrable armour you've so carefully built around yourself."

"Connection?" The mastermind laughed, a hollow, brittle sound that echoed unnervingly off the vast, empty walls of the warehouse. "You honestly think your pathetic belief in the inherent good of people can save you, Mark? Can save Nathan?"

"It already has, mate," Mark said firmly, taking a deliberate step closer, narrowing the distance between them. He could feel the invisible, intricate threads of thought, of intention, of emotion weaving and tightening around them both, his mind working furiously overtime to predict, to anticipate, and to counteract the mastermind's every move, every thought. "Nathan believes in it, you see, believes in me, believes in the possibility of good. And deep down, mate, somewhere in that cold heart of yours, you crave that belief too, don't you?"

"Enough!" The mastermind lunged forward suddenly, violently, but Mark was ready, anticipating the move, sidestepping with a precision born of foresight, of knowing what was coming. His heart pounded frantically against his ribs, each beat a deafening countdown to an uncertain, terrifying future.

"Your anger, your fear, your desperation, I sense it all, mate," Mark continued, dodging another wild, desperate strike. "You're terrified of being seen, truly seen, for who you really are, because then you'd finally have to face yourself, the person you've become."

The mastermind hesitated, a crucial, fleeting moment of doubt flickering across their face, and in that instant, that tiny crack in their facade, Mark saw his chance, his only opportunity. With every single fibre of his being stretched taut to its absolute limit, he delved deeper, further, into the extraordinary, often overwhelming, power of his gift, his consciousness expanding, reaching out, to encompass the turbulent, chaotic thoughts swirling within the mastermind's mind.

"Think about why you even started all this, mate," Mark pressed on, his voice unwavering, steady, as he navigated the treacherous, dangerous landscape of the mastermind's fractured psyche, their buried memories. "Was it truly worth it? All the pain, the destruction, the suffering you've caused, just to hide from your own truth, from who you once were?"

"Shut up! Just shut your mouth!" The mastermind's composure finally shattered completely, their movements becoming erratic, desperate, less calculated, less controlled. It was now or never, Mark knew. This was the moment everything hinged upon.

"Let me help you, mate," Mark offered, the words surprisingly gentle, nearly lost amidst the crescendo of tension, the sounds of their struggle. "It's not too late, you know. It's not too late to choose a different path, a different ending."

The mastermind faltered visibly, their eyes flickering wildly with an intense inner battle, a profound conflict that mirrored the physical one they were clearly losing. Mark stood firm, an anchoring, unwavering presence amidst the swirling chaos, his unwavering belief in the possibility of redemption, of change, his most potent weapon, his greatest strength.

"Choose," he whispered, his voice barely audible, feeling the last precious reserves of his strength drain away, leaving him feeling utterly depleted, as he pushed his gift, his mind, to its absolute final edge, beyond what he had ever attempted before. "Choose who, who you truly want to be, mate."

The room pulsed with an almost palpable electric undercurrent, charged with the inevitable, final clash of wills, of ideologies. Mark's breath steadied, his heightened senses cutting through the dark, suffocating ambiguity that swathed the mastermind's lair, their chosen battleground. The choices he made now, in this critical moment, were the culmination of every struggle, every obstacle he had overcome, every lesson learned. It was not just his own life that hung precariously in the balance, but Nathan's too, and the countless others who had been, and would continue to be, ensnared by this web of deceit, by the mastermind's machinations.

"Your move now, mate," Mark stated firmly, his voice calm, resolute, locking eyes with the adversary who had orchestrated so much turmoil, so much suffering. His voice, a quiet island amidst the storm, bore the undeniable weight of his conviction, his purpose.

"Help me?" The mastermind sneered again, the word laced with pure venom, with bitter sarcasm. "You honestly think you can just waltz in here, Mark, and play the bloody saviour? You're nothing but a freak, mate. Your 'gift' is your bloody cage, a prison you can't escape!"

Mark's resolve tightened instantly, like a coil of steel spring being wound tighter and tighter. The mastermind's desperate attempt to rattle him, to undermine him, only served as a stark, potent reminder of how far he had truly come, of the journey he had undertaken. They didn't understand, couldn't possibly understand, that what they deemed his ultimate weakness was, in fact, his greatest, most profound strength. Mark's empathy, once a source of overwhelming confusion and pain, had blossomed, transformed, into a profound, almost supernatural understanding of the human condition, of what truly drove people – that was his true gift, his real power.

"Maybe," Mark conceded quietly, with a slight tilt of his head, acknowledging his own vulnerability, his own limitations, "but it has shown me more about humanity, mate, than you'll ever, ever know or understand."

"Humanity?" The mastermind scoffed again, a sound of pure derision. "Look where your precious humanity has gotten you, Mark. Cornered, desperate... bleeding."

"Alive," Mark interjected sharply, cutting them off, his gaze unwavering, direct. "Still alive, mate. And with the chance to make things right, to try and fix the damage. That's far more than can be said for those who choose to follow your dark path, isn't it?"

A flicker of genuine uncertainty, of doubt, crossed the mastermind's features before they managed to compose themselves once more, rebuilding their fragile facade. Mark sensed the subtle shift, the tiny crack in the armour, and he dug deeper, further, into his empathic reservoir, reaching out with his mind.

"Behind all this, mate," Mark spoke softly, each word carefully chosen, delivered with deliberate weight, "behind all the anger, the control, the manipulation... you're just scared, aren't you? Terrified. Scared of being insignificant, of being utterly forgotten by the world."

The Mind Whisperer

"Silence! I said silence!" the mastermind bellowed, their control finally snapping completely, their voice rising to a roar as Mark's words found their intended mark, piercing their defences.

Yet Mark pressed on, his voice steady, unwavering, a quiet force in the face of their rage. "But you have made an impact, mate. A profound one. Not as a shadow lurking in the darkness, but as a teacher, a dark lesson. You've taught me, you've taught us all, the absolute importance of standing up, of fighting back against injustice, against those who seek to control others."

"Enough! I've heard enough of your rubbish!" the mastermind roared again, lunging forward with a fierce, desperate determination, a final, desperate attack.

In that critical split second, that fraction of time, Mark reached out with his mind, not to defend himself physically, but to connect, to reach the person buried beneath the monster. He envisioned the intricate network of thoughts, emotions, and memories that formed the complex tapestry woven throughout the mastermind's entire life, their experiences, their choices. With a deft, precise mental touch, he unravelled a single thread, one that he sensed held the key to their undoing, to their potential redemption.

"Remember this, mate?" Mark whispered, projecting a vivid image directly into the mastermind's consciousness, an image of a younger version of themself, vibrant with hope, with dreams uncorrupted, unburdened by the darkness that had consumed them. "This... this is who you are, deep down. Who you can still be, if you choose."

The mastermind halted abruptly, their body tensing violently as the powerful memory invaded their consciousness, unbidden yet undeniable, a ghost from the past. The truth of their original intentions, once pure and noble, clashed violently with the monstrous figure they had become, the path they had chosen. A pained gasp escaped them, their psychological armour crumbling, shattering around them.

"Look at what you've built from fear, mate," Mark said softly, stepping closer now, no longer seeing a threat but a damaged soul, as their eyes locked in silent communion, a shared understanding passing between them. "Now... now imagine what you could build from hope, from belief."

It was the turning point, the undeniable climax of their battle of wills, of ideologies. Mark stood there, not as an adversary, not as an enemy, but as a mirror, reflecting back the part of the mastermind they had long since buried, long since denied. And in that reflection, in that moment of brutal self-recognition, lay their ultimate redemption, or their utter ruin.

The mastermind's expression softened subtly, their posture slackening, losing its rigid tension, as the devastating realisation dawned upon them, washing over them like a cold wave. Mark had turned the tables completely, not through brute force or violence, but through the sheer, unexpected power of connection, of empathy. Their true nature, the person they had once been, lay exposed, vulnerable, in the face of Mark's relentless compassion, his unwavering belief in the possibility of change.

The air in the hideout, though no longer thick with immediate danger, was still heavy, laden with the weight of unspoken truths, of buried regrets, now laid bare for all to see. With each shallow, shaky breath, Mark could feel the lingering tension dissipating slowly, replaced by a fragile, uncertain tranquillity that settled over the room like the first hesitant light of dawn breaking through the darkness. The mastermind, their eyes wide with the shock of profound self-recognition, of seeing the monster they had become, stepped back as if to distance themselves from the harsh reality Mark had so brutally unveiled.

"Is... is it over, Mark?" Nathan's voice, tentative, hoarse from disuse, broke the heavy silence, a hesitant question hanging in the air. He emerged slowly from the shadows where he had been a silent, terrified witness to the intense emotional exchange that had just unfolded before him.

Mark nodded, a slow, weary movement, his gaze never leaving the defeated figure of the mastermind. "It's over, Nathan. For now, we're free. We're safe."

A fragile smile fought its way onto Nathan's weary face, a flicker of relief, and for a brief moment, there was an echo of victory, hollow and uncertain, in the vast, empty room. They had survived; they had triumphed against odds that would have crushed lesser souls, broken weaker wills. But Mark's heart did not soar with triumph, with exhilaration. Instead, it was heavily laden with the gravity of what had just transpired, with the weight of the choices made, the path taken.

"Are you okay, Mark?" Nathan asked, stepping closer to Mark, his dark eyes searching Mark's face, looking for answers, for reassurance.

"Victory comes at a cost, Nathan," Mark replied quietly, his hands trembling ever so slightly at his sides, a physical manifestation of the mental strain he had just endured. His gift had carried them through the darkness, had brought them to a fragile safety, but at the immense expense of delving into the darkest, most painful recesses of another's soul, of witnessing their despair.

"Your gift..." Nathan began, his voice filled with awe and concern, but Mark cut him off gently with a weary shake of his head.

"It's more than just a gift, Nathan. It's a bloody heavy responsibility, a burden. I've seen into the abyss, felt the chilling echoes of the pain, the fear, the desperation that can drive people to do terrible, unspeakable things." Mark paused, his brow furrowed deeply as he grappled with the sheer enormity of his ability, its implications. "Every single time I use it, Nathan, I change a little. I can't help but take a piece of their story, their pain, their truth, with me."

Nathan moved closer, placing a comforting hand gently on Mark's shoulder, offering silent support. "But you see the good in people, Mark, even when they can't see it themselves anymore. That's what makes you different, what makes you special."

"Perhaps," Mark conceded quietly, allowing himself a brief moment to bask in the unexpected warmth of Nathan's unwavering support, his friendship. "But even with this bloody power, Nathan, I'm not immune to doubt, to uncertainty. With every choice I make, every time I use it, I wonder... am I truly doing the right thing? Is this the right path?"

"You saved us, Mark," Nathan insisted fiercely, his voice steadfast, unwavering. "You faced down the bloody mastermind with nothing but your wits, your courage, and your heart. That has to count for something, mate. It has to mean something important."

"Maybe it does, Nathan," Mark said with a small, wistful smile, a flicker of hope. He turned away from the defeated, motionless figure of the mastermind, who remained frozen, lost, it seemed, in their own vast sea of regret, of lost potential.

"Let's go home, Nathan," Mark said after a long, heavy silence, feeling the immense weight of the night's revelations settling upon him, pressing down.

"Home," Nathan echoed, and there was a fragile hope in that single word, a promise of healing, of safety, and perhaps, just perhaps, of new beginnings. As they walked slowly out of the hideout together, leaving the darkness and the defeated mastermind behind, the cold, suffocating grip of the past loosened, giving way to the tentative possibility of a future neither of them had dared to envision amidst the chaos, the danger.

Mark knew, with a chilling certainty, that his journey had forever altered him, fundamentally changed him, imprinting lessons, memories, and a profound understanding that would inevitably shape his path forward, defining the person he would become. With every weary step, he felt the heavy toll of his choices, the sacrifices made, and the lives irrevocably changed by his actions, by his gift. Yet, amidst the swirling emotions, the lingering pain, there remained a steady, quiet resolve, the deep-seated knowledge that, when faced with darkness, with despair, he would always, always choose to kindle the light, to fight for hope.

The night's chill had settled heavily over the city as Mark and Nathan made their way slowly through the shadowed, deserted streets, the echo of their footsteps a sharp, staccato accompaniment to the thrumming, pervasive silence that surrounded them. The residual excitement, the lingering tension of the evening's terrifying events, still crackled between them, an almost palpable electric current that buzzed with unanswered questions, with unspoken fears and uncertainties.

"Mark," Nathan said, his breath forming visible clouds in the cold, damp air, "do you honestly think it's really over? Truly finished?"

Pausing under the dim, flickering glow of a lone streetlamp, Mark considered the question carefully, weighing the possibilities. His mind replayed the intense confrontation with the mastermind, the calculated risks he had taken, and the terrifying moment when victory had seemed both utterly inevitable and yet completely out of reach. "I don't know, Nathan," he admitted honestly, his voice barely above a whisper, a raw sound. "But we've definitely disrupted their bloody plans, haven't we? We've thrown a spanner in the works. That has to count for something, surely."

"Disrupted, yes," Nathan agreed, but his brow furrowed deeply as he glanced nervously over his shoulder, a shiver that wasn't from the cold running down his spine, a prickle of unease. "But people like that, Mark, people like the mastermind... they don't just give up, do they? Not easily, anyway."

Mark's eyes followed Nathan's gaze, scanning the surrounding darkness, searching for any sign of pursuit, any hint that the battle they'd fought, the victory they had snatched from the jaws of defeat, was merely a prelude to the larger, more dangerous war that might inevitably follow. "They might not, you're probably right," he conceded, feeling the heavy weight of responsibility settle upon him anew, a familiar burden. "But I'll be ready for them, Nathan. And we'll be ready. Together."

"Your gift..." Nathan began again, his voice hesitant, then stopped, his expression fraught with deep concern, with worry for Mark. "It's incredible, Mark, truly amazing, but it takes so much out of you, doesn't it? Physically, mentally... Can you keep doing this, Mark? Should you keep doing this?"

"Should I?" Mark echoed, turning to face Nathan squarely, meeting his gaze directly. A small smile tugged at the corners of his mouth, faint but undeniably genuine, a flicker of warmth. "When I see someone in danger, Nathan, when I know, truly know, that I can help them, that I have the ability to make a difference... there's no choice to make, is there? It's just something I have to do." He placed a gentle, reassuring hand on Nathan's shoulder. "As long as I have this ability, Nathan, this gift... I'll use it to protect those who need it, to fight for those who can't fight for themselves."

Nathan nodded slowly, reassured, comforted by the quiet conviction in Mark's voice, by the strength of his resolve, but as they resumed walking side by side, a new, unsettling tension knotted his stomach, a sense of unease. They were approaching the familiar front of their shared apartment building, the place they called home, their sanctuary, yet something felt subtly amiss, like a single note played jarringly off-key in an otherwise harmonious symphony.

"Wait, Mark," Nathan said abruptly, halting suddenly in his tracks, his voice sharp with sudden apprehension. "Do you feel that? Something's not right."

Mark paused instantly, attuning his heightened senses, his gift, to the surrounding environment, searching for the source of Nathan's unease. There was something, he realised, a subtle shift in the air, a palpable sense of expectation, of waiting, hanging heavy and oppressive around them, almost suffocating. Before he could respond, a flicker of movement, quick and unexpected, caught his eye from the dark, narrow alley beside their building.

"Get down! Now!" he shouted, his voice sharp with urgency, pulling Nathan violently down with him as the sudden, loud sound of shattering glass pierced the quiet night, echoing like a gunshot. They hit the cold pavement hard, rolling instinctively into the relative cover of a nearby doorway, seeking shelter. Heart pounding furiously in his chest, Mark peered cautiously into the dark alley, his gift scanning, reaching out, searching for intentions, for the thoughts, the emotions, of whoever lurked within the shadows.

"Are they after us, Mark? Is it the mastermind's people? Have they found us already?" Nathan whispered frantically, his voice trembling with fear.

"Shh," Mark urged, his focus narrowing, intensifying, as he reached out with his mind, trying desperately to discern the motives, the intentions, of their unseen assailant, their attacker. But there was nothing there, no malice, no intent, no discernible human thoughts to read, only a chilling emptiness.

"Maybe... maybe it's not about us, Nathan," Mark ventured, his pulse slowly beginning to steady as the immediate threat seemed to inexplicably dissipate, to vanish. "Could it have just been a stray cat knocking something over, or... or maybe it was just the wind?"

"Or... or maybe it's a message, Mark," Nathan finished grimly, his voice low and serious. "A bloody warning that it's not over, Mark. That we're not safe here. Not yet."

As the two men huddled together in the relative safety of the doorway, the silence of the night returned, settling around them, heavy and foreboding. Mark knew, deep down, that Nathan might be right, that the shattered glass, the unexplained noise, might be the first ripple of a dangerous tide coming to sweep them away, to drag them back into the darkness. Yet, as he looked at Nathan, at his friend's face etched with a mixture of fear and unwavering determination, he made a silent, solemn vow to himself.

"Whatever comes next, Nathan," Mark said, his voice low, steady, and filled with quiet resolve, "we'll face it together. Every step of the way. And we'll end it, Nathan. For good. Once and for all."

The distant, mournful wail of sirens began to cut through the stillness of the night, its approaching cry a haunting promise that the dawn, whenever it arrived, would undoubtedly bring new challenges, new dangers to face. As Mark helped Nathan to his feet, pulling him up from the cold pavement, he couldn't shake the unsettling feeling, the deep-seated intuition, that the true test of his gift, of his resolve, and of their friendship, was still yet to come.

Chapter 18
The Reckoning

The atmosphere was dense with the pungent scent of rust and desolation as Mark Jennings entered the vast, echoing expanse of the warehouse. His footsteps resonated softly against the concrete floor, each step a measured beat in the silent tension that hung in the air. Shadows clung to the walls like spectres, their forms shifting and flickering in the dimness, disturbed only by the faint, weak shafts of moonlight slicing through the broken panes of glass. His breath appeared in visible puffs, the cold seeping into his exposed skin, tightening his muscles and sharpening his senses.

A voice, smooth and sinister as silk yet laced with venom, slithered from the darkness. "Mark Jennings," it hissed, curling around the shadows like a serpent. "You've been quite the thorn in my side."

Mark's eyes narrowed, focusing intently on the silhouette emerging from the gloom. The figure, the mastermind, cloaked in the obscurity of the dimly lit warehouse, moved with an unsettling grace, calculated, predatory. The faint glow of moonlight caught on their features, revealing a face marked by confidence and menace.

"Tell me," Mark said, his voice calm and steady despite the palpable tension, "what is it you want?"

The mastermind chuckled softly, a sound that was amused and condescending all at once. "Want?" The word was delivered with a sneer, a mixture of amusement and disdain. "It's not about want, dear Mark. It's about need. The world needs reshaping, and I am the sculptor. Power, control, everything is within my grasp."

A chill ran down Mark's spine as the weight of the mastermind's words pressed down on him, heavy and oppressive. It was as though the very air around them had thickened, suffocating in its intensity.

"You see," the mastermind continued, voice dropping to a whisper, "while you cling to your precious morals, I embrace the true nature of humanity, the desire to dominate, to conquer. And I will be the one to lead them."

The taunt was designed to disorient, to sow fear and doubt. But Mark remained unmoved, his eyes unwavering, locked onto the figure before him. He understood the stakes; he could feel the danger emanating from every word the mastermind uttered. Yet, he held his ground.

"Your vision is flawed," Mark replied, his tone edged with confidence, unwavering. "Power doesn't give you the right to control others."

The mastermind's lips curled into a sneer. "Ah, but you're wrong," they retorted, taking a deliberate step forward. The distance between them diminished, like the waning hope of a peaceful resolution slipping away. "Might makes right. And I possess might in spades. People like you, with your soft hearts and idealistic dreams, will always lose in the end."

A shiver of anticipation rippled through the warehouse, a silent witness to the confrontation unfolding within its walls. The game of cat and mouse had reached its climax. Mark knew that the next move would be critical.

"Then let's see whose beliefs truly hold power," Mark declared, his voice resolute, a beacon of steadfastness in the encroaching darkness.

The words hung in the air, the symbolic line drawn in this deadly game. Mark's gaze never left the mastermind's, his mind reaching out like tendrils of smoke, subtle, insidious, probing the thoughts swirling within the mastermind's mind. The warehouse seemed to hold its breath, the only sound the distant drip of water from a leaky pipe echoing through the silence.

Mark's gift unfurled, an invisible wave pulsing outward, a mental sonar that allowed him to see beyond the physical realm. He began to perceive the torrent of thoughts racing through the mastermind's head, plans, fears, ambitions, fragmented pieces of a dangerous puzzle.

"Planning to use the city's reliance on technology against itself," Mark murmured almost to himself, piecing together the fragments. "A digital coup d'état, hidden behind a veneer of chaos."

The mastermind's eyebrow twitched, a shadow of unease crossing their otherwise composed features. "Clever... but knowing my plan won't save you or your little protégé," they sneered, though a tremor of uncertainty betrayed them.

"Vulnerabilities," Mark whispered, gaining confidence as insight flooded his mind. "You haven't accounted for the human element, the unpredictability, the resilience." He stepped forward deliberately. "You underestimate people. Their capacity to unite in crisis, to fight back."

The mastermind spat dismissively, "Empty words from a desperate man." But a flicker of doubt crossed their face, a tell Mark did not miss.

"Am I?" Mark challenged, a hint of a smile curling at his lips. "Nathan!" he called, his voice echoing off the walls. "Remember what we talked about, hope, fighting back. It's time!"

From the shadows, Nathan emerged, eyes wide but burning with newfound resolve. Mark felt a surge of pride and connection as the young man's determination aligned with his own, an unspoken pledge forged in adversity. The atmosphere seemed to hum with the energy of their shared intent.

"Hope is more than just a word," Mark declared, stepping beside Nathan. "It's our weapon. Together, we will dismantle your plans and expose the truth."

The mastermind laughed, but it was hollow, bitter. "Two against one? You think you can topple an empire with platitudes and daydreams?"

"It's not the size of the force but the strength of the belief," Mark replied firmly. "And believe me, the goodness of humanity will prevail over your cynicism."

The mastermind hissed, "Let's put that belief to the test, shall we?" with a predatory grace, eyes gleaming with lethal intent, poised to strike.

But Mark stood firm, shoulder to shoulder with Nathan, his mind a lighthouse cutting through the darkness. He was ready to shield his friend, to prove that even in the bleakest places, hope could ignite a revolution.

"Your faith in humanity is nothing more than a child's bedtime story," the mastermind sneered, circling like a vulture. "People are selfish, corruptible, easily manipulated. I merely give them the nudge they need."

Mark felt the sting of those words, an assault crafted to fracture his resolve. The air thickened with malice, and for a moment, the mastermind's contempt seemed to seep into the very walls of the warehouse.

"Perhaps some are as you say," Mark acknowledged quietly, voice steady despite the venom, "but even the darkest night gives way to dawn. You focus on shadows, but I see the stars."

The mastermind paused, their silhouette outlined by the scant light filtering through broken windows. "Ah, shadows are my domain, Mr. Jennings," they murmured. "And in them, your so-called 'stars' are snuffed out like candles in the wind."

"Shadows exist only because of light," Mark retorted, feeling Nathan's steady presence behind him, an anchor of resolve. His own fears wrestled within him, but he wove his next words with conviction, rooted in the hope that had brought him this far. "You underestimate the power of the human spirit. It's resilient, unyielding. Even now, people out there fight against the darkness you cherish."

A harsh, grating laugh echoed through the space. "And what will they do when I reveal the chaos you've hidden from them? When their illusions shatter?"

"They will do what humans have done since time immemorial," Mark replied. "They adapt, they overcome. They find hope amid the rubble."

"Hope?" the mastermind scoffed. "A flimsy shield against the might I wield."

"Stronger than you realise," Mark countered, heart pounding but his voice unwavering. "It's hope that unites us, that drives us to protect one another, to strive for a better world. That's what you're up against, not just me, but the collective will of humanity."

The mastermind's eyes flickered with disdain. "Beautiful sentiment. Let's see if it holds when I strip it all away," they hissed, their stance poised to strike at Mark's deepest convictions.

But Mark remained unwavering. He stood firm, feeling the currents of thoughts and emotions swirling around him, a symphony of human resilience. He knew fear and despair could be weapons, but so could empathy and courage.

"Every person has the capacity for good, for change," he declared, locking eyes with the dark figure. "I believe in that potential. I believe in us. And that belief is the foundation on which we will build a new world, one where your twisted vision has no place."

The mastermind's composure flickered, a moment of doubt breaking through his otherwise impassive facade. Mark sensed the crack, pressing forward.

"Your plans will fail because you've forgotten one fundamental truth: we're stronger together," Mark affirmed. Somewhere in the depths of the warehouse, the silence seemed to echo his words, as if the very walls agreed.

His breaths were short, controlled, as he faced the mastermind, both of them illuminated only by the faint, fractured light from the broken windows. The silence was heavy, pregnant with anticipation. Mark could feel the weight of darkness pressing against him, a tangible force trying to drown his resolve.

"Predictable," the mastermind sneered, a thin smile curling on his lips. "You stand there yammering about hope and unity, but are you prepared to face death, Mr. Jennings?"

"Ready as I'll ever be," Mark replied, his mind a whirlwind of focus. His advantage was clear: his extraordinary ability to anticipate thoughts before they turned into actions. It was more than instinct; it was a dance of synapses, allowing him to see the moves before they were made.

Suddenly, the mastermind lunged, a hidden blade gleaming malevolently in the dim light. But Mark had already perceived the intent, the subtle shift in weight, the tightening of muscles, the flicker of malice in their eyes. Time seemed to stretch and slow, giving him just enough to sidestep, feeling the rush of air as the blade sliced past inches from his skin.

"Nice try," Mark exhaled, heart pounding, his movements fluid amid adrenaline. The mastermind recovered swiftly, circling like a predator stalking its prey, each step deliberate and measured.

"Your mind tricks won't save you forever," the mastermind taunted, their voice echoing in the cavernous space.

"Maybe not," Mark admitted, wiping sweat from his brow. "But they're buying me time. Time for you to slip up."

"Or for you to make a mistake," the mastermind hissed venomously.

The mental duel intensified, a tug-of-war of wills and thoughts. Mark understood that the mastermind was trying to wear him down, psychologically testing him, seeking to break his focus. But Mark drew strength from within, from the compassion and hope that fuelled him.

"Isn't it tiring?" Mark asked softly, despite the fatigue gnawing at his limbs. "All this hatred, all this scheming... where does it lead you?"

"Power," the mastermind spat. "Control. A world shaped by my hand."

"And yet here you are," Mark said quietly, "fighting someone who believes in something greater than himself. Doesn't that say anything?"

"Enough!" The mastermind's voice boomed as he launched himself forward once more, launching into a flurry of calculated strikes designed to disorient and overwhelm. His movements were swift, precise, each punch a deliberate attempt to break Mark's defence.

Mark responded instinctively, parrying each feint and jab with a calm that belied the chaos. His senses sharpened; he read microexpressions, muscle twitches, and subtle breathing patterns, elements that betrayed his opponent's intentions. Years of honing his ability to tune into others' emotional frequencies had made him a formidable opponent, even in these desperate moments. Yet, the relentless barrage drained his reserves, each dodge and counter sapping more strength.

"Getting tired, Mr. Jennings?" The mastermind's voice dripped with mockery, a cruel smirk curling his lips as he sensed victory within reach.

"Exhausted," Mark admitted, voice steady despite the pounding in his chest, "but not defeated. Not yet." His words were a lifeline, a reminder to himself that as long as he could stand, he could still fight.

"Then let's end this," the mastermind growled, eyes blazing with anticipation. He prepared for what he believed would be the final, decisive blow.

But Mark was ready. His gift surged within him, an internal compass that pinpointed the exact moment to strike. His resolve hardened as he drew on a newfound determination, bracing himself for the upcoming, gruelling phase of the confrontation.

Meanwhile, Nathan was pressed against a cold, steel pillar, his breaths shallow and rapid, chest heaving with the panic that clung to him like a second skin. He watched helplessly as Mark deftly dodged another telegraphed punch. A flicker of something shifted within him, an ember of resolve igniting amid the despair that had settled deep in his heart. He could no longer afford to be a passive spectator to his own fate.

"Mark!" Nathan's voice cracked with raw determination, breaking through the tension. "I'm with you!"

At the sound of Nathan's rallying cry, Mark cast a quick glance, sharing a silent moment of connection that spoke volumes. There were no words needed; the message was clear: *Together.*

Refocusing inward, Mark extended his senses beyond the physical confines of the warehouse, reaching into the collective consciousness around him. Fear, anticipation, hope, all swirled into an ethereal tapestry that only he could perceive. It was as if he was conducting an orchestra of human emotion, each note resonating deeply within his spirit.

"Your mind tricks won't work on me forever, Jennings," the mastermind spat, circling with predatory focus, eyes narrowing as he readied his next move.

"Maybe not," Mark replied, eyes narrowing further as he sifted through the cacophony of thoughts. "But they're not just my tricks."

The mastermind faltered for a split second, confusion flickering across his face. That was the moment Mark seized. Not with fists, but with words, words infused with the collective will of those who opposed him.

"Can you feel it?" Mark's voice rang out through the warehouse, resonating with power. It was more than an echo; it was a chorus.

"Every person you've tried to break, every life you've disrupted, they're here with me."

Nathan, moved by the moment, found his own rhythm, almost unconsciously synchronising with Mark's. It was as if the energy that pulsed through Mark now flowed into him, lending courage and sharpening focus.

"Your vision for the future," Mark continued, circling the mastermind as he had, "it's hollow. Because it's missing the one thing that makes us truly human: our connection to one another."

"Silence!" The mastermind lunged, but his movements grew frantic and desperate. The unity of purpose between Mark and Nathan disrupted his concentration, and his confidence waned under the weight of their combined resolve.

"Look around you," Nathan added, stepping closer, shoulder to shoulder with Mark. "This isn't strength. It's fear."

"Enough of this!" The mastermind's voice cracked under the strain, the veneer of composure cracking as the psychic assault intensified.

Mark's gift reached its crescendo, a surge of empathic power that rippled through the space. He felt the mastermind's resolve faltering, the discordant, chaotic thoughts betraying his inner turmoil. Nathan's presence beside him was a tangible anchor, an unspoken reminder that they fought as one.

"Your hold is breaking," Mark declared, voice steady and unwavering, imbued with the conviction of many. "We stand united, and we will not let darkness prevail."

The mastermind staggered back, visibly struggling to maintain control. The atmosphere around them shifted, a palpable sense of impending victory, not rooted in physical dominance but in the resilience of the human spirit.

Mark's senses zeroed in on the mastermind's erratic heartbeat, the jagged rhythm of his thoughts exposing a mind in chaos. The warehouse echoed with their heavy breathing, the oppressive silence amplifying the tension, static crackling in the air like an electric storm.

"Your grand scheme," Mark said, voice echoing against the crumbling walls, "is built on a foundation of sand." He took a deliberate step forward, the sound of his footsteps a drumbeat to his words. "I've seen inside your mind. Your plans are unraveling, even as we speak."

"Impossible!" The mastermind spat, his composure slipping as shadows flickered across his face under the flickering overhead lights.

"Is it?" Mark's gaze remained unwavering. "You sought to control through fear, but fear is a fragile weapon. It fractures under the weight of hope."

With a sudden, decisive movement, Mark reached out, not with his hands, but with his extraordinary gift. It was as if he pulled back the veil on the mastermind's deepest secrets, laying bare the truth for all to see. Across the interconnected web of consciousness, the mastermind's deception spread like wildfire, illuminating his lies.

"Your lies are exposed," Mark announced, his voice rising to a clarion call that seemed to reverberate beyond the warehouse's walls. "The world sees you for what you truly are."

The mastermind howled in frustration, animalistic and primal, as rage and defiance overtook him. He lunged at Mark, intent on silencing him, but Mark was prepared. His ability to anticipate actions before they unfolded gave him the upper hand.

"Humanity will always rise above those who seek to divide it," Mark said, sidestepping the attack with a grace born of certainty. "We are stronger together."

The mastermind's wild eyes flickered with fury. "I will not be undone by the likes of you!"

"By the likes of us," Nathan corrected, voice firm and resolute. He had found his footing beside Mark, his own resolve solidified by the fight they fought side by side.

Mark nodded in acknowledgment, a silent pledge passing between them. The mastermind charged once more, desperation driving his final assault. But Mark was a step ahead, moving with deliberate precision. As the mastermind surged past, Mark used his momentum against him, executing a targeted push that sent him crashing into a stack of crates. The impact reverberated through the warehouse, leaving the mastermind disoriented and defeated, gasping raggedly.

"We choose light over darkness," Mark declared firmly, standing tall despite the exhaustion that clung to him. "We choose hope over despair."

Nathan approached the fallen figure, a mixture of pity and triumph in his eyes. "And we stand together."

Breathing heavily, Mark allowed himself a brief moment to absorb the scene. They had won, not through violence, but through the indomitable strength of compassion and unity. Nathan looked at him, a silent nod passing between them, a recognition of the bond forged through shared ordeal.

The mastermind's plans lay shattered, his grip on power broken. Mark knew the fight for a better world was far from over, but tonight, they had delivered a significant blow in defence of humanity. The goodness in people's hearts had been their greatest weapon, and it would continue to be their guiding light.

"Let's go," Mark said quietly to Nathan, voice steady with purpose.

"There's much to do, and this is only the beginning," Nathan replied, determination etched into his features.

Together, they walked out of the warehouse, leaving darkness behind and stepping into the promise of a new dawn.

Outside, the night air was crisp and invigorating. Mark's breath came out in visible puffs as he leaned against the cold brick wall, his energy waning but his spirit still ablaze.

"Did we just…" Nathan's voice trailed off, disbelief evident in the tone.

Mark offered a tired but genuine smile. "Yes, we did," he confirmed, feeling the weight of their victory settle around them like a warm blanket. "Together."

Nathan chuckled softly, raking a hand through his dark hair, a nervous gesture but one that hinted at newfound peace. "I never thought… I mean, with your mind-reading thing and all…"

"Gift," Mark corrected gently. He pushed himself off the wall, steadying himself. "And it's not just mine. Everyone has something special about them. Sometimes, it takes a crisis to bring it out."

"Guess you're right." Nathan looked up at the stars emerging above, his eyes reflecting hope. "You always believed in that, didn't you? The goodness in people?"

"Always," Mark affirmed, his gaze following Nathan's upward glance. "It's what keeps us going. It's what makes us fight against impossible odds."

"Man, you sound like a superhero or something," Nathan said with a small laugh, though the respect in his voice was unmistakable.

"Maybe we all are, in our own way," Mark replied thoughtfully. His mind drifted to those they had inspired tonight. "We just need to find our power and use it for good."

"Like empathy and understanding?" Nathan asked, turning to fully face Mark.

"Exactly," Mark nodded. "Empathy is my superpower. It connects me to others. But more than that, it allows me to see the world through their eyes. If I can do that, anyone can."

"Thanks to you, they'll want to try," Nathan said quietly, a new confidence shining in his eyes. He had entered this battle haunted by doubt, but now he stood beside Mark, ready to face whatever lay ahead.

"Perhaps that's the real victory tonight," Mark mused aloud. "Not just saving you or defeating the mastermind, but igniting a spark of belief in others."

"Belief in what?" Nathan asked, sceptical yet intrigued.

"In themselves," Mark replied with conviction. "In the difference they can make. In the light they can choose over darkness."

"Damn," Nathan breathed out, a smile spreading across his face. "You really are something else, Mark Jennings."

"Thank you, Nathan." Mark's eyes twinkled. "But remember, so are you."

They lingered for a moment longer, the bond forged through struggle and triumph unbreakable. Then, with a collective breath, they turned away from the warehouse, stepping into the night to share their message of hope and resilience with a world that desperately needed it.

The cool night air brushed against them as they strode purposefully, their footsteps falling in unison on the pavement. The world around them was a tapestry of shadows and silver moonlight, but to Nathan, the darkness no longer felt oppressive, it was merely a backdrop for the stars.

"Can you feel it, Nathan?" Mark's voice broke the silence, tinged with excitement that made each word feel like a revelation. "The pulse of the city, the heartbeat of a million dreams waiting to be realised?"

Nathan glanced sideways, eyes adjusting to the optimism shining from within Mark. "Yeah, I do," he admitted. It was a strange, new sensation, the faint thrum of potential coursing through him.

"Every person we pass is a story," Mark continued, his gaze sweeping over the quiet streets. "A universe of thoughts and feelings. Just imagine what we could achieve if everyone understood that."

"Like some sort of thought revolution?" Nathan quipped, though his words lacked humour, tinged instead with sincerity.

"Exactly!" Mark said, clapping him on the back with brotherly warmth. "A revolution of empathy and compassion. It starts small, but it grows. You and I are just the beginning."

Nathan felt himself swept up in Mark's vision, the contagious hope that radiated from him. "We're going to need a plan, though. This isn't something that'll happen overnight."

"Of course," Mark agreed, already thinking through strategies and ideas. "But every act of kindness, every moment of understanding, those are the building blocks. They become part of a larger movement."

"Spread enough ripples," Nathan said thoughtfully, "and eventually, you get a wave."

"Exactly," Mark replied, a bright smile on his face even in the dim light. "And waves can reshape the shore."

"Then let's make sure it's for the better," Nathan declared with resolve, determination etched into his features.

Their conversation drifted effortlessly as they wandered through the city, mapping out a future neither had dared to dream of before, outreach programmes, workshops to harness Mark's abilities, stories to inspire others.

"Tomorrow," Mark announced as they reached a bridge overlooking the river, "we begin again. We reach out, teach, learn. And most importantly, never give up."

"Sounds like a plan, Mark," Nathan responded, his voice firm and committed. It was more than words; it was a vow.

The Mind Whisperer

Mark extended his hand. "Ready for this?"

Nathan grasped it, a firm, resolute grip. "Let's do it."

Together, they looked out at the horizon, where the first hints of dawn promised a new day, an opportunity to forge a better world.

With hearts full of hope and minds focused on their mission, Mark Jennings and Nathan Walker stepped forward into the emerging light, united in purpose to weave a tapestry of understanding across a world in desperate need of it.

Chapter 19
Renewal

Mark sat hunched over the worn wooden table, his fingertips tracing the grain as if it might somehow reveal a hidden answer. A furrow of concentration creased his brow, a visible testament to the internal cacophony of doubt that relentlessly plagued him. The weight of expectation pressed down upon his shoulders like a heavy cloak, woven from countless threads of past failures and missteps. The room surrounding him was silent, yet his mind was anything but quiet.

"Mark?" Susan's voice sliced through the stillness, gentle yet firm, a reminder that he was not alone in his contemplation.

He looked up slowly, meeting her concerned gaze with eyes that seemed older than his years. "Susan... I just don't know anymore. What if this gift of mine is more of a curse?" His hands fell to his lap, the question lingering between them like a spectre.

"Talk to me, Mark," she urged, pulling up a chair beside him. She took his hand softly, her touch a lifeline in the turbulent sea of his uncertainty.

"It's just... I've been trying to help, you know that. But there are so many times when it feels like I'm not making any difference at all. Maybe I'm not meant to do this." The words tumbled out, each one laden with the burden of unspoken fears.

"Mark, you're always too hard on yourself. You care so deeply, perhaps even too much sometimes." Susan's voice was gentle, but beneath it lay steel, strength born of years of being his anchor.

"Is it enough, though? To care?" Mark's voice cracked, exposing the raw vulnerability beneath his carefully maintained exterior. "What if my predictions are wrong? What if I can't see the path clearly?"

"Then you'll find another way," she answered without hesitation. "You always have. Your gift... it's remarkable, Mark. But it's not infallible, and neither are you. That doesn't diminish the good you've already done."

"But what about the harm? The people I couldn't save, the mistakes I've made..." He couldn't mask the despair tinting his confession.

"Listen to me, brother. You are human, and your gift is a tool, nothing more. It's not who you are. You are kind, intelligent, and one of the most amazing people I know. You've touched lives, Mark, changed them for the better. That counts for something."

Her conviction was a soothing balm to the sting of his self-doubt, a gentle warmth that began to thaw the ice of his fears. She believed in him unequivocally, and in that moment, her unwavering faith served as a beacon, guiding him back from the precipice of his troubled thoughts.

"Thank you, Susan. I just... I want to make a difference. I need to know that all this, everything I'm doing, isn't for nothing."

"Trust me, it's not," she replied softly. "I see it every day, the impact you have. And you'll see it too, in time. Just don't give up, alright?" Her smile was like the dawn breaking through the night, promising hope amidst darkness.

"Okay," he echoed, a small smile beginning to form on his lips. In his heart, the seed of hope Susan had planted started to take root, pushing against the soil of his doubts, yearning for the light.

Mark walked alone, his footsteps echoing softly on the cobblestone path that meandered through the community park. Her words lingered in his mind, weaving through his thoughts like threads of silver light. As he passed a bench, an elderly couple smiled at him, their hands intertwined. The sight nudged Mark into a gentle reverie.

"Mr. Jennings," Mrs. Henderson had said just weeks before, her voice frail yet imbued with strength. "You found my granddaughter when no one else could. You brought her back to us." Her eyes, brimming with tears, had locked onto his, and he felt the depth of her gratitude. That memory filled him with quiet joy. He had helped them, and truly made a difference in their lives.

A child's laughter pulled him from his reflection. On a nearby playground, a boy who once struggled to fit in now played tag with friends, a scene Mark had quietly orchestrated months ago, with just a few whispers of encouragement and understanding. The boy's mother hugged him, whispering, "He smiles again, all because of you."

Yet, as these vignettes of success danced in his mind, a shadow crept over them. With a heavy heart, Mark settled onto an empty bench, gazing at the lake where ripples disturbed the otherwise placid surface. Could he truly save everyone? The question was a weighty anchor dragging along the bottom of his soul. His ability to read thoughts, to predict actions, it was extraordinary, yet undeniably finite.

"Even with this gift," Mark muttered to himself, "there are forces beyond my reach, decisions I can't influence, paths I cannot alter."

A swan glided across the water, serene in its solitary grace. In the elegant arc of its neck, Mark saw the embodiment of nature's indifference to human struggles. It moved unaffected by the complexities of human life, and in that simplicity, Mark envied it. He had seen too much, felt too deeply the tremors of thoughts not his own.

"Can I be content with touching some lives while others slip away?" he asked the breeze, though it offered no answer.

"Mark?"

He turned, searching for the source of the voice, but found only rustling leaves and distant chatter of families enjoying the afternoon sun.

"Is it enough?" he pondered aloud, fully aware that the question was directed inward, a plea for reassurance from the depths of his uncertain heart.

The Mind Whisperer

"Is it enough to save a few and not all?" The question lingered in the air, unanswered, yet Mark sensed the beginning of acceptance, a surrender to the limitations of his own humanity. There would always be battles he couldn't win and people he couldn't rescue from their fates. But those he could reach, those he could help, they were his victories, small beacons of light against the encroaching darkness.

"Perhaps," he whispered as a pair of ducks took flight, their silhouettes casting shadows against the sky. "That has to be enough."

His fingers brushed over the back of a park bench, his mind still echoing with questions that had no clear answers. The sun was beginning its descent, splashing golden hues across the path before him. In this fading light, Mark saw a figure approaching, initially just a silhouette, then a familiar face.

"Mr. Jennings?" called a voice tinged with hope and weariness.

He turned, his sharp eyes focusing on a woman in her late twenties. She wore a coat that had seen better days, her hair pulled back in a haphazard ponytail. Recognition dawned. She was Emily, he remembered her from a year ago, a troubled soul whose thoughts had been as tangled as knots in her hair.

"Emily," he said softly, the name slipping from his lips like a whisper of the past. "How have you been?"

"Better," she replied, her eyes brimming with unshed tears. "So much better since I met you. I... I never got the chance to thank you properly."

"Helping you was my pleasure," Mark said gently, his empathy embracing the space between them. "You don't owe me thanks."

"But I do!" Emily insisted, taking a tentative step forward. "You might not realise it, Mr. Jennings, but you saved me. That day at the coffee shop, when you told me to trust my instincts about leaving my job, it changed everything."

He vividly remembered that encounter. He had sensed her inner turmoil, the weight of a decision that could alter her whole life. His advice had been a simple nudge, but to her, it had felt like so much more.

"Your courage changed your life, Emily," he corrected softly. "I merely helped you see what was already there."

"Maybe so," she said with a small smile, "but without you... I wouldn't be here, about to start my own business." A beam of joy broke through her face, a fragile hope in a tumultuous world. "You have this incredible gift, Mr. Jennings. Please, never doubt that."

Her words pierced the fog of his doubts, resonating within him. Emily's gratitude was a warm balm to the cold insecurities that had crept into his heart. She was the embodiment of hope he feared was fading.

"Thank you, Emily," Mark said, feeling the corners of his mouth lift for the first time in days. "Knowing you're doing well means more than you can imagine."

"Then let that be enough," she urged. "Even heroes can't save everyone. But for people like me, you don't just touch our lives, you transform them."

As she walked away, steps lighter than when she had arrived, Mark felt a seed of realisation take root. He couldn't hold the world in his palms, couldn't whisper away every sorrow or right every wrong. But Emily was proof of the power he did possess, the ability to bring comfort and hope to those he encountered.

"Perhaps," he mused aloud, his voice steadier now, "the true measure of a gift lies not in its reach but in its touch."

He watched her figure disappear around a bend, etched against the dimming sky. For the first time in a long while, Mark felt a sense of peace settle over him. His gift might have limits, but its impact was boundless. In that realisation, he found the strength to embrace the twilight, ready to meet the darkness with resilience and an open heart.

He settled onto the old, worn cushion he kept in the corner of his living room, a place for moments like this. The day's fading light filtered through the blinds, casting striped shadows across the floor and walls. He picked up the leather-bound journal that had become both confidant and witness to his tumultuous journey of thoughts.

"October 20th," he began, his pen hovering over the page as if uncertain where to land. "Today, I met Emily again. She reminded me why... why I do this."

He paused, memories bubbling to the surface. The pen danced across the paper, capturing his introspection. Words flowed, articulating the doubts gnawing at his mind and the gratitude that seemed to be a balm to his weary spirit.

"Is it enough?" he wrote, the question stark against the white page. "Is the touch of comfort more meaningful than the breadth of salvation?"

The journal closed with a soft thud, a temporary end to an ongoing dialogue. Mark leaned back against the wall, allowing stillness to envelop him. His breathing deepened, eyes closing as he listened to the whispers of his own heart.

A sudden ruckus outside drew his attention. He rose and parted the blinds, peering out into the street just in time to see a young boy drop his ice cream onto the pavement. Tears welled in the child's eyes as he stared at the melting mess.

"Hey, it's okay!" called a girl no older than the boy, strolling past. She knelt beside him, a gentle smile on her face. "Look, I've got one too. Let's share mine, okay?"

The boy's face lit up; tears replaced by a wide-eyed hope. Mark watched as they sat on the curb together, the girl carefully splitting her treat and handing half to him. They laughed, a simple moment of tenderness that transcended the chaos around them.

"See, Mark?" he whispered to himself, warmth spreading in his chest. "Kindness… it exists in the smallest gestures."

With renewed energy, he returned to his cushion, flipping open his journal once more.

"Today, I witnessed a simple act of sharing, an echo of my own purpose," he wrote, his hand steady. "It's not about grand heroics. It's about these moments… small, yet infinite in their significance."

Each word became an affirmation, a pledge to his path. His gift stirred within him, not as a burden, but as a beacon, a light to guide others through darkness, one kind act at a time.

"Let this be my promise," he concluded, etching the words into the page. "To use my gift not as a shield against despair, but as a reminder of the goodness that thrives amidst it all."

He snapped the journal shut, its contents a testament to Mark's resolve. Outside, the sky darkened, but inside, he felt illuminated by an unshakeable belief in the power of compassion, both his own and that which lived in the hearts of those around him.

Mark paced the perimeter of the small, verdant park, his eyes tracing the flight of a solitary sparrow dancing on the breeze. He paused, leaning against the gnarled trunk of an oak tree that stood as a silent sentinel over the landscape. The leaves whispered secrets only they understood, and he felt a kinship with their hushed tones.

"Beautiful day, isn't it?" The voice belonged to Susan, who approached him with a gentle smile, her gaze softening as she took in her brother's troubled expression.

"Is it?" Mark responded, more to himself than to her. "Sometimes I wonder if I'm truly seeing it."

"What's on your mind, Mark? Talk to me," Susan prompted softly, her hand gently resting on his arm, offering grounding reassurance.

The Mind Whisperer

He looked at her intently, truly looked, and glimpsed the well of patience and unconditional love that never seemed to run dry. "I feel like I'm floundering, Susan. My gift... sometimes it feels more like a curse. Like I'm drowning in a sea of other people's thoughts, with no lifeline in sight."

"Mark, you've helped so many," she replied gently, her voice soothing.

"But what about those I couldn't reach?" His voice cracked, revealing the fissures beneath his carefully maintained exterior. "What about the times I was too late, or I misread the signs? Those faces haunt me, Sue. They're always there, just behind my eyelids, waiting."

Susan reached up, tenderly sweeping aside the hair that had fallen across his brow. "You're only one person, Mark. One incredibly gifted, caring person. You can't carry the weight of the entire world's pain on your shoulders."

"It's hard not to feel responsible," he admitted quietly, his gaze drifting downward, where ants marched in determined lines across the earth.

"Let's walk," she suggested softly, understanding that movement often helped soothe his restless energy.

Together, they strolled along the winding path through the park, passing families laughing on picnic blankets and joggers moving in rhythm to unseen melodies. The sunlight filtered through the canopy above, casting shifting patterns on the ground beneath their feet.

"Look around, Mark," Susan urged gently. "This is life, messy, unpredictable, but undeniably beautiful."

He nodded slowly, taking in the cacophony of everyday existence. It was overwhelming, yet, somehow, exactly what he needed.

They found themselves at the edge of a tranquil lake, its surface a mirror reflecting the azure sky and fluffy cotton-candy clouds.

"Sit with me?" Mark gestured towards a weathered bench carved from warm, honey-toned wood.

"Always," Susan replied, settling beside him.

The gentle lapping of water at the shoreline became a rhythmic lullaby, inviting a moment of quiet contemplation. A family of ducks glided across the lake, leaving ripples in their wake, ephemeral, yet profoundly visible.

"Nature doesn't rush," Mark mused aloud, feeling the tightness in his chest begin to ease. "And yet, everything gets done."

"Take a leaf from its book, then," Susan said with a playful bump to his shoulder. "You don't have to save everyone all at once. Just one person, one moment, at a time."

"Maybe you're right," he acknowledged, offering a tentative smile. "Perhaps it's enough to be a drop in this vast lake, creating ripples where I can."

"More than enough," she affirmed, linking her arm with his.

As they sat together in peaceful silence, Mark felt the heaviness of his fears lift, carried away on the soft breeze. The clarity he sought didn't come in a sudden epiphany but in the realisation that his gift was not an anchor but a sail, to catch the wind and navigate the turbulent seas of life, no matter how stormy.

His eyes drifted across the park to a commotion nearby, a small crowd had gathered around a young boy. His leg was trapped between the wooden slats of a bench, and his wails pierced the quiet afternoon. Mark moved closer, attempting to attune himself to the boy's thoughts, to anticipate how best to ease his panic and pain.

"Hey there," Mark said softly, kneeling beside the trembling child. "I'm Mark. What's your name?"

"J-Jamie," the boy hiccupped through sobs.

"Alright, Jamie, we're going to get you out, okay? Just try to stay still."

The Mind Whisperer

Mark's hands hovered over the boy's leg, his mind reaching out, searching for the silent clues that would guide his actions. But amidst the chaos of the boy's fear and the anxious chatter of bystanders, his gift faltered. There were no clear thoughts to read, no decisive signals, only a fog of helplessness.

"It hurts!" Jamie cried out.

"Shh, I've got you," Mark reassured, though doubt gnawed at him. His fingers fumbled with the boy's leg, trying to manoeuvre it free, but it was firmly wedged.

"Come on, think!" he urged himself, frustration mounting with each passing second that yielded no progress. His heart hammered in his chest; each failed attempt was a stark reminder of his limitations. There was no foresight, no intuitive path, only the painful realisation that he might not be able to help after all.

"Maybe if we lift the bench?" suggested a voice from the crowd. Mark looked up, cheeks flushed with effort and embarrassment. A man stepped forward, muscles coiled in readiness. Without a word, others joined him, and together they heaved the heavy wooden bench just enough for Mark to slip Jamie's leg free.

"Thank you," Mark breathed, a wave of relief washing over him as he checked Jamie's leg for injuries. It was bruised but not broken. The collective sigh of the onlookers mirrored his own release of tension.

"Sometimes, it takes more than one pair of hands," the man who had led the effort said, clapping Mark on the shoulder.

This small act of communal bravery, the selfless collaboration of strangers, kindled something within Mark. His chest swelled as he watched Jamie run back into his mother's arms. They had done it together. Witnessing this spontaneous act of concern and cooperation rekindled his faith in humanity.

"See? Jamie's safe now because everyone helped," he said aloud, loud enough for Susan to hear as she approached.

"Exactly," Susan replied, her eyes shining with pride. "It's not about doing everything alone, Mark. It's about inspiring that same hope in others that you carry in yourself."

Mark nodded, a faint smile creeping onto his lips as he absorbed the lesson. His gift might have its limits, but the kindness of people was boundless. This realisation buoyed his spirit, inspiring him to move forward with renewed purpose. The sun dipped lower, casting a warm, golden glow over the scene, a gentle reminder that even when shadows fall, light persists.

His fingertips brushed the rough surface of the park bench as his mind swirled with emotion. The clouds of doubt that had once clouded his thoughts now gave way to rays of understanding and purpose.

"Hey," he said, turning to Susan with a spark in his eye. "I've been thinking about this, about my ability."

She tilted her head, curiosity piqued. "What about it?"

"I can't see the future. I can't fix every problem. But I've realised something important," Mark said, his voice gaining momentum like a rolling stone gathering speed. "My gift isn't about changing destinies; it's about illuminating the dark corners where hope seems lost."

"Mark, that's... That's beautiful," Susan responded softly, her voice filled with emotion.

He nodded, his gaze steady and determined. "People carry so much pain, silent, invisible. If I can sense that, if I can reach out and let them know they're not alone, it's worth every setback, don't you think?"

"More than worth it. It makes all the difference," she affirmed, her hand squeezing his in support.

"Then I'll keep trying," he declared with firm resolve. "No matter how many times I stumble. No matter the odds."

"Because you care," Susan said softly. "And because you believe in the inherent goodness of people."

"Exactly," Mark agreed, a smile of pure determination spreading across his face.

The park grew quiet as the day drew to a close, families and joggers heading home. A gentle breeze whispered through the leaves, carrying the distant sounds of children's laughter and the soft murmur of passersby, a symphony of life's simple pleasures.

Mark rose from the bench, brushing dust from his trousers. He drew a deep breath, filling his lungs with the crisp evening air, drawing strength from the very essence of the world around him.

"See that kid over there?" he asked, nodding subtly toward a young boy sitting alone on the swing set, his small shoulders hunched.

Susan glanced over, her eyes softening. "Looks like he could use a friend."

"Exactly what I was thinking," Mark replied, a warmth rising in his voice.

With measured steps, he approached the boy, each footfall a testament to his resolve. "Hey there, champ," he greeted gently, his tone kind and reassuring. "Mind if I sit here?"

The boy looked up, eyes wide with surprise, then offered a tentative smile. "Okay."

As Mark swung gently beside him, chatting about superheroes and school, the worried lines on the child's face began to soften. Laughter bubbled up between them, light and genuine, a simple moment of connection that felt like a victory in itself.

In this quiet exchange, Mark found reaffirmation.

Each word, each shared smile, was a small victory, a symbol of his ongoing mission to harness his extraordinary gift for connection. And though the journey ahead might be challenging, Mark Jennings knew one thing for certain: he was ready to face it head-on, with heart and hope as his guides.

Chapter 20
Origins

The room fell silent save for the soft rustle of paper as Mark Jennings sat hunched over his desk, a proper whirlwind of photographs and aged documents surrounding him. His study, usually a haven for a bit of peace and quiet and a good think, felt particularly heavy tonight with the weight of unanswered questions hanging in the air like a damp fog. Every image, every letter, was a bit of his past, a past that seemed to hold the key to just what his extraordinary gift was all about.

"Come on," he muttered under his breath, running a hand through his short brown hair. "There's got to be something here, surely."

Mark's fingers moved with a careful precision, his touch as gentle as you like as he handled those delicate memories. He'd always been one for being thorough, a trait that stood him in good stead both in his own searches and when helping others with his uncanny knack for predicting what they'd do next. It was this very meticulousness that kept him at it late into the night, trying to get to the bottom of his gift, a gift that allowed him to see right into the minds and future actions of those around him.

"Who are you?" he whispered, pausing as his eyes landed on a particular photograph. The edges were worn down a bit, the colours faded, but the eyes... well, they were undeniably familiar. They were his own, or so it seemed, staring back at him from a face he couldn't for the life of him recall. A young lad, no older than five or six, stood in a garden dappled with sunlight, a look of proper carefree innocence all over his face.

"Never clapped eyes on this kid before," Mark said, his heart giving a bit of a thump. He leaned in closer, scrutinising every little detail, trying to find any hint of recognition beyond those hauntingly familiar eyes. But nothing. This boy was a complete stranger, and yet, something deep down in Mark resonated with the image.

"Could it be..." His voice trailed off as all sorts of possibilities started whizzing through his mind. Was this child a relation? Could he hold the answer to Mark's unique abilities? His hands trembled ever so slightly as a bit of excitement coursed through him. The mystery that had been lying low within his family line was now calling out, urging him to unravel its secrets.

"Right, let's get this sorted then." Mark's gaze hardened with a bit of proper resolve. He carefully placed the photograph to one side, making it the main focus of his investigation. "I have to know who you are, how we're connected." He spoke to the boy in the picture as if he were right there, listening, a silent guide leading him towards the truth of things.

He reached for his journal, the one where he jotted down all his thoughts, his discoveries, his very soul, you might say. Flipping to a fresh page, he wrote down the date and began to describe the photograph in proper vivid detail. His handwriting was neat and purposeful, each word filled with the enthusiasm of his brand new mission.

"This is it, isn't it? You're the key." Mark's eyes sparkled with determination. He'd always believed in the good in people, in the connections that tied everyone together. Perhaps this photograph was more than just a memory. Perhaps it was a clue, a beacon to light up the path that lay hidden in the shadows of his past.

"Let's solve this mystery then," he said, his voice a mix of hope and anticipation. And with that, Mark Jennings, the man with a comforting way about him and a gift like no other, set off on a journey that promised to reveal just where his extraordinary abilities came from.

Mark's saloon car crunched down the gravel path, a sound that seemed to punctuate the quiet anticipation building inside him. The car rolled to a stop in front of the weathered building that had been his childhood home. His hands lingered on the steering wheel for a moment longer than needed, as if they could somehow put off the inevitable face off with his past.

"Right, Mark," he muttered to himself, a bit of a ritual to get his courage up. "Time to find some answers then."

He stepped out into the crisp air and made his way towards the house, his heart thumping away like mad against his ribs. Each footstep felt heavy, carrying the weight of what he might discover within those walls. The once bright blue paint was now all chipped and faded, clinging to the wood like the last leaves in autumn, not wanting to face the winter.

"Hello, old friend," he said softly, reaching out to touch the peeling frame of the front door.

With a gentle push, the door creaked open, letting out the musty smell of years gone by. He stepped inside, his eyes taking a moment to get used to the dim light filtering through dusty windows. The hallway stretched out before him, with doors on either side leading to rooms filled with echoes of laughter and whispers of secrets that had been kept quiet for ages.

"Remember when we used to slide down the banister?" He spoke to the empty house, half expecting the walls to answer back.

He ventured further in, his fingertips lightly touching the wallpaper, tracing the patterns he'd known off by heart as a child. Each step was like going back in time, each room a chapter from a life that felt both really familiar and strangely distant.

"Mum's piano," he whispered, stopping in front of the instrument, its keys all yellowed with age. "Dad's chair." His eyes settled on the armchair by the fireplace, where so many nights had been spent wrapped up in stories and warmth.

"Where are you hiding the clues then?" he asked the silent companions of his youth.

His exploring took him upstairs to the doorway of his old bedroom. Taking a deep breath, he pushed the door open. The room was bathed in the golden light of the late afternoon sun, casting long shadows across the wooden floor. He stepped inside, a proper mix of feelings washing over him.

"Here it is... my fortress of solitude," Mark chuckled, even though there was a bit of a tightness in his throat. "So many thoughts read, so many actions predicted within these walls."

He moved slowly towards the window, resting his palm against the cool glass. Gazing out at the overgrown garden, he let the waves of nostalgia and a bit of worry wash over him.

"Did you know, even then?" he wondered aloud, speaking to his younger self, a ghostly figure in the reflection. "About this gift of mine?"

The house stayed silent, keeping its secrets locked away with a stubbornness. And yet, Mark could feel the little tendrils of memory starting to stir, whispering to him that the key to unlocking his past was here, somewhere amongst the bits and pieces of his childhood.

"Come on, Mark. Think. There's got to be something more," he urged himself, his voice echoing slightly in the emptiness.

The study, with its shelves crammed with books that had fuelled his imagination, beckoned him next. Even though the books were now covered in a layer of dust, their spines still proudly showed off titles that had once been gateways to worlds beyond his own.

"Was it here all along then?" The question hung in the air, unanswered.

A sense of purpose settled over him like a warm coat, comforting and giving him strength. Mark knew that within this decaying shell of a home lay the bits of his truth. All he needed was the courage to put them back together.

"Let's uncover your secrets then," he said, determination shining in his eyes as he got ready to delve deeper into the mysteries hidden by time.

Mark climbed the creaking stairs to the attic, each step a reminder of the years that had gone by. The air was thick with dust, and the weak light from the small window cast long shadows across the forgotten space. His eyes scanned the room, finally landing on an old chest that he remembered as a pirate's treasure trove from his childhood games.

"Hello, what's this then?" Mark murmured, brushing away cobwebs from a corner where the wall seemed to have a faint outline that didn't quite match the rest of the panelling. His curiosity well and truly piqued, he pressed against the wood, and to his surprise, it gave way, revealing a hidden compartment.

"Secrets upon secrets," he whispered, his heart racing a bit as he pulled out a weathered box filled with letters and journals all tied up by the passage of time.

Settling down cross-legged on the floor, like a child about to open their presents, Mark broke the brittle seal of the box. A musty smell wafted out, the very scent of history itself. His hands trembled slightly as he lifted the top envelope, addressed in elegant handwriting to "My dearest."

"Mum and Dad," he read aloud, "what have you left for me then?"

The letters were written with love and a bit of sadness, each word a piece of a puzzle Mark had never known he was part of. They spoke of a child born with stars in his eyes and a future yet to be written, a child they had loved as their own.

"Adopted?" His voice cracked a little, the word sounding foreign yet deeply personal. "I... I'm adopted then?"

He sifted through more envelopes, each revelation hitting him harder than the last, until he found one that felt heavier, more significant. The letter inside was different; it didn't have a greeting but launched straight into a confession that seemed to echo through time.

"Your birth parents," it started, "had a gift, a wondrous ability that was both a blessing and a curse. It seems you've inherited more than their smile, dear Mark."

"Gift?" Mark said to the empty attic. "Is this why then? Is this why I can see what others can't?"

His mind raced, thoughts tumbling over each other like dominoes in a proper relentless cascade. The memories he had, the feelings he could sense, the actions he could predict, all suddenly made sense in a completely new way. The extraordinary gift that had always set him apart now had a history, a heritage that both made him uneasy and filled him with a strange sort of energy.

"Connection..." He trailed off, a rush of adrenaline going through him. "There's a connection. I knew it! I'm not just... different. There's a reason for it all."

As the weight of the truth settled in his chest, a laugh bubbled up, surprising even himself. It was a laugh that had a bit of disbelief in it, a bit of relief, and a growing sense of who he was. He scooped up the journals next, eager for every little bit of insight they might offer.

"Let's see what else you're hiding then," he said, flicking through pages covered in the thoughts and events from parents who had loved him enough to let him go, to give him a life they believed he deserved.

"Thank you," he whispered, a tear escaping without him even realising. "For everything. For this journey."

"Right then, Mark Jennings," he declared, standing up with a brand new sense of purpose. "It's time to embrace who you are, where you come from, and what you're meant to do with this incredible gift."

Mark's hands trembled ever so slightly as he placed the last journal down on the dust covered floorboards of the attic. The dim light from the small window cast long shadows across the pages, shadows that seemed to echo the proper mix of emotions swirling inside him. For a moment, he simply sat there, letting the revelation wash over him in waves.

"Adopted," he murmured to himself, the word sounding foreign yet deeply personal as it hung in the air. He had always known he was a bit different, but this knowledge... well, it was like a key turning in a lock, opening doors to parts of himself he hadn't even known existed.

"Could every choice, every path I've walked, have been leading me here then?" he wondered aloud, his voice a whisper amongst the silence of the past surrounding him. His gift had often felt like a bit of a burden, a secret that kept him at a distance from others. Yet now, it seemed to be something he'd inherited, a legacy from birth parents whose faces were a complete mystery to him.

"Did they know? Did they see the world the way I do?" The questions bubbled up from a well of curiosity that had been dry for far too many years.

His thoughts were interrupted by the creak of the old house settling, a reminder of the present. Mark ran his fingers through his short brown hair, a gesture of contemplation, and stood up with a purposeful exhale. It was time for some answers; no more shadows, no more secrets.

"Mum, Dad," Mark practised, his voice sounding stronger now, "there's something we need to have a chat about." He pictured their kind faces and the loving home they'd given him, but the image was now tinged with the unknown. They had never mentioned his adoption, never even hinted at the truth behind his abilities.

Picking up his mobile, Mark scrolled through his contacts until he found the familiar numbers. His heart raced a bit as he pressed 'call', listening to the dial tone with bated breath.

"Hi, Mum? It's Mark," he said when the line connected. "Could we meet up? There's something important we need to discuss."

"Of course, darling. Is everything alright?" Her voice had a touch of worry in it, always tuned in to his emotions despite the distance.

"Everything's fine. I just... I found some things. About my past," Mark replied, choosing his words carefully. "Could you and Dad meet me at The Cozy Corner Café tomorrow morning?"

"Sure, love. We'll be there. You know we're always here for you," she reassured him, her words wrapping around him like a warm hug.

"Thanks, Mum. See you then," Mark said, the finality of arranging the meeting setting his resolve. "Take care, dear," she said before hanging up.

As Mark ended the call, the full weight of the upcoming conversation loomed before him. It would be emotional, no doubt about that, but it was necessary. He needed to understand the whole picture to piece together the puzzle of his own identity.

"Tomorrow then," he whispered to himself, feeling a mix of worry and anticipation. "Tomorrow, everything changes."

Taking a deep breath, Mark gathered the letters and journals, holding them close as if they were fragile lifelines connecting him to a past he'd only just begun to uncover. He left the attic, leaving behind the dust and shadows for the clarity he hoped tomorrow would bring.

The bell above the door gave a little chime as Mark pushed his way into The Cozy Corner Café, the familiar smell of roasted coffee beans and cinnamon pastries wrapping around him. His parents were already there, sitting at a table by the window, their hands clasped together in a way that showed they were a bit nervous. Mark's heart thumped with a proper mix of love and uncertainty as he made his way over.

"Mum, Dad," Mark greeted them, his voice sounding steady despite the turmoil inside.

"Mark, my boy," his father said, standing up to give him a hug that was both comforting and a bit tight.

"Sit down, love," his mother urged softly, nodding towards the chair opposite them. Her eyes, so like his own, looked like they might well up.

"Thanks for coming," Mark began, folding his hands on the table, hoping to stop them from shaking.

"Anything for you, son," his father assured him, his voice firm but with a hint of something Mark couldn't quite read.

"About my adoption," Mark started, trying not to let his voice wobble, "there are things I need to know." His mother reached out, her fingers just touching the edge of the old photograph Mark had placed on the table. It showed a young boy with eyes just like Mark's but whose smile belonged to someone he didn't know.

"Mark," she sighed, her voice laced with a familiar sorrow, "we always wanted to protect you."

"Protect me?" Mark echoed, the word thin and hollow, barely a whisper against the café's gentle hum.

"Your birth parents," his father interjected, his gaze unwavering but heavy with a truth long withheld, "they possessed this... ability. Like yours." He paused, visibly wrestling with the immense weight of the revelation. "They feared it might draw unwanted attention to you, even danger."

"Is that why they gave me up?" Mark asked, a raw lump forming in his throat, threatening to choke him.

"Partly," his mother whispered, her eyes softening with a deep, maternal pain. "Your gift, it frightened them at times. They loved you so profoundly, but they genuinely believed you would be safer with us, shielded from those who might seek to exploit your extraordinary abilities."

"Safer," Mark repeated, the word tasting strange on his tongue, a stark contrast between the secure, ordinary safety of his upbringing and the profound, unsettling mystery of his origins.

"Your birth parents made us promise to keep it a secret," his father explained, each word delivered with the solemnity of years spent in silence, "to raise you as our own, untainted by the shadow of your gift defining you."

"Did they ever try to reach out? To see if I was alright?" Mark's question hung suspended in the air between them, thick with a yearning he had never known he possessed.

His mother slowly shook her head, sorrow etched into every delicate line of her face. "No, my love. They passed away when you were very young," she said, her voice fracturing on the final, devastating words.

"Passed away," Mark echoed, the reality settling in his chest like a crushing stone. The faint, fragile possibility of ever meeting them, of finally asking them about this bewildering gift, evaporated like smoke, leaving only an ache.

"Mark, we never, ever wanted to hurt you," his father said firmly, his hand reaching across the table to cover Mark's. "We have loved you as our own son since the very first moment we brought you home. You are our son, with or without this gift."

Tears welled, blurring Mark's vision as he gazed at the two people who had meticulously shaped his life with unwavering love and boundless care. In that moment, he truly understood the enormity of their sacrifice and the profound depth of their protective embrace.

"Thank you," he managed, his voice thick and uneven with overwhelming emotion. "For everything."

"Always, Mark," his mother replied, her grip firm and reassuring on his hand. "Always."

The café buzzed around them, the gentle clinking of cups and the soft murmur of conversation fading into a distant, indistinct backdrop to their intensely intimate tableau. Mark felt the undeniable pull of his newly revealed past, the alluring mystery of the unknown, but also the steadfast, grounding presence of the two people who had nurtured him, guided him, and given him a true home. Gratitude wrestled fiercely with raw curiosity, deep affection contended with a burgeoning longing, as he sat suspended between the fading remnants of one life and the daunting, exhilarating threshold of another.

Mark pushed open the café door, the cool, crisp spring air embracing him like a soothing balm. The gentle clamour of the small establishment receded behind him as he stepped onto the bustling pavement, his heart thrumming with a rhythm of tumultuous, conflicting thoughts. With every deliberate step away from the comforting warmth of familial love and the stinging revelation of hidden truths, the city's ambient noise gradually dimmed, replaced by an internal cacophony that desperately begged for silence, for clarity, for understanding.

"Need to think," he murmured to himself, his voice barely audible above the ceaseless hum of life around him. He found his feet instinctively carrying him towards the nearby park, a familiar oasis of vibrant green nestled amidst the stark concrete landscape, a place where he often sought refuge from the world's demands.

The park welcomed Mark with an almost tangible embrace, its familiar gravel paths winding invitingly before him. Ancient trees swayed gently, their nascent leaves rustling softly in the breeze, while the distant, carefree laughter of children playing echoed like a faint, sweet melody. He meandered aimlessly along the winding walkway, each deliberate step an earnest attempt to unravel the tightly tangled skein of his tumultuous emotions.

"Adopted," he whispered, the word tasting foreign and yet painfully intimate on his tongue. "Gifted."

The Mind Whisperer

A weathered wooden bench by the tranquil duck pond offered a welcome solace, and he sank onto it, the cool slats a comforting presence against his shirt. He closed his eyes, drawing a deep, cleansing breath and exhaling slowly, deliberately. The fresh scent of newly cut grass mingled with the gentle, rhythmic quacking of ducks, weaving a delicate tapestry of tranquillity around him, gently coaxing his mind to unfurl its tight, anxious grip on the present.

And then, without warning, the past surged forward, a vivid, unbidden memory that seized him with startling, almost painful clarity.

"Watch me, Mark! Watch me!" A child's voice, bright and brimming with playful challenge.

He was instantly transported back to his childhood garden, his younger self perched beneath the sprawling shade of an old oak tree, a book of intricate puzzles forgotten in his lap. Across the verdant lawn, his childhood friend, Tommy, bounced a worn rubber ball with determined concentration, his brow furrowed in intense focus, his lips moving silently as he counted.

"Tommy is going to trip," the thought surfaced, clear and distinct, in young Mark's mind just moments before his friend stumbled awkwardly over an exposed root, the ball flying wildly from his grasp. Young Mark gasped, not from surprise, but from a profound, unsettling recognition, the chilling realisation that the thought had arrived before the action, an echo preceding the sound.

"Are you okay?" young Mark called out, already scrambling to his feet and rushing instinctively towards his friend, his innate empathy driving him to offer comfort.

"I am fine," Tommy grumbled, rubbing his scraped knee, utterly oblivious to the extraordinary moment that had just unfolded, a pivotal instant that would subtly, yet profoundly, shape the trajectory of Mark's entire life.

Back on the park bench, adult Mark's eyes snapped open, the vivid memory slowly receding but leaving behind a profound, undeniable revelation. His ability had always been there, a quiet, insistent whisper of insight subtly colouring his interactions, gently guiding his compassion. It was far more than mere intuition; it was a genuine gift, a profound connection, perhaps, to the birth parents he would now never have the chance to know.

"Connection," he repeated to himself, the word now infused with a startling, powerful new meaning. It was not merely about genetics or shared bloodlines; it was about the unseen, intricate threads that inextricably tied one soul to another, the inexplicable knowing that bound human beings far beyond the tangible.

With the immense weight of the past momentarily lifted, Mark slowly stood up, a burgeoning sense of quiet determination settling deep within him. He gazed out across the placid pond, watching the ducks glide effortlessly across the water's surface, each leaving a delicate, expanding ripple in their wake. Like them, he too would move forward, creating his own unique ripples and forging his own distinct path, guided by the extraordinary gifts bequeathed to him by unknown hands but profoundly nurtured by the boundless love of those who had chosen to call him son.

"Thank you," he said aloud, his voice clear, gratitude for both sets of parents swelling in his chest as he turned away from the pond, ready to embrace whatever lay ahead, his gift now a trusted compass in a vast, mysterious world.

Mark's key slid into the lock with a familiar, reassuring click, the sound echoing softly in the quiet hallway of his flat. He pushed the door open, the soft creak of the hinges a testament to the countless times he had returned here seeking refuge from the world's relentless cacophony. But this time felt profoundly different; this time, he crossed the threshold not seeking escape, but with a newfound clarity and an unwavering determination.

He tossed his keys onto the small, ornate table by the door and made his way directly to his desk, where a leatherbound journal lay waiting, its pages already filled with neat, methodical script, a tangible testament to the intricate inner workings of his mind. Mark flipped it open to a pristine, blank page, the cream coloured sheet staring back at him like an uncharted territory, vast and ready to be discovered.

"Where to start?" he murmured to himself, drawing a deep, steadying breath as he uncapped his pen. The faint, metallic scent of ink was grounding, a tangible link to reality as he began to transcribe the tumultuous, transformative journey of the day, meticulously recording every revelation, every emotional crest and trough.

"I met with them today," he wrote, the words flowing onto the page, "my adoptive parents. They told me everything. My birth parents... they had this gift, too."

His handwriting, usually so precise and controlled, wavered noticeably with the raw weight of emotion that each word carried. It was not merely a chronicle of events; it was an uninhibited outpouring of his very soul onto the waiting paper.

"Knowing the truth changes everything," Mark continued, pausing, his pen hovering above the page, as he deeply considered the profound magnitude of what he had learned. "And yet, paradoxically, it changes nothing about who I choose to be."

He leaned back in his chair, a long, contemplative sigh escaping his lips as he gazed into the uncertain future. Who was he now, armed with this astonishing knowledge? Did it fundamentally redefine him, or did it simply add another intricate, vibrant layer to the complex mosaic of his already multifaceted identity?

"Their blood runs through my veins; their gift is my undeniable legacy. But the love... the boundless, unconditional love that Mum and Dad gave me, that shaped me more profoundly than any inherited ability ever could." The words spilled out, a spontaneous stream of consciousness that was both intensely cathartic and brilliantly enlightening.

"Predicting actions, reading thoughts, it is not just about the 'how' anymore," he whispered to himself, a nascent excitement bubbling up inside him, light and effervescent. "It is about the 'why'. Why me? What profound difference can I make with this gift?"

The questions, though rhetorical, ignited a fierce, burning fire deep within him. His gift had always felt like an inscrutable enigma, a complex puzzle to be meticulously solved. Now, it resonated with the unmistakable clarity of a profound calling.

"Perhaps I am meant to help people, to wield this extraordinary connection for something far bigger than myself," he mused, the pen dancing across the page once more, imbued with a new sense of purpose. "I can be a bridge between understanding and confusion, between the crushing weight of loneliness and the warmth of companionship."

He stopped writing, his heart pounding with a thrilling mix of anxiety and exhilaration. The possibilities stretched before him, seemingly endless and daunting, yet undeniably thrilling. With every powerful beat of his heart, he felt more profoundly aligned with his true purpose, more intimately in tune with the intricate, unseen web of life that connected him inextricably to others. "Tomorrow," he said, setting the pen down with a gentle, decisive finality, "tomorrow, I start anew. For now, it is enough, simply enough, to know that I am on the right path."

In the profound silence of his study, surrounded by the tangible artefacts of his past and the boundless promise of his future, Mark felt the intricate threads of destiny that bound him to an unseen fate. And with a quiet, resolute strength, he embraced it.

Mark leaned back in his chair, the supple leather creaking softly under his weight. The journal lay open before him, its pages filled with his neat, precise handwriting that somehow managed to capture the torrent of his deepest thoughts and most intense feelings. He could almost feel the subtle hum of possibility permeating the room, like static electricity, causing the fine hairs on his arms to stand on end.

"Who would have thought," he whispered to the quiet room, his voice a soft murmur, meant only for the walls that had borne witness to his greatest struggles and now his most profound insights, "that my past would unlock so much potential?"

He turned to the last page he had written on, his eyes tracing over the powerful words that signified the definitive start of a brand new chapter in his life. "I am more than the sum of my experiences... I am a beacon for those lost in the dark." Speaking the words aloud gave them a tangible power, making them undeniably real.

The study remained silent, save for the gentle, rhythmic tapping as he absently drummed his fingers on the polished wooden desk, contemplating his imminent next steps. Each tap seemed to echo the steady rhythm of his heartbeat, a comforting, consistent pulse grounding him firmly in the present moment.

"Tomorrow," he declared with renewed determination, rising from his seat, "I will start by reaching out. There are people out there, people who desperately need someone to understand, to truly listen." His gift, once a persistent source of inner conflict and confusion, now felt like the undeniable key to countless doors he never even knew existed.

"Hey," Mark chuckled, speaking to the empty room as if it were an old, trusted friend, "you know what? I am actually looking forward to this." A genuine excitement bubbled up inside him, a stark and welcome contrast to the usual anxieties that so often accompanied significant change.

He picked up the journal and held it close to his chest, feeling the comforting warmth of the leather and the silent promise of the blank pages that eagerly awaited his future entries. With a decisive, resolute motion, he closed the book, the soft click echoing slightly in the hushed stillness of the study.

Mark gently set the journal down, running his hands thoughtfully over its worn cover before placing it back in its rightful, cherished place on the shelf. He took a deep, cleansing breath, each inhalation filling him with a profound tranquillity that felt both strangely foreign and deeply familiar.

"Thank you," he whispered, not entirely certain to whom his gratitude was directed: his birth parents, his adoptive parents, or perhaps the vast, mysterious universe itself for setting him so firmly on this path. It did not truly matter. What mattered, above all else, was the profound sense of acceptance that warmed him from within, the deep, abiding peace that settled over him like a comforting, enveloping blanket.

He glanced around the study one last time, his eyes lingering on the various objects that, in their silent way, told the intricate story of his life. They no longer seemed like scattered fragments of a forgotten past but rather perfectly fitting pieces of a grand puzzle he was finally, completely putting together.

"Time to share this gift," he said, nodding to himself, a quiet vow. And with that, Mark Jennings stepped out of the study, leaving behind the fading echoes of his old life and stepping boldly into the limitless possibilities of his new one.

Chapter 21
New Beginnings

Mark Jennings sat on the weathered park bench, the once chaotic threads of thought from passersby now a softened murmur against the edges of his consciousness. It had been a relentless, overwhelming cascade of events. His extraordinary gift, once a solitary oddity, had transformed into both a potent beacon of hope and a dangerous target for those who sought to exploit its power. Mark had gradually grown accustomed to the ceaseless cacophony of minds around him, yet nothing could have truly prepared him for Nathan Walker's profound, unsettling silence, nor for the intricate conspiracy that had so irrevocably entwined their fates.

"Hard to believe it is truly over, isn't it?" Nathan said, his voice a quiet ripple breaking the park's gentle stillness. He sat beside Mark, his dark eyes meticulously scanning the distant horizon, searching for a deep, abiding peace he had yet to discover.

"Over, yes. But I think it is more of a beginning, a fresh start," Mark replied, turning his head to meet Nathan's steady gaze. The final, brutal confrontation had undeniably left its scars, meticulously unravelling a sinister plot that had sought to manipulate the very fabric of human will. "We have fundamentally changed the course of things. For the better, I fervently hope."

Nathan nodded slowly, a fleeting ghost of a smile flickering across his face, quickly gone. "You saved countless lives, Mark." His voice was now tinged with a newfound, profound respect. "That has to count for something significant."

"Perhaps," Mark admitted, feeling the immense, lingering weight of each mind he had touched, every potential disaster he had subtly pre empted with his peculiar, prescient insight. He keenly observed Nathan's tightly clenched fists and the palpable tension in his shoulders. "And you, Nathan? How are you truly holding up after all this?"

"Me?" Nathan scoffed lightly, his gaze drifting away into the middle distance. "I am just profoundly glad it is done. That... whole mess, it messed with my head far more than I would ever care to admit."

"Understandable," Mark said softly, his tone imbued with deep empathy. "It was not merely a physical battle we fought. It was a fierce clash of ideals, a fundamental disagreement about what we believed humanity should ultimately be."

"Your gift," Nathan began, then paused, carefully collecting his scattered thoughts. "It completely turned my world upside down. It forced me to question things I desperately did not want to. But seeing you navigate it all with such... grace, such unwavering conviction. It is difficult not to believe there is still some inherent good in this incredibly messed up world."

Mark's hands rested calmly on his knees, though a gentle, almost imperceptible tremor betrayed the lingering adrenaline still coursing through his system. "Thank you, Nathan. But it was not just me. You were there, steadfast, every single step of the way. Doubt, when embraced, can be a surprisingly powerful ally if it ultimately leads us to seek the unvarnished truth."

"Still," Nathan insisted, his voice firm, "what you accomplished back there, how you navigated through that absolute chaos, reading their intentions like an open book... You are truly one of a kind, Mark Jennings."

The park around them continued to buzz with the vibrant symphony of life: children's joyous laughter, dogs' excited barks, and the gentle, rhythmic rustle of leaves in the soft breeze. A world utterly oblivious to the invisible, silent war they had so bravely waged and decisively won. Mark watched a mother tenderly console her crying child, her soothing words reaching his ears with startling clarity, as if he stood directly beside them.

"Sometimes, I wonder," Mark confessed, his voice barely above a whisper, a rare glimpse into his inner turmoil. "What if I misread someone? What if I make a catastrophic mistake that I can never undo?"

"Nobody is perfect, Mark." Nathan's voice was firm, reassuring, a solid anchor in the swirling currents of Mark's doubt. "But you, with this... extraordinary ability of yours, you possess a genuine chance to enact real, lasting change. Most of us can only ever dream of that."

"Responsibility," Mark mused aloud, the weighty term resonating deeply within him like a solemn, unbreakable vow. "With great power..."

"Comes great responsibility," Nathan finished, rolling his eyes playfully, a hint of their old banter returning. "Yes, I have seen the films too."

A burst of genuine laughter bubbled up between them, a momentary, welcome reprieve from the profound gravity of their situation. It was a shared laughter, rich with the intimate knowledge of darkness faced and ultimately overcome, of lives irrevocably intertwined by the capricious hand of fate and the unwavering strength of choice.

"Films aside," Mark said, the last chuckles subsiding, his expression becoming serious once more, "it is profoundly true. And I fully intend to use it well. To help wherever I possibly can."

"Of course you do," Nathan said, standing up and offering a strong hand to help Mark to his feet. "You are the closest thing to a superhero I know."

"Superhero," Mark echoed, a bashful grin spreading across his face as he accepted Nathan's steadying help. "Let us just stick with 'helper,' shall we?"

"Helper it is," Nathan agreed, clapping Mark affectionately on the shoulder. "Now, come on. We have a world out there that is none the wiser to your unique brand of heroism. And I have a distinct feeling it is going to need you again very soon."

Together, they walked away from the bench, two men whose paths had intersected under the strangest of circumstances, now united by a conspiracy finally unravelled, their steps light with the boundless promise of a future yet unwritten.

Mark meticulously shuffled the deck of cards in his hands, a look of intense concentration etched on his brow. Nathan and the others' familiar faces were gathered intimately around the small kitchen table, their expressions a comfortable mix of contentment and eager anticipation. There was an easy, natural camaraderie in the room, the kind forged only from shared adversity and hard won triumph.

"Okay, I think I have it," Mark announced, breaking the comfortable silence with a playful flourish. "Nathan, pick a card, any card you like."

"Is this another one of your infamous mind tricks?" Nathan quipped with a wry, half smile, plucking a card from the deck and scrutinising it closely, a twinkle in his eye.

"No tricks," Mark replied, his eyes twinkling in return. "Just trying to keep things light for a change, for everyone's sake."

Nathan showed the chosen card to the rest of the group, careful to keep it completely hidden from Mark's view. "Alright, now what do I do?"

"Put it back into the deck," Mark instructed. Nathan complied, and Mark deftly shuffled the cards once more, with an almost magical grace. With a dramatic flourish, he pulled a single card from the very middle of the deck and held it up for all to see. It was the Queen of Hearts.

"Is this your card?" Mark asked, his voice laced with mock suspense, a mischievous grin playing on his lips.

"Unbelievable!" Nathan exclaimed, genuine laughter bubbling up within him as the others cheered in delight. "Every single time, Mark. Every single time."

"Ah, but that is not all," Mark said, his smile widening, a deeper meaning in his words. He turned to the others, his gaze sweeping over their faces. "You see, it is not merely about reading minds or foreseeing future events. It is about knowing when someone truly needs a lift, a moment of unexpected joy."

"Speaking of which," a soft voice chimed in from the doorway, drawing their attention, "I think we could all use a bit more of that magic outside this room, in the wider world."

They all turned to see Mrs. Collins, the elderly neighbour from two doors down. Her eyes were weary, lined with unspoken worries, but there was a distinct spark of fragile hope in them that had not been there before.

"Mrs. Collins," Mark said warmly, rising immediately to greet her, his concern evident. "What can I do for you today?"

"It is my grandson, Jimmy," she began, wringing her hands nervously, her voice a thin, reedy whisper. "He has been struggling so much since his parents... since they passed away. I simply do not know how to reach him anymore."

"Let me talk to him," Mark offered gently, the depth of his innate empathy evident in every syllable of his tone. "Sometimes, it is easier for a young person to open up to a stranger, to someone outside their immediate circle."

"Would you? Oh, thank you, Mark. You truly have a gift; you truly do," she said, her voice thick with gratitude.

"Come on, let us go and find Jimmy," Mark said, glancing back at his friends with a reassuring nod, a silent promise of his return.

As they left the kitchen, Nathan quickly caught up to Mark, clapping him firmly on the back. "You are genuinely making a difference, man. One heart at a time, one person at a time."

"Is not that what it is all about?" Mark mused, a serene, thoughtful smile playing on his lips. "Helping others, forging connections, healing wounds..."

"Exactly," Nathan affirmed, pride and deep affection for his friend shining brightly in his eyes. "And who knows how many lives you will touch with that extraordinary gift of yours?"

"Who knows indeed," Mark agreed, stepping out into the wider world where countless hearts awaited the gentle, transformative touch of his unique understanding.

Mark strode purposefully through the bustling community centre, his gaze sweeping across the room for faces that conveyed a silent need for comfort or guidance. The general hum of conversation buzzed around him, a constant background noise, but beneath it, he distinctly heard silent cries for help, subtle emotional currents that only he could discern with his extraordinary gift.

"Hey, Mark!" a young woman called out, waving him over with a bright, welcoming smile.

"Hi, Lisa," he greeted her, immediately noting the distinct undercurrent of stress in her otherwise cheerful voice. "What is on your mind today?"

"It is the fundraiser," she explained, tucking a stray lock of hair behind her ear, a gesture of nervous habit. "We are desperately short staffed, and I honestly do not know if we will manage to pull it off successfully."

"Let me see what I can do to assist," he offered, his words imbued with a quiet, unwavering confidence that instantly put her at ease.

As he effortlessly mingled with the volunteers, coordinating their disparate efforts with an uncanny knack for anticipating problems long before they even arose, Mark felt a profound sense of purpose swell within him, a deep, resonant satisfaction. This was far more than simply helping; this was guiding a collective effort towards a genuinely greater good.

But as the day wore on, a challenge unlike any other loomed ominously on the horizon. A desperate mother approached him, her hands trembling slightly as she cradled a faded photograph of her missing son like a precious, irreplaceable relic.

"Mr. Jennings," she said, her voice quivering with barely contained panic, raw and exposed. "My boy, Alex... he is gone. They say you have a way of finding people, of seeing things others simply cannot."

Mark gently took the photograph, his heart sinking with a heavy dread as he met the innocent eyes of the child in the picture. He concentrated intensely, trying to reach out with his mind, to find some faint trail to follow, some whisper of his whereabouts. But there was only an unnerving silence, a stark void where normally a torrent of thoughts and emotions would be.

"I, I am so sorry," Mark stammered, the frustration evident, a bitter taste on his tongue. "I cannot sense anything. Sometimes, it simply does not work the way I want it to, the way I need it to."

The mother's face crumpled instantly, her hope visibly shattering, and Mark felt a sharp, excruciating stab of helplessness, a familiar, unwelcome companion. It gnawed at him, this glaring limitation, this stark, painful reminder that even his extraordinary gift had undeniable boundaries.

"Please," she pleaded, her hands gripping his arm with a desperate, almost painful strength. "You have to try again. You must."

Mark nodded, closing his eyes, taking a deep, fortifying breath. He reached out once more, pushing past the suffocating fog of uncertainty, willing his gift to surface, to manifest for this desperate, suffering soul.

"Okay," he murmured, opening his eyes, his gaze now resolute. "I will do everything I possibly can."

"Thank you," she whispered, tears streaming freely down her cheeks, a silent testament to her fragile hope.

That night, Mark lay wide awake, staring intently at the ceiling, the darkness offering no solace. His mind raced ceaselessly with countless possibilities, with the crushing weight of expectations, and with the daunting, humbling reality that he was not, in fact, omnipotent. Yet, even as insidious doubt crept in, his resolve hardened, solidifying like steel.

"Tomorrow," he whispered into the oppressive darkness, a silent promise to himself, "I will try again."

Mark sat at the old oak table, his fingers tracing the worn wood grain as a silent, yet profound, cacophony of thoughts swirled gently around him. The musty air of Nathan's book laden study was punctuated by the subtle clinks of China as his friend meticulously poured tea into delicate cups. Across from him, the rest of the team buzzed with a subdued, anticipatory energy, their eyes fixed on Mark with a comforting mixture of concern and unwavering conviction.

"Mark," Nathan began, his voice steady and reassuring, a calm anchor in the storm, "we have seen you accomplish truly incredible things. This is merely a setback, a temporary obstacle, not the absolute end."

"Indeed," chimed in Elise, her sharp intellect often softened by her profound compassion. "Your gift, it is like a powerful beacon in the deepest fog for those lost souls. You have guided so many safely to shore, to peace."

"Plus, you have us," added Alex, his youthful exuberance undimmed by the gravity of their current situation. "We are your crew, your unwavering support, ready to navigate through any storm, no matter how fierce."

Their words were a soothing balm to his frayed nerves, and Mark allowed himself to fully absorb the comforting warmth of their collective support. He nodded slowly, feeling the immense weight on his shoulders lighten ever so slightly, a tangible relief.

"Thank you," he said simply, his gaze meeting each of theirs, a silent acknowledgement of their unwavering loyalty. "I will not give up. Not when there is still even a glimmer of hope."

"Speaking of hope," Nathan said, sliding an ancient looking tome carefully across the table towards Mark, its leather binding cracked with age, "I think it is time we expanded your understanding of what you can truly do, of the full scope of your abilities."

Mark opened the heavy book with meticulous care, his eyes widening in awe as he scanned the cryptic symbols and intricate diagrams within its aged pages. Nathan pointed to a particular passage, his finger tracing the complex, intricate script.

"See here? Your abilities are far more than just a simple mind reading act. They touch upon something truly fundamental, an intrinsic connection to the very fabric of existence itself."

"The multiverse?" Mark asked, the word tasting strange yet oddly familiar on his tongue, a concept both alien and deeply resonant.

"Exactly," Nathan confirmed, his eyes alight with intellectual excitement. "Each decision, every single thought, creates ripples that span across countless dimensions. You possess the incredibly rare talent to sense these echoes, to influence them even, to guide them."

"Like threading a needle through multiple layers, pulling them together into a cohesive whole," Elise mused, her own sharp curiosity visibly piqued by the revelation.

"Or tuning an instrument to play a perfect harmony that resonates across worlds, across realities," added Alex, his eyes alight with genuine wonder and boundless possibility.

Mark felt a powerful surge of excitement, inextricably mixed with a daunting sense of immense responsibility. The potential of his gift now seemed truly limitless, yet so much remained profoundly unknown. But with Nathan's astute guidance, Elise's insightful intellect, and Alex's unwavering, youthful support, he felt an undeniable readiness to explore these vast, uncharted horizons.

"Then let us begin learning," Mark declared, his voice firm with renewed determination, a quiet strength. "There is a child out there who desperately needs us, and I fully intend to find them. With this," he tapped the ancient book, a symbol of newfound knowledge, "and with all of you by my side."

The room hummed with a palpable, newfound energy, a collective resolve that fortified them all, binding them tighter. Together, they would delve deeper into the profound mysteries of Mark's extraordinary gift and the boundless possibilities it held. And with each revelation, each new piece of understanding, they would face whatever challenges lay ahead as an unyielding, united front.

Mark's fingers hovered gently over the worn, parchment like pages of the ancient tome, a soft, ethereal glow emanating subtly from beneath his touch. The intricate symbols seemed to dance before his eyes, revealing profound secrets of the cosmos that few, if any, had ever truly seen. The room was steeped in a deep, profound silence, save for the whisper of turning pages and Mark's steady, rhythmic breathing.

"Are you okay?" Nathan's voice cut through the stillness, tinged with a distinct note of concern, a gentle intrusion.

Mark blinked, pulling his hand back as if stung by an unseen force. He had not noticed the crushing fatigue until this very moment, his eyes gritty and strained, his entire body aching with an unfamiliar weariness. A thin sheen of perspiration clung to his forehead, a testament to his exertion.

"I am fine," he lied, offering a weak, unconvincing smile. "Just a little tired, that is all."

Elise glanced at him, her gaze sharp and discerning, seeing beyond his facade. "You are pushing yourself far too hard again, Mark. The immense toll it takes on you..." She did not have to finish her sentence; they all knew precisely what she meant, the unspoken cost of his power.

Alex stepped closer, placing a warm, supportive hand on Mark's shoulder, a gesture of quiet solidarity. "The journey has only just begun, my friend. You absolutely need to pace yourself. This is a marathon, not a frantic sprint."

Mark nodded, a reluctant acknowledgement, knowing they were absolutely right. His gift was a true double edged sword, granting him extraordinary, almost godlike abilities but demanding an equal, reciprocal measure of his very essence in return. Each use left him profoundly drained, a bit more hollow than before, a vessel tirelessly filled and then relentlessly emptied.

"Perhaps it is time for a proper break," Nathan suggested, his voice gentle but firm. "Reflection, at times, can be as powerful and transformative as direct action."

Reluctantly, Mark agreed. They settled into comfortable chairs arranged intimately around the low coffee table, mugs of hot, steaming tea warming their hands, a small comfort in the quiet. The soft, distant hum of the world outside seemed a universe away, a forgotten echo.

"Sometimes, I truly wonder if it is worth it," Mark confessed, his gaze fixed on the amber depths of his steaming cup, his voice barely audible. "The things I see, the thoughts I hear... it is utterly overwhelming. Am I truly changing things for the better, or for the worse?"

"You have saved lives, Mark," Elise reminded him gently, her voice a soothing balm. "Those people, those grateful souls, would vehemently disagree with any doubt you harbour, any self recrimination."

"Indeed," Alex chimed in, his youthful voice earnest. "Your gift, it is not just about the big, dramatic battles. It is the small, subtle moments, the gentle nudges that steer someone back from the precipice of despair, from the edge of the ledge."

"Yet, every choice, every intervention, carries immense weight," Mark muttered, the persistent moral quandary gnawing relentlessly at his conscience. "Every time I intervene, I undeniably alter someone's predetermined path. Is it truly my right to do so?"

"Your compassion makes it your inherent responsibility," Nathan said firmly, his voice resonating with conviction. "You feel their pain, their joy; it inextricably connects you to them, to all of us. Your gift does not just affect the present. It profoundly echoes into the future, actively shaping it."

The room fell silent once more, each person lost in their own contemplative thoughts. Mark felt the immense weight of his responsibilities like a physical, tangible presence, pressing down on him. There were lives he had touched, and those he simply could not reach. The delicate balance between intervention and fate was a precarious one, a path he was still painstakingly learning to navigate.

"Thank you," he whispered, genuine gratitude lacing his words, heartfelt and sincere. "For being here, for believing in me when I struggle so profoundly to believe in myself."

"Always," Elise replied with a warm, comforting smile.

"Without a doubt," Alex added, squeezing his shoulder reassuringly, a gesture of unwavering support.

"Forever," Nathan concluded, his eyes holding the silent promise of unending, steadfast support, a bond forged in fire.

As night descended upon the quaint town, its unsuspecting residents utterly oblivious to the cosmic threads being meticulously woven within Mark's modest living room, four friends sat together, bonded by a shared, extraordinary journey that transcended both space and time. And in the very heart of that unbreakable bond lay a simple, profound truth: they were immeasurably stronger together. Mark's gift might indeed take its toll, but with allies like these, he would never, ever face the encroaching darkness alone.

Mark stood by the window, the first tender light of dawn brushing gently against his face like a soft, reassuring promise. The overnight storm had completely cleared, leaving behind a breathtaking canvas of vibrant pinks and oranges that painted the sky with an undeniable sense of renewed hope.

"Looks like it is going to be a truly beautiful day," Elise remarked, joining him by the window with a steaming cup of tea in hand, her gaze mirroring his.

"New beginnings," Mark replied, his voice soft but steady, imbued with a quiet resolve. His gaze was fixed intently on the horizon, where the sun edged slowly over the rooftops, casting long, retreating shadows that seemed to melt away like the lingering doubts of yesterday.

"Exactly," Nathan chimed in from behind them, his voice full of optimism. "And we have a whole lot of those ahead of us, a future brimming with them."

"Speaking of which," Alex said, flipping through a local newspaper, his attention caught by an article, "there has been talk about setting up a new community centre. They are looking for volunteers to help out."

Mark turned from the window, his interest immediately piqued by the suggestion. "That sounds like something we could genuinely do. Together."

"Count me in," Elise said, her smile bright and encouraging, a clear sign of her enthusiasm. "It will be good for the town, and good for us too, in many ways."

"Us most of all," Nathan agreed, a knowing look in his eyes. "Helping others... it is healing, is it not?"

"Absolutely," Mark nodded, feeling the profound truth of Nathan's words resonate deeply within him, a comforting echo. It was this very sense of purpose, of contributing to something far larger than himself, that had always driven him forward, even when the immense weight of his gift felt almost too heavy to bear.

The group moved seamlessly to the kitchen, the true heart of Mark's home, where plans were eagerly made, and laughter mingled freely with the gentle clink of cutlery. There was an undeniable ease between them, a deep seated camaraderie born of shared struggles and hard won victories, a bond that only deepened with the passage of time.

As they talked, Mark used his ability discreetly, almost unconsciously, tuning into the subtle undercurrents of emotion around him. He sensed no fear, no lingering pain, only a powerful, collective determination to make a tangible difference. And for once, the myriad voices in his head did not overwhelm him; instead, they flowed through him like harmonious music, a beautiful symphony of the human spirit.

"Mark?" Elise asked, her voice gentle, snapping him back to the present moment, her eyes questioning. "What are you thinking about so intently?"

He smiled at her, the genuine warmth reaching his eyes, reflecting his inner peace. "I am thinking that we have a truly incredible chance to do something good, something profoundly meaningful. My... our journey does not end here, not by a long shot."

"Never does," Alex said, winking, a playful note in his voice.

"Then let us not waste any more time," Nathan declared, his voice decisive and resolute. "The future is waiting for us to shape it, to mould it into something better." They raised their cups in a silent toast to the days ahead, to the unknown possibilities. Each of them had their own individual dreams, their own unique paths to forge, but they would walk them together. That much was absolutely certain.

The Mind Whisperer

As the scene drew to a close, Mark stood once again by the window, watching as the town slowly awoke to the boundless possibilities of a brand new day. Children's laughter floated up from the street below, a sweet, innocent sound, a poignant reminder of the simplicity and pure joy that life could still hold. He knew that challenges lay ahead, inevitable and perhaps daunting, but he also knew, with unwavering certainty, that every single step taken, every life touched, truly mattered. They were all intricate threads in an ever expanding tapestry, meticulously weaving a story of profound resilience and enduring hope.

"Ready, Mark?" Elise called out, her voice laced with an infectious excitement.

"More than ever," he replied, turning away from the window with a renewed sense of purpose, his spirit invigorated. As the sun climbed higher, bathing the room in a warm, golden light, Mark Jennings stepped forward into the day, his heart full of boundless optimism and his spirit utterly unbreakable. The journey continued, and with each powerful heartbeat, he cherished the infinite possibilities that awaited.

About The Author

R. B. Hill has extensive experience and expertise in various fields, particularly social care. With over 20 years of experience, including 11 years specifically focused on working as a social worker with older adults in diverse teams. He has accumulated a wealth of knowledge and understanding. His versatility is evident in his roles as an independent social worker and best interest assessor and his involvement in supporting students and social work consultancy. His commitment to continuous growth and expanding his skill set is commendable. his decision to become a hearing aid dispenser in audiology further exemplifies his dedication to providing comprehensive support to those in need. By diversifying his expertise, R. B. Hill ensures that he can address a wider range of challenges faced by individuals and offer them the best possible care. What truly sets this author apart is his genuine passion for helping and supporting others, which stems from his own personal journey of overcoming obstacles in life. Having faced and conquered challenges himself, he possesses a deep empathy and understanding for those he works with.

R. B. Hill draws upon his own experiences to forge meaningful connections with individuals, enabling him to guide them through their own challenge and empower them to realise their full potential. he has a sharp, perceptive mind and wealth of experience make him an irreplaceable asset in his profession. He is a master in his field, with a deep understanding of its complexities and an unwavering drive for perfection. this truly sets him apart is his multifaceted background and his genuine empathy for others. These qualities combine to make him a compassionate and highly effective advocate for those he serves. his devotion to helping others and his exceptional skills make him a true standout in his industry.